COLDIRON

# Thunder of Cannon

## Books by F.M. Parker

**Coldiron** *series*
Coldiron
Shadow of the Wolf
The Shanghaiers
Thunder of Cannon
The Thieves

**Novels**
Skinner
Nighthawk
The Searcher
The Highbinders
The Far Battleground
The Shadow Man
The Slavers
The Assassins The Predators
Winter Woman
The Seekers
The Highwayman
The Last Orphan Train
Wife Stealer
The Harvester
Soldiers of Conquest
Dream Hitcher

COLDIRON

# Thunder of Cannon

F. M. Parker

SPEAKING VOLUMES, LLC
NAPLES, FLORIDA
2021

Thunder of Cannon

ISBN 978-1-64540-493-4

# The Creation of the Mississippi River
## A Prologue

The drifting snow of the white ice desert of the great glacier was less hospitable than the drifting sands of the hottest desert.

For tens of thousands of years the water of the oceans had been sucked up by the winds of the earth and flung down as snow onto the breast of the continent. The snow turned to ice, more than two million cubic miles of it smothering the land. The level of the oceans dropped three hundred feet.

Piled nearly two miles thick in its central dome, the ice became plastic under its own crushing weight. Mobile now, the ice flowed outward to cover two-thirds of the land surface, and extended far out into the Arctic and Atlantic Oceans. The glacier drowned mountains six thousand feet tall, obliterated two mighty rivers— one flowing east and another north—and beheaded a third river that went off to the south. Even the strong rock crust of the planet was depressed nine hundred feet. The rebound of the crust from that great depression is still happening today.

Millennium after millennium passed as the glacier held the continent captive. Powerful winds blew constantly off the huge ice field, stirring raging blizzards in summer as well as winter. The beheaded, south-flowing river was often frozen solid to its rocky bottom.

The shifting balance of heat and cold on the earth tilted to the warm side. The quantity of ice flowing to the periphery of the glacier became equal to that which was melting. The glacier halted its advance across the continent and stood and did battle with the sun for thousands of years.

The glacier lost the battle and surrendered to the sun. In six thousand years the front of the ice retreated five hundred miles.

A multitude of streams of water rushed away from the seventeen hundred miles of melting glacier terminus, spreading like a tangled skein of blue-green silk through rock and sand moraines. The giant rivers that had been overrun by the ice flowed strongly again. They fought each other for mastery of the continent's broad watershed.

Once, an arm of the thick ice blocked the east river for eight thousand years and created a gigantic lake. To the west, large depressions were uncovered by the re-treating glacier. Ice melt poured into the deep cavities to form a series of mighty lakes, the ancestors of the Great Lakes of today.

The land surface began to rebound from the depressed level to which the glacier had crushed it. The bottoms of the lakes rose. At times the high walls of the lakes were breached, and a flood of unimaginable quantity spilled out. Most of the water poured into the river flowing south, and it became the mightiest river on the planet.

The braided network of the upper reaches of the south river finally coalesced downstream into one tremendous channel several miles wide and hundreds of feet deep. The channel ran brimful of swift water straining to return to the sea.

For long distances behind the retreating glacier, the land lay barren and abandoned by all the plants and animals. Choking dust storms raged, swirling away, carrying the fine loess soil two miles into the air and many hundreds of miles beyond its source. The sun was obscured for months. In the darkness, massive sand dunes fifty feet tall and miles long were birthed.

The south river cared nothing about the darkness but hurried onward, pulled relentlessly by the implacable gravity of the planet. It dumped its titanic load of sand and silt into the Gulf of Mexico. A delta of massive proportions grew swiftly, now below sea level, now above.

The lusty river full of tumbling, churning water refused to be held to one channel and it frequently shifted its huge, meandering body into new courses. It flung its mouth from side to side, sometimes tens of miles apart in a day, and spewed out its load of continental debris—first here and then there. Often the delta expanded thousands of feet in a year, until it was scores of miles wide and extended ten times that far into the Gulf. The river changed the very size and shape of the continent.

The glacier died. The river shrank. Yet it was still a great stream, and near its mouth was half a mile wide and two hundred and fifty feet deep. For ten thousand years the river flowed thus.

Natural levees formed on the banks of the river. Each time the stream poured over its banks, the current slowed at the margin of the channel and dropped its load of fine silt. Embankments, levees, were thus built. The river in normal flow was confined within these impervious banks of clay. Outside the levees, and lying below the level of the river, was a region of extensive swamps and lakes, a labyrinth of water and land.

At times deep crevasses broke the levees and the river plunged through, flooding the land for vast distances and holding it in a watery prison for weeks. The land animals drowned.

Then one year white men found the river. They traveled its length and named it Mississippi from the name the Indians gave it, misi-great and sipi-water. In their foolhardy, reckless way, the white men began to build a town in the mud flats laying twice the height of a tall man below the level of the river. Only a fragile levee protected the town, call New Orleans, from the gargantuan destructive powers of the river.

As was its habit, the river often rampaged through the town because the presence of the white men did not prevent the levees from failing.

# Chapter One

The 8-inch Columbiad cannon roared, spewing flame and hurling its solid iron ball out through the gun port of the armored embrasure and downriver. The recoil of the big gun rammed it backward to the end of its reinforced chocks.

"Wheelmen, roll her back into position," the gun captain shouted out above the booming crash of the other cannon firing from the fort.

The two men sprang to the Columbiad and threw their shoulders against the rear of the iron-rimmed wheels. They caught hold of the oak spokes and heaved mightily. The heavy gun rolled forward.

Roy Penn dropped his hands from over his ears. He grabbed up one of the iron balls from the meager supply of them piled on the ground. He saw the powder monkey, a twelve-year-old boy, five years younger than himself, snatch up a bag of gunpowder and stand ready on the opposite side of the cannon. The boy looked across at Roy with eyes mere thin, bloody slits in his smoke-blackened face.

Roy turned away from the strained, frightened face of the powder monkey and looked out through a gaping crack in the wall of the shell-battered embrasure. Downstream, the clouds of gun smoke made by the exploding guns of the Yankee enemy stretched away in a long, gray cloud until it vanished over the horizon. Fort Jackson had been under siege by a Union flotilla of warships for five days. The sound of cannon fire, the flat, dry crack of the rifled cannon, and the hollow boom of the big naval howitzers had never stopped, had gone on madly for all those long days.

The Union warships, heavily armed steam sloops, gunboats, and mortar schooners were anchored in the Mississippi River on the west side, one and one-half miles below the fort. They were beyond a bend of the river and screened behind tall trees. The Union sailors had fastened branches to the top sections of their ship's masts so as to camouflage them to blend in with the trees. The Yankee guns, firing with deadly accuracy, poured more than a hundred rounds an hour into the fort.

Fort Jackson was manned by seven hundred men. Rather, there had been that many men at the beginning of the battle. Portions of Roy's 1st Louisiana Artillery and the Saint Mary Cannoneers were here, and eleven local boys from New Orleans who had volunteered to be powder monkeys.

The fort was in the shape of a star and made strongly of stone and mortar. It had seventy-four big cannons. In the center of the fort was the Citadel, where the gunpowder was stored. A water-filled moat surrounded the Citadel. The drawbridge to the Citadel had been destroyed, making it difficult to bring up gunpowder. The hot-shot furnaces and fresh water cistern were in ruins.

The Confederate fortification of Saint Phillip on the opposite side of the river and half a mile further upstream had received far less cannonballs from the Union ships. The deepest current of the Mississippi and the best passage for the Union fleet lay close to the west side, and under the guns of Fort Jackson. The Union gunners had from the very first shot concentrated most of their devastating attack on Fort Jackson. They wanted to destroy all the Confederate guns there or kill the gun crews so that the invading force could steam upriver and capture New Orleans.

Roy knew the guns of the Confederates were not hurting the Yankees much. Half the shells fired from Fort Jackson never even reached the enemy. The powder was of poor quality, and often he could see the splash of the shells in the river on his side of the screen of trees.

A cannonball struck just outside the embrasure and exploded. The already weakened redoubt shuddered like a dying thing. The last of the roof came crashing down. Half of the north wall collapsed, the stones tumbling and rolling among the men.

The half-dazed gun crew jumped and dodged until the stones came to rest. Then the smoke-begrimed men hurriedly looked around, checking the other cannoneers. That look of expecting to find their comrades dead was like no look Roy had ever seen. Did he appear as strange to them? They were all caught up in the brewing for-mula of death. And death waited, confident of getting them.

The gun captain saw that his men were still alive and had their arms and legs. He gestured at the young pow-der monkey. "Load!" he commanded.

The boy leapt forward and stuffed the bag of powder down the open barrel of the cannon.

"Load the ball!" the gun captain shouted.

Roy had stepped into loading position upon the command to the powder monkey. Now he hoisted the twenty pound ball and shoved it into the throat of the gun. He swiftly backed away to the side of the tall right wheel.

The rodman inserted his piece and rammed the ball tightly against the powder. The gun captain stepped close to his huge gun and bent to sight the thick, iron barrel.

Roy looked in the direction where the gun pointed. His mind froze at what his eyes saw. A flock of enormous naval shells with smoking fuses were tearing out of the blanket of smoke that hid the Yankee ships. Every enemy cannon must have fired all at once. The shells arched upward, seemed to halt at their zeniths, then turned earthward.

The sky fell, round, iron balls with hissing red fuses streaming down on the men in Fort Jackson.

A cannonball plunged into the embrasure just to the left of the Columbiad. The exploding shell burst with a brilliant, orange flame. The earth leapt. Blocks of stone flew through the air.

A mighty wind of concussion flung Roy across the embrasure, and he landed on his back on the ground. The wind vanished, sucking his breath away. He lay in a vacuum.

Roy saw the gun captain go cartwheeling past overhead. The man's head was missing, and the stub of his neck spouted blood. Some of the blood rained down on Roy's upturned face.

Bits and pieces of the powder monkey flew straight up. Dirt and broken stones trailed close behind him, all tossed so negligently, uncaringly, into the air. The powder monkey and the stones fell back to earth.

Roy struggled to his feet. He stood swaying drunkenly and looking at the overturned cannon. Its bulk had shielded him from most of the killing blast of the explosion.

He saw only one body, other than the parts of the powder monkey. The wheelman, who had been closest to Roy, lay grotesquely plastered against a mound of rubble. His guts were spilled out on the ground. All the other men were blown away or buried under the fallen wall of the embrasure.

Roy felt his ears, for he heard a ferocious, high intensity ringing. Such a sound could not possibly exist. His hands came away bloody. His eardrums had been burst by the exploding cannon shell.

He ran from the destruction and death of the embrasure, into the madness and despair of the fort compound. Stunned men with eyes like coal chips wandered about. Some had been blown into the moat that surrounded the Citadel. The live ones, leaving blood-streaked water behind them, were crawling upon the bank. Many crumpled forms that had once been men lay scattered about on the ground.

Roy walked unsteadily, avoiding gaping shell holes in the ground and other men limping or crawling in the same direction as he went. All were trying to reach the pharmacy that had been turned into a makeshift hospital where the surgeon worked. Roy saw that the building still stood, but large cracks ran from the top to the bottom of its stone walls.

He ducked and hunkered low as he felt the air above his head part abruptly and wash aside as a low flying cannonball zoomed by. The missile struck beyond him and exploded, flinging up a geyser of dirt and stone. Another shell hit the ground, but did not explode. It bounced away to come to a jarring stop at the base of the farther wall of the fort.

Roy went on, passing a man lying limp and still on the ground. He could see no wounds, but he knew the poor fellow was dead. A man in death looked so pitifully lonely.

The cannonballs of the Union guns shifted and began to pound the section of the fort behind Roy. An eight foot section of the perimeter wall came apart, sending fragments flying like shrapnel. Something struck Roy's left hand a stinging blow. Instantly he sprang to the side and dove into a shell hole.

He tumbled and rolled down the bank. He thrust out his hands to stop his fall. Only his right hand responded. He ended up jarred, flat on his back, in the bottom of the hole.

Roy looked at his left hand. It hung to his wrist by a thin strip of skin. In numb disbelief, he lifted the arm to better see the wound. As he did so, the skin broke and the hand fell into the dirt.

"God! No!" Roy cried. He grabbed his wrist to stop the blood spurting from the end of the severed arteries. The blood did not want to stop. He squeezed harder. He climbed from the shell hole and ran weakly, crab-like, toward the pharmacy.

The steps up to the pharmacy were red with blood, like a butcher's block. He slipped on the slick steps, caught himself, and staggered into the pharmacy. The long, low-ceilinged room was crowded with gray-faced wounded, some moaning, some with silent moving mouths. A large man stared at Roy, eyes sunk in deep purple sockets.

The surgeon was scarlet from head to foot. His hair was caked with blood. Beneath the blood, his face was a colorless paper mask.

Two burly medical orderlies held a man down on the red, dripping table. The surgeon sawed on the bone of the man's mangled right leg. He worked with feverish haste, for the shock of the amputation could kill the soldier should it continue past a few seconds. Through his pain, Roy thought of the statement often repeated by the veteran soldiers that if a surgeon was good, he could cut off a leg in seven seconds.

Roy sagged against the wall of the pharmacy. He continued to squeeze the end of his severed arm and gritted his teeth to keep from crying out with the pain. Hurry! Hurry! he pleaded silently to the surgeon.

On the operating table the wounded soldier shuddered and fell unconscious. The surgeon cauterized the end of the leg stump to stop the bleeding. He pulled a pad of flesh and skin over the raw end and stitched it in place. The orderlies lifted the soldier and lay him on the floor near the wall.

The surgeon turned to Roy. "What's wrong with you?"

Roy held up the stub of his wrist. "I've lost my hand," he said, and fell half unconscious across the bloody operating table.

The orderlies scooped Roy up and stretched him out on the table. One of them grabbed the spurting wrist.

The surgeon bent over Roy. "I have no laudanum to deaden the pain. Hang on the best you can while I tend to your wound."

"Stop the bleeding," Roy whispered weakly, looking up into the surgeon's face.

"Yes. I'll stop the bleeding."

As the surgeon reached for his instruments, wild, striking bombs exploded. The floor of the pharmacy bucked like a ship at sea. The cracked walls collapsed. Some of the wounded men tried to shield themselves from the falling stones. Others tried to crawl, like the crippled animals they were, out of the way. Some lay still, said nothing, and looked without interest at the crumbling walls.

The last of the stones stopped falling. Roy shut his eyes as the thick dust fell out of the air. He felt the grit grinding his eyeballs.

But the dust was nothing. Even the falling stones had brought no fright to Roy. Deep inside him, a sickening nausea was growing. God! To be a cripple. To be only part of a man. Without a hand, would he become a beggar on the streets?

The surgeon began to cut at the shredded flesh of Roy's wrist. The light faded for Roy, and black unconsciousness engulfed him.

Roy came awake to hellish pain. His thoughts were chaotic, enmeshed and intertwined like twisting streamers of fog reaching out of the night. He shook his head, trying to clear away the befuddlement.

He lay on the floor near the wall with several other wounded men. Black night had fallen and filled the corners of the pharmacy. In the dim light cast by a shielded lantern, the surgeon still worked at the operating table.

Roy looked at his bandaged arm. The shortness of it startled him. He wanted to cry.

A man dressed in seamen's clothes came in the open door of the pharmacy. He stared around at the damage done to the building, and to the men. Then, walking carefully among the wounded soldiers, he drew close to the surgeon. "Doctor, I've come with my boat," he said. "I've got a load of medical supplies. And I can take some of the wounded men back to New Orleans with me."

"I'm damn glad to see you," the surgeon said. "How many can you take?"

"Thirty or so."

"The orderlies will help you unload the supplies from your boat. Bring the laudanum first. After I dose the worst of the wounded, you can take them aboard."

Roy hoped he would be one of those to be sent to New Orleans. He drifted off in his own hellish world of pain, and the memory of the exploding cannon shells.

"Drink this," the surgeon's voice said, and a hand touched Roy's shoulder. "It's laudanum but only enough to take away some of your pain. I want you awake to walk to the boat."

Roy caught the surgeon's hand with a trembling hold and brought the small glass to his lips. He drank. Now, perhaps he might be able to shut his eyes and not see the scarlet and yellow explosions of bombs.

The surgeon left and an orderly came. "Get up," the man said. His tone was gentle. He pulled Roy to his feet. "Lean on me."

They went down the narrow aisle between the rows of wounded men. Roy stepped on some of them. No one complained. He wanted to tell them he was sorry, but his tongue refused to form the words.

The orderly and Roy reached the outside and moved across the fort compound. Scores of shell holes like open, dead mouths surrounded them on all sides. To avoid them, the two men, the partial one leaning upon the whole one, wove a zigzag course toward the river.

With the orderly holding him on his feet, Roy stumbled down the low bank to the river. He heard the cold current growling and tugging at the bank, and it almost swept his weak legs from under him when he waded in. The water rose to his waist before he reached the side of the boat that had been run in close to shore. The orderly lifted Roy into the vessel.

"Lie down and rest," the orderly said. "In a few hours you'll be in The Sisters of Charity Hospital in New Orleans."

Roy lay flat on his back with the hard oak decking for a pillow. The artillery bombardment was continuing in the night. Overhead bomb shells crossed each other. Some with fuses cut too short, exploded in the air. It seemed as if a battle was being fought in the heavens as well as on the earth.

Roy cuddled his handless arm to his chest. "I don't want to die," he told the night. "Not until I've taken my revenge on the God damn Yankees."

# Chapter Two

**April 23, 1862.**
**A few miles northeast of New Orleans.**

The forest of giant cypress and gum trees stood totally silent. Not one limb swayed. Not one leaf stirred. Overhead, the dome of the sky seemed unnaturally far away, as if it had drawn back uncaring of the happenings on the earth.

Susan Dauphin sat astride her roan mare and listened to the silence. Now and again, as today, the forest became so still she could hear the heart beat in her bosom. Sometimes the quiet was peaceful but not today, for she felt there was an eeriness, an aura of danger about the forest. However, she must be wrong about that, because the danger was not here but miles away at the mouth of the Mississippi River where the Union war fleet and the Confederate forts battled each other with huge cannons.

She looked ahead at the bayou of dark, flat water that stretched off to the southeast. The bayou was some twenty yards wide, and completely blanketed by the shadows cast down by the dense foliage of the tall trees.

The twisting, sensuous body of the bayou vanished from her view among the dark boles of the trees in less than a quarter mile. She knew it continued on for miles, meandering through the forest until it reached Lake Borgne.

Susan swung down from the mare and tethered it to a low hanging limb. She pulled her shotgun from its scabbard on the saddle and turned toward the bayou. The wood and iron of the 12-gauge, double-barreled gun felt familiar and comfortable in her hands.

Susan had ridden beyond the extreme eastern boundary of her father's plantation, beyond the fields and pastures, and now was within the forest and swampland where man had changed nothing. She was alone in this primeval place, alone except for her horse and the shotgun.

Susan's blood flowed more swiftly with a sense of exhilaration at her daring. No other woman in New Orleans would hunt alone in the forest as she did. She lifted the shotgun to her shoulder. Her head dropped and she pressed her cheek to the stock. Her eye was in exact alignment looking down the rib between the barrels, just as the eye should be for a skilled marksman. All that remained was to swing the gun until the front bead sight found the thing that was to be killed.

As Susan sighted down the twin barrels of the gun and thought of the heavy charges of powder and lead shot, she knew the feeling of strength, of safety that an armed man must feel. Still, around the periphery of her mind she retained the memory of the many warnings that all girls are given about the danger from scoundrel men and wild animals in unprotected places. Even so, the sensation of strength was grand. Any other woman here in the deep woods without a man close beside her would certainly know fear.

Guns were familiar to Susan, and so too, was the forest. The year she became eight-years-old, her mother had died. After that sad event she and her father, Wade Dauphin, had turned to each other for comfort. Her father, always an avid hunter and an excellent marksman, began to take her with him on his stalks after game in the fields and forest. She trailed along behind, sometimes running to keep up with his long strides. Often he stopped and called her to him. They knelt together as he pointed out tracks and droppings on the ground and told her the characteristics that identified the animal that had made them. She loved him dearly at those times—and the pleasant memories of being with him that would be hers until she died.

As the years passed and her strength increased, her father taught her to shoot with rifle, shotgun, and pistol. She had hunted waterfowl in this same bayou. Not two miles north of where she stood today, she had killed her first deer.

Her Aunt Sophia Dauphin, her father's sister, had assumed the task of teaching Susan the proper manners of a girl, and later of a young lady. Aunt Sophia had disagreed with Susan's use of firearms, stating strongly that such activity was unbecoming to a woman, that the masculine skill might scare off suitors. Susan and her father had laughed at that notion. However, Susan had not forgotten her aunt's warning, and never openly made a show of her prowess with guns.

Wade Dauphin forbade Susan to hunt alone in the forest and the black water swamps. He explained that a pretty young woman such as she was would be in great danger at the hands of some of the rogues roaming the vast wilderness. The rules and laws of civilization stretched and broke at the boundary where the wilderness commenced.

But what if she dressed and looked like a man, Susan had privately wondered. At seventeen she had grown to within a couple of inches of her father's height. She took a suit of her father's cast-off hunting clothes and cut them down to fit her, leaving the garments slightly oversize to mask her womanly build. She wore a vest to hide the swell of her bosom.

She recalled the day she had donned the altered garments, piled her hair up on top of her head and covered it with a brimmed, felt hat. The coarse cloth that her father had worn seemed to instantly wrap her in security. She examined herself in a mirror. She made a stern face at the reflection. With her height, and if she could keep her distance from another hunter in the woods, she could possibly pass as a young man.

Sometimes Susan did encounter other hunters in the forest, most often on the trails between the swamps, where men and animals alike were forced to travel in constricted pathways. At those times, she held her gun so that it was plainly visible to the man, raised her hand in greeting, and glided away through the trees before a conversation could begin.

She was now twenty-six years old. Aunt Sophia had told her many times that she was past the age when young women should be married. Susan was attracted to men, and they to her. She had taken lovers. However, none of them had stirred her deeply enough for her to accept their proposal of marriage. She would one day marry, of that she was confident. That would greatly please her aunt. Her father had put no pressure on her to hurry the act. Bless him for that.

Susan, holding her shotgun ready, stole closer to the bayou. Countless numbers of waterfowl left the frigid north country each autumn and migrated down the Mississippi River valley to spend the winters in the numerous bayous, lakes, and salt marshes of Louisiana. That vast horde of birds had now left to return to their summer nesting sites. Some waterfowl liked the south country and remained year round. Perhaps the bayou held some of those birds.

Slowly she crept up behind the waist high brush that bordered and screened the bayou. When she had gone only a short distance she halted abruptly and froze. A heron stood stock still on its long, stick-like legs in the shallow water of the edge of the bayou. Its grayish-purple plumage blended perfectly with the forest shadows and had made it difficult to spot. The bird had not yet discovered Susan. Its eyes were turned down watching for an unwary fish to come within reach of its strong beak.

Susan did not want to kill the heron. She stooped lower and went to the right. Should the heron be frightened into flight, that could cause any other waterfowl present to take wing before she was within shooting range.

More of the bayou came into view. The surface of the water was flat, as unmoving as the surface of a mirror. She went a few steps further. Close to the fringe of the brush on her right there was a series of tiny, concentric ripples radiating outward. Soundlessly, she stole nearer and peered through a small opening in the brush.

Two green-winged teal, a male and a female, preened themselves on the water. The small, fast-flying ducks were unaware of Susan's presence and continued with tidying their plumage. They rotated their heads to critically examine their feathers. Then, taking each one in their flat beaks, they oiled it from glands in their mouths, shaped it, and placed it back into position, just right for best flight.

Susan stood up in full view to flush the teal into flight. The birds instantly launched themselves off the water, their strong wings pumping, whirring with power. Her blood rushed at the sound as the teal climbed rapidly away on the soft ladder of air.

She brought the shotgun to her shoulder. Her finger found the front trigger that fired the right hand barrel. The twin barrels swung to follow the speeding ducks. She waited, watching the two birds, their wing tips almost brushing each other as they sped away like arrows. If she fired too soon, the teal would fall into the bayou and she would not be able to retrieve them from the water.

As the teals' range increased, they gradually drew closer to the bank of the bayou. Then the teal on the right was over land, the second close behind.

Susan moved her point of aim ahead to lead the duck. She fired, the boom of the shotgun crashing out, shattering the stillness of the forest.

The swift beat of the teal's wings ceased. Feathers blossomed around the bird's body like an explosion of flower petals. The teal plummeted down.

Instantly, before the first teal struck the ground, Susan swung the shotgun upon the last bird. Her finger found the trigger of the second barrel. The front bead sight touched the teal and then moved ahead.

Susan pressed the trigger. The bird was knocked cartwheeling, falling, in a feather-strewn arc to the ground.

She pivoted to look all around her as she loaded the shotgun with powder and shot and slipped caps over the nipples. She was unprotected, vulnerable until the weapon was once again primed.

The cap slipped over the last nipple. The weapon was reloaded. She was strong and safe.

She retrieved the pair of teals from the leaf-covered forest floor. She walked to her horse and placed the birds in a saddlebag. She pulled herself astride the mare and rode west through the woods. Miles later, she broke free of the brooding forest and came out into a broad, grassy pasture that extended to a large, white plantation house.

# Chapter Three

**April 23, 1862.**
**New Orleans, Louisiana.**

The huge, side-wheel river steamboat heeled abruptly to port as the strong frontal winds of the approaching rain squall struck it broadside. The streams of smoke from the twin smokestacks were shredded and whipped away. Thousands of choppy waves wrinkled the surface of the wide Mississippi River. Large, cold drops of rain began to drum on the wooden decking.

At the roll of the steamboat, the herd of two hundred horses whinnied in fright, and their iron-shod hooves stomped the tossing deck. They were used to fierce winds and cold rain, but never had the very earth moved beneath their feet.

"Tend your horses," Luke Coldiron called out to the seventeen Comanche wranglers and the white man, Hammond.

He knew the order was unnecessary. The skilled wranglers were already moving among their charges, talking to the nervous beasts in low, soothing voices. They rubbed the muscular necks and withers and stroked the stiff, flicking ears. The men's words and hands were calming opiates to the animals.

Each wrangler had two strings of horses—seven animals in each and tied nose to tail. The lead animal, always the most gentle of each string, was fastened by a leather strap to the saddle of the man's riding mount. The horses had long since grown accustomed to being led in this manner.

The swift winds whipped away and the boat settled more solidly onto its keel. The horses became quiet. Only their stiff ears and bright eyes still showed their uneasiness.

Luke looked ahead past the bow of the steamboat. Visible beyond the rain squall, the Queen City of the South, New Orleans, extended along the left shore for miles. It was a great seaport, the volume of its trade second only to that of New York. New Orleans was also the largest slave market in the world.

He felt relief and a sense of accomplishment at having reached the city. In thirty days he had brought his herd of horses twelve hundred miles. They had come down from his horse ranch in Gachupin Basin high in the Sangre de Cristo Mountains of the New Mexico Territory, crossed the high plains of north Texas, and reached Natchez on the Mississippi River. The commander of the Confederate forces in that city had helped him to contract a riverboat, a vessel with a broad main deck built to haul cotton, well suited for transporting horses. Luke and his crew had loaded the horses and sailed immediately downriver.

The rain slackened to a drizzle, and the city could be seen more clearly. New Orleans, with a population of one hundred and seventy thousand people, looked deserted. The miles of city docks and levees normally lined with ocean-going steamships and tall-masted sailing ships, thronged with stevedores loading cotton, sugar, rice, and hundreds of other trade goods were all abandoned. Luke saw only two river steamboats, both tied up at the dock lying farthest upstream. The rebel commandant at Natchez had said the Mississippi was being blockaded by a Union naval flotilla. He had not said the blockade was so totally effective.

Two Moons, the leader of the Comanche wranglers, came to stand beside Luke. As he looked forward at the sprawling city with its numerous large warehouses, factories, and multitude of homes, the same skittish look that the horses possessed came into his black eyes.

"Luke, this New Orleans is a very great village," Two Moons said in an awed tone.

"That it is," Luke replied. Two Moons had spent his entire life in the wild upper reaches of the Red River of western Texas. New Orleans must indeed be a most magnificent city to him.

"I hope we do not have to fight the white men who live here for they will have many warriors." Two Moons rested his hand on the butt of his pistol in its holster.

"They do have many warriors, and they are ready for battle. But they only prepare to fight other white men. We come in peace to sell them horses. There should be no battle between them and us."

"That is good," Two Moons said solemnly. "The women of my people do not like for their men to die."

"No woman of any people wants her man to die." Two Moons's statement about fighting had a dark reality. A band of Indians armed with pistols, rifles, and long-bladed skinning knives could easily draw the attack of the white people through whose land they traveled. For that reason, Luke had hired the trusted white man, Hammond, from Santa Fe, to journey with them.

Should Luke remain in New Orleans, Hammond's presence on the long return trek would forestall any misunderstanding of the Indians' purpose. However, even with the potential trouble that the Comanches might bring upon him, Luke was pleased that Two Moons and his braves had agreed to help bring the horses to New Orleans. The Comanches were the most skilled horsemen on all the Great Plains. Not one horse had been lost in the journey from New Mexico. The two extra horses Luke had brought to insure the proper number reached the destination were not needed.

The riverboat moved on and shortly left the drizzling rain behind. The captain angled his craft in from the deeper reach of the river and toward the shore. As it drew closer to land, Luke could make out people on the dock, two long lines filing up the gangways of the two berthed boats. Each person was heavily laden with possessions, many with valises, bundles, or packs on their backs.

" 'Pears hundreds of people are leaving the city," Hammond said to Luke. "I wonder how close the Union forces are."

"We'll soon find out."

The steamboat slowed as it came into the dock. The captain reversed the engine. The paddlewheels halted, then began to rotate in the opposite direction. The water boiled with white foam.

"Lines away," ordered the captain. "Make her fast."

"Stay on board with the horses," Luke called to his men as the steamboat grated against the dock. "I want to be sure we still have a sale before we unload."

He jumped ashore and hastened toward the levee, passing the long lines of people inching up the gangways of the two steamboats.

Twenty or so spectators—mostly men and boys scattered along the top of the levee—watched the river and the boarding of the steamboat. An Indian, dressed in worn, white man's clothing and holding a wooden bucket in each hand, stood off by himself. Some of the people watched Luke climb the bank toward them.

A young, boyish soldier in a gray Confederate cavalry uniform separated from the spectators. Leading his horse, he walked toward Luke. He raised his hand in greeting.

"You're Mr. Coldiron, if my judgment is correct," the cavalryman said.

"Yes. How did you know that?"

"Mr. Dauphin has had me waiting on the levee to meet you for nearly a week. He got your message some time ago that you were about ready to start with your horses for New Orleans."

"I'm glad you are here," Luke said.

However, Luke was not glad that he was in New Orleans. Four months ago, he had journeyed from his horse ranch in the New Mexico Territory to St. Louis, Missouri, for the purpose of selling horses. There he had met Wade Dauphin, owner of a large farm east of the city and a plantation in Louisiana. They had struck an agreement for Dauphin to purchase two hundred horses from Luke for fifty thousand dollars.

Luke had not been surprised at Dauphin's purchase of the horses, for he knew the funding of the Confederate war effort was substantially different from that of the Union government. With no strong central government, the Confederates had little ability to impose and collect taxes to buy war goods. To fill the void, Southern states, cities, and individuals took action. Rich men spent huge sums of their personal wealth to outfit squads, companies, and entire regiments with uniforms, weapons, and mounts. Wade Dauphin was one of those committed to helping the South win the war.

Luke prepared to make delivery of the horses by May 30, 1862, as the contract stated. The place of delivery had been specified as the city piers on the banks of the Mississippi River. He had understood this to mean the piers at St. Louis, since the place of reaching the sale agreement had been that city. He believed Dauphin had also understood that the place of delivery was to be St. Louis. However, by the end of March a large flotilla of Union gunboats had left Cairo, Illinois, and had almost reached St. Louis. Dauphin had sent a message to Luke that the point of delivery of the horses must be the piers at New Orleans, or there would be no sale. Worried that the Confederates might confiscate his horses, Luke had cursed the change of destination.

Still, an agreement was a thing of honor and must be fulfilled. Luke had embarked on the longer trek to New Orleans.

"My name's Riley, sir," the cavalryman said. "My instructions are to guide you to Mr. Dauphin, or to help you in any way I can."

"What's happening? What's the military situation?" Luke was staring down from the levee into the city. The streets lay some ten feet below him and below the level of the river. Now, in the spring, with the river full of runoff from the broad interior of the continent, the city would have been under water had it not been for the levee.

From his vantage point, he could look directly up broad Canal Street. People on foot and in vehicles of all sorts moved along the streets to the northwest. They seemed subdued, fearful, so different from the carefree, boisterous atmosphere which Luke had come to expect in New Orleans. Where were the clowns who wandered the streets and entertained the pedestrians for small coins, or the Negro liverymen dressed in fine, purple linen and driving their masters' carriages from the high seats, or the pimps watching their whores proposition-ing the sailors on the waterfront ways? In fact, where were the sailors? He thought the military news would not be good, from the Confederate point of view.

The cavalryman spoke. "As you can see, people are leaving the city and going upriver to Natchez and Vicksburg, and many other towns. They've been leaving for days now, ever since Admiral Farragut with his Yankee warships began their attack on Fort Jackson and Saint Phillip."

"When did that begin?"

"Nearly a week ago."

"The forts are still holding?"

"At the last report they are. That was early this morning. Shall I take you to Mr. Dauphin? He's at his plantation."

"No. Ride there and ask him to come to the docks. I'd like him to examine the horses and take delivery here."

"That's a good idea. Then we can take the horses directly to the camp of the cavalry company. They'll be damned pleased to have mounts."

"How long will it take you to make the round trip to the plantation and back?"

"Half an hour, maybe a little more."

"Then be on your way."

"Yes, sir."

Riley swung astride his horse and left at a gallop down the levee bank and northwest along Canal Street.

***

"Sweet honey for sale," Panther, the Chickasaw Indian, called. His eyes were fastened on the white man who had arrived on the riverboat with the horses. The Indian had drawn close and waited patiently for the man's conversation with the soldier to end.

Luke turned at the call of the Indian vendor. The man's face was dark mahogany and broad, with a large, high nose. His jet-black eyes were bright, penetrating, like those of a hunter. The man was no longer young, and white streaked the shoulder-length, black hair tied behind his head with a red cord.

The Chickasaw was out of place selling honey on the streets of New Orleans, Luke thought. Twenty-five years before, in 1837, the U. S. Army had rounded up the members of the tribe and forced them to leave their villages and make the long journey to a reservation in the Oklahoma Territory. Many Indians had died from the hardship of that terrible march, especially the old and the very young. This man would have been in his prime at that time. He must have been hiding for years in the swamps surrounding New Orleans. What had brought him from the forests to walk the streets with his buckets of honey?

"Sweet honey and chewy comb, fresh from a honey tree this morning," the Chickasaw said. He sat his two tin buckets of honey down on the ground and whipped aside the snow-white, cotton cloth Blackberry Woman had given him to cover the buckets and keep the flies and dirt from the honey. He was proud of the cleanliness of his offering.

Luke glanced at the buckets of honey. Large, golden-brown chunks of comb protruded from the amber liquid nearly filling the gallon containers. His mouth moistened at the thought of the rare, enticing treat.

"How much for both buckets?" Luke asked.

"Four dollars," the Chickasaw replied. "Paid in gold or silver." He wanted none of the nearly worthless paper money being issued by the white men of New Orleans.

"Both buckets are sold." Luke dug into a pocket and brought out a handful of coins. He gave the Indian four silver dollars. "Bring them and come with me." He pointed at the honey and turned down the levee toward the dock and the steamboat.

Panther was pleased at his sale. He draped the cotton cloths over the buckets of honey, picked them up, and followed after the white man.

"Dig out your tin plates and spoons," Luke called out to the men standing with the horses on the boat.

"I've got a sweet surprise for you. Hammond, bring my utensils, along with yours."

The Comanches and Hammond quickly did as directed and hurried off the boat. They crowded around Luke and looked expectantly at the buckets the Chickasaw had set on the dock. Luke lifted aside the cloth covering to show the honey.

"Sink your sweet tooth in that," he said.

"That looks great," Hammond said.

"Yeah. Let's get at it," Luke said.

Luke took his plate from Hammond and squatted with the other men around the buckets. He reached out with his knife and speared a piece of honeycomb.

The Chickasaw had drawn back a few steps. He stood very straight, and his broad chest was squared. He was closely measuring the Comanches. Garbed in buckskin breeches, cotton shirts, and high moccasins tied just below the knees, they were armed with both pistols and knives. Those long blades began to flash as they were drawn and then stabbed out to lift chunks of honey from the buckets and onto plates.

"Have some with us," Luke told the Chickasaw, and he pointed at the honey with his knife.

Panther shook his head. "I've had my fill," He was surprised at the invitation, and at the ease with which the two white men ate with the Indians.

He studied the white leader. The man was strongly built. His face was open, with widely spaced eyes. They were of a strange, yellowish blue color. He was clothed in faded wool trousers and cotton shirt, a vest, and heeled boots. A brimmed hat topped his head. Same as the Comanches, he was armed with a Colt revolver in a holster and a long-bladed knife. Both weapons seemed perfectly natural on him. Panther thought the man would be a fierce fighter.

The Comanche wranglers ate steadily. They smacked their lips with pleasure. The levels of the honey in the buckets fell swiftly.

Luke ate slowly, enjoying the delicious food. Now and again he glanced at the top of the levee, checking for Riley's arrival with Dauphin. The Chickasaw, waiting for his buckets, remained standing ramrod straight and watching the Comanches with a keen, concentrated stare.

Loaded railing to railing with people fleeing the city, the two steamboats pulled away from the dock. Spouting black smoke from their twin stacks, the vessels drove upstream under full power. More people, with all the personal possessions they could carry, came from the city and began to talk with the captain of the boat that had transported Luke's horses.

Mounted riders, fifteen or so, came up over the levee and swiftly down on the dock. All but two were in gray uniforms. One of the civilians was a woman riding a roan, mare. She wore a long-skirted riding habit, and rode astride like a man.

Luke set his plate down by the nearly empty buckets and stood up as the riders brought their mounts to a halt near him. He wiped some spilled honey from his hands onto his pants leg and stepped forward to greet the new arrivals.

"Hello, Mr. Dauphin," Luke said to the tall, angular civilian who had swung down from his horse.

"Luke Coldiron. Glad you have made it to New Orleans," Dauphin said with evident pleasure.

Luke turned to the woman and whipped off his hat. He bowed slightly. "I'm pleased to see you again, Miss Dauphin." Susan Dauphin was even more beautiful than when he had seen her in St. Louis. She had inherited her father's height and was tall for a woman, but she had none of her father's bony sharpness. Rather, she was womanly rounded with large, brown eyes. Her wide, smiling mouth was like a lovely, red butterfly resting on her white face.

"And I am very glad to see you again, Mr. Coldiron," Susan said, gazing back into the penetrating eyes of the man from the New Mexico Territory.

Luke studied the woman. Men talked to men and watched their eyes to determine if they were friend or enemy. However, men looked into women's eyes searching for truth, to see that a woman had a soul, that she was true. Luke read in Susan's eyes that what she said was indeed true. She was pleased at his arrival in the city. She was uniquely straightforward for a woman, so very confident of herself. What would making love to her be like? At that moment he decided he would spend a few days in New Orleans, regardless of the threat from the Yankee fleet.

Dauphin spoke. "I knew I could depend on you to bring the horses as you promised."

Luke reluctantly looked away from the lovely Susan and at Dauphin. He felt put upon by the man. However, he knew there was nothing to be gained by bringing up the matter of the place of delivery of the horses. He was in New Orleans with the animals, and that was that.

"I have the two hundred horses we agreed on. Also, I have two extra ones. I thought we would have losses coming so far over rough country, but we didn't."

"I'll take the two extra horses, and glad to get them. The price will be the same as for each of the others."

"That's agreeable with me."

"This is Captain Thacker," Dauphin said. He gestured at the officer just stepping down from his mount.

"Hello, Captain," Luke said.

"I'm glad you've come, Mr. Coldiron. My troopers need the horses."

"Captain Thacker will take the horses to his camp after we have inspected them," Dauphin said.

"All right. My wranglers will bring them off the boat and you can examine and count them."

Dauphin looked to the west, where the yellow ball of the sun had fallen from the sky and lay close to the horizon. "Let's do it quickly. There's only a little daylight left."

"Hammond, Two Moons, bring the horses," Luke called to the waiting wranglers.

Two Moons spoke to his band in their language and led them off to the boat. Hammond followed.

"I'll let you two men alone to complete your business," Susan said. "I must be on my way to the hospital."

"Someone is ill in your family?" Luke asked.

"No. We have wounded soldiers at the hospital. The bombardment of Fort Jackson and Fort Saint Phillip has caused many causalities. They are brought upriver to the two hospitals here in New Orleans. I am working at the Sisters of Charity Hospital as a nurse."

"She is a fine nurse," Dauphin said.

"I believe that," Luke said.

"Mr. Coldiron, my father will ask you to come to dinner tonight. Please do come. I won't be there, for I must work until midnight, but I'm certain you would like a good meal after a long journey. We can breakfast together in the morning. Perhaps you will spend a few days with us here in New Orleans?"

"My daughter is very outspoken," Dauphin said with a proud smile, "but she speaks for both of us. It would be our pleasure for you to stay for a time."

"I gladly accept the invitation."

"Then it is done," Dauphin said.

Susan gave Luke a smiling nod. Luke liked the expression in her eyes. She reined her mount away.

Two Moons came down the gangway leading his two strings of horses.

"I have raised every horse, and they carry my Steel Trap Brand," Luke said. He pointed at the right hip of the nearest horse. A brand in the shape of a steel trap with the jaws open and trigger set, was burnt clearly into the skin. "Point out any animal that doesn't satisfy you," he said.

"That we will. But I don't expect there will be many. Your horses are known for their excellent qualities."

Luke had carefully chosen the horses as cavalry mounts. They were all of approximately the same size, with good legs and deep chests. Their color ranged from gray, to roan, to nearly black. They were well-broken and would take little further training to be stable in battle.

The horses had great endurance, for they had been raised in the high mountain valley of Gachupin Basin in the Sangre de Cristo mountains. He had discovered the valley nearly twenty years before in 1843, when he was a young fur trapper and had been transporting his catch of beaver pelts down from the towering mountains to Santa Fe. More than a thousand horses had been grazing the meadows of the canyon, far more than the land could feed. Many were thin and stunted. He found scores of skeletons and decaying carcasses of horses that had died of starvation during the winter. Luke recognized the huge potential of the mountain valley to produce excellent horses, if their numbers were kept in check.

A month later he returned from Santa Fe with two packhorses straining under heavy burdens of powder and shot. During that first summer, he slew more than eight hundred horses, those that were sick, lame, or had poor body form, and almost all of the stallions. So many animals were slain that the coyotes and wolves stopped hunting, merely following the killer human around and growing fat from eating the choicest tidbits of the carcasses left at his ambushes. Out of all that large herd, he allowed only two hundred horses to live, the start of his famous Steel Trap Brand.

He had slain men—white men and Indians—for trying to steal his horses. Once he had chased bandits deep into Mexico and killed them for rustling a band of his brood mares. He knew with certainty that he would be forced to kill again to protect what he had created.

Luke looked at the horses as they moved past Dauphin and Thacker. He had sold many horses over the years, and every time he felt sad to see them go. He had watched them grow to full size and he had personally gentled each one. They were like old friends.

The last horse filed past and Dauphin and Captain Thacker conferred briefly.

Dauphin turned to Luke. "We can't find fault with any of the horses. You've made a sale for the entire herd."

"That's good," Luke said.

"If it's all right with you, Captain Thacker will take possession now. You can ride back to my plantation house with me and I'll pay you. I've kept the money there, for banks aren't safe in times of war."

"Fine," Luke said. "Hammond, Two Moons, I'm going to stay two or three days in New Orleans. Two Moons, I suggest you leave now and take your braves upriver on the steamboat that brought us here. There may not be another one you can travel on. Hammond, as we agreed before we left Santa Fe, your job is to see that no one bothers the Comanches. I want no trouble for Two Moons, no fighting with white men along the way home."

"I'll get them safely back to the Red River country."

"Good. Let's all go aboard. I want to pay the Comanches and get my horse."

Luke led the way onto the steamboat. He went directly to his horse and extracted a leather pouch from a saddlebag. He passed among the Comanches and counted out gold coins into their hands. He came last to Two Moons. "Now you are paid in full. I have already given each of you a choice horse."

"All is as you promised," Two Moons said. "Stop at my village and rest and talk when you return."

"I'll do that."

"I'll see you in Santa Fe later on," Hammond said to Luke.

"Right." Luke pulled himself astride his black horse and rode off the steamboat.

Panther, the Chickasaw, stood for a moment longer watching after the Comanches. Then he took up his buckets and walked swiftly from the dock.

# Chapter Four

Coldiron rode his horse beside Dauphin's horse on the wide road paved with crushed white seashells. The way ran north from New Orleans through groves of big trees and broad, open fields toward Lake Pontchartrain. In the growing dusk of evening, the seashell road glowed with a strange, pale luminescence.

Luke had never been to Lake Pontchartrain, and he looked about, examining the land. Dauphin talked about the war.

"New Orleans is an important city for the Confederacy," Dauphin said. "It has the resources of modern warfare with large workshops that can manufacture many things such as small arms. Our shipyards can build wooden and iron ships, our foundries can cast heavy guns. The Union knows this, and that is why they are attacking the forts at the mouth of the Mississippi. They hope to fight their way upriver and occupy the city and turn it into a supply house for their own forces."

"How strong are the forts?" Luke asked. He knew they were located seventy-five miles downstream, one on each side of the Mississippi. Fort Jackson had been only recently built, while Saint Phillip was an old fort constructed by the Spanish in the 1790's and strengthened two decades later.

"Fort Jackson is the stronger of the two," Dauphin said. "It alone has seventy-four big cannons. Saint Phillip has nearly as many. Some military men have said that one gun in a fort is worth five on a ship. I believe the forts are impregnable. Also a strong iron chain, resting on rafts and the hulks of old boats, has been strung across the river just south of the forts and within range of their cannons. The chain will stop Admiral Farragut and his Union ships from coming up the river. Nothing that floats can get past the forts. Nothing that walks can get through the swamps."

Luke glanced to the side at the man. Such certainty could be very dangerous. "Do you have an army in New Orleans, in case the Union forces do break through?"

"General Mansfield Lovell has six thousand men, but I'm afraid they're not well-trained and only partially armed. To add to the difficulty, the city has been infiltrated by Union soldiers disguised as 'civilians,' and there are a substantial number of Union sympathizers. Both have grown very bold since the Yankee navy moved upriver to bombard the forts. Men such as myself who are clothing and arming companies of soldiers to fight in the war are often targets of attacks by the infiltrators and the sympathizers. But that does not worry me, and certainly won't stop me."

Dauphin seemed completely caught up in the war. Luke could understand why young men went so willingly to the battlefields. They searched for adventure, and to test their courage against other men in battle.

In 1846 he had gone to Mexico with the American army and helped conquer that nation. He had fought in the attack on Vera Cruz on the Gulf of Mexico. Victorious on the coast, the American army marched up into the mountains and crushed the Mexican armies at Cerro Gordo, Jalapa, and Puebla, and moved onward until Mexico City, the nation's magnificent capitol, lay under siege. A final, overpowering charge had breached the mighty stone walls of the ancient city. Luke had remained there in the occupying force until the late spring of 1847.

But he felt older men should be wiser and know the horrors of war and not be so willingly to participate.

However, this was not Luke's war. He remained quiet and said nothing to Dauphin. Let him and the other men like him fight the war as they wanted.

"Where are the Union infiltrators coming from?" Luke asked.

"An army of Yankee soldiers is being assembled on Ship Island in the Gulf of Mexico, south of Biloxi. I believe the infiltrators are coming from there. They sail into Breton Sound, and then come by small boats up some of the hundreds of bayous that lace the swamps and forest. The Confederate army does not seem able to catch them. In fact, the situation is becoming so bad that neither the army nor the local law officials can even stop the outbreaks of looting in the city."

Luke rode on silently. Though he wanted no part of the war, he felt the Confederates were indeed rebels and President Lincoln probably had a right to crush them if he could. He shoved the thoughts of war aside. After a few days of the pleasant company of the beautiful Susan, he would return to his mountains.

"What's that," Dauphin called sharply. He jerked his mount to a halt and stood erect in the saddle to listen ahead.

"Gunshots," Luke said, cupping his hands around his ears to better hear the distant, muted firing.

"Goddamned infiltrators," Dauphin cursed. "They're attacking the plantation," He struck his horse savagely with his riding crop.

The startled and hurt beast lunged forward. Its driving hooves flung white seashells behind it.

Luke spoke to his mount and the animal sprang forward to run parallel to Dauphin's.

"They waited for Thacker and his cavalrymen to leave, and for it to become almost dark," Dauphin called across to Luke. He lashed his horse to the top of its speed.

The horses thundered along the road. They swept past broad, cultivated fields and pastures. The two riders passed a group of Negro field hands staring off in the direction of the gunshots.

"There's the house." Dauphin pointed ahead. At a distance of some one-half mile, a large plantation house painted a brilliant white sat in a grove of tall trees.

Dauphin pulled a pistol from inside his jacket and held it ready in his hand. "Help me fight them, Coldiron," he said. "Your money is there in the house."

Luke lifted his revolver from its holster. It was one thing to want to avoid war, but it was quite another to be attacked and robbed.

The gunshots had ceased. A thick plume of smoke rose from the main section of the house, and another column from the right wing. Black men and women calling out in frightened voices and herding their children in front of them, were hurrying away from the house and out into the fields. They whirled to look to the rear when a loud explosion at the house boomed out, shaking the air.

The distance to the house diminished swiftly, and Luke could see up the long, tree-lined driveway and in under the wide spreading limbs of the trees. Near the house, a man in civilian clothing sat his horse and held the bridle reins of several other saddled mounts. He whistled shrilly through his teeth as Luke and Dauphin raced into sight in the lane.

A moment later, five men dressed similarly to the first ran from the open door of the mansion and out between the tall, wooden columns of the porch. Every man carried a bulging sack in his arms. The raiders tied their stolen loot to the pommels of their saddles and jerked themselves up on the backs of their mounts.

One man had swung up astride a tall, gray horse. He threw a look down the lane at the two approaching riders and called out something to the other men that Luke could not hear. He pointed out across a meadow stretching off to a wood. The entire group kicked their horses into a run away from the house.

Dauphin reined his horse to the right out of the lane and into the meadow and rushed to intercept the raiders. He screamed a high, shrill cry and thrust his pistol out before him.

You are a damn fool, thought Coldiron, but a brave fool. Two men should not fight six. That could be suicide. I'm just as foolish. He pulled his pistol and ran his horse up beside Dauphin's.

The distance separating the groups of men shortened to a hundred yards. Luke and Dauphin continued to bore in at a steep angle to the course of the raiders.

The leader shouted to the members of his band. They raised their mounts to an all-outrun. Some drew rifles and others pistols in preparation to fire upon the two riders charging in on them.

"Veer off! Veer off," Luke cried out at Dauphin. The man seemed intent upon riding right into the muzzles of his enemies' guns.

Luke swerved his mount to the left to provide a space of forty yards or so between the raiders and himself. His eyes locked upon the rider on the gray horse, a large, bearded man. That was the leader. Luke would shoot him first.

Dauphin's pistol cracked. The raiders instantly began to fire back. Luke heard the whistling of bullets.

Luke raised his pistol to point at the leader of the raiders. His finger pressed on the trigger. As he fired, one of the other horsemen suddenly rode between Luke and his target. Luke's bullet slammed into the nearer raider.

The man, hard hit by the speeding lead ball, rocked to the side. He struggled to maintain his seat in the saddle, held on for a brief moment, then fell from his horse.

The two groups of men, astride their running horses, reached their closest point of approach. Luke snapped a shot across the few yards of space that separated them.

The leader of the raiders, now knowing he was Luke's target, threw himself to hang along the far side of his horse. He held himself there, exposing only his hand on the pommel and his heel over the back of his horse. From behind the protective, bony bulk of his steed, he threw a shot at Luke.

The bullet tore a hole in the air near Luke's head as he ducked low and slid down like his opponent to hang Indian fashion behind his horse. He lowered himself to look from under the neck of his mount. He tried to spot a vital piece of his enemy to shoot, but could not.

Luke shifted to the next raider in line. That man sat upright. A perfect target. Luke shot him from the back of his running horse. The man, dead as he fell, rolled and bounced with a jumble of legs and arms along the ground.

The raiders sped away. The riderless horses ran on with them. The shooting ceased.

Luke pulled himself upright in the saddle. He yanked his horse to a stop as the raiders vanished into the woods.

Three bodies lay in crumpled mounds in the meadow. Dauphin had also killed a man.

Luke swung down and went to kneel beside the nearest raider. The man was alive, but badly wounded. A bullet had entered his side high up. Blood oozed steadily from the jagged hole.

The man reached feebly for his revolver, which lay on the ground near him. Luke grabbed the weapon and tossed it out of reach. "None of that. Who are you? Who sent you to attack Dauphin?"

"Go to hell," the man growled, his face fierce.

"You're going there before me. Now who are you?" Luke grabbed the front of the man's clothing and shook him roughly.

Pain clouded the raider's face. His mouth worked trying to form words. "Stop, you're killing me. My name's Simon Hanks. I . . ." His head rolled to the side as life ran out of him.

Luke studied the man's features for a few seconds, imprinting it on his memory. As he rose to his feet he heard Dauphin groan. He had forgotten about the planter. He turned toward him.

Dauphin was slumped far forward in the saddle. He straightened himself with an effort and looked at Luke. His face was pale and pinched with pain.

"You're hit?" Luke said. He moved swiftly to Dauphin.

"I'm afraid so."

"Let me take a look."

"Later. First I must get a bucket brigade organized to put the fire out."

Dauphin rode off slowly across the meadow. Luke, worried at the planter's appearance, guided his horse to ride close beside the man.

Luke evaluated the elegant, two story plantation house setting in among ancient hardwood trees. He judged the structure must contain twenty-five to thirty rooms. Six large, round, wooden columns reached to the roof, which was surfaced with gray slate. A wide open veranda stretched across the full width of the house.

Dauphin climbed weakly down from his horse at the front entrance. He halted beside the body of a man lying on the steps leading up to the porch. A pistol lay by the man's hand.

"That's Simpson, my overseer," Dauphin said.

Luke bent over the man and examined him. "Dead," he announced.

Dauphin nodded and went up the steps. Luke followed and entered an immense room with a high, domed ceiling. Hand-painted murals decorated two of the walls and the underside of the dome. Hand-carved mahogany banisters adorned the winding staircase leading up to the second floor, and marble covered the mantles and window sills.

Smoke was pouring into the room through a door on the right side and another in the rear. It hung in a dark, dense cloud beneath the dome. Luke could hear the roar of a raging fire somewhere deeper in the big house.

"Luke, call the blacks back to the house and get them started fighting the fires. Then help me."

"All right."

Luke hastened to the outside. The slaves were returning hesitatingly from the surrounding fields. He shouted at them to come quickly.

They hastened their steps and gathered in the yard. The men moved to the front of the group and looked at him expectantly.

Luke swiftly organized two bucket brigades, one for each fire. The men and women began to work swiftly, hoisting water up from a large cistern at the rear of the house. The slopping buckets of water were sent up the lines hand-to-hand to the men facing the fires.

Luke hurried back inside and along a smoke-filled hallway toward Dauphin in the front. Partway along, a shattered door hung on one hinge. He glanced inside.

The room had once been a grand library, but now it was a shambles. The explosion earlier had flung the furniture back against the wall, and books lay scattered everywhere. The door of a metal safe set in a corner, gaped open. The safe was empty.

Luke turned away. The money that would have been used to pay him for his horses was gone. He stomped angrily down the hallway.

Dauphin sat on the floor, propped against the wall. His breath came labored and shallow.

"Let me see your wound," Luke said, kneeling beside the man.

"I think it's a bad one," Dauphin's voice came with a wet, bubbly sound.

Luke ripped open the man's shirt. A bullet hole in Dauphin's chest steadily leaked blood, blood that was frothed with white. The planter's lungs had been punctured.

"You need a surgeon, and quickly," Luke said.

"No surgeon can help me. I'm a dead man. Tell Susan what happened here," Dauphin became silent, staring fixedly out the open door.

With a will, the planter pulled himself back from whatever he was seeing, and looked at Luke. "She will be able to take care of herself. Behind that beautiful face, she's sword steel. And she's a fine marksman."

"I'll tell her. But now I must get a buggy hitched up and get you to a hospital."

"Wait. I want you to know the payment for your horses is in my safe in the library. Susan can open it for you."

"The safe has been blown open. It's empty. The raiders must have known you had a large sum of money there."

"Some of the slaves must be helping the infiltrators and sympathizers. The house blacks know everything that goes on here, and they've told my enemies. I'm sorry that you lost your payment. This is not your fight. Go find Captain Thacker and take back your horses."

"Your loss is much greater than mine."

Dauphin looked at Luke. The bright fire of battle was gone from his eyes. He started to speak, but his voice caught and he began to cough. Blood filled his mouth and bubbles burst on his lips. He fought to breathe, his chest arching, then his head sank.

Luke remained kneeling for a moment beside the dead man. His eyes burned with the acrid fumes of the smoke that had thickened and hung barely above his head. The house was filled with the roar of the fires. Almost inaudible in the sound, was a scared, nervous chant the men and women of the bucket brigade had begun.

He carried Dauphin's body into the yard, and brought the corpse of the overseer to lie beside it.

Luke checked the two fires, finding that the fire at the rear of the house was the largest. The aged, dry wood of the structure burned fiercely. He moved to the front of the bucket line, and the sweating black man moved back to give him a place where the fire was hottest.

The chant that bound the chain of laboring slaves broke as every worker shifted a step to the rear. Then the rhythmic cadence began again.

As the buckets of water were handed forward to Luke he began to hum to the chant of the blacks. As he flung the buckets of water at the leaping flames, his hum hardened, becoming a full-voiced cry in the rear of his throat. He became part of the group, part of the mighty labor to put out the fiery inferno that growled and raged and shot flaming embers at him. But even as he worked, he knew the battle was lost. The water he threw upon the orange flames immediately exploded into steam and did nothing to slow the ravaging advance of the fire.

Then the ultimate words of defeat came. "No more water. The cistern is empty." The words went from mouth to mouth up the chain of men and women.

Luke and the slaves backed away from the flames and into the yard. "Save as much of the furniture as you can," he called out to them. The two doors he knew about were full of flames. "Climb in through the windows and hand out as many things as you can. Are there other doors we can use?"

"There's a door on the west end of the house that might not be afire," a man said.

"Show me. The rest of you do what you can."

The group of people broke and scattered around the house. Luke ran with the man who had told of the other door. He heard glass breaking as windows were broken out.

For the next few hectic minutes, the men and women carried and dragged what items they could from the burning house. Smaller furniture, several firearms, linens, bric-a-brac, clothing, and half a hundred other items were brought into the yard. Finally, choking and coughing with the smoke and seared by the flames, the men and women drew away from the raging inferno.

Luke stood with the blacks and watched the beautiful mansion be consumed by the fire monster. The flames roared on, burning through the exterior walls. The high, slate roof caved in with a tremendous crash. Sparks and flying embers erupted, spewing out into the yard and geysering up into the limbs of the trees.

A sad, mournful cry sprang from the throats of the people. Some of the women were crying. Luke wondered if one of the slaves had told of the coming purchase of horses and the money in the safe as Dauphin had said. And was that person present here now?

Luke went to his horse, mounted, and rode away from the burned home. Night had fallen, but with the aid of the moon he found the location where the fight with the raiders had occurred.

He began to curse savagely as he looked at the empty meadow. The bodies were gone. The raiders had returned for their dead. The only information Luke had was a dying man saying his name was Simon Hanks. That might well be a lie.

\*\*\*

Dauphin's Negro slave, riding the horse ahead of Luke, seemed to have cat's eyes in the dark. He led at a trot along the night-blackened roads, making turns onto other roads that were nearly invisible to Luke.

"Gettin' close now, suh," the Negro called over his shoulder. "They's camped just yonder on the shore of Pontchartrain."

"Lead on," Luke replied. He had not been paid for his horses, and now must retrieve them from Thacker before the company of Confederate cavalry rode off on them. He had no idea how he would get them back to the New Mexico Territory. Perhaps he could yet find a buyer for them in New Orleans. The possibility of that was very remote.

"There's the camp," said the Negro, halting his horse.

Luke could make out the dim, white pyramids of several canvas tents placed in two rows. There was no light. The only sound was the chitter of night insects and the buzz of mosquitoes. Strange that at this military encampment no sentry had challenged their approach.

"Hello the camp!" Luke called.

Somewhere among the tents wind flapped a piece of canvas. Then the silence held sway again.

"Hello the camp!" he shouted loudly.

"For God's sake, come and help me," a voice cried faintly from the darkness.

"Where are you?" Luke called as he dismounted.

"Back here in the edge of the brush. My leg's all shot to hell."

"Keep talking so I can find you," Luke said as he moved to the left of the tents and along a stretch of bushes.

"Is that you, Mr. Coldiron?"

"Yes. Are you Riley?"

"Sure enough."

"I see you," Luke hurried forward and squatted beside the man. "What happened?"

"Bunch of men, ten or twelve, jumped us. Hit us just at dark. I think I'm the only one left alive."

"You mean the whole company was beat by ten men?"

"No. Captain Thacker let all the men go into town for this last night, except for four of us. We were to patrol the camp and guard the horses. The company was going to ride north to Vicksburg in the morning."

"Were the attackers Union soldiers?"

"Might've been soldiers, but they were in civilian clothes so I couldn't say for sure."

"Where are the other men who were on guard with you?"

"Down toward the far end of the camp. I think they're all dead. After the fighting was over and the men and horses were gone, I called and called. Nobody answered."

Luke spoke to the Negro standing nearby. "Find a lantern in one of the tents and make a light."

"Yes, suh," the man replied. He hurried off in the darkness.

Shortly a flame made a hole in the night. "Light's lit," the Negro said.

"Good. Bring it over here."

Luke spoke to Riley. "I'm going to fix your leg the best that I can and take you to a hospital."

"All right. Then you must go and find Captain Thacker and tell him about the horses being stolen."

"Which way were they taken?"

"East along the shore of the lake. But you'll never find them in all that swamp country."

"I'll find them, or the men who took them," Luke felt his anger cold, hard, and determined.

"Why you?"

"I never got paid for them. I want them back."

"Why didn't Mr. Dauphin pay you?"

"He's dead. His plantation was attacked and robbed. The big house was burned to the ground. Somebody planned very well. They had total success both there and here."

"Damn Union spies or sympathizers did it," Riley said.

"I'd guess so," Luke said. "Hold on." He lifted the wounded cavalryman in his arms.

# Chapter Five

"My father, dead!" Susan Dauphin cried. She seemed to shrink into herself. Her hands fluttered up like wounded birds to press upon her breast over her heart. Tears welled up from their tiny salt springs, gathered in her eyes and, overflowing, coursed down her pale, white cheeks.

"Yes. I'm sorry to have to tell you that," Luke said. He had brought the cavalryman Riley to Charity Hospital and a surgeon was now tending to the man's wound. Luke had found Susan in the ward of the wounded Confederate soldiers.

"How? Where did it happen?"

"At your home. Raiders were attacking the house when your father and I got there. Your father charged them, firing his pistol. They shot him."

"They all escaped?"

"We killed three of them. Three got away."

Susan looked at Luke through her tears. "There is something else that you're not telling me."

"They've burned your home. Your slaves and I tried to put the fires out, but it had too much of a start before we could get to it. We were able to save some of the furniture and other household items."

Susan turned away and stared out the window of the hospital. She stifled her sobs and spoke over her shoulder. "And what of your horses? Were you paid?"

"The raiders had blasted the safe open. All the money was gone. Also, a second band of men killed the guards at the cavalry camp and stole all the horses. Both attacks were well planned and coordinated."

"My father was a generous, loving man. I will miss him so terribly. Did he know before he died that the money was gone, and he could not provide horses for his company of troopers?"

"Yes."

"Damn them all to hell!" Susan exclaimed. She shook with the terrible hate that swept over her. The need for vengeance rose black and ugly. Union men had slain her father and destroyed her home. They would pay a horrible price for that. Her hands clenched at her sides. Besides the punishment she would wreak upon them, she would find the money to equip Captain Thacker's company of cavalry.

Susan dashed her tears away and looked at the man from the New Mexico Territory. He was watching her intently.

Luke was shocked by the change that had occurred in Susan upon learning of the death of her father. After the first shocked expression and a brief flow of tears, a dark veil seemed to have fallen over her through which he could see nothing of the previous woman. She had become pale and stiff, corpse-like. Her eyes were cold and her face hard, with the bones coming closer to the skin. She was sword steel, as her father had said.

"And what of you, Mr. Coldiron? What do you plan to do?" Susan's voice was flat, without emotion.

"Get my horses back," Luke replied. Susan appeared to have little interest in how he might answer. She seemed to have turned inward, as if focusing on some private plan.

"Where can I find General Lovell's headquarters? I want to report to Captain Thacker what has happened."

"On Jackson Square in New Orleans. That's near the waterfront. The general's headquarters are in the Cabildo. There has been quite a bit of activity there all evening. Rumors are everywhere that the Union army has landed on the coast southeast of the forts and are moving inland."

Luke nodded his understanding as he gazed steadily at Susan. "You invited me to stay a few days in New Orleans. I would still like to do that. When I return with my horses, may I come to see you?"

"Yes, Mr. Coldiron, you may do that if you want to," Susan said in her controlled voice. "Don't get yourself killed fighting the horse thieves."

"I'll do my best not to let that happen. Where will you live now that the plantation house has burned?"

"I have an aunt—Sophia Dauphin. She lives on Napoleon Avenue in the Garden District of the city. I could stay with her. However, there is a cottage in the woods just behind the plantation house. You can find me there, or here at the hospital."

"You can expect to see me soon."

"If you don't get your horses back, you must join me to make the Yankees pay."

*** 

Coldiron watched the half dozen lanterns weave eerily through the darkness lying dense around the army tents. The squad of Confederate cavalrymen, their bodies ghostly silhouettes against the patches of light, made not a sound as they searched the camp for their dead comrades.

Abruptly a voice called out angrily. "Here's another one, Captain It's Purdy. And he's dead, too, just as Coldiron said."

"Look for the last one," Captain Thacker called back.

Coldiron and the cavalry captain sat their horses in the center of the encampment on the shore of Lake Pontchartrain. They had arrived only minutes earlier from New Orleans with a wagon to retrieve the men killed by the raiders.

"Goddamned Yankee infiltrators," Thacker cursed. "They hit and run. We can't catch them."

"It is war, Captain," Luke replied. "And I believe it will become very bad."

"Are you going to sign up and help us whip the Yankees?"

"No. There may be a cause big enough for the war, but I am sure it is not my concern."

"I see," said the captain in a sarcastic voice.

"We've found the third man, captain," a cavalryman called. "He's dead too."

"Put him in the wagon with the others," Thacker directed. "Have the troopers form up here by me. We're going back to New Orleans. We'll have a squad of men come and strike the tents tomorrow."

The soldiers came, two carrying the corpse. The dead man was placed in the wagon.

The squad gathered around its captain. The lights of the lanterns joined into a diffused yellow glow that illuminated the tense faces of the cavalrymen.

A sergeant stepped forward. "Your orders, sir," he said.

"Sergeant, take the dead men to the morgue in the city. See that they are properly identified. Assemble the company of troopers at first light in Jackson Square. We will fight as an infantry unit until we can obtain horses. I will inform General Lovell of our situation."

Coldiron spoke. "Captain, there are two hundred horses within a few miles of us. They'll be easy to trail. We can take them back from the raiders."

Thacker looked at Coldiron. "You told me Dauphin never paid you for the horses before he was killed and his money stolen. Therefore, the horses are still yours. Do you plan to give them to us should we be able to recapture them"

"I'd want pay for them."

"We have no money to buy them. Nor can we find someone with the money. Surely not the Dauphins. They've already sold their farm in Missouri and mortgaged their plantation here to the limit. They will be penniless if the Yankees win the war. So the horses remain yours. You get them back as best you can. I've a war to fight, and no time for you."

Thacker reined his mount away from Coldiron. "Sergeant, move the men out."

"Yes, sir," the sergeant said. "Two lantern men take the lead, two in the rear. Form up and move out."

A Stygian blackness settled upon Coldiron and the deserted camp as the squad of cavalrymen with their flaming lanterns drew away behind the trees along the road. He dismounted and stood by the head of his horse. The sky was totally hidden by thick clouds, and the air heavy with moisture. The dampness and the darkness had a tangible density, a weight that he could feel on his face.

Luke untied his bedroll from behind the saddle. He considered sleeping in one of the tents, but decided against that and spread his gum blanket on the ground. The front legs of the horse were hobbled with a leather strap, the iron bit slipped from between its teeth, and the cinch loosened. He slapped the animal away to graze. He lay down on his bed and stared up at the invisible sky.

Luke could not sleep. He slapped at the mosquitoes and watched the pale, yellow glows of fireflies as they made slow, erratic flights through the darkness. The horse made low, tearing sounds as it cropped the wild, spring grass. Farther away, the waves of the waters of Lake Pontchartrain lapped wetly upon its grainy shore.

He was still awake when the gray light of the false dawn came and then died. Shortly, the true dawn arrived, the darkness sliding away and the light hardening. The shadowy forms of the trees of the forest took shape, and the broad, flat surface of Pontchartrain could be seen stretching away for miles to the north.

He arose and rolled his bedding. The horse came obediently at his whistle.

Luke rode off along the dark tunnels of the forest.

# Chapter Six

"Quiet, there," Admiral David Farragut said sternly as some heavy object thudded to the deck of the war sloop Hartford. "The rebels will hear you."

"Sorry, sir," a chastened voice replied out of the darkness. "It slipped."

The admiral was leaning against one of the starboard cannons of his flagship and peering hard to pierce the night lying black upon the Mississippi River. He could see the outlines of the Brooklyn and Richmond, powerfully armed sloops anchored nearby. The two ships would accompany him in the second division to run upriver past the Confederate Fort St. Phillip and Fort Jackson. The first and third divisions, made up of three heavy sloops, three light sloops, and nine gunboats, were only vague forms farther away on the breast of the river.

He had been forced to leave the frigate Colorado, the largest and most heavily armed ship of his squadron, behind at the mouth of the Mississippi. The frigate drew twenty-three feet of water and could not cross the bar, that ridge of sand deposited where the river's current met the quiet waters of the Gulf of Mexico. Numerous times the ship had charged the bar, but she could not bull her way through. The big cannons aboard the Colorado would be sorely missed.

The admiral turned his attention to the two dark and silent forts that blocked the path of the Union flotilla of warships. Fort Jackson, a modern pentagon structure and the strongest, lay upriver from the flotilla of Union warships and on the west bank. Old Fort St. Phillip lay on the east bank. The Confederate soldiers in the forts were brave fellows, thought the admiral, and stubborn. They had shown their mettle by withstanding six days of bombardment from his ships' heavy guns. He had rained three thousand shells a day upon the rebels.

The main deck of the Hartford was alive with men. They spoke in low voices, and their feet made low, scuffing sounds as they moved about making the last preparations for the coming dash through the gauntlet of Confederate cannon. Battle lanterns, hooded so that their light could barely be seen the width of the ship, gave but little aid in the darkness, yet the decks were familiar to the seamen and the Marines, and they went on with their duties.

The admiral watched the crew at their tasks. Two seamen went by carrying a bucket of sand in each hand. Their shadowy faces were sober. They seemed mere lads, almost children, to the sixty-one-year-old admiral.

The seamen began to spread the sand behind the 30-pound rifle on a horizontal pivot on the stern of the ship. The same preparations were being taken at the 30-pound rifle on the bow, on the small deck, and the cannons on the gun deck just below. The sand would prevent the members of the gun crews from slipping on the blood of their wounded comrades. He had had the chore of spreading sand as a midshipman at the age of eleven, when he had fought in the War of 1812.

The admiral walked aft. Seamen were lowering a section of thick, iron chains over the side of the ship to protect its engines and powder magazines. The chains scraped as they slid down the wooden hull. The men grunted under the strain of the heavy weight.

"Hang it three feet below waterline and eight feet above," the lieutenant in charge of the operation directed.

"Aye, aye, sir," the chief petty officer replied.

"Admiral, this is the last section," the lieutenant said.

"Thank you, Lieutenant," the admiral said. He thought the positioning of the mesh chains was not unlike that of a medieval knight being helped into his suit of chain mail. And, like the knight, the Hartford would be shielded from lighter blows. Nothing could protect her wooden hulls from a direct hit by a ball from one of the enemy's larger guns.

The pace of the activity on the ship slowed. Officers sought out the admiral and reported their readiness for battle. Colonel Trotter, senior officer of the Marines, came last for he could not place his men until all other ship's tasks had been completed.

"Admiral, my Marines are stationed to repel borders, though I do not expect any unless there is some Confederate force upstream we do not know about. We will assist the ship's crew as best we can while running past the forts."

"Very well, Colonel," the admiral said. The colonel had ordered an extra fifty Marines aboard from the other ships to protect him and insure he did not fall into Confederate hands.

The admiral again looked upstream at the forts. Should he wait for General Butler? For months, the general had been building a Union army on Barren Ship Island just off the coast. The general had now embarked with his force of sixteen thousand soldiers, and was sailing to the Isle au Breton Sound. He would put ashore there and march overland to strike the forts from the rear. It could take days for the general to arrive. Time was critical in war.

The admiral stepped to a lantern and looked at his watch in the light. "Two o'clock," he said, as if to himself. Then, in a louder voice he called to the chief signalman standing waiting nearby. "Chief, send a man aloft with the signal. We're going upriver."

"Aye, sir. I'll do it myself."

Two ship's lanterns with red globes were lighted. The chief signalman tied them to his belt and mounted the ratlines. A minute later the lights swung from a high yardarm.

From off in the darkness came the rumble of several steam engines. The first division of ships began to move upriver.

The admiral stood rigid, awaiting the sound of an alarm at the Confederate forts. Seconds passed. None came. The enemy had not yet heard his ships' engines.

The admiral walked forward to the bow of the Hartford. He could see the black forms of the ships of the first division crawling north on the even blacker water. Good luck to you.

The admiral knew he was taking the biggest gamble of his long naval career. Most of his officers opposed the attempt to run the ships through the crossfire of the cannons of the Confederates. They had argued the bombardment of the enemy should continue until the forts were destroyed, or surrendered.

The officers reasoning had a sound basis. The Union flotilla was composed of wooden-hulled, deep-drafted ocean-going ships. They were equipped with both sail and steam engines to propel them. The sails were of no use on the relatively narrow Mississippi River. The steam-powered screws were vulnerable to damage in the shallow water.

The Confederate enemy was formidable, armed with big bore cannon behind strong masonry fortifications. Also, the massive chain stretching across the river just south of the forts was a great impediment. Fortunately, a pair of gunboats had stolen close to one of the hulks two nights earlier and cut the chains. A gap had been created, but only wide enough to allow the passage of one ship at a time. As they steamed through the passageway, the Union ships would be a long line of targets for the rebel cannoneers.

The ships of the first division were now in formation and steaming full speed toward the chain barrier. The admiral watched them for a moment longer as they faded into the darkness. Men did not like to die in darkness, but only the blackness of the night could save his ships and men.

The admiral returned to the quarter deck. In two hours or so he would know if his gamble had failed or succeeded.

"Hoist anchor," he ordered. "Slowly. Make as little noise as possible," The capstan had a habit of groaning loudly as pressure was applied to it to lift the anchor.

The capstan began to rotate. It was quiet. Someone had gotten to the right spot with grease. The anchor chain crept up through the hawsehole and down into the chain locker. The big anchor came clear of the water and was lashed firmly against the ship's bow.

"Full speed ahead," the admiral ordered.

The Hartford steamed into the current of the river. The Brooklyn and Richmond took station in single file close astern.

"I'm going aloft," the admiral told the quarter deck officer. "Hold a heading directly for the passage through the chain barrier. Listen for my orders."

"Aye, aye, sir."

The admiral tucked his spyglass under his belt and climbed up the ratlines of the main mast. He found a high perch on the futtuck shrouds a little distance below the maintop. He braced himself and extended his telescope to scan the ships ahead.

The last ship of the first division was just clearing the chain barrier. No alarm had yet been sounded at either fort. Luck had been better than expected. The Hartford plowed onward, fast approaching the barrier.

A cannon roared out at Fort Jackson. Immediately other cannon at the fort opened fire. Guns at Fort St. Phillip commenced to crash. Cannonballs came streaking in, exploding around the Union ships. Several exploded near the flagship.

The Hartford shook beneath the admiral's feet as the ship's twenty-five 9-inch Dahlgren smoothbore cannon fired. Only seconds behind, the two 30-pound rifles boomed. Flame lanced out from the bores of the cannons on port and starboard as the gun crews fired at both forts. The admiral saw the flashes of the guns of the other Union ships as they joined the battle.

The black night was torn with bright red spears of flame from the cannon blast and round flashes of bursting shells. The river reverberated to the cannon fire, and became bathed with lurid red.

On the shore near the forts, huge bonfires sprang into life, casting light out onto the river to help the Confederate gunners to better see their targets. Above the chains some one quarter mile, fire rafts were set ablaze and shoved out into the current to float down upon the Union ships. The river seemed full of rafts with their loads of leaping flames rising in orange columns some two hundred feet high.

Admiral Farragut braced his knees against the mast and leaned back against one of the stays. He pointed his spyglass at the fire rafts. Two of the rafts were being pushed by tugs.

"Admiral, come down," Colonel Trotter shouted from the deck. "The aim of the rebel gunners is damn accurate. It's not safe up there."

The admiral did not reply. He swung his telescope to look at the ships of the first division. They were above the barrier and steaming out of range of the forts' guns. He turned to the rear. The Brooklyn and Richmond were holding station astern. The lead ship of the third division was coming swiftly. In the flickering light of the exploding shells and the fires on the shore, he tried to spot any damage to his ships. The light was too uncertain and the smoke of burnt gunpowder too dense to be sure of much of anything.

"Admiral, come down!" Trotter shouted with considerable urgency through the din of cannon roar.

The admiral collapsed his telescope in his hand and took one sweeping look with naked eyes over the battle zone. He knew the horrifying death that was being caused by the bursting shells. Men were being blown apart in the forts and on the ships. Yet there was magnificence in such a great battle. He came down the ratlines to the deck like a young man.

"Thank you, Admiral," the colonel said with relief evident in his voice.

A solid, round cannonball struck the main mast where Farragut had stood but a moment before. A splintered yardarm and pieces of the rigging came drumming down on the deck. The admiral and the colonel dodged away across the deck. They stopped by the railing and looked up at the mast.

"It seems that I should thank you, Colonel," the admiral said. "A minute longer on the mast and I'd have been as broken as that yardarm."

He pivoted and hastened to the quarter deck. The Hartford was just passing beyond the break in the chain barrier. Every gun was firing at the forts. The return fire was heavy. The rebel gunners had got the range of the line of ships. Exploding shells flung shrieking pieces of shrapnel over the Hartford. A shell ripped through the foremast. Solid balls flung up great geysers of water close on all sides. The air cringed at the deadly crash of guns.

"Helmsman, a point to starboard," the admiral ordered, watching one of the tugs shoving a fire raft to intercept them. The new course would take the ship closer to the shore, but he had no choice if he were to avoid the fire raft.

He shouted at the men at the nearest deck gun. "Chief gunner, sink that tug and fire raft coming in on the port side," Neither the 30-pound rifle on the main deck nor the big guns on the gun deck could be brought to bear on the low riding tug. The small cannon on the main deck would have to do the job.

"Aye, sir," The barrel of the gun began to swing and to lower.

The tug came doggedly on, altering its course to force a collision with the ship. The blazing pitch wood on the raft sent flames leaping as high as the mast of the Hartford. The flames, reflecting in the water, seemed to be burning the river.

The Hartford came to an abrupt, jolting stop. The masts swayed and groaned. A stay broke with a sound like a rifle firing. Men were flung off their feet and sent sprawling on the deck.

"We've hit a sandbar," Admiral Farragut shouted. "Reverse engines. Get us off!"

The rebel tug took a shot, and then another, from the small deck cannon of the ship. The sturdy tug steamed on, shoving the fire.

The raft and its blazing pitch pine crashed into the side of the Hartford near the deck cannon by the admiral. Flames leapt up the side of the ship. The tug continued to drive forward, holding the fire against the ship's hull.

"Don't flinch from the fire, boys," the admiral shouted at the gun crew, who were now surrounded by flames. "Load and give that rascally tug another shot." '

One of the gun crew, braving the searing flames, rammed powder and a ball into the bore of the cannon. The gun captain fired point blank into the tug. Fragments of tug decking and hull flew in every direction. Her two-man crew sprang into the river.

The tug's engine continued to turn the screw for a handful of seconds. Then the cold river water rising up through the hole in the bottom of the hull quenched its fire. The tug listed rapidly to the side and sank.

The blazing raft hung a moment against the hull of the ship. Then, inch by inch, it drifted away on the current of the river.

The fire fighting crew instantly sprang forward with their buckets of water and swarmed up the rigging, dousing the flames.

The admiral shouted encouragement. "Good, lads!"

He hurried to the speaking tube to the engine room. "Back us up. Give her everything she's got. Sit on the damn safety valve if you have to."

The Hartford fought the sandbar, the steam engine pounding like a great heart deep within the ship and the big screw churning water and mud. The Hartford vibrated as if she would shake herself apart. Then, with a great lurch, she pulled free.

The admiral ran his ship beyond the range of the Confederate guns. He halted, holding against the current of the Mississippi near the Richmond and Brooklyn. The ships of the first division were nearby.

He surveyed the battle through his telescope. The cannon in both forts were still firing rapidly, their fire concentrated on the last half of the third division. The gunboat Iroquois, barely through the barrier, was taking the brunt of the shells. She had been assigned the last position of the Union flotilla.

The plucky Iroquois, running through a blizzard of shells, steamed past the chain barrier and out of range of the Confederate guns. As the last cannon fired and silence fell, the admiral lowered his telescope. His ships had run the gauntlet of the Confederate forts. The extent of the damage to them was not yet known. He did not think it serious.

You did your best, Admiral Farragut said silently to the fighters in the forts. However, it had not been good enough. The magnificent enemy city of New Orleans would be under his guns in a few hours.

# Chapter Seven

"The honeyguide was in its tree most of yesterday," Blackberry Woman said to Panther as he seated himself at the breakfast table.

Panther glanced out the open door of the log cabin. Dawn was creeping in from the east and driving the night shadows from the aisles among the big forest trees. Thick clouds hung low, hiding the sky. It would rain before the day ended.

He checked the dead, leafless tree that was the favorite of the honey-guide. The limb upon which it always perched when watching for Panther was empty.

"The bird will be back," Blackberry Woman said, seeing the direction of the man's eyes.

"I hope so," Panther said. "I sold all my honey yesterday."

Blackberry Woman merely nodded. She had washed the buckets and cloths used to cover the honey, and all were ready by the door for the next beehive hunt.

Panther began to eat. The venison, he had killed himself. The sassafras roots for the hot tea, he had dug. The canned berries, richly sweetened with the white man's sugar, had been prepared by the woman the previous summer. Her hot biscuits and the gravy made from the drippings of the venison were delicious.

He chewed slowly, watching the day come alive in the forest.

The woman sat down opposite the man. She folded her hands on the top of the small, hand built table and looked steadily at Panther.

"Be very careful in the woods today," Blackberry Woman said. "I feel danger for you."

Panther stopped eating and looked into the woman's black eyes. He had spent his entire life in the forest and knew it as well as the animal whose name he bore. Blackberry Woman did not know the dense woods as well as he. However, she sensed things that he could not. For that reason he gave much weight to her words.

"There are strange men hiding in the woods," Panther said. "They come up the bayous from the south, and I think they must be the Yankees the people of the city talk about and fear. There will be a great battle soon."

"A battle has just ended one place, and is drawing close to us."

The Chickasaw continued to study the Negro woman. Her name was Alice Laveau. She had lived with him for twenty years, cooking his food and laying with him at night. Some of the few Negro men with whom Panther sometimes talked had asked him about Alice, questioning him about her powers to know the future. They pointed out that her mother had been a much respected voodoo woman. Panther always told the men that Alice had no powers. He had not told them the truth, for he did not want the attention of others focused upon his woman, and thus on him.

Panther recalled a long ago time, a time of great sorrow, and a time before he first knew Blackberry Woman. That was twenty-five summers past. The white man's army came and forcibly rounded up the Chickasaw people of every village and herded them away to The Oklahoma Territory far to the west. Panther and a few other young braves refused to leave the land where the Chickasaw nation had lived from the beginning of time. They fled into the swamps, hiding in the dangerous, watery labyrinth. The soldiers failed to find them.

For five years Panther hid in the solitary forest and avoided the soldiers. That was not difficult, for the white men were afraid of the swamps and did not venture far from the traveled roads in their searches. The forest that had been a joyous home to Panther had become a place of heart-searing loneliness after the people were gone.

Panther came to know that he should have fought the white soldiers instead of fleeing. There were hundreds of them, and they would have slain him in the end.

But would that not have been better than hiding like a coward in the swamps?

There in the lonely forest a burning, unquenchable desire for a woman came upon Panther. As he roamed the forest he thought of the lovely Chickasaw maidens he had known, and he dreamed of them at night. He wanted a wife, a woman of his own people. But that could not be, for only a very few women had fled into the forest with the men. None were for him.

He had first seen Alice picking blackberries along the edge of the forest east of New Orleans. She had been young and pretty. He moved out into the open where she could see him. To show her he meant her no harm, he laid his bow and arrows and knife down on the ground and walked away from them. For a time she stood poised to flee, at the same time examining him with her keen eyes. Then she relaxed, seeming to have decided he was indeed no danger to tier.

Alice had been born of a free black woman, and was thus free in her own right. She could go and come as she pleased. To earn her living she picked blackberries for sale in the city. Often she and Panther met at the edge of the forest. She told Panther the white soldiers no longer searched for the remaining Chickasaws to march them off to that place called the Oklahoma Territory. That summer he began to venture into the town to sell honey, and in the winter that followed to sell furs.

The pleasant, enduring companionship of Blackberry Woman gave him some consolation, and allayed a little of his painful remorse at not having fought the white soldiers when his people had been torn from their land.

At the end of the first year Alice, always Blackberry Woman to him, came to live with him in the forest. Panther had not one complaint about the woman. She was pleasant and giving. However, he did possess a regret that he could not mention to her. He could never sire a true Chickasaw boy or girl.

Panther finished his food and went to the door. The honeyguide sat on its limb, watching the house.

"The bird is back," Panther said. "It's time for me to go."

He reached out his free arm and drew Blackberry Woman close to him. He lowered his face into the curve where her neck met her shoulder. He smelled the good, musky woman smell of her. He released her and she moved back a step.

Panther fastened a strap to the bails of the buckets, one vessel nested inside the other. The sharp edge of the ax with which he would chop down the bee tree was wrapped in burlap and stowed in the buckets. He slung everything over his shoulder.

He picked up his rifle. The pouch containing cartridges and firing caps were hung over a shoulder. "I might stumble onto some men who don't want to be seen," he explained to Blackberry Woman.

In the yard, Panther whistled a trilling call, starting high and trending swiftly downward over several notes. He waited for the honeyguide to signal that it, too, was ready for the hunt.

The bird was totally gray except for white outer tail feathers. It was slightly larger than a dove but less streamlined, with a somewhat longer tail. It stretched both wings and flared the feathers of its handsome body. It lifted its head and warbled a call similar to the Chickasaw's but more tuneful, melodious, very pleasant to hear.

"Then let's go," the Indian said, and touched his head in salute to the bird.

The bird rose in the air, circled at treetop level and flew off over the woods to the southeast. Panther kept close watch on the bird. It went almost out of sight before it landed on the topmost branch of a tall tree.

Panther knew that the bird, with the excellence of its aerial scouting, had located every beehive within its territory. The distance the bird flew before it landed gave him a rough estimate of how far away the nearest bee tree was. This one must be very far. He moved silently toward the bird, which waited patiently for him.

Panther had first taken close notice of the honeyguide in those lonely days before Blackberry Woman came into his life. He had seen three of the birds circling a tree and calling their shrill, trilling calls to each other. He spotted the bees leaving and entering the hive high up on a hollow tree. He laughed in comradeship with the birds. "You are honey hunters, like myself," As they almost always did, the bees had selected a place for their hive with an entrance much too small for the honey loving birds to enter and feed. Imitating the call of the birds, he began to chop on the trunk of the bee tree.

The tree had fallen and Panther took the quantity of honey he wanted. As he departed, the honeyguides swooped down from the treetop where they spied on him and began to devour the bee larva and scraps of comb he had left. He halted and watched the hungry birds. He whistled their song again, touched his forehead to them, and left.

Panther began to look for the birds so they could show him a honey tree. Always he whistled their tune as he searched through the forest. Often they appeared and followed him, anticipating him finding a tree.

One day as he hunted, he noted that a particular bird had grown impatient and flown off ahead. Then it returned, checked his progress, and again flew off ahead. To his amazement, as he followed and observed the bird's antics, he discovered it had each time flown in the direction of the nearest bee tree. Thus his partnership with the honeyguides was born.

That first bird had grown old and died. Another had taken its place. Six generations of honeyguides had hunted bee trees in the forest with him.

Panther continued on, trailing through the forest after the bird. They had come nearly two miles. The distance the bird flew off ahead had grown very short, less than fifty yards. Also, its call had become softer toned with longer intervals between successive notes. The bee tree was close.

He veered off to the left to skirt around a swamp where giant trees rose black out of the stagnant water. In two places within his sight, the tall grass was matted down and the edges of the land grooved with a slide trail where alligators crawled onto the shore.

Panther cautiously examined the alligator trails. A moment later he spotted a misshapen form, like a partially rotted log, lying motionless in the swamp grass. An alligator nearly fourteen feet long waited in ambush for an unwary animal to come within reach of its large, tooth-filled jaws. The swamp was a place where things large or small died violent deaths. If you fell, you were devoured. Panther circled around the fearsome beast.

The honeyguide trilled its honey hunting call excitedly as it noticed the man's change of direction. Panther smiled at the almost human emotion in the bird's tone. He whistled back, reassuring the bird of his intention to follow.

## Chapter Eight

Luke rode warily through the giant trees of the silent forest. The oaks and beeches and the cypress in the swamp on his right moved not a leaf. The long strands of Spanish moss draped on every limb of the aged trees hung limp. The forest appeared abandoned, empty of all life, with neither bird nor animal stirring.

Gray whorls of fog rose from the damp earth and stood like spirits among the boles of the trees. The heavy overcast of dark clouds pressed down close above his head. The tops of the taller trees penetrated the body of the cloud layer, and it seemed that only their support kept the clouds from falling from the sky onto the earth.

The course of the stolen horses and the raiders bore easterly, varying direction only to avoid the water-filled swamps. The trail was as easy to follow as a highway.

Somewhere ahead, the thieving raiders would have set an ambush for pursuers. But not yet, not this close to the place where they had attacked the Confederate cavalry.

Luke came to a section of the forest where a tornado had reached down its savage arm and cut a swath. For a space a hundred yards wide and nearly half a mile long, the trees were a deadfall of broken, fallen timbers like spilled matchsticks. Even the mightiest of the giant oaks had been wrenched from their hold upon the earth by the twister and thrown down. He slowed his horse to a walk and pulled his rifle from its scabbard. His eyes raked the tangle of tree trunks. No better place for an ambush could be found.

Still, he reached the end of the deadfall and no gun had fired upon him.

A medium-size gray bird swooped in to land in the top of a tall tree in the woods just beyond the deadfall. The bird's attention swung back down its course and became fixed on something on the ground. The bird warbled a tuneful series of notes.

Luke looked in the same direction that the bird did. His eyes caught movement. A figure materialized from the deep forest, gray from gray. An Indian stepped into the opening between the deadfall and the undamaged woods.

The Indian halted instantly as his sight fell upon the horseman. He jerked up the rifle he carried in his hands.

Coldiron threw himself low across the neck of his horse and kicked it sharply in the ribs. As the animal leapt forward toward the nearest wall of the forest, Luke swung his rifle to point at the man raising his weapon.

The Indian halted his threatening move, dropping his rifle into his left hand. His right snapped up palm outward in a gesture of peace.

Luke caught his finger pressing on the trigger of his gun. Damnation, how close he had come to shooting the man! Or being shot by him, for he was very quick. Luke rose in the saddle and reined the horse to a halt.

He examined the Indian standing motionless, blending with the shadows that filled the woods. He seemed more apparition than real. The Indian stared silently back. A strap over the man's shoulder held something on his back. Luke recognized the Chickasaw who had sold him the honey on the docks of New Orleans.

Panther watched the rider swing down from the back of his horse, and walk toward him, leading the animal. The white man's face was expressionless. He halted a few paces distant.

The air was abruptly jarred around them as the booming sound of cannon fire spilled down from the heavens. The bird in the tree let out a squawk and crouched low on its limb. Both men pivoted to look to the south.

"Chalmette," Panther said. "The Yankees are attacking Chalmette."

"Then that means the Union battleships have beaten Fort Jackson and Saint Phillip," Luke replied. He had once visited Chalmette, the site of Andrew Jackson's defeat of the British Army half a century earlier. If the Union ships could get past the forts, then the lesser number of guns at Chalmette could not stop them for long.

"New Orleans is lost to the Confederates," Luke said.

The Chickasaw shrugged his shoulders. He spoke through the booming of the distant cannon. "I care nothing about white men or white men's battles."

Panther's black eyes focused on Luke. "You follow the trail of the men and the herd of horses that went in that direction," He pointed.

"Yes. They were stolen, and I want them back. Did you see them pass?"

"No. We arrived only a few minutes ago."

"We?" Luke questioned, glancing around.

"The honeyguide and thus old Indian," Panther chucked a thumb up at the bird in the tree.

Luke glanced at the bird and then back at the man. The Indian gave no indication he was joking about being with the bird.

"Well, I must be going," Luke said, and he gathered up the bridle reins of his mount. He wished the man had seen the thieves and could tell him their number.

"I wouldn't go along that trail."

"Why not?"

"There are three men with rifles just off there in the woods where the hard ground goes in between two swamps. I believe they would shoot you."

Luke studied the Chickasaw. "Why do you warn me of this when you don't care about white men?"

Panther considered the question. Why, indeed, did he warn this white man? Because he sat and ate from the honey bucket with the Comanche as their equal, and only their equal. Never before had Panther seen a white man treat an Indian in that manner. Panther could not tell the man this.

Ignoring the question, Panther spoke. "There is another path to the east around the swamp. Go that direction a half mile and you will find it. Once past the wet ground, you can swing back to the south and again find the trail of your horses."

"Thanks. Do you live near here?"

Panther nodded, just one short bob of his head, and his eyes flicked into the woods lying to the west. Then without another word, he turned and with a soundless, moccasin step crossed the space made barren by the tornado and vanished back into the trees from which he had come.

The bird launched itself from its perch and flapped off, hurrying ahead of the Chickasaw.

Luke remained a moment gazing into the forest after the pair, the Indian and the bird. He smiled a short smile. The Indian had indeed meant we.

The cannon continued to thunder miles away beyond New Orleans. The sound waned and then rebounded strongly as a rising wind played with it. Men were dying there at Chalmette. Luke felt sad at the thought of death, and yet strangely at the same time he knew he would kill the men who had stolen his horses and shot Dauphin.

He went east, then south a short distance, and found the game trail that the Chickasaw had told him went around the border of the swamp. In an hour he was again on the broad path left by the horses and the men who drove them.

Half a mile later a horse nickered at Luke from among the trees beside the trail. The animal carried the Steel Trap Brand on its hip. One of his horses had escaped from the herd. The animal recognized Luke and allowed him to approach and place a rope around its neck. It followed along obediently.

The battle of the cannons at Chalmette ceased, and the forest fell silent. Luke judged the Union battleships had destroyed the Confederate guns, or had run the gauntlet and were steaming up river to lay siege to New Orleans.

The overcast had gradually darkened. To the south a gray wet curtain of rain began to leak from the clouds. In minutes, rain began to fall upon Luke, fine, misty droplets settling out of the gray heavens. He pulled his rain slicker from behind the saddle and dragged it on.

A stiff wind had come in with the drizzly rain and now whipped the limbs of the trees and the long, hanging ropes of Spanish, moss. The woods seemed totally alive, and angry. Luke rode on, dodging the flailing arms of the forest.

He broke through a thick stand of trees and came abruptly upon a clearing of four acres or so. He yanked his horses to a quick stop in the edge of the timber. The opening was full of men, perhaps three hundred, and his horses. A number of large rowboats were drawn upon the bank of a bayou extending in from the southeast. All but ten of the men wore blue uniforms. The thieving infiltrators had joined with a company of invading Union soldiers.

The soldiers were fashioning crude halters for the horses from their belts and short lengths of rope. They began to climb upon the backs of the animals.

Luke guided his horses back along the trail and tied them. He slipped forward on foot, going off to the left through the dripping woods around the border of the meadow, to where he had seen an officer. The wind and rain hid the little sound he made. He crept as close as he dared to the officer, a lieutenant, who was talking to one of the men in civilian clothing.

Both men were mounted, and watching the soldiers working with the horses. They had their backs to Luke. The collars of their rain slickers were turned up and their hats pulled low against the rain. Luke could not see either man's face. He heard the rumble of their voices and strained to make out the words.

"What are your orders from General Butler?" the man in civilian clothing asked.

"I'm to proceed to New Orleans," the lieutenant replied. "There I'm to keep my men hidden north of the city until Admiral Farragut has arrived with his fleet. Then I'm to report to the admiral and place my detachment under his command. What of the Confederate Army under General Lovell? Will they stand and defend the city?"

"He's not going to fight. Already he's moving his men from the city and north upriver to Vicksburg, to reinforce the garrison there. By this evening there'll be no rebel army to oppose our occupation of New Orleans."

"That's surely good news," the lieutenant said. He inclined his head at the men in the clearing. "My company is mounted and ready to move."

"Kassor will take the lead and guide you north of the city," the civilian said. He pointed at a tall figure in civilian clothing standing off in the edge of the clearing.

The man was gaunt, with narrow shoulders and a cadaverous, bony face looking out from beneath the brim of his hat. He had no slicker, and stood unprotected in the rain. A covered rifle rested in the crook of his arm. He was watching the soldiers with a sardonic expression.

The lieutenant rode his horse across the meadow and came up to Kassor. They spoke for a moment. Then Kassor twisted around with a quick movement and went with gliding strides from the clearing.

"Form up a single file and follow me," the lieutenant called to the mounted soldiers. He waited half a minute to be certain all his men had heard the order, then followed after Kassor.

One by one the soldiers vanished into the wall of the forest.

At a call from the civilian who had talked with the officer, the remaining men gathered near him. They went off on a westerly course toward New Orleans.

Luke felt a cold anger. Trailing the thieves had turned out to be a useless effort. The Union army now had his horses. There was no way he could take his property from so many soldiers. He must devise a new tactic.

He turned back into the woods. He, too, would go to New Orleans.

\*\*\*

Panther sat in the doorway of his cabin and looked out across the small natural opening surrounding it. The rain had slackened to a drizzle. Night was arriving early, falling swiftly in the drippy, foggy forest. The trunks of the trees were fading into the darkness.

Blackberry Woman moved around behind him near the stove. The aroma of cooking food, which usually pleasantly teased his nose, did not this night. A great uneasiness lay heavily upon him. He sensed that he should be doing something, something he could not define.

The day had gone well. The honeyguide had led him to a bee tree full of honey. He climbed the trunk and plugged the entrance hole to the hive with a wad of cloth. Only minutes had been needed to fell the tree with the sharp ax. After filling his buckets with the sweet labor of the bees, he had returned home. Not one bee had stung him.

Blackberry Woman came to the doorway and stood beside him. She put her hand on his shoulder. Neither man nor woman spoke as they watched the daylight die.

Blackberry Woman's hand tightened its grip on Panther's shoulder. She leaned forward to look past the doorframe. Her head turned from side to side as her eyes swept the woods beyond the clearing.

"I believe someone is in the trees," she whispered.

"I don't see anybody," Panther said.

"Neither do I. But he's there."

Panther did not question the woman's statement. He reached out and lifted his rifle from where it leaned against the log wall near the door. This was a dangerous time, for there were ruthless raiders and foreign soldiers roaming the forest.

His eyes scanned the perimeter of the clearing. He saw nothing. Then, at the far eastern border a blacker piece of the forest separated from the great bulk of it. The object moved, coming toward the cabin.

The black thing became two, a man on the back of a horse and a horse trailing.

"Stay inside the cabin," Panther said to Blackberry Woman. He rose to his feet with his rifle. He stepped out of the doorway and stood beside the cabin wall.

The man came on. When he had closed the distance by half, Panther recognized Coldiron. How had he found the cabin? No white man ever had before.

The man and his horses halted. "Hello, the house. May I come closer?" The voice was low, and died swiftly in the woods.

"Come in," Panther said. He stepped out into the yard.

Luke drew rein in front of the Chickasaw. "I've brought you a gift. I found of my horses and want to give it to you."

"You owe me nothing."

"You warned me of danger. Maybe I could've killed the men before they killed me. Then again, maybe not. If not, then I owe you my life."

Luke stepped down and untied the horse and handed the short lead rope to Panther. "Please accept the horse. Give me a pencil and paper and I'll write you a bill of sale."

"My woman will have those things, for she can read and write." Panther looked up into the wet sky. "Come in out of the rain. It will not end soon. Have food with us and, if you will, spend the night under my roof."

"I thank you, and I accept."

"Good. We can talk."

Panther faced the cabin and called. "Blackberry Woman, a friend has come. He will eat with us."

Panther spoke to Luke. "I have rope we can use to stake out the horses so they can graze."

The task of caring for the horses was soon accomplished. Luke lifted his saddle onto his shoulder and followed the Chickasaw to the cabin. As they entered, the woman lit a coal oil lamp sitting on a small table.

Luke placed the saddle just inside the door where it would dry. He removed his soggy hat.

"I am Panther. I know you are called Coldiron, for I heard the soldier call you that."

"Yes, Luke Coldiron."

"This is Blackberry Woman." Panther gestured at the woman.

Luke bowed to the Negro woman. He had expected an Indian woman. "Pleased to meet you," he said. Panther was very dark-skinned. However, the woman was darker, so black her skin seemed to have a purplish tint. Her eyes, set far apart, regarded him steadily. There was a sharp intelligence behind those eyes.

"How do you do, Mr. Coldiron?" Blackberry Woman said. "Thank you for the gift to Panther. The food will soon be ready. Please seat yourself."

Luke took the chair indicated by the woman. He glanced around at the interior of the cabin. The furnishings were simple and sparse, and most were handmade. Everything was spotlessly clean. A door led into a second room.

The woman cooked on a flat-topped, metal stove with an oven. He smelled the food. His hunger surged, for he had not eaten all day.

"How did you find this place?" Panther asked.

"The bird told me," Luke replied.

A questioning expression swept over the Chickasaw's face. Then he smiled, the very first time Luke had seen him do so. It broke the stern countenance and reformed it into a pleasant face. "Yes, it did. You saw the direction it came from."

"That's right." Luke did not tell Panther that he also had shown the direction to his home, by that flick of his eyes into the woods when he had been asked where he lived. Luke had judged that the man looked toward his home.

The woman came and placed food on the table in front of the two men. They began to eat. She took a plate and sat eating near the stove.

The food consisted of meat, beans, hot cornbread, honey, and dried apple pie, all excellently prepared. Luke ate with high enthusiasm. Finally, he shoved back from the table.

"If I had another horse, I would give it to you for such a delicious meal," he said to Blackberry Woman.

She did not reply, or smile, as Luke thought she might. Instead she spoke to Panther. "I think Mr.

Coldiron would like a fresh glass of water from the rain barrel. I know that I would. Please bring some in."

Panther rose. Luke noted the slight puzzlement on his face, but the man said nothing. He picked up the bucket from its stand and went out the door.

Luke looked at the Negro woman. He knew she wanted to say something to him, words that Panther was not to hear. Her eyes were moist, and they shone with reflected lamplight. She leaned tensely toward him.

"Don't kill my man," Blackberry Woman said in a whisper, a whisper so full of emotion that it quivered.

Luke straightened in shock at the woman's words. "I mean him no harm. He is not my enemy. Why do you say such a thing to me?"

"When you two are together I feel the presence of death. I believe it is Panther's death."

Luke sat dumbfounded. The woman must be addled, even though she appeared perfectly sane.

"You are greatly mistaken. Panther is in no danger from me. He probably saved my life, and I owe him."

The black woman waved aside his remark with a quick motion of her hand. Her eyes glittered.

"Don't kill my man," she repeated. There was no mistaking the threat in her eyes.

Panther came in the door and sat the bucket on the water stand. He glanced at the two people he had left alone in the room. Coldiron was looking at Blackberry Woman. There was a troubled expression on his face. She was bending to put wood in the stove, and he could not see her expression.

Panther wondered what had been said between them. Later he would ask Blackberry Woman. She might tell him. Then again, she might not. She could be a tight-lipped woman at times.

## Chapter Nine

Luke and Panther broke free of the forest three miles north of New Orleans. They halted their mounts where a big cypress tree threw its shadow upon them.

"Coldiron, I have no need to go further," the Chickasaw said, looking at the city, the buildings miniaturized by distance. "Tomorrow will be soon enough for me to go and sell my honey."

"All right," Luke said. "Thanks for showing me the shortest route to town."

"Come again to my home," Panther said. A smile came that softened his craggy, somber features. "Now that you know the path."

"I'll do that."

"Then, until we meet again," Panther said, and reined his horse back into the forest.

Luke touched the black with his heels and rode on toward New Orleans. He reflected upon the Chickasaw's woman. Blackberry Woman had said not another word to him after warning him not to harm Panther. Luke shook his head in puzzlement, with no further understanding as to why she thought he would in any way injure the Chickasaw. Luke liked the man.

He entered the city and rode along Dumaine Street toward the riverfront. The buildings lining the street were two and three story bricks with limed or stucco walls. The bottom floors were used for businesses, groceries, cafes, coffeehouses, haberdasheries, and offices, and for scores of other purposes. The upper levels were the homes of the people.

The thoroughfare and the cross streets were full of people. Hundreds of men, women, and family groups were streaming north, fleeing the city. Some walked, carrying bundles in their arms, while others rode upon many types of vehicles from wagons to buggies, surreys, and hackneys. Here and there men and women pulled handcarts piled with their personal possessions. A great din of shouts, curses, and the cries of frightened children filled the streets. Luke felt a deep sorrow as he looked at the faces twisted with fear and worry.

A string of cargo drays—heavy clattering vehicles drawn by sweating mules, their axles groaning under tremendous loads—went by Luke in the opposite direction. Some of the drivers were armed with shotguns, others with rifles or pistols. From horseback, Luke could look down into the vehicles as they passed. They were loaded with bags of sugar, coffee, tea, beans, and hams, cheese wrapped in cloth, and canned goods. Merchants were removing foodstuffs from the city. A group of slaves—thirty or so males guarded by a white man with a pistol and carrying a whip—hurried along the street. A Union attack must be imminent, Luke reasoned.

A gathering of men, perhaps a hundred, were in a vacant lot at the corner of Bourbon and Dumaine Streets. Not one man was in uniform. Everyone carried a weapon which he brandished in a reckless manner. The men spoke in fierce voices among themselves.

Luke noted they did not have a leader. Without one, they were useless as a fighting force.

Ahead in the direction of the Mississippi River, black smoke rose in thick, wavy columns above the city. Luke directed his horse toward the smoke, guiding it through the throng of people and the vehicles wheeling along the ways.

As he drew nearer the waterfront, the naked masts of many ships became visible above the rooftops. Two days before, the river had been deserted. He went a few blocks farther and came out on the levee.

A fleet of Union warships lay at anchor on the river. Luke counted seventeen vessels of various types. The stars and stripes fluttered briskly from their topmasts. The ships' huge cannons were aimed at the heart of New Orleans. He could see the gunners standing ready with their slow-matches to touch the cannons off and hurl solid ball and exploding canisters upon the city and its people.

Several boats were being lowered from the larger ships. A small brass cannon, riding between iron-rimmed wheels, was swung out on a davit and lowered into one of the boats already on the water. Men in the red of marine uniforms descended slanting gangways and climbed into waiting boats.

As the Union Marines pulled toward the shore, a mad buzz of voices rose from the crush of people on the docks. Armed men lifted their weapons threateningly.

"Damn Yankees. Here they come again," said the man standing next to Luke.

"What do you mean?" Luke asked.

The man glanced to the side at Luke. "Admiral Far-ragut and his Yankees anchored out there about one o'clock yesterday, after running past the cannons at Chalmette. He sent an officer and a squad of sailors ashore to demand the surrender of the city. Mayor Mon-roe met with them, but refused to give up the city. I think today, with the Marines coming, the Yankees intend to occupy it by force."

"What about the Confederate Army? I thought the city was under military protection."

"Our brave General Lovell has abandoned us and slipped away with his army to the north. The last of them left yesterday. But the Yankees won't get much from taking our city. We've destroyed most everything they can use. We've sunk the ships we were building at the yards, and wrecked the machinery in the factories."

The man pointed across the docks and along the levee. "Yesterday and this morning we brought all the cotton, tens of thousands of bales, from the warehouses and presses and burned it and everything else that had not been hauled away."

Coldiron saw the large mounds of smoking ashes remaining from the burned cotton, and crates and boxes of other valuable goods. Hundreds of broken molasses barrels lay in broad pools of the brown liquid.

"Many tons of rice were dumped in the river," the man said proudly.

"A terrible waste," Luke said.

"Better that than letting that damn Admiral Farragut and his men get it."

Luke did not reply. The first boats, the oars pulled by seamen, landed with the cannon. The Marines quickly sprang out onto the dock. The marine officers, a captain and a lieutenant, studied the huge throng of people that lined the riverfront as far as the eye could see. The flinty eyes of the officers settled on the knot of armed men at the head of the dock.

At an order from the marine captain, four sailors hoisted the gun out onto the dock and swung it to point directly at the group of men of the city. One of the seamen crammed powder and a bag of rifle balls down the throat of the gun.

The chief cannoneer petted the barrel of his gun and grinned with a determined expression. He lifted his smoldering, slow match, to show the men of New Orleans he was ready to blow them to smithereens.

The remaining boats landed, and tied up. The Marines unloaded swiftly.

"Form up four abreast," the marine captain ordered. "Lieutenant, take point position."

The lieutenant stepped to the front. The forty Marines swiftly fell into formation. The honed edges of the bayonets fastened to their rifles flashed sharp silver in the sun.

"Make way," the captain called to the men barring the end of the dock.

The civilians did not move. "Like hell, we will!" a man shouted back at the marine officer.

The captain looked at his cannoneer and shouted loudly, his voice ringing out clearly so that the men of New Orleans could hear him. "Gunner, stand ready to fire upon those men if one marine is hurt."

"If you're going to shoot, then shoot these," a southern man shouted.

Two young women, one with a babe in her arms, stepped out in front of the men. They set their feet and stared resolutely at the Marines.

The captain stabbed his arm at the angry man, confronting him. "Listen to me. We are going to enter the city. Those women will not stop us." He pointed out over the river at the Union warships bristling with cannon. "If my cannon fires, every gun on those ships will open up on New Orleans. There won't be anything left of your homes, or of this fine city. Think hard about that."

The captain, his face hard, gestured to the lieutenant. "Clear those men from the dock. Use bayonets if necessary."

"Bayonets ready," the lieutenant commanded his squad of Marines. "Don't hurt the women if you can help it. Forward, march."

The contingent of Marines advanced in a solid mass. Their eyes were set and hard as they sighted over the bayonets fastened to the extended rifles. The regimental guidon, held aloft on its staff by the lead marine, flapped in the breeze.

The men of New Orleans shouted fierce encouragement to each other. "Stand firm! Give no ground! Women, the bastard Yankees dare not hurt you."

The bayoneted rifles, thrust forward with strong arms, advanced inexorably closer. The women's eyes filled with fright. They pressed back against the men. The bayonets drew within stabbing range of the women's bosoms.

Hands suddenly reached out from the packed group of men and jerked the women aside. The men held their ground for a brief moment. Then they wavered, broke, and pulled back to allow a narrow lane.

The Marines marched into the opening. One civilian crowded too close, and a burly marine slammed him in the chest with the butt of his rifle. With a cry of pain, the man fell back against his comrades.

The Marines passed through the angry crush of men and onward in the direction of Jackson Square. The cannon, drawn by four seamen, rolled along behind with its iron-rimmed wheels rattling on the stone-paved quay.

***

"Hurry, Roy," Susan Dauphin told the wounded soldier. "All the others who can walk are gone, and you must leave before the Yankees come and make you a prisoner."

"I'm not going to run from those bastards like the other fellows did," Roy replied. His missing hand ached horribly, and his head spun as he sat on the cot in the soldiers' ward of Sisters of Charity Hospital. He had been in a stupor for the past day, and now this crazy nurse was trying to get him to walk when he could hardly sit.

"Our army will keep the Yankees from landing," he said, shaking his head to stop its spinning. The movement only increased the rate of spin and intensified the pain in his arm.

"We have no army. The last of our soldiers have left the city. The Yankees are here. They've been there on the river since yesterday noon. Look!" she ordered harshly and stabbed a finger out the window.

"Our army retreated without a fight?" Roy said in disbelief. He twisted around. From the second floor of the hospital, the river and the Union ships armed with heavy cannons were plainly visible four blocks away. All the death and suffering the men at the forts had endured to protect New Orleans had been for nothing. He had lost a hand for nothing. He stifled a sob.

"Damn the Yankees. I'm not running," Roy said stubbornly.

"Don't be a fool," Susan said more kindly. "They've already come ashore from their ships. Mayor Monroe is negotiating the surrender of the city to Admiral Farragut's representative at this very time." Her voice hardened. "Get on your feet."

Roy struggled to rise. The powerful laudanum circulating in his blood and the weakening effects of his wound had turned his muscles to wet strings. He swayed drunkenly. "Help me," he said.

Susan caught Roy around the chest as he fell. She staggered under his loose-limbed weight. What was she to do with him?

\*\*\*

"Miss Dauphin is in the soldiers' ward on the second floor," the Sister of Charity told Luke in answer to his question.

"Thank you," he said to the elderly woman sitting primly in her white habit behind the desk in the entryway of the hospital. She appeared exhausted, but there was no expression of defeat or resignation on her face such as he had seen on most of all the other people in the city. He had always felt a little in awe of the fortitude of truly religious people.

Luke entered the soldiers' ward and cast a glance down the long room with its double rows of cots. All the beds were empty except for two. At the far end of the ward, Susan was struggling to hold a soldier with a bandaged left arm on his feet.

Spying Luke in the doorway, Susan called out, "Mr. Coldiron, come quickly and help me."

Luke hastened forward. Taking hold of the soldier, he stood him upright and held him there.

"What do you want to do with him?" he asked.

"He must be gotten out of the hospital before the Yankees come. They'll make all the soldiers they find prisoners of war."

"I'll fight them," Roy said, leaning heavily upon Luke's arms.

"What can a one-handed man with no gun do against a platoon of Marines?" Luke asked the soldier.

"I don't care how many of them there are."

"Enough of your foolishness," Susan said with exasperation. "We will fight them and hurt them for what they have done, but at a time when we can win. Do you have any family or friends in New Orleans who can hide you and treat your wound?"

Roy shook his head. "I have only a father, and he lives on a farm east of Vicksburg."

"There is no way we can get you to Vicksburg. You'll have to go with me. Mr. Coldiron, will you help me take Roy to my house? He'll be safe there. I've a buggy in the stables behind the hospital."

"Lead the way," Luke said. He put Roy's arm over his shoulder and, mostly carrying the young soldier, followed Susan down the stairs and from the hospital.

## Chapter Ten

The streets of the French Quarter were deserted as Luke rode toward the riverfront. The angry mob that had resisted the Union landing early in the day had vanished. The people were hidden in their homes, afraid or too ashamed to show their faces now that the Yankees had conquered the city.

Luke moved along a narrow way lined with two-story houses. Iron-railed balconies extended out from the upper floor of most of the houses and overhung the sidewalk. A young, pale-skinned woman with black hair stood on the galleria on Luke's left. She caught hold of the top of the railing and leaned over to look down at him.

"Kind gentleman, it is lonely up here," the woman said with a whore's smile. "Please come up and visit me. There is a door just below."

"Thank you, but no," Luke said.

"You are a handsome man, so my price will be very reasonable," the woman said encouragingly.

Before Luke could reply to the whore the sound of glass breaking and wood splintering sounded from the building half a block in front of him. Two men disappeared into the building.

"Only looters," the whore said. "They have become brave now that there are no policemen, and the Yankees have not yet sent out patrols in the town. Please come up. I truly am lonely."

"I have a woman," Luke said. Some occupations never cease, even in war.

The whore was quiet, looking down at Luke. She no longer smiled. "Your woman is very lucky."

Luke wondered if he had lied to the whore. Had he read the expression in Susan's eyes correctly? He rode on.

The two looters burst from the broken door of the building, a combination general merchandise store and apothecary shop. On their backs they carried bags bulging with stolen merchandise. They slid to a stop on the sidewalk at the sight of Luke. They watched him suspiciously. Then, seeing he was not going to take action to stop them, they darted off along the street with their bags.

Luke entered the broad, stone-paved area lying between the Cabildo and Jackson Square. The squads of armed Marines, four men in each, marched on patrol in opposite directions around the Cabildo. They had swept the streets surrounding the building clear of all the townsfolk. Only the darkening shadows of the falling evening, and the Union Jack flapping on the flagstaff on top of the Cabildo, kept the sentries company.

As he came closer to the entrance of the Cabildo, the two Marines stationed there watched him warily. The corporal of the pair moved forward when Coldiron swung down and tied his horse to one of the iron hitching posts.

"What do you want?" the corporal challenged him.

"Who is your commanding officer?"

"Colonel Trotter is senior officer ashore tonight."

"Go tell him I've got some horses to sell that would make excellent cavalry mounts."

The marine looked coldly at Coldiron. "Wait here. I'll find out if the colonel will see you," The man turned and entered the Cabildo.

Luke rolled a cigarette and surveyed the large building. The aged Cabildo, constructed originally by the French in 1790 and later added to by the Spanish, was three stores high with nine stone arches stretching across the front and reaching to the top of the first floor. Behind the arches was a walkway. Then came the entryway, barred by an iron gate. Luke knew that the Cabildo normally housed the offices of the city officials, but those men had been evicted by the Marines and now the building was the headquarters of the Union occupying forces.

On Jackson Square, just beyond a wide, paved street, men of New Orleans began to gather. They made not a sound, simply staring through the late evening shadows at the marine sentries. The town's men looked cowed.

The corporal came from the Cabildo. "Colonel Trotter will see you," he said to Coldiron.

"All right. Show me the way."

The Corporal led him in under the arches and through the iron gate to the heart of the stone building. He halted at the head of a passageway and pointed. "You'll find Colonel Trotter down at the end in the mayor's office," he said.

"Thanks, corporal. Watch my horse. There are thieves around."

Luke walked the length of the passageway. A sentry stood at a door bearing a sign: Mayor's Office.

The man looked Luke over closely. "Are you armed?" he asked.

"No." Luke opened his vest to show the marine. He knew that he would not be allowed armed into the commandant's office, and had left his pistol outside in his saddlebags.

The marine knocked on the door and pushed it open. "Mr. Coldiron is here, Colonel."

"Send him in."

Luke entered as a marine officer rose behind a big oak desk. "I'm Colonel Trotter."

"I'm Luke Coldiron." He sensed the guard close to his back.

The colonel looked past Coldiron. "It's all right, marine, you may return to your post. I don't believe Mr. Coldiron has brought the battle of New Orleans in here with him."

"You are correct, Colonel. I want only to talk business."

"You have horses for sale?" said the colonel, reseating himself behind his conquered desk. He motioned Luke to a chair.

"Yes. Some very good horses." Luke took the chair.

"You do not talk like a Southerner," the colonel said.

"I was born and raised in Ohio. Now I'm from the New Mexico Territory," As Luke spoke he heard someone come into the room behind him.

"Captain Rawls, you have arrived just in time," the colonel said. "I want you to meet Mr. Coldiron."

Luke climbed to his feet and turned to face the new arrival. He instantly recognized the officer as the captain commanding the Marines that had landed from the

Union ships earlier in the day. The man was large and clean-shaven with a ruddy complexion. His red officer's uniform was immaculately clean and excellently tailored to fit his body. His polished leather boots gleamed like new metal. A pistol was in a holster on his belt. He stood ramrod straight, as if on a parade ground. But as Luke looked into the man's strangely mud-colored eyes, and remembered his orders to his men for the use of bayonets and cannon at the dock, he knew Rawls should never be taken for a mere parade ground soldier.

"Coldiron," Rawls said, inclining his head the slightest bit.

"Rawls," Luke said. Rawls had not addressed him as Mr. Coldiron, so Luke would not recognize his rank.

"Mr. Coldiron has some cavalry horses to sell to us," the colonel said.

"Is that so?" Rawls said. "How many do you have?"

"Two hundred."

"Where are these horses?" Rawls asked. "When could you make delivery?"

Luke thought he saw a momentary flicker of amusement in Rawls's eyes. "They are north of the city. The Union army already has possession of them."

"What do you mean by that statement?" Colonel Trotter asked.

Luke did not reply immediately. Rawls was not amused now, Luke noted. He seemed surprised at Luke's knowledge of the whereabouts of the horses. Then Rawls's eyes became hooded and he became relaxed, and infinitely dangerous.

"I've heard the name Coldiron before," Rawls said. "He sold a herd of horses to a company of rebel cavalry. He's as much an enemy as any rebel."

The colonel looked sharply at Luke. "Is it true that you sold horses to the Confederates?" he asked.

"No, that's not true. I would've sold the horses to a man named Wade Dauphin, but he was robbed and his plantation house burned. He was killed when he tried to stop the thieves. He took possession of the horses from me at the waterfront and turned them over to a captain of cavalry. But I was never paid, so the horses are still mine."

"Captain Rawls, the horses Mr. Coldiron is talking about must be the same ones you took from a camp of Confederates on the shore of Lake Pontchartrain," Colonel Trotter had sent the captain, Lieutenant Springer, and a platoon of Marines into New Orleans weeks earlier. They were to harass the rebels and to send information they gathered about the Confederate strength to Admiral Farragut. Only this morning had Rawls and his subordinates returned to duty in uniform.

"The very same, sir, the ones I turned over to General Butler's advance company of soldiers," the captain replied.

Luke looked at the marine captain. So he was one of the Union infiltrators who had attacked Captain Thacker's camp and killed the patrol on duty. It was a strange coincidence that Dauphin's plantation had been raided at approximately the same time the horses were being taken. Was Rawls responsible for both actions? Was he at Dauphin's instead of at the Confederate cavalry camp?

Luke focused more closely on Rawls. The raiders had been dressed in coarse civilian clothing and had been bearded. Also, it had been almost dark. Still, Luke did not think Rawls had been one of the men at Dauphin's plantation.

"Colonel Trotter, Coldiron is a man from Union territory who sells war goods to the rebels," Rawls said. "He's a war profiteer, and. has committed treason. I'll lock him up to stand trial," Rawls pulled his pistol from its holster.

Coldiron tensed. He would not allow them to take him prisoner without a. struggle. The war might go on for years, and he could be imprisoned for all that long time.

"Just a minute, Captain," the colonel said. "Mr. Coldiron, are you a Confederate sympathizer?"

"No. I met Wade Dauphin in St. Louis last February. I had horses for sale. He had money and wanted to buy them. I did not know his politics."

"I say he's a Union traitor," Rawls said. "Why else would he bring horses to New Orleans?"

"Coldiron, you've admitted bringing horses here," the colonel said. "Explain yourself."

"I fought in the Mexican War in forty-six and forty-seven," Luke said. "If I was to join either side in this war, it would be the Union army. But I'm not going to take sides."

"Many men who fought in the Mexican War are now fighting in the Confederate army," Rawls said sarcastically. "So the fact you were in Mexico means nothing."

"Tell us how you got involved in being in New Orleans with horses for the Confederacy," Trotter said.

"Dauphin and I made a contract of sale in St. Louis for delivery of horses at the docks of the city. Unfortunately, the city was not specified. I understood it was St. Louis. In late March, Dauphin sent me a message stating the place of delivery must be New Orleans. I had given my word to deliver horses, so I brought them to New Orleans."

"Even knowing New Orleans was a Confederate city, eh?" Trotter said. He rubbed the edge of his jaw and looked hard at Luke. "What did you hope to accomplish by coming here to talk with me? You really have no horses to sell."

"A band of men attacked Dauphin's home and robbed a safe containing the money that was to pay me for my horses. Those men burned the house, hoping to hide their crime, or for just plain meanness. The fifty thousand dollars that was stolen was to be my payment. The Union army has my horses, so it should pay."

"Captain Rawls took the horses by force from a company of rebel cavalry. That is an action he should have taken. No money is owed for the animals. Confiscation of supplies during war is not theft."

"I think the band of men who robbed Wade Dauphin and killed him were also Union infiltrators," Luke said. He looked directly at Captain Rawls. "So, the Union has my horses, and they also have the fifty thousand dollars. Robbery and murder of civilians is not lawful even in war."

"Do you have any proof that Union infiltrators attacked Dauphin?" the colonel questioned.

"No. I have no proof," Luke replied, holding his anger under tight rein.

"Then, Coldiron, you have no case. You'll get no money from the Union government. You say you are neutral in this war. I'm willing to believe that. I suggest, and I do so very strongly, that you leave New Orleans and go back to the New Mexico Territory. Go today."

"Not without payment for my horses."

"Coldiron, you have my decision on this matter. I have no more time for you. Go home."

Luke pivoted away from the colonel and to the captain. He saw the smug cunning in Rawls's eyes before the man could hide it. That look convinced Luke that Rawls knew more than he had told. God, how Luke wanted to smash that face with his fist!

Luke forced himself to turn from the captain. He left the colonel's office and went along the hallway and out of the Cabildo. As he untied his horse he surveyed the building with a keen scrutiny. He watched a patrol of sentries go past and disappear around the corner of the Cabildo. He turned away, leading his horse, and went northwest on St. Peter Street. His hot anger coalesced into a burning determination.

Luke stopped. The Union colonel had refused to pay for the horses. Luke could not find fault with him for that. Still, Luke's money was gone. Now there was only one way left for him to get his payment.

He took his holstered pistol from a saddlebag and buckled it on. He knew the name of one of the three dead raiders—Simon Hanks. With that information, he might be able to learn who the others were who had ridden in the attack on Dauphin. Those men still alive had his money. Luke would not be surprised if the marine captain Rawls did not have part of it.

# Chapter Eleven

"Captain Rawls, you have made yourself and the Union army an enemy," Colonel Trotter said as he stared at the door through which Coldiron had just left.

"I was just doing my duty as a marine officer, sir."

"Your action was correct in taking the horses from the Confederate cavalry. They will be very useful to General Butler. What do you know about the attack on the Dauphin plantation?"

"Nothing, sir," the captain said in a firm voice. "The first I heard about it was when Coldiron told of it here tonight. Looters must have struck Dauphin."

Colonel Trotter evaluated his captain. Rawls was a hard man, but an excellent officer. The marine would follow him anywhere. Trotter believed Coldiron's story, and he had seen the expression on Coldiron's and Rawls's face. They had taken an instant dislike to each other. Was that entirely from the taking of the horses? Still, Coldiron had not accused Rawls of anything. That was good, for the colonel needed Rawls.

Trotter knew that the seven hundred Marines who had accompanied the Union fleet and the three hundred soldiers who had recently arrived were insufficient forces to put New Orleans totally under martial law. Yet the large enemy city must be controlled until General Butler could bring his army ninety miles north through the swamps and forest from the Gulf of Mexico, conquering Forts Jackson and St. Phillip on the way, and relieve Trotter. Until then, Trotter and Rawls must quell any revolt by the Southern rebels.

"Is there anything else you want of me, sir?" the captain asked.

"I'm glad to have you back in uniform."

"Thank you, sir."

"You have established an excellent organization for supplying military information to Admiral Farragut. Continue to expand your network of black informers and Union sympathizers. Find a black in the household of every important family in New Orleans. Leaders of resistance groups will probably come from such families. We must know what schemes are being hatched by the Confederates."

"Yes, sir. I shall do that."

"You are dismissed, Captain."

"Yes, sir," Rawls saluted and left with long strides.

Colonel Trotter took up the papers he had been working on when Coldiron's appearance had interrupted him. He reflected upon the man from the Territory who had attempted to sell horses to a Confederate citizen. He hoped the fellow would go home and cause no more trouble. The colonel dismissed thoughts of Coldiron, and his brow became furrowed as he began to design the plan for occupying New Orleans. Admiral Farragut had ordered that the plan be ready for his review at first light of the morrow.

\*\*\*

Rawls went quickly to the city council conference chambers, where some fifty Marines stood by with their arms, ready to repel any attack that might be launched upon the Union headquarters. He stepped through the doorway and looked about. Lieutenant Springer and Sergeant Luttrel, the senior noncommissioned officer, were talking together. Rawls lifted his hand to catch their attention.

"I'd like a word with you two," the captain said.

"Yes, sir," the lieutenant replied.

The sergeant said nothing. Both men crossed the room to the captain.

"Come with me," Rawls said.

"Yes, sir," The lieutenant replied.

Rawls had recruited both men. He had been a career marine on active duty when the war began. Immediately he had obtained permission to return to his hometown in Massachusetts and recruit men to bring his company up to full strength. He had carefully selected Springer as his lieutenant and Luttrel as top sergeant, both men known from his childhood. They in turn had helped enlist forty other men. All were very special, willing to fight hard but with a mutual understanding that their objective was to become rich men by the end of the war. They would take as many valuables as possible from the beaten rebels. Already, they had made good progress toward their goal during the battles with Admiral Farragut along the east coast. Now the richest prize of all was open to them. However, a man threatened their good fortune. Three of their number were dead because of him.

The captain set a fast pace along the passageway and out the front entrance. He threw a hasty look down the streets that converged on the Cabildo. He struck off on St. Peter Street, heading northwest.

"There, see that man leading the black horse?" the captain said.

"Yes, sir," the lieutenant replied.

"His name's Luke Coldiron. It was his horses I took from the Confederate cavalry. He was the man who fought against you two at Wade Dauphin's."

"I remember the bastard," the lieutenant said. "He almost shot me."

"He's causing more problems. He was just in the Cabildo telling Colonel Trotter about the horses and the attack on Dauphin's plantation."

"What did he say about the fight and our dead men?" the lieutenant asked.

"This Coldiron is smart. He only mentioned the raiders killing Dauphin and taking money from the safe. He said nothing about shooting any of the raiders. So our report that three Marines were killed by Southern resistance fighters goes unchallenged. Coldiron is going to take things into his own hands and try to find out who the men are who have his money."

"He must not be allowed to interfere with our plans," the lieutenant said.

"Agreed," Rawls replied. "We have conquered this town, and we're going to take whatever we want from it. That has been the rule of conquest for thousands of years, and I don't plan to change it. Coldiron must not get another chance to talk with Colonel Trotter, or to cause trouble of any kind."

"I can take care of that job," Sergeant Luttrel said.

"Don't use our Marines," the Captain said. "Find Kassor and have him kill Coldiron. Now, I don't think he'll be an easy target. Have Kassor take a couple of his toughest thugs with him. Get rid of Coldiron's body after he's dead."

"Captain, Kassor's finding out too much about what we're doing," the lieutenant said. "He's dangerous to us."

"I know that," Rawls said. "But we need him and his gang of thugs. No better man can be found to kill Coldiron and make him vanish. Also, we need Kassor's fence Hammlin to buy what we steal. We have three to four weeks before we go upriver to help in the attack on Vicksburg. I want to rob this town blind by then. We'll use Kassor during the time we're here. Before we leave, we'll kill him. General Butler has an iron fist and will destroy the remaining thugs. There'll be no trouble left behind to follow us."

"That's a sound plan. Do you know where Coldiron is going?"

The captain checked Coldiron's progress along the street. "St. Peter hooks into Shell Road. Shell Road then runs past the Dauphin plantation. Since Coldiron is a friend of the Dauphins, I'd guess he's headed there."

"Good," the lieutenant said. "That'll make it easier for Kassor to find him."

"I want Coldiron caught before he leaves the city. I could be wrong about where he is going. We don't want to lose him."

"Half an hour or so ago, I saw Kassor go into the Mississippi Gal Saloon just down the street," the sergeant said. "He's probably still there."

"Then get him started after Coldiron now." Rawls extracted a roll of bills from a pocket. "Here's two hundred dollars in greenbacks. Tell Kassor there'll be three hundred more when the job's done."

"Yes, sir." The sergeant took the money.

\*\*\*

Luttrel found Kassor at the bar talking with a heavily rouged young woman. He caught the thug leader's eye and nodded at a table in the rear near the wall.

Luttrel took a seat and watched Kassor say a last few words to the woman. The sergeant had never met a man he liked less. Kassor had been recruited months earlier by Union spies to provide information about the rebel strength in New Orleans. When the captain and the other Marines had infiltrated the city, Kassor had immediately attached himself to them. He had proved useful, for he knew every trail through the swamps and he had men who would fight, for pay. The information about Dauphin's purchase of horses had come from Kassor. The man had helped the captain take them from the rebel cavalry. A black informant had told Rawls that he had seen his master, Dauphin, stash a large amount of money in a safe in his home.

Kassor came and sat down opposite Luttrel. He stank of whiskey and old sweat. "What do you want, Sergeant?" he asked.

"How would you like to make five hundred dollars?"

Kassor was only partially listening. He was looking past the sergeant at the young woman he had left at the bar. She had begun to talk to another man. She smiled sweetly at him.

"Damn her," Kassor said. "She's at it already," He rose abruptly, jarring the table with his knee.

Kassor stalked across the saloon and up to the pair. Without warning, he struck the man on the side of the head. The man crashed into the bar, then slid down to lie on the floor.

Kassor caught the woman roughly by the shoulders and jerked her close against him. He whispered in her ear, then released her. She hurried from the saloon, her face tight with fright.

The thug swaggered back and sat down at the table with the sergeant. He rubbed his skinned knuckles.

"What was that all about?" Luttrel asked.

"I plan to bed that woman in a little while," Kassor said. "I didn't want her used. Now what was you saying about five hundred dollars?"

"I've got a job that'd pay that amount."

"For doing what?"

"Making a nuisance disappear."

"How am I to do that?"

"Kill him is the best way. And then throw him in the river."

"Well the old river has hauled away many corpses. I guess it could do it again. Who's to take the wet journey?"

"A man named Coldiron."

"The same man that brought the horses for sale to Dauphin?"

"The same. Here's two hundred dollars. The other three will be yours when Coldiron is in the river."

"I need the money. You didn't give me anything for the horses I helped you take, because you gave them to the Union army. My boys are complaining."

"They'd better not complain too loud, or I'll take my Marines and show them how tough real fighting men are. Now, hear me. Coldiron's going to try and get even with those men who took his horses. You are one of them. He'll be coming after you as well as me."

"You'd tell him about me?"

"Sure." Luttrel smiled broadly.

Kassor's face hardened. Then he shrugged. "Five hundred dollars seems a fair price for one man. I'll do it."

"Take a couple of good men to be certain it gets done right."

"All my men are tough. Where can this fellow be found? I'd like to get it over with."

"I would, too. He's just down the street. Come with me. He can't have gone very far. I'll point him out to you."

Luttrel led the way from the saloon and turned up St. Peter Street. He walked swiftly with Kassor keeping pace. For a couple of minutes, Luttrel thought Coldiron had escaped him. Then he spotted the man in the evening shadows ahead.

"That man leading the horse, that's Coldiron," Luttrel said.

"Is he armed?" Kassor asked.

"Always think a man has a gun and knows how to use it. That way you'll never be surprised to death."

Kassor snorted at Luttrel's remark. "Doesn't make any difference," he said. "I don't aim to give him a chance to fight back. You go on about your business. He'll not get away from me."

"This is important. Don't fail."

"He'll be dead in a little while. It'll take but a minute to round up some help. I've got men in every saloon and whorehouse in New Orleans."

# Chapter Twelve

Slaughterhouse Point was a fitting place to fight and kill a man, thought Walt Bouchard. Still he was glad the wind was blowing the stench of animal dung and rotting flesh away from him and off to the east. He was between the river and the huge slaughterhouse with its holding pens sprawling over more than ten acres. The building was deserted, and the pens empty. There was no rackety noise of cattle bellowing and hogs squealing as they waited to be run down the chutes to the man who crushed their skulls with a sledgehammer. All the live-stock had been driven away north past Lake Pontchar-train, out of the reach of the conquering Union military.

Walt felt a reluctance to fight John Alder, his oppo-nent in the duel, and was even more reluctant to kill him. Yet that was what he had been paid to do. Dueling for money was Walt's profession. Alder was young and handsome. And he was reckless. He had made love to the young mistress of an older, richer man. The woman had not been discreet. Their tryst had been found out. But was loving a woman such a sin that a man should die for it—especially when the woman was so beautiful, and so willing?

Walt leaned against one of the big sycamore trees that grew between the slaughterhouse and the Mississippi River. He listened to the sound of the great river as it passed by just beyond the levee. The evening sun was growing old and turning orange as it drew near the horizon. The other participants of the duel would arrive at any moment.

He reflected upon this strange feeling of not wanting to kill an opponent. Why should Alder be any different? He hardly knew the man, and the fee to fight him had already been paid. The amount was substantial.

Walt knew the transience of life, for he had slain fifty-five men in sixty-three duels. Sometimes he was hired to frighten a man, to teach him a lesson and not to kill him. These men he only wounded. He fought some men on his own account, wounding or killing them depending on how grievous he believed the affront was.

He searched his mind for fear of the coming duel. Perhaps that was causing the gloomy thoughts. There was no fear. Though he was fifty-years-old, his reflexes and accuracy with weapons had not diminished. Of that he was sure. Never had he met an opponent as quick or accurate as himself. No, it was something else. The reason would come to him.

He climbed up on the top of the levee and watched the sun's rays turn the broad Mississippi to a plain of rippling orange.

His attention shifted to the docks that extended along the river for at least three miles and faded away in the distance. He loved the river and the city. His great-great-grandmother had come up the river to New Orleans in 1727, after a long sea voyage from France. She was one of the "filles a la cassette" -Casket Girls- a term applied to the young women who crossed the tempestuous sea to become wives of the male colonists. The name came about due to the chests of clothes the French government gave to the women for agreeing to make the arduous journey.

Downstream, the flotilla of Union warships lay anchored on the water. He could see the big deck cannons and hear the drifting voices of the seamen. The battle for New Orleans was over. However, the private battles of man against man were not. The duel this evening would be carried through to its conclusion.

Since Walt was almost always the challenger in a duel, his opponent had the choice of weapons. Knowing his skill as a duelist, men sometimes chose strange weapons. They hoped to find one with which they were more familiar than he. A forester had wanted axes to be used in the contest with Walt. A farmer chose scythes.

Men good at hunting often chose rifles. Walt always won, and he made terrible wounds in his adversaries. The forester had been cleaved nearly from shoulder to hip by Walt's swing of the ax. The farmer had his legs cut from under him, leaving him alive but a cripple. Walt had felt no remorse for his actions. It was his occupation.

Alder had taken lessons from one of the several dueling masters in the city. It was said he was very good. He had chosen pistols. Walt was glad of that. Pistol balls made the least obvious wounds and yet caused death.

"Mr. Bouchard, are you ready to begin?" a man called from the direction of the slaughterhouse.

Walt recognized the voice of Renault, his second for the duel. He watched the river for a few seconds longer, then turned away. He came down from the levee and joined the group of men standing in a little clearing.

Walt studied Alder and answered the dueling judge at the proper time and with the proper words. Alder had to know of Walt's reputation as a fighter, yet the man's eyes as he looked back were steady. He even nodded a short greeting. Walt liked that. He believed Alder would die with dignity, and that was the test of a man, the ultimate point of life. Walt turned back-to-back with Alder at the judge's directions.

The judge and the two surgeons retreated the usual eight paces back, at right angles to the lines of fire.

"Do you want to live or die?" Walt said in a low voice over his shoulder to Alder.

"Live." Alder's voice was a hoarse whisper.

"Then stand steady like a man and you may indeed live."

"What do you mean?" Alder asked.

Bouchard did not answer. He might yet change his mind.

"Take ten paces and turn," the judge of duels directed.

The two duelists stepped off on the count and pivoted, each placing the thin sides of his bodies to the gun of his opponent. They lifted their cap and ball, single shot dueling pistols to point at the sky. Walt felt the thrill of the deadly contest. There was no higher wager than one's life. He truly enjoyed a duel.

Walt heard the judge's call to fire. In one smooth, nearly invisible motion, his arm snapped down. His pistol exploded.

Alder was brave, and quick with the quickness of youth. Walt saw his pistol jerk down in response to the judge's order to fire.

Then Walt's bullet hit Alder, spinning him. Alder's gun crashed, but he was facing away to the right at an angle, and his ball thudded into the ridge of dirt that made the levee.

Alder leaned forward, holding the front of his chest. He dropped his pistol to the ground and stood, swaying.

Walt went swiftly to the young man and put his arm about him to hold him erect. "I told you, you would live through this. Now, mend your ways and stay away from other men's women."

Alder looked at Walt. Then his teeth showed as he smiled through his pain. "She was worth it. But I shall take your advice."

Alder's surgeon hurried up. "Let me see him," he said.

"I only creased him across the chest," Walt told the surgeon and released his hold on Alder. "He should heal nicely."

Walt walked to Renault and handed the dueling pistol to him. "Thanks for standing with me again."

"Why didn't you kill him, as you agreed," Renault asked as he passed Walt his Colt revolver in a shoulder holster.

"Today is my birthday. I thought I'd be generous and give a foolish young man his life," Walt said. He walked away along the road that ran past the slaughter-house, and onward in the direction of the city.

"How old are you?" Renault called after him.

Walt did not reply out loud. I'm half a century old, he said to himself.

He thought about the meeting he would have with the man who had hired him to fight the duel. Walt would have to give back the fee that had been paid to him. He laughed at that thought. To laugh at returning his fee was strange for he always took money seriously. He was not himself this evening.

Walt entered the city and walked steadily on through the aged building of the Vieux Carre, the Old Square. He had a large house with servants in the Garden District. However, he rarely spent a night there. His destination was the Ramparts in the northern part of New Orleans.

Months before at the beginning of the war, the United States Mint had closed. A few months later, the Union blockade of the Mississippi had closed like a prison gate, and the commerce of the South's largest trading city had strangled. Gold and silver disappeared, hoarded by the banks, the moneylenders, and people alike. Confederate money—"Shinplasters"— was the currency, and mostly valueless.

Law and order had broken down as the threat of the Yankee invasion increased. The terror of the "Thugs," a ruthless band of robbers and murderers, swelled into the void and they ruled the streets. Looting was common.

People became busy with the business of hiding valuables. Maybe the Yankees would restore a semblance of order and safety.

Walt came to a cross street and glanced along it. The street was nearly empty. A man wearing a broad-brimmed hat and leading a black horse of excellent quality was walking in Walt's direction. Looking neither left or right, the man seemed deep in thought. The iron-shod hooves of the horse rang with a dull iron sound on the cobblestones of the street. The noises masked the footsteps of three men walking swiftly and overtaking the horsemen.

Walt noted the intent expressions of the three men.

All their eyes were focused on the man ahead. He recognized one of the three, a thug named Kassor. He had seen Kassor around the waterfront. As Walt started to look away and continue on toward the Ramparts, Kassor turned his head and spoke to his cohorts. All three reached for the pistols in their belts.

The threat to the man with the horse was obvious. For the second time that day, Walt did an unusual thing. He became involved with the life, not the death, of another man.

"Watch out behind you!" Bouchard shouted.

\*\*\*

Luke heard the warning cry and flung a look ahead. A man was pointing back past him along the street. Luke spun to the rear and moved to the side of his horse to put the body of the animal between him and the man. It could all be a trick. He looked back the way he had come.

Three men were forty or so paces distant. They broke stride and halted as Luke came round face-to-face with them. They held pistols partially drawn from their belts.

Luke slid his pistol from its holster and held it as he measured the menacing men. He recognized the tall one on the right. He had been part of the civilians in the forest with the soldiers and horses. The man had been called Kassor.

The men were not just simply out to hassle somebody. Their intent was deadly. Luke was their target, of that he was certain. Who had sent them? He'd worry about that later.

Who was the stranger who had shouted at him? Because of that warning, Luke now had a chance to survive, but a small one. The odds were three to one against him. His nerves tightened, and every sense became focused on the enemies in front of him.

"Goddamn you, Bouchard," Kassor muttered. Coldiron had reacted to Bouchard's shout by quickly moving to put his horse between him and the duelist. That told Kassor that Coldiron did not know the man, and thought he might also be an enemy. Now Coldiron stood poised and primed to fight, with his pistol half raised and aimed along the street.

Bouchard troubled Kassor more than did Coldiron. The duelist was the best pistoleer in all New Orleans. He stood motionless on the street several yards beyond Coldiron and slightly off to the side. Would he take part in a fight? Or did he merely want to see who died here this night?

"Did you fellows lose your nerve?" Luke called. His lips drew back, and his teeth showed cruelly white. He felt joyous in a ferocious sort of way. This was the first chance he'd had to strike at those who had stolen his horses.

"Let's kill the bastard," the man on Kassor's right said. "That's what we're being paid to do."

"I don't know about that, Reed," Kassor said. "That other fellow might take a hand to help Coldiron."

"Hell. He's off there a long distance," said the third man. "I bet he couldn't hit one of us even if he tried."

"That's Bouchard," Kassor said. "He's dangerous with a gun at any range."

"I don't care if it is Bouchard. We can't stand here all day. I vote to take Coldiron. Reed, let us do it if Kassor's afraid."

"Right," Reed said. "Get set. Go!" he called sharply.

# Chapter Thirteen

Coldiron snapped his pistol up level with his eye. Hurry, for the three men have their weapons free. Shoot the man on the left first, for he is moving most quickly. He pressed the trigger as the barrel of the pistol came into alignment on the man.

Luke's gun roared and bucked with its recoil. The man went over backward, his arms flinging out and the pistol falling from his grasp. His head slammed the cobblestones of the street with a thud.

Luke swung his pistol, searching for the next target. As he brought his gun to bear on a second foe, the man crumpled to the pavement.

The third man fled, sprinting to the side of the street toward the opening of an alley. He had made no attempt to help his cohorts. Luke knew the man should not be allowed to escape alive. He aimed a shot at the racing figure. The bullet shattered brick on the corner of the alley as the running man vanished into the murk-filled passageway.

\*\*\*

Bouchard surveyed the thugs talking among themselves on the street. He could not make out their words. Surely it was about the attack upon the man with the horse. Why did they want to kill him?

The men ceased talking. Two pulled their pistols.

Walt, conditioned by many duels, reacted instantly, his own hand grabbing for a weapon. Even as he brought his revolver into firing position, he knew he was in no danger. The reason for joining in the battle was one of curiosity, to see if he could hit a man with a quick shot at such a long distance. His pistol exploded.

The bullet struck the thug, and he went to his knees. He held himself there half erect for a moment. He began to tremble with an effort to keep from falling. He collapsed face down onto the pavement.

Bouchard saw Kassor plunge into the alleyway at a breakneck run. He had a short twinge of doubt about his action of killing one of the thugs. They were many in the city, all very brave now with the police gone. He shrugged the worry away. They would not dare bother him.

He holstered his pistol and walked toward the horseman who had come out from behind his animal. The man watched him closely.

"Thanks for the help," Luke said. "I hadn't planned on getting any."

"Three to one seemed unfair," Bouchard replied. "And anyway, I don't like the thugs."

"Thugs? Who are they?"

"Bullyboys when they want only fun. At other times they rob and kill. A great bunch of men to stay clear of. Why where they after you?"

"I suspect because that man who ran into the alley helped steal a herd of my horses."

"That was Kassor. I've never heard of him stealing horses. Still, he's stolen everything else, so why not horses? But there must be more to it than that."

"I believe he was with Union Marines in civilian clothing when it happened."

"I see. Union infiltrators. Yes, the thugs would want to join up with the Yankees. They probably think the North will win the war. Both groups will work hard to loot the city of everything valuable."

"War is hell on the conquered," Luke replied.

"Watch out for Kassor. He'll not want anyone alive to know he ran."

"I'll do that. Can I buy you a drink as payment for the help?"

"No, thanks. But I'd like to know your name."

"Luke Coldiron."

"Mine's Walt Bouchard. Good luck to you, Cold-iron," Bouchard turned back to his original course toward the Ramparts. He began to whistle. It was a fine day.

Luke climbed astride and rode swiftly away from the two dead men on the street. The attack had been ordered by the marine captain, Rawls. Only he knew of Luke's discussion with the colonel. The captain felt threatened by Luke's knowledge. Luke must not be caught so off guard again.

He came off the stone-paved street and struck the white shell road. He spoke to the black horse and raised it to a gallop.

\*\*\*

Susan, looking out from the cottage window, saw Luke come into view in the lane. He paused by the burned ruins of the plantation house and sat his horse for a short time, looking at the mound of ashes. At the sight of him, she felt a momentary lift of her spirits. Then the dark, heart-cramping sadness closed upon her again. Nothing would ever make her whole again. She went out on the porch of the cottage.

"Hello, Susan," Luke said, swinging down from the back of his mount. The woman had a strained, haunted look, like someone looking at death. Her beauty was being destroyed, devoured by her grief and burning desire for revenge.

"Did you have good luck with the Union commandant," she asked. "Will he pay you for your horses?"

"No. He told me to get out of New Orleans. Then three men jumped me on the way here. I think that was the doing of Captain Rawls."

"Captain Rawls?"

"A marine colonel is commandant of the occupying force in New Orleans. Captain Rawls is a Marine captain under him. Rawls was the leader of the men who took the horses from Captain Thacker. I'm certain he had a hand in killing your father and taking the money from his safe. If Rawls knew about the horses, he could have also known about the money to pay for them."

"Then why didn't you kill the murderer," Susan asked in a flinty voice.

"We were in the commandant's office. I didn't want to be stood before a firing squad and shot for killing a Union officer."

"I guess you did the right thing," she said in a disappointed voice. "I wasn't thinking of the consequences. I just wanted the murderer of my father punished."

Susan's eyes lost some of their hardness. "But enough talk of that until later. Come inside. I've kept some food warm for you."

"I am half starved," Luke said. It was pleasant to have a woman waiting for him. Even a cold woman. He followed her inside.

The entryway led directly into the living room of the cottage. To his right, beyond an open door, Roy Penn lay upon a cot. He opened his eyes and looked at Luke.

"Hello, Roy," Luke said. The young man's face was startlingly pale, and seemed caved in with his pain and the suffering from the loss of his hand. His eyes were burned out ashes.

"Hi, Luke. I never thanked you for bringing me here from the hospital. Well, I do. Now Susan has given me a gun. I'll be ready when the Yankees come. Maybe my war isn't over. A one-handed man can still shoot a pistol."

"Yes, I suppose so," Luke saw the pistol lying on the bed near Roy's good hand. "How are you doing?"

Roy held up the bandaged stump of his arm. "Susan keeps the bandages fresh, and me laced with laudanum. So I'm making do." He grinned crookedly without mirth.

"The food is ready," Susan called from the kitchen just off the living room. "There's a washbasin here by the side door."

"Coming," Luke replied.

He poured water into the basin and washed his hands and face. As he dried himself, he glanced into the mirror on the back of the washstand. He became suddenly conscious of his soiled clothing and unshaven face. He would have to do something about both.

Susan sat down across the table from Luke. "This is not the kind of dinner I had planned for you when I invited you to stay a few days," she said with a wistful smile.

"The food is excellent, and the company is the best," Luke said. He saw the effort it had taken for Susan to make even a weak smile. She had lost her father, a grievous loss indeed. And added to that was the fact that the great mansion had been burned and the land was heavily mortgaged. There was little likelihood the mortgage could be paid off in time of war. The land would be taken from her. Susan had lost practically everything of value in her life.

"Tell me about this Marine captain Rawls," Susan said.

"He looks like a tough fellow, and he acted quickly to send men to kill me. That is more evidence he doesn't want me around to tell about the robbery of your plantation house. The colonel knew about the horses, so the only thing that could cause Rawls trouble has to be the theft of the money."

160

"How did you get away from Rawls's men?"

"A stranger helped me. Shouted a warning. Then, when the gunwork started and while I was busy, he shot one of the men. Damn fine shot from a long distance. He aimed a little high, but the bullet killed the man."

"That's odd that a stranger would get involved. Did he give his name?"

"Yes, Walt Bouchard."

"I've' heard of him. He's a duelist, one of the best. He often fights for hire. Now and then one of his duels is written up in the newspaper when he kills someone of importance. He also teaches the use of sword and pistol at his gymnasium in Exchange Alley. He keeps a placee on the Ramparts.

"I'm damn glad he happened along. I owe him."

Luke knew of the placees, quadroon mistresses of white men. They were girls born of a white man and a woman whose parents were a white man and a black woman. Their mothers decided early in the girls' lives that they would become white men's mistresses. To insure this, the girls were sent to France for education and refinement, to learn to dance and play a musical instrument. Their mothers taught them how to satisfy a man in all the ways a woman could.

The mothers brought the beautiful, dusky-skinned girls to the lavish quadroon balls held in New Orleans.

There the white men inspected the girls, danced with them, and selected ones who pleased them. The mother was paid a flat fee of several thousands of dollars. The girl received a cottage free and clear on the Ramparts, where all the placees lived, and a yearly stipend for her services.

For a black man to appear at the ball, or to object to the proceedings in any manner, meant his certain death.

"So what do you plan to do now about Rawls? About everything?" Susan asked.

Luke's eyes, cold as frozen spheres of pale water, fastened upon Susan. "Rawls tried to have me killed. I can't let that go by. So I'll hunt him down. And Kassor, too, if he doesn't run and hide where I can't find him. I hope they'll have some of my money on them when we meet."

"And then?"

"I'll go home to the New Mexico Territory."

"Shouldn't the Yankees be made to pay? They have your horses."

"I've already tried that."

"There are other ways than merely asking for payment."

"What do you have in mind?"

"Join with me. We'll spy on them and pass the information upriver to General Lovell. And we'll steal their money."

"That's a foolish suggestion. I've been in one war. I fought in all the battles from Vera Cruz to Mexico City when we conquered Mexico. I killed men who were really not my enemies. I'll not fight another war, and especially this one."

Susan's eyes clouded with resentment at Luke's words. Hard lines formed around her mouth. She spoke sharply. "Why not? Simply killing Rawls and Kassor won't be enough revenge."

"That'd be enough for me. In a year, I'll have a new generation of colts to replace those horses stolen. And anyway, how could two people damage the Union navy and army? And what money do they have that we could steal?"

"The army and navy payroll. I would think they'd pay the men every month or two. It is near the end of April, now. They'll surely pay the soldiers that will be stationed here in New Orleans. We find out where that money is and take it."

"Just like that? Why, they'd have a whole platoon of Marines guarding it."

"No, not just like that. We need a plan, and we need men."

"What men? Cripples like Roy?" Luke looked at Roy lying on the cot in the adjoining room. The young man had heard his words. It showed on his hollow face. Luke should not have spoken so bluntly.

"They might be part of the men we'd need. There are two, maybe three hundred wounded Confederate soldiers hidden in New Orleans. Some are not badly wounded. I can find them. They'd be glad to help. And there are civilian patriots, who would help."

Luke evaluated Susan with amazement. "You'd try such a scheme?"

"If you'd help me. And it's not as crazy a scheme as you're thinking," she said with heat.

"You're correct. It's no more crazy than this whole war. How would you find out about the payroll? How much would be in it?"

"I've heard the Yankee General Butler has sixteen thousand men, and should reach New Orleans in three or four days. The navy has at least a thousand more, counting the Marines. If each man's pay is approximately twenty dollars, that would mean a payroll of over three hundred thousand dollars."

"My other question is, how would we find out about the payroll?"

"I'll go and work as a nurse at Charity Hospital. The Yankees have taken it over and their wounded are there.

Men say many things when they are under the influence of laudanum. Someone will tell me."

"It'll be Union money," Luke said.

"That's for the best, for it has the most value," Susan said. "And all of it will be paper money, and easy to carry. What do you say? Will you help me?"

"Let me think about it," Luke said. He wanted to tell Susan that he would never try to rob the Union payroll, but he could not voice the words. Not with that hopeful expression on her face.

Susan smiled at him. "All right. I know we can do it."

Luke began to eat again. Susan's plan was a hare-brained scheme with no chance of success.

***

Luke lay in the darkness on the overstuffed couch in the cottage living room. He had slept at first upon going to bed, then had awakened as a stiff wind came with the deepening night. The cottage seemed full of the low, mournful, moaning sound the wind made as it fluted across the peak of the roof.

He heard Roy tossing about on his bed in the room nearby. Now and then the wounded soldier called out garbled words.

The door to Susan's bedroom across the room from Luke creaked slightly as it opened. He did not hear the soft fall of her feet, but he saw her upright form take shape out of the darkness. She came within a step of the couch, halted, and looked down at him.

She was nude. Her white skin glowed with a soft luminescence all its own. He could see her long, graceful legs, the swell of her hips, the globes of her breasts.

"Are you awake?" she whispered.

"Yes."

"Would you hold me, Luke? I'm chilled, and need someone to hold me and keep me warm." Her voice broke.

"Are you certain?" He felt his heart thumping. He had not loved a woman in a very long time. And Susan was very beautiful.

"Yes." Her voice was barely a whisper on the night.

"Come. Lie down beside me."

"No. There is more room in my bed." She held out her hand to him.

Luke rose to his feet and took Susan's offered hand. It was very cold. He felt a tremble in it. Then the fingers closed firmly upon his—and led him through the darkness.

## Chapter Fourteen

Night had come and robbed the world of substance and filled it with a thousand shadows by the time Bouchard reached Rampart Street. His step quickened in anticipation of seeing Annette.

He saw other men on the street, white men with expensive, well-cut clothing. He had read in the newspaper that there were nearly four thousand placees housed in the Ramparts, an area encompassing Rampart Street and two adjoining streets. He thought the number exaggerated, but there were indeed many placees living in this circumscribed world of dusky female and white male.

Bouchard turned into the stone-paved driveway of a handsome stucco cottage painted a pale yellow. He opened the gate, closed it behind him, and continued along the side of the house, treading the familiar way to the courtyard at the rear.

Tall stone walls enclosed the courtyard, holding the deep darkness as they would a black liquid. From the far side of the courtyard came the pleasant sound of a trickle of water tinkling into a tiny stone pond fed from a roof reservoir kept replenished by the frequent rains. He breathed deeply of the odor of the blossoms of the flowers he could not see. Annette had planted many varieties, and they grew in great profusion. There were magnolias, crepe myrtles, oleanders, azaleas, gardenias, jasmine, and honeysuckle blossoms all the time. She was still enlarging the flower beds. The soft glow of light in a window at the far end of the cottage drew him, and he went on.

Annette opened the door at his knock, as she always did for him. Her maid greeted all other visitors.

"Walter, I am very pleased to see you," she said, and her wide, happy smile told Bouchard that was the truth of it. "Please come in."

He stepped through the door. She took his hat and hung it on the coat rack. She came instantly into his arms, soft flesh and red velvet dress.

He held her, feeling her breast against his chest. He ran his hands down the smooth contour of her back and out over her rounded hips. She stimulated him as no other woman ever had. God, how he desired her! But he would wait. It would be better for the waiting.

He moved her back a step. She watched him with large, dark eyes. He caught her face in both hands and ran his thumbs over her high cheekbones. Her skin was silk beneath his touch.

"You are not hurt," she asked.

"No, I'm immortal," he said, and smiled. She always knew of his duels, even though he never told her. The placees possessed a network for transferring news among themselves that was truly unworldly. Nothing happened to one of their white men that they did not learn about almost immediately.

"I'm glad. You must never be injured."

"So it will always be."

She laughed and pulled away and spun around, her dress sweeping out in a wide, flaring red circle. The swirling velvet cloth had the sound of bird's wings. "You make me want to dance," she said.

"I will dance with you. But later. And we will enjoy other entertaining antics."

"I will hold you to your promise. Both of them." She came back into his arms.

"Tibbie has cooked us a wonderful meal," she said, looking up at the wall. "A friend of hers from the country sold her a young capon. And we have fresh vegetables, butter, and hot bread."

"And wine?" he asked. He was glad that the shortage of food items that had developed in the city during the past month had not yet affected Annette's and Tibbie's ability to keep the larder stocked.

"Of course."

"Then let us eat."

"So that we may have energy for the night."

\*\*\*

Walt looked at Annette as she slept. He was always amazed at the smallness of her, the fragility of her neck and shoulders. She possessed a small girl quality, yet a sturdiness that carried them through their violent love-making. He smiled at that last thought.

Her sleeping face was lovely. Her lips were slightly parted as if in awe at what she saw in her dream. An odd tenderness and compassion took shape in Bouchard. He felt protective of her. He wanted to always be kind to her, this woman who gave him so much. Yet he had actually bought her, so what were her deepest feelings toward him?

He had first seen her at the Quadroon Ball held in the Salle d'Orleans, next to the Theatre d'Orleans, a building handsomely paneled in hardwoods. He had been laughingly badgered into coming along by Madame Dubois, who knew about placees and other things. He had taken one of the loges for onlookers, and for a few minutes he had sat there with some male friends and drunk brandy and sampled the excellent food brought to them by a waiter. Below them the orchestra played, couples danced—white men and quadroon girls—and Madame Dubois wove her path about, overseeing the event.

The quadroon girls were accomplished dancers, and could play musical instruments. Most had been educated in France, and could carry on conversations in fluent French and English, and on many subjects. Though every one was a virgin, each knew how to please a man.

Then Walt had seen Annette enter, accompanied by an older, shades darker woman. She was dressed in a long, black gown, against which her skin shone as dusky ivory. A simple pearl necklace was her only adornment. She was seventeen, but looked like a child imitating a woman—a woman in totality, he was to learn.

He rose to his feet and stared down from the loge. At his movement, she had glanced up, clear bright eyes fastening on him.

The woman with Annette had spoken quickly. Annette had lowered her eyes as a slight smile came to her lips. They continued on across the ballroom to join other mothers and daughters.

Walt went immediately and, taking Madame Dubois by the arm, led her to Annette for an introduction.

Annette and he had danced, gliding among the other couples. Walt was intoxicated by the loveliness of the girl. Other men had noted her outstanding beauty and approached to request dances. Walt ignored the men, refusing even to glance at them. They left, not wanting to bring his wrath down upon them.

Walt had held a discreet talk with Annette's mother. They had agreed upon a flat sum of eight thousand dollars and yearly stipends for the mother and daughter. He had given Annette the five room cottage, free and clear in her name, on the Ramparts. He purchased a slave for her, a middle-aged woman who would serve as a cook and maid.

He remembered the first night with her, how delicious her young body had been that first time. Even now there was a feeling of unexplored newness each time they loved. He adored his placee. No other woman interested him. What a grand thing to have no feeling of lacking, a complete, full life. Annette had been with him for four years. During that period, not once had he regretted his acquisition.

He became aware that she had woken and was watching him. He couldn't quite determine her expression in the night shadow. He thought it was a questioning look, with a touch of sadness.

"I have been thinking about you, Walter, this dueling you do as an occupation."

"My occupation does not bother me," Walt replied.

"I know that. But I think you do not like people very much."

"Are you certain of that? Today I only wounded a man who I had planned to kill. Then later, I aided a man in a fight with three other men with pistols. Maybe I saved his life. What do you think of that?" What she thought meant a great deal to Walt.

"Did you do those things for them, or for yourself?"

Walt reflected on the question. She was correct. He had no true desire to help the men to live, in fact no feelings toward them at all. He had allowed Alder to live and helped Coldiron in the fight with Kassor for his own amusement.

He had grown up on the tough waterfront streets of New Orleans. Very early he learned that to show fear made others feel brave and they stepped on you, crowding you, taking your few pennies. The streets had ground away his fear. He fought, and with his strong, wiry body and quick fists, he seldom lost. Finally he stopped losing altogether. He trained himself in the use of sword and pistol. There again, he found himself more quick and accurate than other men who came against him. Perhaps in all the toughening process, the streets had stolen his compassion toward others.

"Let us talk of other things," Walt said. He did not like the direction of the conversation. He wanted their life together to be always light and amusing.

"As you wish, Walter." She moved close to him and placed her head on his bare chest.

She spoke without looking at Walt. "I feel afraid now that the Yankees have conquered New Orleans. Can we continue to live here?"

"I see no reason why we can't. However, I may not be able to earn money by dueling, as in the past."

"Would that be so bad? You have your gymnasium."

"Yes, I could concentrate on teaching. There will always be those men who want to learn how to use weapons."

"Then perhaps the Yankees being here is not so terribly bad?"

"We don't know what kind of man General Butler is. He may enforce curfews on the population and ration food and other items to such an extent that we could not endure them. Then we would have to leave."

"The Union army may not allow the people to leave."

"I have a friend who owns a very fast boat. He is a smuggler. He hides his boats in the bayous during the day. At night they transport goods into and out of the city, right under the Yankees' noses. I've bought half interest in the boat, and made arrangements with him to take us from the city whenever we want. In case we do, where would you want to go?"

"Not Baton Rouge or Vicksburg, for they are too small. Let's go all the way to St. Louis. I think I could be happy there."

"That's in Union country."

"Does that make any difference to us?"

"No, not really."

"Then it is settled."

***

Luke awoke jerkily, his mind chilled by a premonition of danger. His hand snaked out for his pistol. It was not there beside him. He had left the weapon behind when he had come to Susan's bed. He immediately sat up.

"What's the matter?" Susan asked, rolling to face him.

Luke cocked his head to listen, then stared around the dark bedroom. He heard nothing except the wind rattling a limb of a tree on the window.

He put his hand out and touched the white cameo of Susan's face. "I should not be here. Rawls might figure out where I would go and send men to kill me. That would be very dangerous for you."

"He has no way of knowing you would come here," Susan said.

"He knows about the horses, and that I was a friend of your father. Rawls is a crooked bastard, but he is intelligent and could figure out where I would go. Or one of your blacks might have seen me and told him. I must leave before daylight."

"Where will you go?"

"I don't know. I'll find a place to stay until I can have a meeting with Rawls and Kassor."

He climbed from the bed and began to dress in the darkness. He heard Susan donning her clothing on the opposite side of the bed.

\*\*\*

Roy's eyes twitched beneath their covering of eyelids. His mouth opened, emitting frightened mewing sounds. He laid soaked in sour, cold sweat. Within his mind the faces of his dead comrades' with vacant eyeholes and open and bleeding mouths, moved over him and came down and swallowed him, and he spun round and round in the black sea of his nightmare.

He awoke breathing in sharp, shallow breaths. For a moment he was disoriented, not knowing where he was. Then he heard Coldiron talking to Susan. their voices muffled. Protecting the stub of his left wrist, he climbed from his cot and opened his door. The voices came from Susan's bedroom.

Good for you, Coldiron, Roy thought. Any man would be glad to be in that woman's bed.

Roy moved hastily back into the darkness of his room as Luke and Susan came into the living room. He did not want to embarrass them by letting them know he was aware of where Luke had slept. He began to pull on his clothing awkwardly with his one hand. He was stronger today, his legs more steady.

Susan lit a coal oil lamp and turned to Luke, regarding him steadily. "I want you to help me to rob the Yankees," she said. "I want to hurt them in a hundred ways."

"Your plan has almost no chance of succeeding. You risk too much. I want nothing to do with helping you kill yourself."

An expression of sadness and disappointment clouded Susan's face. Her eyes grew moist. She blinked to hold back tears. "Sooner or later you must take a stand, pick a side. Sooner or later everyone has to become involved with everybody else, and with what is happening. Please help me, for I need you."

Luke studied Susan. God, how beautiful she was. It was hard to deny her anything—especially after the night with her. But he would not attack the Union forces in New Orleans.

"I can't," Luke said. "I have a better plan. You come with me to my ranch in the New Mexico Territory. You'll like the high mountains with their pines, and flowing streams. Leave this warring land with its savagery. When all the fighting is over we'll come back here and rebuild the plantation house. I am rich enough to do that. We'll leave this very minute. I'll not even take time to search for Rawls and Kassor."

"I can't do that. Oh, I can't!" Susan cried. "I must do something about the death of my father. About my home being burned to the ground. You must see that. I'm going to organize a band of men to help me. We'll rob the Yankees with or without your help."

Susan and Luke fell silent as Roy came from his bedroom. He crossed to the front door and went through to the outside. He walked to the far end of the porch. The conversation between Luke and Susan was not for his ears.

He relieved himself, making his stream out onto the yard. He heard the wind in the trees and coming down over the roof with a sliding sound. He shivered as the wind evaporated the sweat of the nightmare from his body.

The night was spent, and in the east a drop of dawn made a hole in the black sky. The trees were taking form. The ruins of the destroyed plantation mansion could be made out.

Roy leaned forward, his eyes wrestling with the darkness. Something had moved near the ruins of the house. There, it moved again. And a second form appeared following the first, and a third. All carried long slender objects, like rifles. They were men, and from what he could see they all appeared to be dressed alike, in uniform.

Roy's film of sweat was suddenly ice upon his skin. His enemies had found him. He lunged back into the house.

"Luke, Susan, Yankees are coming!" Roy called. "I saw them out by the ruins of the big house. There're at least three, and probably a lot more."

"There'll be a squad of them," Luke said. "Grab your gear. We'll leave out the back way and be into the woods before they can surround the house."

Luke spoke to Susan as he rolled his bedroll. "You'd better come, too. They may arrest you."

"I don't think they will if you and Roy aren't found here. I'll be all right. But I know where you should take

Roy. There's a family named Dosset on the Big Bayou Road. His name's Jack. For years he was overseer of our plantation, but now farms his own land. Go northwest three miles or so, and you'll run into a main road. Then go north to a wooden bridge. The lane to the Dosset house is just beyond the bridge and on the right."

"All right." Luke said. "Let's go, Roy."

"Can I take your pistol?" Roy asked Susan.

"Yes. Yes. Go!"

"Susan, I'll not leave New Orleans without seeing you again," Luke said.

Susan nodded. "All right. Perhaps you'll even change your mind."

Luke followed swiftly after Roy out the rear door and the few steps to the stable. He saddled in seconds and tied his bedroll on.

"Climb in the saddle," Luke directed Roy. He gave the wounded soldier a boost.

Luke swung up on the horse's rump behind the saddle. He reached around Roy and took the reins. He jammed his heels into the flanks of the black horse. The big animal bolted out the stable door and into the night and the wind.

They raced away from the cottage and toward a dense grove of trees some one hundred yards away. The big horse stretched his long, powerful legs. His hooves thundered upon the earth.

Luke looked hard past Roy. He heard the black horse sucking air deeply into its lungs. Give the horse five seconds, and he would have them safely into the woods.

"There's one of them!" Roy cried.

Luke saw the figure of a man running in from the right. The man halted and snapped his rifle to his shoulder.

Roy jerked up his pistol. Luke saw the lift of the weapon. If the soldier was shot, Susan would be held accountable, an accessory to murder.

"Don't shoot!" Luke shouted into Roy's ear.

The pistol cracked. The soldier fell.

Roy let out a wild, happy yell. "Got the son of a bitch."

The big, black horse sped past the crumpled form on the ground and vanished into the woods.

## Chapter Fifteen

"Captain Rawls, shall I arrest the Dauphin woman?" Sergeant Luttrel asked. The sergeant stood with the officer in the living room of the cottage near the door that led onto the porch.

The captain did not reply, but continued to stare at Susan, who sat on the sofa. She looked back at him, her eyes as noncommittal as a blind woman's. She had been straightening the covers on the big double bed in one of the bedrooms of the house when he and his Marines had burst inside. Steadfastly she had denied knowing of the presence of the two men who had wounded one of the Marines as they fled on horseback.

"How bad is the man injured, sergeant?" the captain asked.

"The bullet went through his side," the sergeant said. "We've bandaged him the best we can. He should be gotten to a surgeon right away, for he's losing a fair amount of blood. I've got the men making a litter to carry him back to the transport wagons."

Susan listened to the two Yankee Marines. She could not look away from the officer's eyes, set in deep sockets beneath bushy eyebrows. They glittered with malevolence. She hid her fear, clamping her hands tightly together in her lap to keep them from trembling. She had heard the sergeant call him Captain Rawls. He was the man Luke thought was responsible for the murder of her father and the burning of the plantation house. He must know Luke would have told her that. He would arrest her in a minute for sheltering Luke and Roy, and thus being a party to the wounding of the marine. Her punishment would be quick and brutal, for this was wartime.

"Come outside, Sergeant," the captain said.

"Yes, sir."

Rawls led out into the yard and halted where Susan could not hear them talk. He spoke to the sergeant. "Coldiron was here. Two people had slept in the big bed. That would be Coldiron and the woman. That's why she was in a hurry to make it. There were bandages on the side table near the cot in the smaller bedroom. I'd guess the second man was a wounded Confederate soldier."

"More than enough reason to place her under arrest if we were really looking for Confederate soldiers."

"But we're not," Rawls said. "Damn Kassor to hell. He had the perfect chance to kill Coldiron and missed it. Now we are getting involved with our men."

"Kassor picks his fights when he has the best odds for winning without getting hurt. He's more dangerous than a man who'll stand up and fight. I'll bet he kills Bouchard, just as he said he would."

"Bouchard is not important to us," the captain said. He gestured toward the cottage. Susan was visible through the open doorway. "The woman is quite pretty—Coldiron may be back. But I doubt it. He won't make the same mistake twice. We've got him on the run. However, he'll not leave the city willingly. We'll keep a watch on her from time to time. Assemble the men. We'll leave for now."

Susan heard the sergeant calling orders to his squad of Marines. She could see them forming up in a double column. Then the thud of their feet drew away from the cottage.

She hastened to the door and looked out. The Yankees were marching off toward the city. The wounded marine was being carried on a stretcher. Rawls and the sergeant were with them. They had not arrested her after all. She stared after them in puzzlement.

\*\*\*

Colonel Trotter sat on the bow seat of the ship's cutter that carried him toward Admiral Farragut's flagship anchored in the center of the Mississippi River. The day was breaking, the sun a silent explosion of orange on the eastern horizon. An upriver wind blew cool and damp. A flock of white seagulls, hungry after the enforced fast during the long, black night, shrieked and glided over the boat.

He stared past the two rowing oarsmen and the coxswain at the tiller to the city. The waterfront was deserted except for one squad of four Marines on patrol. Beyond the levee and the warehouses of the riverfront, several feeble stringers of smoke struggled up from homes where cooking fires had been lit. It's a sad city, the colonel thought. He was glad the warships had not fired their big cannons onto the beautiful homes and public buildings of New Orleans.

"Coxs'n, have you been to New Orleans before the war?" the colonel asked.

"No, sir. I've spent all my navy time in the East."

"I was here two years ago. She was a grand city then."

"Yes, sir. I've heard that."

"The city is dead now," the colonel said. He lapsed into silence.

The two seamen rowing steadily, brought the cutter close to the side of the Hartford.

"Hook us on," the coxswain said.

The seaman on the side next to the Hartford shipped his oars and went forward with the boathook. He caught hold of the Jacob's ladder. The second seaman shipped his oars as the coxswain threw the tiller over and swung the boat in against the Hartford's hull.

Colonel Trotter grabbed the Jacob's ladder and went nimbly up the rungs to the deck. He hoped the admiral was in a good mood. He could be a crotchety old bastard at times.

"Good morning, Colonel Trotter," the marine at the top of the ladder said as the officer stepped onto the deck of the ship.

The colonel saluted aft at the flag and then spoke to the marine. "Good morning to you, Corporal. Has the admiral come on deck yet?"

"Yes, sir. He's in the main cabin. He ordered me to tell you to report directly to him there."

The colonel crossed the deck and entered an open door. Admiral Farragut and a young army lieutenant sat studying a map spread on the long table that extended nearly the length of the room.

"Ah, Colonel Trotter, right on time," the admiral said.

"Yes, sir." The colonel saluted the senior officer.

"This is Lieutenant Swisher of General Butler's command," the admiral said.

"I judged as much, sir. Captain Rawls told me of the lieutenant's arrival."

The colonel spoke to the army officer. "Good to see you, Lieutenant."

"Hello, Colonel Trotter. My men appreciated the horses Captain Rawls gave us."

"Be seated, Colonel," the admiral said. "Do you have the plan for occupation of the city ready for my review?"

"Yes, sir." The colonel withdrew a packet of folded and bound sheets of paper from inside the front of his tunic and handed them to the admiral.

Admiral Farragut sat for a time, his glasses perched upon his nose, and studied the papers. At last he looked up at the colonel. "Very thorough and well thought out plan. Implement it at once. Put New Orleans under martial law. Take the entire battalion of Marines ashore with you. Get as many patrols on the street as possible. Put your roving patrols on horseback so they can travel swiftly if the need arises. Block all roads leading from the city. Allow nothing to leave that can be of use to us. Stop the looting in the city. Confiscate all firearms."

The admiral turned to the army officer. "Lieutenant Swisher, place yourself and your men under Colonel Trotter's command. You will assist him in the occupation of New Orleans."

"Yes, sir."

"Colonel, find the former policemen of the city, or at least as many of them as you can, and get them back on duty to enforce the civil laws. The same action applies for the civil judges. Get them back in their courtrooms to hear the cases. Locate the editors of the newspapers and put the presses to running. We will need the newspapers to tell the citizens of the city the orders of occupation, and for other reasons. The editors can print news, but you will review and approve what is printed."

"Yes, sir."

"There is a railroad extending south down the east side of the Mississippi nearly to Fort St. Phillip. We could hurry General Butler's arrival if we could send a train to transport him and his men. Are there any locomotives with railroad cars in the city?"

"No, sir. General Lovell took all the engines and cars north with him."

"That's too bad. General Butler and his soldiers will have to use shank's mare. However, there's something we can do for the army. Find quarters for the officers in the buildings near the Cabildo. The general will want his officers close to headquarters. Evict the occupants of the Montalba Rowhouses as you need to. Also find space for the camp of the soldiers. Gather food supplies for them. Have everything in readiness. The paymaster has received my orders to prepare to pay the men, and will be reporting to you."

"Admiral, I've already started the collection of food and other camp provisions," the colonel said.

"Good. I'll be gone for a couple of days. I'm going downriver to inspect the forts. The gunboat Itasca will transport me. After the forts, I'll continue on to the mouth of the river to see the captain of the Colorado. Since the ship can't be gotten over the bar, she's of no value to me and should return to the East Coast. She's needed for blockade duty there. You'll be in command ashore until I return."

"Yes, sir," the colonel said.

"Gentlemen, you are dismissed."

# Chapter Sixteen

Walt arose early, as was his custom, yet Annette was gone from the bed. She would have bathed and now be seeing to the preparation of his breakfast. He went to the adjoining bath and washed in the tub of warm water waiting for him. He dressed in the fresh clothing she had laid out.

Annette smiled radiantly at Walter as he came into the kitchen and sat down opposite her. He smiled back. He could not help himself. She had such an infectious smile. Today would be another grand day, just like the long line of them that had passed since she had come into his life.

He marveled at the beauty of her. Beauty was rare, if it was genuine. Beauty was a currency of a kind. You could trade it for success, and for amusement. And you could use it to get love. With love, you weren't destitute.

Walt's currency was gold. Annette's was her beauty. They traded currency with each other. Some foolish men thought women should give their beauty without charge. Foolish, indeed. Men did not give their strength for nothing.

The maid served them and left. They ate and talked of many things, but not of war, nor of duels.

Walt left the cottage and walked leisurely along the narrow streets of the Old Square, once the walled French city of Nouvelle Orleans. The morning shadows were still long, and a cool breeze blew in from the river. Even with the Yankees occupying New Orleans, the day was grand.

He reached Exchange Alley and turned down it, passing other dueling academies on the street. All were still closed. The instructors had not yet arrived. Ahead on the street, three young men stood talking among themselves. They saw Walt and called out greetings to him. He lifted his hand in acknowledgment.

"You young gentlemen are here early today. Now, why is that?"

One of the men spoke in a solemn voice. "We leave New Orleans for Vicksburg at noon. We have stayed here because we thought there would be a battle for the city. But we now know the battle will be at Vicksburg. Our forces are all dug in there. We thought we'd get in a last couple of hours practice until time to leave."

"Then we must not waste time in beginning," Walt said. "But I suggest you wait until dark to go north. The Yankees may have the roads and railroad guarded, and will take your weapons."

The three men glanced at each other. "That's good advice," one of them said. The others nodded agreement.

The men were Bouchard's latest students. He never accepted more than three at any one time. Also, they must be very skilled. He had no time or interest in teaching the basics of the use of knife, sword, or pistol. Young men and sometimes older ones came to him to put the finest edge of killing on their already high levels of proficiency with weapons. His fee was very high.

Bouchard opened the door to his dueling gymnasium and all filed inside. For the next two hours, he taught the men, practicing with first one of them and then another while the remaining two fenced with each other. He called a halt at the end of the period.

Walt said good-bye to the men, and shook their hands. They strolled across the gymnasium and out the door. For an instant, as Walt watched the men, he had a sensation of loss. He would never see them again, for they were going to a war they would lose, in which they would die.

He hung his rapier on the wall with his other weapons and gazed about the practice hall. He had owned it for more than twenty-five years. He was more relaxed, more comfortable here than any other place in the world. He could sit quietly for hours among the swords and pistols in the aged and worn place and be perfectly content. The cottage with Annette was a close second, but that was only because of the girl.

He locked the outside door of the gymnasium and pocketed the key. He left Exchange Alley and turned left toward his favorite cafe for a cup of strong coffee.

Walt did not see the four men in civilian clothing enter Exchange Alley from the opposite end and stare after him.

\*\*\*

The tall, cadaverous body of Hammlin Fouveaux leaned to the side like that of a stricken crane ready to fall. The parchment skin of his face was taut with his pain, and his huge beak of a nose protruded like a hatchet blade. He put out a hand to brace himself on the desk of his office.

"Damnation, Kassor," he growled through the searing pain in his warped spine, "you had the opportunity to kill Bouchard and failed." He shuffled around behind the desk and eased himself into the big padded chair. From a desk drawer he extracted a bottle of laudanum. He swallowed a mouthful.

He felt the sharpest edge of the pain slowly receding, but it would never go completely away. He would never be able to straighten his back. That had not been possible for the past fourteen years, ever since Bouchard's bullet had shattered his spinal column.

Fouveaux's eyes flicked across the room to rest on the chief of thugs sitting quietly and watching. He tried to control his anger at the man, for it was the tension that came strongly with anger that brought on the most horrible episodes of pain. He spoke in a calmer voice. "Kassor, you know I want Bouchard dead."

"Bouchard is a hard man to kill." Fouveaux should know that. He had not succeeded in his attempt to shoot the man during a duel, and was now a cripple for the remainder of his life.

"You had two men with you," Fouveaux said in an accusative tone.

"And we had that horse breeder Coldiron to deal with at the same time as Bouchard."

"So you let your two men die without trying to help them. Do I have the wrong man as my partner?"

"I warned those two not to start the fight with Coldiron while Bouchard was watching," Kassor snapped. He leaned forward and stabbed a finger at Fouveaux. "Listen," he hissed, "I took a tongue lashing from those damned Union Marines over this because I need them. But I don't have to take any bull from you. We've made a lot of money together, with me supplying the stolen goods and you using your shipping company as a front to get rid of it. But hear me, you need me more than I need you. I can find another fence."

"All right. All right. Take it easy. I want to remain partners with you."

Fouveaux saw the dangerous glint in Kassor's eyes. It was not wise to bait the violent thug. He picked up the bottle of laudanum and put it back into the drawer, slowly placing it beside the pistol that lay there. He left the drawer open.

"What are Rawls and Springer planning now?" Fouveaux asked.

Kassor answered in a sour voice. "They have lined up several plantations for us to rob," Then the thug seemed to make a decision. He spoke in a level tone. "We should be bringing you some things tonight."

"Good. You and the Union men must continue to strike as many places as you can, and in the shortest possible time. Also, the Marines must not be given any excuse not to use our services. If that should happen, I don't think we would be safe for long."

"I don't have to be told that."

"I'm sure you don't."

"The first thing I'm going to do is kill Bouchard. He took a stand against the thugs and must pay for that."

"Yes, that should come first. He must be made to suffer."

"I'll take some men and shoot him to pieces."

"Oh, no," Fouveaux said. "He must die a little at a time."

"What do you mean?"

"A quick death is too good for Bouchard. He has a beautiful placee on Rampart Street. A man like Bouchard would set great value on his woman. She must die first, and in a most terrible manner. Then, in time, Bouchard will join her in death."

"I like that plan," Kassor said. "You have seen her, and she is beautiful?"

"Yes. Very."

"Then making Bouchard pay will be a lot of fun."

"Do it early today. Bouchard should be at his dueling academy and will not be home. However, you should first go and be sure he is there."

"Right," Kassor climbed to his feet. He would take three men with him, just in case they should encounter Bouchard and have to fight.

\*\*\*

Kassor and his cohorts came into Exchange Alley as Bouchard left his gymnasium. The duelist locked the door behind him and walked off along the street. "Let's go, fellows," Rassor said. "A pretty woman waits for us. She just doesn't know it."

He struck off, leading his men north on Toulouse Street toward the Ramparts. Only four blocks to go. He smiled broadly in anticipation of the pleasure that would soon be his. Bouchard's placee would be the most lovely of all of those women chosen for their beauty. She would not be a beauty when he finished.

# Chapter Seventeen

Annette halted her conversation with Tibbie when she heard footsteps on the stoop of the rear door. She began to smile happily. "Walter has returned home early today," she said.

"Maybe it's a peddler, or some other stranger," Tibbie said. "Let me answer the door."

"I will do it. I like to welcome Walter."

She hastened to the door and swept it open. Her smile vanished like fog hit by a stiff wind.

A tall, thin man stood on the stoop. He grinned crookedly at her through a ragged beard.

"Hello, beauty," the man said.

Kassor lunged forward, scooping Annette's slim body up in one arm and clamping her mouth shut with a hand. He continued his movement onward into the room. The men with him, who had stood out of sight on either side of the doorway, swarmed inside. One sprang upon Tibbie and bore her to the floor.

"You're just like Fouveaux told me you would be," Kassor said, staring down into Annette's black eyes, enormously enlarged by her fear.

Annette struggled to free herself, but the man's arms were steel bands encircling her. She tried to bite his hand. He clamped her jaws tightly shut with a hard hand.

"Now for the fun part," Kassor said gleefully.

"I'm going to be busy for a little while," he said to the men standing and watching him. "You two guard the front and back doors." He glanced at the man holding Tibbie. "Keep that old woman quiet any way you have to."

"Right, Kassor," the man said. He slid a knife from his belt.

Kassor carried Annette, struggling and kicking in his arms, from the room and down the hallway. He shoved a door open. He laughed when he saw the big bed. Bouchard, I'll use it for the same purpose you do, Kassor thought. He laughed long and loud at that.

*\*\**

The eight horsemen came into sight in the lane leading to Jack Dosset's home. They halted in the shade of the big walnut tree in the yard and looked at the farmhouse.

"They've come, Jack," Susan said. She had been by the open door for the past hour, waiting. The success of her plan depended upon these men.

"Do you think they'll help me fight the Yankees?" she asked.

"They've told me they want to fight," Jack Dosset replied. "They hate the Northerners for blasting the forts and capturing New Orleans. I believe your plan has a good chance of succeeding and that the men will think so, too."

"I like your plan," Roy Penn said.

"Let's go out and talk with them," Jack said.

He stepped through the doorway with Susan by his side.

Roy walked beside Susan. He had discarded his artilleryman's uniform, and now wore civilian clothing. The pistol Susan had given him was stuck in the waistband of his trousers. His stub of an arm rested in a cloth sling fastened around his neck. The arm hurt like hell when it hung down his side.

"They have to help us," Susan said softly, as if to herself. "We can't do it by ourselves." She squared her shoulders and stood as tall as possible. The men must accept her. She had dressed in the pants, shirt, and brimmed hat that she wore when hunting. Her face was scrubbed and plain, without rouge.

Jack had chosen these eight from the wide number of men he knew in the city. All were unmarried, and young, younger than Susan by several years. Five were ruffians who had not yet joined the Confederate military. Three were soldiers who had escaped from Fort Jackson and had made their way upriver.

Susan recognized two of the men—Johnson, a roofer, and Perkins, a horse trader. Both men had been at her family's plantation at one time or another for business with her father.

"That fellow standing out in front is Fletcher Swift," Jack said. "He'll be the hardest to convince. He likes to argue. He's a brawler, and tough."

"I knew him in Fort Jackson," Roy said. "He was always in trouble with the officers, for he couldn't take orders."

Susan evaluated Fletcher. He was a short, powerfully built man. A large chaw of tobacco bulged one cheek. His log-like legs appeared to have rooted themselves in the ground.

The eyes of the men became focused upon Susan. She saw their expressions of surprise as one after the other came to the realization that she was a woman.

"Hello, Fletcher, and you, O'Doyle," Jack said to the two men nearest him. "And to the rest of you."

The men nodded or spoke their greetings, while still looking at Susan. She saw their faces become filled with skepticism about her presence here. That did not bode well for the outcome of the meeting.

"Thanks for coming on short notice," Jack said.

"You said you had something important to talk to us about," Fletcher said.

"What's to be said is important," Jack said. "But first I want to introduce you to Susan Dauphin and Roy Penn. Susan's father was killed a couple of days ago, and her plantation house burned."

"I heard about that," Fletcher said. He glanced at Roy. "Hello, Penn. I see that you got out of Fort Jackson, too."

"Hello, Fletcher," Roy said.

"I'm sorry your father got killed," Johnson said to Susan. "Wade Dauphin was a good man."

"And a good horse trader," Perkins said. "Miss Susan, how do you like that mare I sold your dad for you?"

"A very good mount, Mr. Perkins," Susan replied. "That's her there by the fence."

"I recognized her when I rode up. I never forget a horse I've once traded."

"That's enough chatter," Fletcher said coarsely. "What's the important news that all of us fellows have come to hear?"

"Before we go on, I'd like to know the names of these other men," Susan said.

"That one there is Tidwell," Jack said, pointing. "And that's Waller, and Compton, and Stamper."

"Hello," Susan said.

The men acknowledged the introductions.

"Now to business," Jack said. "It's about striking back at the Yankees. I'm sure all of you would like to do that."

A chorus of voices rose in agreement.

"I'm glad you're organizing it," Fletcher said. "We all trust you."

"It's not my plan, but I'm for it. The plan is Miss Dauphin's."

"I don't want to hear any plan that a woman has cooked up," Fletcher said with disdain. "She doesn't know anything about fighting."

Susan moved a step out in front of Jack and Roy and closer to the group of men. "New Orleans has been conquered and it's too late to fight and stop that," she said. "Now we must hurt the Yankees in other ways."

"Whatever we do will end up being a fight with the Yankees," Fletcher said. "I want someone to lead us who has been in a war. Dossett was a sergeant in the Mexican War and won a medal. What did you ever kill except maybe a rabbit or squirrel? Can you even shoot a gun?"

"She's as good a shot as most of you men," Jack said. "I've hunted with her and her father. She killed her first deer at fourteen. She was with me when we chased a sheep-killing panther with dogs. She killed the panther with one shot while it was running. She hunts alone in the woods."

Fletcher looked Susan over from the top of her head down to her boots. "Maybe you can shoot and hunt. You can even dress like a man. But that don't make you one. I want only men fighting beside me." Fletcher's voice was harsh.

"Don't talk to Miss Susan in that tone," Roy said. He moved to stand by her side. "She's brave as any one of you. And probably smarter."

"Watch your mouth, Penn, before I tear off your other arm and beat the hell out of you with it," Fletcher growled. His big hands folded into bony fists.

Roy laid his hand on the butt of the pistol in his belt. "I'm telling you to watch how you talk to Miss Susan."

"It's all right, Roy." Susan placed a restraining hand on Roy's arm. Fletcher was very strong. She did not want Roy hurt. "There mustn't be any trouble among us," she said.

She raised her head defiantly toward the group of men. "You haven't even heard my plan and already it's no good, and that's just because I'm a woman. Well, there's no way I can change what I am."

Dossett spoke. "Fletcher has made his say. How about the rest of you men? Are you game to join together against the Yankees? Susan has a plan to take a lot of money from them. I think the plan has a good chance to succeed."

"Will she be going with us?" O'Doyle asked, avoiding Susan's eyes and looking at Jack.

"I certainly am," Susan said, speaking for herself. "I'll not be kept back. And you can't do it without my help."

"I'll not go if a woman is part of the group," O'Doyle said. "I agree with Fletcher on that. I can't think of a way she'd be so important that we couldn't do it without her."

Susan looked into the faces of the men and knew she had lost. The strongest mouth always won, and that was Fletcher. O'Doyle had joined with him. Now no man would go against them and join with her. She could have persuaded Jack to present the plan as his own, but dam-nit, it was hers. Besides, she had used Jack's friendship enough. He was a married man with five children, and was already putting himself in danger by being part of a resistance group against the Yankees.

"Miss Susan, you got to see our side in this here argument," Johnson said. "Us men all know each other, and as Fletcher said some of us even fought together in Mexico. And at the Forts. So you see how it is."

"I see, all right," Susan replied. "I've not proved myself to you. Well I'm sorry that I haven't, for there's much we could do to hurt the Yankees."

"You can prove yourself," Fletcher said.

Susan saw the sly grin stretch Fletcher's lips across his tobacco-stained teeth. She knew his remark was a trap for her. How dangerous was it? Did she really have any options but to play along with the game?

"How?" Susan said.

"Why, just go into New Orleans and kill a Yankee marine," Fletcher said. "There's plenty of them around the Cabildo and the riverfront."

"That's crazy, Fletcher," Jack said.

"Don't listen to him, Miss Susan," Roy said. "There's no need for you to do that."

But there is a need, Susan thought. A dark shadow came over her as she pictured herself actually killing a man. Still, the plan she had devised held a strong probability that death would occur to some of the Yankees, and also to some of her comrades. Perhaps even she would be killed. She was prepared to ask these men to risk their lives. Fletcher had proposed she risk hers a little earlier than the others.

Roy was watching Susan closely. He saw the intensity in her eyes, the steely purpose in the line of her jaw. "Don't do it," he said.

"You said a marine, Fletcher," Susan said. "That means one."

"No!" Roy cried out. But Susan's sensitive features hardened, and her skin became pale as bone. She would not be turned aside.

"Just one will do it," Fletcher said. He was smiling around his cud of tobacco. "Ain't that right, boys?"

The men shifted their feet, uncomfortable with the course the conversation had taken. Several dropped their eyes from Susan and stared at the ground.

Johnson spoke. "You don't have to kill anybody, Miss Susan. Let's just forget what's been said here and all go home. Ain't that the best thing, Jack?"

"I agree," Jack said.

"We will not all go home and forget," Susan's voice rose, shrill and full of anger. "I'll not forget what the Yankees did. They killed my father and burned my home. Now I'll kill one of them. Roy, give me your pistol."

"No," Roy said. "You gave the gun to me, so I don't have to," He backed away a step. "Killing in battle is one thing, but to simply go up to a man on the street and shoot him without warning is an entirely different matter." He surely did not want Susan to do such a thing.

"Roy, give me the pistol," Susan said in a tight, firm voice, "or I'll find another one."

Roy looked at Susan's face. It was closed against further argument. He looked around at the men. There was no help there, not even from Jack.

"If you must do this, then use a rifle and not a pistol," Roy said to Susan. "That gives you a longer range for good shooting, and keeps you safer."

"I'll use the pistol. It's not just the killing that Fletcher wants to see, but how I do it."

Roy pulled the revolver from the waistband of his trousers. Feeling a terrible reluctance, he handed the weapon to Susan.

She took the pistol in her hand. Then, very deliberately, she studied the men, resting her eyes on each one until he returned her stare.

"I'm going to shoot a Yankee Marine," she said. "That's what Fletcher said I had to do to prove how brave I am. All of you let him talk for you." Susan's voice dropped, and a threatening tone was in it, "When

I do this, I'm going to think all of you are committed to helping me. No one had better back out."

Johnson started to speak. "Miss Dauphin—"

Susan shut him off with a savage cutting motion of her hand. "It's too late for more talk, Johnson." She controlled her anger at the men, at her personal losses, at the damn Yankees. "But you come with me and witness the deed."

She spun upon Fletcher. "You come, too. I want you to see this killing. We'll go to the Cabildo and I'll shoot one of the sentries on duty there. You and Johnson can then tell the other men what you saw. The rest of you wait here for us to return."

Susan whirled away and hurried to the mare by the fence. She jerked herself astride.

"Come on," she called loudly to Fletcher and Johnson. She galloped the mare off on the lane leading to the road that went to New Orleans.

Fletcher and Johnson hastened to their horses. They seemed surprised at the swiftness of Susan's actions. They kicked their mounts into motion after her.

Jack watched Susan ride away. She was too brave. "Damn you, Fletcher!" he called as the man passed by with Johnson.

Fletcher stared straight ahead.

"Nothing had better happen to her." Roy's warning trailed after the men.

# Chapter Eighteen

As Bouchard came into the rear courtyard of the cottage, he saw the open door. Annette often left the door that way when a wind blew from the south. Thus, the breeze, sweet with the aroma of the flowers growing in the yard, could drift through the house. Walt smiled at the thought and took the two steps up to the stoop in one stride.

He halted abruptly in the doorway. His mind was suddenly frigid, as cold as an Arctic blizzard. Tibbie lay in a large pool of dark, coagulated blood on the floor in the center of the room. Her black face, stiff in death, still held a terrified expression.

"My God!" Walt cried out as a great dread seized him. "Annette," His voice thundered throughout the house.

His hand flashed to his pistol and yanked it out. He leapt across the room to the hallway that led to the other rooms. The murderer might still be here and shoot him as he charged forward. Walt cared nothing for that possible danger. He fervently hoped to find the man responsible for this awful deed still here. The murderer would die.

The parlor was empty. He ran to the next doorway and sprang inside.

Annette lay on her back upon their bed. She was naked, and her girlish body held horrible knife wounds in the chest and stomach. No life was evident in the motionless body. The sheet that had once been snow-white was now soaked with an impossible amount of blood.

"No! Damnit. No!"

Walt went hastily forward and bent over the still figure. His heart jumped, and began to pound on the ribs of his chest—Annette still lived. He could see a tiny pulse beating weakly in the hollow of her throat.

"Annette, can you hear me?" Walt said. He reached out tenderly with both hands and cupped her face, his fingers gently caressing her cold cheeks, her eyelids, her temples. "Please speak to me."

The woman's wonderful black eyes opened. "Walter, is that you?"

"Yes, my love."

"I have waited for you to come. I could not die without seeing you again."

"You shall not die."

For a moment that mischievous expression he was so fond of came into Annette's face. Her lips curved up, and a small dimple appeared in each cheek. Then, as if it were too heavy to hold, the expression faded, and her face became strained as she fought off death.

"You know that I shall die," she said, her voice a fragile sound, like thin ice breaking. "I wanted you to know that I loved you. I would have remained yours whether or not you had money."

Bitter tears burned Walt's eyes. His throat was so constricted with his sorrow that he could not speak. God, how he loved this woman.

"Please hold me," Annette whispered. "The darkness is falling, and I grow cold."

Walt leaned over her and slid his hands beneath her shoulders and head. He lifted her so very gently and held her against him.

"Who did this terrible thing to you?" he asked softly.

"They called him Kassor. He said a man named Fouveaux told him about me. There were three men with him."

The soul-bending truth of the reason for Annette's wounds struck Walt savagely. Kassor had come and taken revenge upon Annette for Walt having helped Coldiron fight him. Walt's action in giving that aid to the man from New Mexico had been an unimportant game to him—a game with no value—but because of the act, Kassor had committed this awful crime against

Annette. Walt's sorrow and regret became so icy cold it burned him.

Annette's head rested more heavily on Walt's shoulder. She sighed, a slow, soft movement of her breath past his ear. It was a sound she sometimes made as she drifted off to sleep.

Walt continued to hold Annette. He was sure she would awaken. She was merely sleeping, tired as after love. The blood was just an error.

He waited, his eyes open but blind. She lay gently in his arms, weighing almost nothing. He was fooling himself. He knew she would not awaken.

Walt lowered Annette back down upon the blood-stained bed. Oh God! How terribly he would miss her! There' would be no more pleasant words from that sweet mouth, no delightful lovemaking. He wanted to lie down beside her, and also die. No one would mourn him after he dropped from life. Did Annette wait for him in death? If he could be certain that she did, he would take his pistol and end his own life to join her. He pulled himself back from the path his thoughts were taking him. There was something very important he must do. He left the bedroom and went to Tibbie.

"I'm sorry, sweet wpman," he said, touching her cold face.

He hastened out into the courtyard and stood in the sunlight. He had seen death come many times. He had caused it most of those times. He had never given death much thought, until now. When somebody you love dies, oh how much that makes a difference.

Walt jerked his head up to look skyward. He thought he could hear God laughing cruelly somewhere behind the sun. The laugh was so very real. Then Walt cursed hoarsely. There was no God, so how could he be laughing?

He walked slowly among the flowers Annette had so lovingly planted and tended. Gradually he pulled himself together and began to smell the fragrant odors of the blossoms and see the myriad beautiful colors. Her small footprints were in the loose soil. The hoe she used to cultivate the flowers leaned against the wall of the stable. She was not gone completely, not yet.

Walt noticed the bloodstains on his clothing from holding Annette. He touched the blood with his fingers. There would be more blood spilled before this day ended—not innocent blood, as hers was. He reentered the cottage and changed to fresh shirt and jacket.

At a writing table, he penned a short note to Annette's mother. It was worded simply: My Annette and your daughter has been foully murdered. Please come at once.

Walt went out on Rampart Street. A hackney was coming along the way. It stopped two cottages distant, and a white man climbed out. The man paid the driver and the vehicle rolled in Walt's direction.

The black driver stopped at Walt's signal. "Where do you wish to go, sir?" he asked.

Walt handed the man the note and a gold coin. "Take this to Marie Rillieux." He told the driver the address. "I've paid you very well, so don't stop or delay anywhere. Bring the woman straight back here. Do you understand?"

"Yes, sir."

"Then be on your way."

Walt could not leave Annette and Tibbie alone in their deaths. He returned to the cottage. At the kitchen table he checked the loads in his pistol, the set of the lead balls against the charge of gunpowder, and the firing caps on the nipples.

The minutes passed slowly. At last he heard the hackney stop in front of the cottage. He walked out into the courtyard.

Annette's mother came swiftly down the driveway beside the cottage and came out into the courtyard. She went to Walt and looked up into his face.

"Tell me, Mr. Bouchard, what has happened?"

"An enemy of mine has taken his vengeance out on Annette and Tibbie."

"Then my daughter is truly dead. I had hoped the note was a cruel hoax," Marie Rillieux began to cry, the tears coursing down her black cheeks.

"It is most terribly true. Please wash Annette and dress her in her prettiest gown. I will return soon, and hold a wake during the night with you and her friends."

He pivoted away to hide his tears. Marie Rillieux's voice ran after Walt as he hurried up the driveway. "Do a proper job of killing the man—but not too swiftly."

# Chapter Nineteen

The bull alligator bellowed savagely, warning all the animals of the forest that he was on guard and would defend his domain against all who dared intrude. The threatening sound came ricocheting off the boles of the big trees, and reached the Chickasaw.

Panther did not stir where he rested in the leaves beneath the outstretched limbs of a giant oak. The alligator was at least two hundred feet away in the edge of the swamp and was no danger to him.

The forest fell silent again, and Panther's reverie continued. The only things that moved within his view were the gray hawks soaring against the blue sky. White sunlight fell in streamers through the canopy of leaves above him. The air was full of the odors of the forest in springtime—the blossoms of the wildflowers, rotting wood, the wetness of the nearby swamp. Every breath was an elixir in Panther's lungs. He felt his innate affinity with the land and its creatures. He was even comfortable within himself, his troubles diminished to their true, insignificant dimensions. He had not felt so totally alive and totally at peace since he had lain under this very same tree as a child.

His blissful mood ran on even as he considered the fact that he was not a child but an aged man with gray in his hair and a face creased and seamed by the years, his eyesight not as keen as it had once been. The years had taken their toll on him, and also on the oak tree. Some of its limbs were broken, battered by the fierce storms that swept in off the sea. There was a lightning wound, a deep gash in the body of the tree, extending from its crown to its roots. A lightning bolt had ridden down the tree from the heavens to the earth. Panther did not feel bad about the aging of the oak, or of himself, for that was the natural order of things.

He rolled his head and looked at the horse the white man Coldiron had given him. The animal was nearby, standing slump-shouldered and sleeping on its feet. It seemed to sense Panther's eyes upon it and lifted its head to look at the man. When the horse decided that he was not going to rise, it began to nibble at the sparse grass growing in the shade of the tree.

A light dust rose as the horse's hooves disturbed the leaves. One of the streamers of sunlight became golden with dancing dust motes. One tiny, illuminated speck hovered just above Panther's face. He held his breath to keep from disturbing the air on which the dust particle floated. It seemed to be rotating, but he could not be certain. It slowly sank toward him.

He pursed his lips and blew a short, quick puff of air. The bright speck vanished into the darkness of the shade. Was his life just as easily snuffed out? He chuckled at that thought. Today he felt very strong and durable.

Panther's laugh broke his mood. He picked up his rifle from the ground and rose to his feet. The weapon was replaced in its scabbard on the horse.

He mounted the horse. What a grand feeling to ride an excellent steed. He went off, winding a course among the trunks of the trees.

Panther thought of Blackberry Woman. She had been very quiet for the past two days, going about her womanly duties with hardly a word to him. He could not lift her out of her melancholy. She would not discuss the cause of it. A very stubborn woman at times. However, since she would not talk to him about what bothered her, he knew it must somehow be related to him. He had reflected long and hard upon his past actions and words, and still could not recall anything he had done to cause her dark mood. He would buy her a present, a length of cloth. Perhaps he could find a pretty, red one. That was her favorite color.

The trees thinned and Panther left the forest behind. He rode through several miles of farmland and came out on the end of Rampart Street. He turned along the way.

The street was lined with one and two-story cottages painted in bright blues, yellows, or greens. The lots were small, and often the side wall of one cottage butted against the wall of its neighbor. These were the homes of the white men's placees.

Panther found pleasure in traversing the street where the young quadroon women tripped about in their colorful, long-tailed dresses. Sometimes, in the evenings, they were in the street by the scores, often in small groups gossiping and laughing. Their cultivated voices were very pleasant to hear.

Very few of the women were on the street today. Of those who were, Panther heard no laughter, nor did he see any smiles. Blackberry Woman knew some of the placees and she had told him that many of the men who owned them had gone off to war. Some men had been killed on the faraway battlefields.

As Panther drew near the intersection of Rampart Street with Barracks Street, three men in red uniforms came into sight. They spoke together for a moment and then turned and walked in Panther's direction. All wore pistols in holsters on their belts. Panther knew the uniformed men were Union Marines. He had encountered others, but always near the riverfront. These Marines were off duty, and exploring the Ramparts. Probably the beautiful placees drew them.

The Marines swaggered and talked loudly as they moved along the street, like the conquerors they were.

One of the men said something to a young, pale-skinned woman passing them. He showed her some object in his hand. The woman's head lifted haughtily. She spoke angrily to the man and hastened on.

The Marine turned to a second man. "Cooper, I thought you said a gold coin could buy one of these women, that they'd do anything for money."

Panther heard the words. The placees were often called whores, but they were not. They were as true to their men as any married woman.

"That's not right, Byrnes. I said Sergeant Luttrel told me maybe some of them could be."

"Well that girl was not one of them," Byrnes said. "Damn, she had a sharp tongue."

Panther reined his horse to go around the Marines in the street. They ceased talking and glanced at him. The Marine with the two stripes on his sleeve—the one called Cooper—fastened a sharp look on the hip of Panther's horse.

"Look what that Indian is riding," Cooper said.

"That horse has the same brand as those we took from the Confederate cavalry."

"The Indian must have stolen it from the soldiers," Byrnes said. "Best we take it away from him and give it back to them."

"We don't know that for sure," the third Marine said. "He could've found it. Captain Rawls did say some horses had escaped in the woods."

"Corporal, do you want me to take the horse," Byrnes asked.

"Why not?" Cooper said. "He's just an old Indian, and don't need a horse. Take it, Byrnes."

Panther wanted no trouble with the white men. He could only lose. At the thought of losing, a cold chill ran through him. The certainty of being defeated had caused him to run and hide in the swamps those years long past when his people had been driven from their land. In that time of great injustice and misery, he had fled without fighting the enemy. A very great shame lay upon him for that cowardly act.

Never again would Panther be afraid. Nor would he ever surrender something that belonged to him. His mind was set on that.

He reached and touched his medicine bundle, the small pouch of buckskin that hung around his neck. It held a collection of secret objects, each with strong spiritual powers. He almost smiled as the strength flowed out from the medicine, traveling up his arm, encompassing his entire body. Great Spirit, I have no time to sing the warriors song to you, even though I want to. The battle begins now.

Panther's rifle was in its scabbard on the right side of the horse, where the Marines could not see it. He dropped his hand and caught hold of the stock.

"The horse is mine," he said to the Marines walking toward him. "Coldiron gave it to me, and I shall keep it."

"Like hell you will," Byrnes said. "We're taking it, and right now."

Byrnes jumped forward, his hand reaching out for the horse's bridle.

Panther threw his left leg over the pommel and slid from the saddle on the side of the horse opposite the men. He yanked the rifle out as his feet touched the ground.

The horse snorted in fright at Byrnes sudden leap at its head, it lunged backward, exposing the two men standing facing each other, not a body length separating them.

Panther raised his rifle, cocking the hammer. At the short range, there was no need to bring the weapon to his shoulder. He thrust it out at Byrnes, and pulled the trigger.

The speeding 50. caliber projectile lifted the Marine off his feet. The bullet shattered his thick sternum bone, plowed onward through the soft lung tissue, and erupted out the man's back. He flopped down on the stones of the street, slack-muscled and lifeless.

Panther threw one quick look at the two remaining Marines. They stood stunned, their faces frozen with shock at the suddenness of the attack. For the moment, they seemed to have forgotten their revolvers, their hands still at their sides. However, Panther knew these were fighting men and their surprise would last but a second.

His single shot Sharps was empty. Something to shield him must be found until he could reload. He sprang to the side of the horse farthest from the men. He caught a tight grip on the pommel of the saddle with his left hand. At the same moment he rammed the barrel of the rifle into the horse's ribs. The hurt beast plunged away.

Panther, towed by the horse, ran, leaping in long, powerful bounds beside it. His hold on the saddle horn was almost torn from his grip with each lunge of the horse. He clutched the horn harder, vising it with every ounce of his strength.

He heard the rapid, crashing fire of the Marines' revolvers. He wished he owned one of the white man's guns that could shoot many times. Then he would simply let go of the horse and fight it out with them.

The horse staggered as a bullet stabbed deeply into its body. The flank of the wounded brute struck Panther and he stumbled, his bounding stride broken and legs tangled. The horse dragged him on. He must not let go his hold on the saddle horn and thus be left in the open in the street. The Marines would surely kill him.

Panther gathered himself, his muscles tensing. He jerked powerfully forward and upward. He thought his arm was being torn from its socket, but his legs came untangled and he again caught his footing.

Even as Panther regained his feet, the horse shuddered under the impact of another bullet. The grievously wounded animal came to a stumbling halt. It splayed its legs, trying to keep from falling. Its big body began to tremble and its head lowered until the muzzle touched the pavement of the street.

Panther spun and looked behind. The two Marines, holding their pistols ready, were running swiftly toward him and at an angle across the street. In a few more feet they would have a clear shot at Panther.

He bolted. Bent low and his legs driving, he raced for the corner of the block.

A bullet struck his right ear. The burning pain spurred him onward. A second projectile plucked at the clothing on his shoulder. Then he whirled around the corner. Safe for the moment.

He straightened and ran on without slowing. No man had ever been able to catch him on foot. He worked the lever on his Sharps and opened the loading chamber. A cartridge was fished out of his ammunition pouch and shoved into the breach of the weapon. He jerked the lever up, closing the breech. A firing cap was pressed over the nipple.

Panther immediately halted and wheeled to the rear. He would run no further. They had killed his horse and shot him. Now it was their time to die.

The Marines came to a sliding stop as the Indian turned upon them. One, sensing the danger to them, jumped to the side and threw himself down by the raised sidewalk.

Panther's rifle jumped to his shoulder. He pressed the trigger. The hammer fell. The round ball of lead sped across the intervening space striking the Marine still standing.

The man dropped his pistol and clutched at his chest. He collapsed on the street.

"Cooper, help me," the wounded man called weakly. Then he became quiet and lay very still.

Panther began to swiftly reload as he watched the last Marine climb to his feet. The man pointed his pistol down the street, aiming carefully.

The range was long for a pistol, thought Panther. Still, the man might be skilled enough to hit him if he remained motionless. Then, he'd give him a moving target. Panther began to stalk across the street as he finished shoving the cartridge into the rifle.

The pistol roared. Panther heard the snarl of the bullet, like some deadly insect zipping past.

He thumbed the firing cap onto the nipple. And raised the rifle to his shoulder.

The Marine's nerve broke. He ran toward the nearby building at the corner of the street. He was gone before Panther could fire.

Panther hurried to the fallen Marine. The man was dead. Panther took his pistol and supply of powder and balls.

A door squeaked as it came open in the nearby cottage. Panther turned hastily. A young woman came outside and stood on the sidewalk.

"That was a very brave thing you did," she said.

Panther said nothing. He must hasten away from this place. He had not seen the last of the Union Marines. This had been only the first battle.

"You are hurt. I see blood," the woman said, and she came toward him.

In the heat of the fight, Panther had forgotten his wound. He felt his ear, determining how much had been shot away. There was a section missing, a half circle notch that he could lay his finger in had been torn from the outer rim of his ear. The wound was bleeding some, but not seriously. He laughed. He had been very fortunate.

"It is nothing," he told the woman.

He walked away toward the forest. There, in his land, a thousand Marines could not trap him—but he could find them, if they dared to come looking for him.

The woman stared after the grim-faced old Indian with the white-streaked hair. He carried two guns. He appeared totally unafraid.

# Chapter Twenty

Susan stopped her mare on Basin Street at the St. Louis Cemetery where her father had been laid to rest in the first hour of daylight of that day. She sat the horse and looked over the tall, brick wall at the many rows of tombs. She located her family's burial crypt. The structure was nearly seven feet tall, constructed of stone and painted white.

Once, as a small child, she had climbed to the top of the tomb and looked out over the cemetery. She had thought the hundreds of little buildings were very pretty with their bouquets of flowers and carved stone angels, crosses, and spires. She had danced a little, happy jig on the flat top of the tomb and called out to her father, telling him how beautiful the little houses were. She asked him why people made them. That's when he first told her of death, and that the structures were the resting places of many thousands of people who died, that each crypt held the bones of several generations of a family. She had felt very sad after that, and she danced no more on the top of the tomb.

"Father," she whispered, "I have a feeling that I will soon join you in your little stone world."

The mare moved on at the touch of Susan's heels upon her flanks. Shortly, horse and rider carne to Toulouse Street and veered onto it and onward in the direction of the riverfront.

Susan glanced to the rear. Fletcher and Johnson were a block behind. What were they thinking? That she would grow too fearful to commit the act of killing a Marine? That she would fail even if she tried?

They were correct to think she was afraid. Her hands trembled. Her lungs were stiff, as if half frozen, and her breaths were shallow. In this condition, could she hit a target with her pistol?

She came off Toulouse and onto Chartres Street. She recalled that her father had liked to come to the Exchange on Chartres. Here men gathered after business hours for talk, to drink wine, and to gamble. Susan looked one block east to where the Cabildo fronted onto Chartres Street. A Marine with a bayoneted rifle on his shoulder was in view at the tall arches of the entrance of the building. She guided her mount along the cobblestone street in his direction.

As she began to shorten the distance to the Cabildo, a squad of four Marines came off St. Anne Street and onto Chartres. She lost sight of them as they entered Jackson Square. Almost immediately an old horse pulling an equally old, dilapidated buggy came into view in front of the Cabildo. A black man sat upon the seat of the buggy. The Marine watched the man pass close in front of the Cabildo but made no challenge to him.

The buggy came abreast of Susan, and she saw that the reins of the horse hung loosely in the black man's hands. She looked at his face. He stared straight ahead, his eyes clouded and whitewashed by cataracts. The old horse was finding its own way along some familiar route, carrying its blind master to some destination only they knew.

Susan felt the old black man with his opaque, unseeing eyes appearing at this crucial time was an ill omen. However, that would not stop her from doing what she must do. She pulled her pistol from its holster and held it down beside her right leg.

As the buggy turned the corner behind her and vanished from view, silence fell upon the street. Even the strike of the iron-shod hooves of the mare upon the cobblestones seemed muted. Susan felt the mare between her legs, but she also seemed to be outside herself and a little distance away, an observer watching the lone rider upon the horse draw nearer and nearer to the red-jacketed Marine.

Susan fought the strange feeling of being in two places at one time. She gathered her scattered senses and willed her mind to pull her back into the body of the rider on the horse. Her sight blurred for a second. Then she was looking clearly from only one set of eyes.

She stared down from the mare's back at the Marine standing a few steps distant under one of the arches of the Cabildo. He took his rifle down from his shoulder and warily watched her.

She lifted her left hand to the Marine. "Hello," she said, to throw him off guard.

He gave a short nod to Susan's greeting. Blond hair protruded from under his military hat, and there was a splash of freckles across his nose. He was a mere boy. It would have been better had he been older, a veteran, a Marine who had killed other soldiers. This youth probably had never fired his rifle in battle. He was so young to die.

Susan's mouth became a grim trap. She jerked her pistol up from where it had been hidden from the Marine's view beside her leg. She thrust the weapon out, pointing it into his startled face.

As she sighted down the barrel of the pistol into the smooth, unblemished face of the Marine, she knew she could not shoot a bullet into such boyish handsomeness. The pistol was quickly lowered to point at the second button of his tunic.

The Marine swiftly raised his rifle. His eyes were wide and bright with the sudden realization that she intended to kill him.

Susan pressed the trigger of the pistol. The button on the man's tunic vanished. Just a button, after all. Try not to think about the boy's body behind it.

The Marine staggered backward under the arch of the Cabildo. His face twisted with shock and sudden agony. The finger on the trigger of the rifle tightened and the weapon fired.

The smoke and burning gunpowder of the Marine's rifle spewed out at Susan. The concussion jarred her. For a split moment of time, she thought she had been hit by the bullet.

The man's eyes never left Susan's as he fell to the side, his shoulder striking against the stone archway. His rifle clattered onto the stone pavement. He tried to hold himself erect by clutching at the stones of the archway.

A questioning, disbelieving expression came to the man's face as he slid down the archway to sit on the ground. His head slowly sank to rest on his chest, his eyes hidden at last from Susan.

She continued to sit the mare and stare down at the bowed, youthful head. Susan was petrified, unable to think or act.

The thud of feet of running men penetrated her dulled senses. The sound came from her right. These men would be the squad of Marines she had seen earlier as she approached the Cabildo. Other Marines inside the building would surely be pouring out the door at any instant to investigate the gunfire.

She must escape this hazardous place at once. She gouged her mount's ribs with her heels, and struck the horse on the shoulder with the heavy pistol.

The mare raced away on Chartres Street. Its iron-shod hooves beat sparks from the cobblestones pavement and sent them flying.

A volley of rifle shots rang out behind Susan. Bullets sang banshee songs as they ricocheted off the pavement. Other bullets whacked the fronts of the nearby buildings lining the street.

Susan felt the chill of fear, and the sharp edge of panic. She flailed at the mare again and again with the pistol. She threw herself forward on the mare's neck and screamed a shrill animal cry into its ear. The brute took the primal call, the long neck stretched, the lungs sucked great droughts of air, and the driving hooves reached for every inch of distance.

Susan swerved the horse left onto St. Anne Street. The gunshots at her rear stopped. The only sound was the clatter of the mare's hooves filling the narrow canyon of the street.

Royal Street was reached, and Susan reined the horse right onto it. A block later, she went left onto Dumaine Street. She slowed the mare's headlong run to a swift gallop for there were miles to go to be truly safe—if she could ever be safe again.

People on the street turned to look at the speeding horseman. Susan hardly noticed the curious, staring faces. The city blocks fell away to the rear. The houses became widely scattered, and then there were none as the street ended. The forest was visible several miles distant beyond wide meadows bounded by rail fences.

She ran the mare across the meadows and deeply into the forest. Finally the weary animal came to a stop, of its own volition. It stood trembling, its sweaty chest heaving. Susan slid from the saddle.

She grabbed the neck of the horse to keep from falling, for the forest was spinning around her. The big trees seemed to close upon her. A heavy, black sky fell crashing down upon her. She tumbled to the ground.

For an unknown time, Susan sprawled senseless on the leaf-covered ground of the forest. She did not know when an Indian carrying a rifle came out of the shadows and knelt beside her. He listened to her breathing and looked for a wound as best he could without touching her. Finding no injury, he checked the sweat-stained horse. He returned and, sat down by her side with a frown of wonderment.

Susan came to consciousness in one tick of time. Someone was near her. She knew it. A wave of fear swept over her. She flung a look around.

A man sat on the ground beside her, an Indian with a dark, mahogany face, broad and craggy. A rifle lay across his lap.

"Who are you?" Susan exclaimed.

"I am Panther." He saw she was frightened. It showed in the stillness of her, as in a frightened animal of the forest. "Sometimes the people in the city call me Honey Man."

Susan recognized the Chickasaw. He had been selling honey on the docks of the river the day Luke Coldiron had brought his horses to New Orleans. She recalled having seen the man a few other times on the city streets. She searched his face, trying to determine if he meant her harm. He sat unmoving, his eyes holding an expression of curiosity and of concern.

Susan recalled the events that had brought her to this place in the forest. The vivid memories of the killing of the Marine flared like flame in her mind. She again rode the mare in the wild run through the city streets, and she heard the sounds of the rifle shots and the bullets flying and striking around her. A shiver shook her as she realized the immense danger she had escaped.

She knew only the first step had been taken on a very long path full of danger, but it had been made. There would be more battles and deaths for she would pave the road to purgatory with the bodies of dead Yankees—if she could stay alive long enough.

Panther saw the rapid change of the white woman's emotions, casting aside fear and ending with an expression of hard, implacable determination. To do what?

"Are you hurt? Did your horse throw you?"

"No," Susan said without explaining as to which question the answer applied. She looked up at the sun, marking its elevation above the horizon. The sun had moved a hand's width down the sky, and she judged that nearly two hours had passed since she had been at the Cabildo.

"I am pleased that you are not hurt," Panther said.

"Thank you for watching over me."

"You are a friend of Coldiron, so I wanted to keep you safe until you awoke."

"Why do you owe Coldiron anything?"

"He gave me a horse, but it is now dead. And he slept under my roof one night. I think he is a friend and a man I can trust, so I must protect those things he holds of value."

Panther rose to his feet. "Now I must go. Be watchful as the deer, for there are cruel men in the forest," He went off like a brown shadow into the trees.

Susan felt no fear of men in the forest. Her spirit soared with exhilaration at the knowledge that the deed, the killing, was finished and she was alive. Fletcher and Johnson would have witnessed the death of the Marine. Now the men must help her to rob the Yankee payroll.

Susan picked up her hat from the ground and climbed erect. She piled her tangled hair once again upon the top of her head, and captured it with her hat.

The mare came to her and watched her expectantly with gold-flecked, brown eyes. Susan walked around the horse checking for gunshot wounds. No bullet had struck the faithful mare. However, the animal's right shoulder was badly bruised and swollen where Susan had hit it with the pistol.

"I'm sorry about doing that," Susan said, and she gingerly touched the bruised area.

The horse nickered as if it understood and was accepting the apology.

Susan mounted and headed in the direction of Dosset's farm. As she rode her mind replayed the shooting and the face of the young man as he died. She was sickened at her act, yet she knew she would kill other Yankees. They would always be her hated enemies.

***

"It's her. She's not dead," Roy exclaimed to the other men sitting under the tree in Dosset's yard. He scrambled to his feet and pointed with his whole arm. "Fletcher, you were wrong."

"I thought she got shot," Fletcher said, climbing erect beside Roy. "I saw her fall across the horse's neck."

"Maybe she is hit," Jack said.

"God, I hope not," Roy said. Fletcher's declaration that he had seen Susan shot had cast a black gloom over him. Now this wonderful reprieve from sorrow.

Roy went to meet Susan. The other men moved forward more slowly behind him.

Susan reined in the mare and sat her saddle. Her eyes swept over the faces of the men. Roy was smiling in a very pleased manner. Her sight came to rest on Fletcher.

"Did you see the Marine die?" she questioned curtly.

"Yes."

"And you, Johnson?"

"Yes."

"Did you tell the others what you saw?"

"We told them," Johnson said. "We thought you got hit. There were plenty of bullets flying after you."

"You're a crazy woman," Fletcher said.

"I'm not crazy. I shot a man because you said I had to prove my bravery. It is done. Now you must listen to my plan."

"Tell us your brilliant strategy for making the Yankees suffer," Fletcher said.

Susan swung down from the saddle. She was immensely tired, but rest would come later.

In a controlled voice, she began to explain her plan for robbing the Union payroll. Now and again, one of the men interrupted with a question. She finished and stood waiting. They had to like the plan. They must. After what she had done.

The men remained silent, their eyes fixed on Susan.

"Well, what do you think?" Susan asked testily.

"I still think you're a crazy woman," Fletcher said. "But the damn plan just might work. I'm with you for now. Let's see how the pieces fall together." He faced about. "How about you other fellows?"

"I'm in," Johnson said.

"Me, too," O'Doyle agreed.

"Same here," said Tidwell.

The remaining men called out their approval. Susan's lips stretched across her teeth in a bleak smile. Her eyes were cold and flat.

# Chapter Twenty-One

"Simon Hanks? Nope, I don't know anyone by that name," the bartender said.

"Thanks, anyway," Luke replied. He turned and left the saloon.

For hours Luke had been walking the streets of the riverfront district and entering the saloons, billiard parlors, and gun shops. He had asked scores of people if they knew the raiders he had identified at Dauphin's plantation. The answer had always been no.

On Decatur Street Luke pushed open the door of the Mississippi Gal Saloon and went inside. The saloon was narrow and deep. The bar was on the left, a long row of tables on the right. Three card tables and a craps table were in the rear. All the gaming tables were deserted.

Luke's attention focused on several Marines at two tables. Muskets leaned against the wall within easy reach. All the men wore pistols. Though apparently off duty, the men carried weapons—a wise action in a hostile enemy city.

Luke pulled his vest closed over the pistol in his belt. The Marines were confiscating all weapons they found, and Luke did not want to lose his. He scanned the faces of the men quickly. All were unknown to him.

He moved toward the bar, where four men in civilian clothing stood drinking. One of the men was in conversation with the bartender.

"Beer, if it's cold," Luke said, placing an elbow on the top of the bar and facing the bartender.

The bartender ceased his conversation with the civilian and looked at Luke. "It's as cold as it ever gets," he said. "And we're lucky to have any with the war on."

"You're right. The beer will do, warm or cold."

The bartender filled a mug and it came sliding it down the bar to Luke. "Fifteen cents," he said.

Luke laid a nickel and dime on the bar. He took a pull at the beer and let it slide down his throat.

"Not bad," he said. "I have a question for you. I'm trying to find Simon Hanks. Have you seen him around lately?"

"Not in the past two or three days," the bartender replied. "What do you want him for?"

Luke's pulse jumped. At last somebody knew the man.

"He owes me money, and has been dodging me."

"You'll not ever get your money from that fellow."

"That'd be downright disappointing. If you haven't seen him, maybe you know who he runs with."

"He runs with Sam Kassor."

"Have you seen Kassor?"

"Not today. He was in here yesterday evening. Talked with a Yankee Marine sergeant right over there." He chucked a thumb at a table in the rear.

"Do you know where Kassor lives?"

"No. But he'll probably be here later tonight The Mississippi Gal Saloon is his favorite hangout, for he's sweet on one of the girls that works here."

"Where else might Kassor and his men be hanging out?"

"I don't know any more than what I've told you. I just serve them drinks and watch them take the girls upstairs."

One of the Marines called out for another round of drinks. The bartender moved back down the bar to the beer keg.

Luke took his drink to a table off some distance from the Union military men and seated himself. Now that he knew where Kassor's girlfriend worked, the task was to wait. He propped his chair against the wall and sipped at his beer.

The evening grew old and the light in the front window paled and died. The bartender lit the wicks of the four coal oil lamps hanging on chains fastened to the ceiling. A dull, yellow glow came alive in the saloon.

The Marines took up their muskets and left. Civilians came drifting in until there were twenty or so.

Two saloon girls in short-skirted, brightly colored dresses arrived. They spoke to the bartender and started to drift among the customers, smiling at the men and asking them to buy drinks.

Luke held up his mug and signaled to the bartender for another beer.

The bartender came and sat the foaming mug down. He picked up the coins Luke had laid on the table.

"You said Kassor is stuck on one of the girls," Luke said. "Which one is it?"

"She's not coming in tonight, or so one of the other girls told me."

"Why not?"

"She said to tell me she was sick, but I'd bet Kassor has beat her up again. He's a mean bastard. And jealous of a saloon girl that can be bought for two dollars. Can you believe that? There's no accounting for a man's taste."

"What's her name? Where does she live?"

"Her name's Cecelia Ross. She lives three squares west of here on Clay Street. She has an apartment in the rear of number sixty three. But she'll not tell you anything about Kassor. She's scared to death of him, and for good reason."

"It won't hurt to ask her."

"Unless you run into Kassor while you're there."

"I just might be that lucky," Luke said.

"Suit yourself," the bartender said with a shrug.

\*\*\*

As Walt Bouchard drew near the riverfront, the black wave of night came stalking and overran the defeated city of New Orleans. The conquering Union fleet faded into the deepening murk on the river. He could barely make out the squad of six Marines stationed on the pier to guard the lighters and other small boats the Union sailors used to transport men and material from the ships to the shore.

He passed evening strollers, silhouettes with dimly seen faces. They hurried as if anxious to get off the darkening streets. No one paid Bouchard any attention. However, he scrutinized the people as best he could in the failing light, checking their features for familiar ones.

Bouchard moved with a relentless stride. He should be tired, for he had walked miles, but he felt no weariness. There was a killing to do before he slept—if he could ever sleep again.

His last view of Annette's lovely face with cold death upon it was forever burned into his mind. How awful to see the blank stare in those wondrous eyes. His hands ached to inflict punishment upon Kassor, and upon any of his men that happened to stumble into his path. The punishment would be terrible. Nothing could stop him.

A few yards ahead, a door opened and lamplight spilled out onto the sidewalk. A man came outside and went off with a fast step on the sidewalk.

Walt quickened his pace. "Coldiron!" he called at the retreating back.

Luke pivoted at the sound of his name. In the same movement, he went to the side and drew his pistol from his belt. He stabbed the weapon out to point at the man hastening toward him.

"Don't shoot—it's Bouchard."

Luke tucked his pistol back inside his vest and watched Walt draw nearer through the night that was cloaking the street.

"Are you ready to let me buy you that drink now?" Luke asked.

"No. I've no time. There's something I must do."

"Then some other time."

"I'm looking for a man we both know. Sam Kassor. Have you seen him?"

"No, I haven't. But I know where his girlfriend lives. I'm heading there now. Why do you want him?"

"He took revenge on me for helping you fight him. He came to the home of my woman and killed her. He killed my Annette in an awful way. And her servant, too."

Luke heard the pain and suffering in the man's choked voice. "God, I'm sorry that happened," he said. "Come with me. Your claim on his cowardly life is greater than mine. You shoot him."

"With the greatest pleasure. Where does this woman live?"

"Near here. I'll show you."

"Lead on."

Luke and Walt walked swiftly. They turned left off Decatur onto Clay Street. A block later, Luke halted them in front of a two-story stucco house.

"This is it, number sixty three," Luke said. "Her name is Cecelia Ross. She has an apartment in the back."

"There's a gate," Walt said and pointing.

Luke stepped upon the sidewalk, shoved the iron rod gate open, and led the way down a brick-paved walkway beside the house. He knocked on the first door at the rear of the building.

There was silence within. Yet Luke sensed that someone had come and now stood close to the door. He rapped again, louder.

"Who is it?" a woman's voice came muffled through the door.

"Luke Coldiron, Miss Ross. I'd like to talk to you."

"I don't know any Luke Coldiron. What do you want to talk about?"

"Sam Kassor."

"Go away, Mr. Coldiron. I have nothing to say about Sam."

"But Miss Ross—"

"I said go away," the woman said with finality.

"Let me try," Walt said.

He knocked lightly on the door. "Miss Ross, my name is Walt Bouchard. Maybe you've heard of me. I've lived in New Orleans all my life, and am fairly well-known."

"Are you the duelist?"

"Yes."

"I have seen you a few times on the street," Cecelia said. "What do you want Sam for?"

"It would be better if we could talk inside. Neither Coldiron nor I want to harm you. We need a little information. Please open the door."

There was no sound from within the apartment. Then, after a few seconds an iron bolt scraped as it was withdrawn from its locking socket. The door opened.

A young woman peered out at Luke and Walt. Luke was shocked at the sight of her. In the light from a lamp on a nearby table, he could see that she had been severely beaten. Her lips were swollen, and there was caked blood in one corner of her mouth. Her eyes were black and blue. The sides of her face were bruised and red. She leaned to the left as if her ribs ached.

"Come in," Cecelia said. The two men entered the room and stood with hats in hand. Cecelia closed the door.

"I see you think I'm beautiful," she said in an ironic tone, looking into the men's faces.

"I'm sorry that someone did that to you," Luke said. She would normally have been quite pretty, he thought, but not now.

"He did it so men would not want me," Cecelia said. Her hands rose to lightly finger her swollen lips. "He really hit me this time, much harder than ever before. My face will never be the same again."

"Who hit you?" Walt asked.

"Why, Sam Kassor, the man you asked about." Her voice shook, and her eyes were shiny with a sudden wash of fear.

"We're looking for Kassor," Walt said. "Do you know where we can find him?"

"Why do you want to find him? Is he a friend of yours?"

"He's as good a friend of ours as he is of yours."

"He is no friend of mine. Would a friend beat you like this?"

"Certainly not," Walt said. "No man who is a man beats a woman."

Cecelia studied Walt in an intent, speculative manner. "I've heard you are good with guns and swords. That you have never lost a fight. Is that correct?"

Walt tried to read the woman's thoughts. "I am good with weapons," he said.

"You are for hire?"

"Say what you mean," Walt said with sharp impatience. "I've business with Kassor that can't wait."

Cecelia's bruised lips parted, and her tongue came out and touched the blood in the corner of her mouth. A look came into her eyes like that of a small, cornered animal that sees a possible avenue of escape.

"Kill the vicious bastard for me!" she cried out with a vehemence that jarred Walt and Luke. "I'll give you all my money, more than three hundred dollars. I can't stand another beating."

Luke looked at Walt. The duelist's eyes were tinged a feline yellow by the lamplight. His body was poised like that of some big cat that has at last spotted its prey and is ready to spring.

"Tell me where I can find Kassor," Walt said in a flat, dead voice.

"Yes. Yes," Cecelia said. "He told me he had business outside the city today, and that this evening he was going to meet with a man named Hammlin Fouveaux. As soon as he is done with that, he will come here."

"Fouveaux, eh?" Walt said.

"He owns The Mississippi Shipping Company," Cecelia said. "He has an office and warehouse at the corner of North Front and Bienville Streets."

"I know where his place is located," Walt said.

"You'll kill Kassor?" Cecelia said, the fear back in her voice. "He will beat me to death for telling you what I have. I'll get the three hundred dollars for your payment."

"I don't want your money," Walt said, his voice rough as if dragged over stones. "Kassor was a dead man hours ago, and has just been waiting to die."

# Chapter Twenty-Two

"Walt, who is Fouveaux?" Luke asked as the two men went along North Front Street.

"An enemy from many years ago. We once fought a duel. My bullet should have killed him. But he lived, as a cripple. I'm sure he hates me very much."

"What dealings do you think he and Kassor have?"

"Fouveaux is probably fencing the goods Kassor steals. Fouveaux's family has been in New Orleans for many generations. He inherited a shipping company from his father. The company has offices here in this city and in Cincinnad and St. Louis. It would be easy for him to ship anything Kassor steals to his agents upriver. Knowing Fouveaux, I'd say he's playing both sides of this war and is transporting goods for both the Yankees and the Confederates. In that way he can mix in his stolen goods and ship them to any destination he chooses."

"It makes sense that Kassor needs a good fence. Such an arrangement could be very profitable for both men."

"This is Bienville Street," Walt said. He pointed at a huge building on the south side of the street. "That's

Fouveaux's warehouse, and I see a light in the window of the office."

"I hear a vehicle coining," Luke said as the rattle of wheels and the tromp of horse's hooves on the pavement reached him.

The two men moved quickly into the recessed doorway of a building on the opposite side of the street.

A horse-drawn wagon came into sight on Bienville Street. A storm lantern was hung on the mounting post on the front of the wagon, and threw a yellow stain on the night. As the wagon rolled past Luke and Walt, they could make out three men sitting upon the spring seat. The vehicle halted at the big sliding door of the warehouse.

"I made out Kassor and two other fellows," Walt whispered in a cold voice.

"I think I might know the two other men," Luke said staring through the deceitful night shadows. "I need a better look with more light to be sure."

Kassor sprang down from the wagon and shoved the warehouse door open. One of the men on the seat clucked to the team of horses and drove the wagon inside. Kassor closed the door.

"The office door will most likely be locked," Walt said. "The warehouse door may not be, for the horses have to be brought back out and taken to a livery."

He led silently to the warehouse and placed his eye to a crack where the edge of the door met the wall. "They're on the far side of the building near the office. Let's go in."

Luke took hold of the door and pushed. On well-oiled rollers, the door moved silently to the side a short space. Both men went swiftly inside and closed the door behind them.

The wagon was visible pulled up close to the office door that opened into the warehouse. A fourth man had joined the first three.

"That new fellow is Fouveaux," Walt said. "He's responsible for the murder of Annette. I feel it. I'll put another bullet in him and finish what I started."

Luke checked Fouveaux. The man was bent far to the side, and walked with an ungainly step. He appeared ready to fall at any instant.

Kassor went to the storm lantern and took it down from its mounting post. He threw aside the tarpaulin that covered the bed of the wagon. With Kassor holding the lantern up, all four men gathered, and stared down into the vehicle.

The voices of the men came drifting across the warehouse to Luke and Walt. Both men cocked their heads to listen.

"I can't make out what they're saying," Luke said. "But from the tone of their voices, they seemed pleased. I think they've robbed somebody."

"If it takes a wagon to haul the loot, there must be a lot of it," Walt replied.

"They're not going to live long enough to enjoy it."

"Have you figured out the other men?"

"They were with the band of raiders that attacked the Dauphin plantation."

"That's good," Walt said. "Let's go and send them all to hell."

Hugging the walls where the shadows were thickest, they stole around the periphery of the warehouse. The four thieves had finished unloading the wagon. They were carrying the last of several bulging sacks toward the office as Luke and Walt came up behind them.

Walt charged out in front of Luke. He struck Kassor, the last man in line, powerfully with his shoulder. Kassor slammed into Fouveaux, who was next in line. The cripple went down hard on the floor.

Walt instantly leapt upon Kassor and struck with his pistol, hitting the man a savage blow across the mouth. Kassor crumpled to his knees against the office wall. His open mouth showed several broken teeth for a second, then blood came gushing out. He began to howl soundlessly.

Luke, holding his pistol ready, sprang forward close behind Walt. The remaining two men spun quickly around, dropped their booty, and started to reach for their pistols. Then they froze, staring directly into the black open bore of Luke's weapon.

"Go ahead and try it," Luke said encouragingly.

The men stood coiled. Their hands did not move.

"No," Lieutenant Springer said.

"All right, then. Hand your pistols over, slowly."

Walt jerked a pistol from a holster on Kassor's belt. He kicked the man flat on the floor. "Don't move," he ordered.

Walt hurried past Luke and knelt over Fouveaux. He removed a pistol from inside the man's jacket. "Stay down there," he said with a menacing look.

"At last we meet again," Luke said to the two raiders.

"I don't know you," Lieutenant Springer said. "We've never met."

"But we have. Now I want to know your name. What is it?"

"Go to hell."

"Walt, ask Fouveaux who this fellow is," Luke said.

Walt jabbed Fouveaux in the ribs with the barrel of his revolver. "Answer my friend."

Fouveaux's hate-filled face turned from Walt to Luke. "His name's Springer."

Walt jabbed Fouveaux again with the pistol. "Tell all of it. Springer—who and what is he? Talk."

"Lieutenant Springer of the Union Marines," Fouveaux growled.

"And this other man?" Luke said.

"Sergeant Luttrel," Fouveaux replied.

"I'll bet your senior officer is Captain Rawls," Luke said. "That makes sense and ties it all together, the horses and the raid on Dauphin."

"You'll never prove in court that we had anything to do with that," Springer said.

Luke laughed in a brittle voice. "I'm not even going to try. Give me your wallets and money belts."

"Like hell I will," Springer said, and did not move.

"Neither will I," Luttrel growled.

"Walt, these fellows don't yet understand the game we're playing," Luke said.

"They'll soon know."

Luke spoke to Springer and Luttrel. "If you don't give them to me, I'll take them off your dead bodies."

Springer looked up at Luke. There was a cold, deadly aura about the New Mexican. Springer hastily extracted a wallet from a pocket and pulled a money belt from inside his shirt. He tossed them to Luke. "Luttrel, you'd better give him yours, too."

The sergeant jerked his wallet and money belt from his clothing and threw them at Luke's feet.

"Barely eleven thousand dollars between you," Luke said after swiftly counting the money. "Where's the rest of the fifty thousand dollars?"

"The captain and Kassor has it," Springer said. "And a lot of it has been spent."

Kassor had stopped moaning. He was leaning against the wall and holding his broken mouth. Blood dripped from between his fingers and onto his shirt. He watched Luke and Walt with pain-filled eyes.

"Give me all your money," Luke said to Kassor.

Kassor lowered his hands, and with fumbling fingers removed a money belt from around his waist inside his clothing. He took a wallet from a back pocket.

"Less than two thousand dollars," Luke said with disgust. "Where's the rest of your share?"

"I gave it to my men," Kassor mumbled through the blood in his mouth.

"Luke, check Fouveaux's office," Walt said. "He had planned to buy these stolen things, and must have brought money to do it. While you're doing that, I'll see how much he has on him."

Luke went to Fouveaux's desk and began to search. In a bottom drawer, he found a leather pouch. He untied it and dumped the contents onto the center of the desk.

"Now that's money," Luke said, and began to count.

"Only a few dollars on Fouveaux," Walt said.

"Twenty thousand dollars even here," Luke said.

"You're getting closer to your fifty thousand."

"Right. I'll get the rest from Rawls. Or take it out of his hide."

"You've got what you come for. Now get out," Fouveaux said angrily.

"Ah, but you are wrong," Walt said. "Luke wanted his money. I came for something else. Something that doesn't have much value, but still something I wanted."

"What's that? Whatever it is, take it and leave."

"I'll do just as you say," The fury that Walt had kept bottled as Luke searched for money began to burn so hot he thought it would consume him. "I'm going to take Kassor's life. And yours."

Fouveaux jerked back at Walt's words. Fear moved like slimy water creatures in the pale, blue pools of his eyes.

Walt knelt beside Fouveaux. He whispered to the man.

"I should have killed you long ago. An enemy should never be left behind alive. You think about that while I tend to Kassor."

In a slow, lazy movement, Walt rose to his feet. He moved the short distance to look down at Kassor.

"You made my Annette suffer terribly, and then she died. I wish there was some way I could kill you a thousand times. To make you suffer in a thousand different ways."

He pointed his pistol at Kassor's right eye. "Watch for the bullet," he said.

Kassor saw death in Bouchard's face. He screamed, the sound pure animal fear with nothing human in it.

The pistol crashed. Kassor's cry ceased abruptly. His head snapped back. A gaping round hole existed where once there had been an eye.

Still moving in a lethargic way, Walt returned to Fouveaux. He brought the barrel of his pistol to touch Fouveaux's head. "Hell waits for you," he said, "but not for long."

"Give me a chance for my life," Fouveaux pleaded.

"You deserve no chance.

"Are you afraid, Bouchard?"

"You want to try the old contest over again? Well, why not? Get to your feet." Walt's voice was that of a very tired, uncaring man. "You may get lucky."

Walt held out Fouveaux's pistol. "Take hold of it by the barrel and go over there to the edge of the light. We'll replay the contest exactly as before."

Fouveaux walked with his body leaning precariously to the side. He halted where the light gave way to darkness, and pivoted.

Walt had backed away to the opposite border of the lighted zone. His pistol was aimed at Fouveaux. "Now reverse your hold and catch the revolver by the butt. Aim it at the floor. That's right."

Walt lowered his weapon to point down. "This is your chance, Fouveaux. Make it good. Luke, I want you to give the signal to begin the duel. Let Fouveaux go free if he wins. Call the order to fire whenever you want to."

Luke looked from Walt to Fouveaux. He did not like the task that had been thrust upon him. Worse, Walt did not seem to care whether he won or lost.

"Stand ready," Luke called.

Fouveaux jerked his pistol up and thrust it out at Walt.

A blow struck Fouveaux, and then, instantly, another. Two pistol shots exploded so close together they seemed to be one continuous sound. Fouveaux flopped backward.

"I knew the tricky bastard would try that," Walt said, coming into the bright light.

He turned and looked through the coils of lazily rising gun smoke at Luke. "Kill your two men, Coldiron, and let's be gone from this place."

Luke stood stunned by Walt's execution of Fouveaux and Kassor. But what other ending could there have been?

At the edge of his vision, Luke sensed Luttrel drawing something from his boot top. The man lunged at him.

Luke thrust out his pistol and fired straight into Luttrel's heart. The Marine sergeant fell at his feet. A knife clattered to the floor.

Luke glanced at Springer. The man was rushing at him. He stumbled and fell, and Luke heard the crash of Walt's revolver.

Luke looked at the four corpses. He felt revolted at the accumulation of death around him, but why should he feel bad? The men deserved to die, and there was still more killing to come.

"It's done," Walt said.

"Not completely," Luke replied. "I've Captain Rawls to find."

"Good luck to you."

"Thanks."

"You will need a place to rest. Here is a key to my training hall." Walt gave Luke directions. "You should be safe there."

*   *   *

"Captain Rawls, there's a black man out front who says you wanted to see him," the Marine sentry said. "His name is Tate."

"He's quite right, private, I do want to see him. Send him in. Then go and tell Corporal Cooper to come to my office."

"Yes, sir."

A moment later a big black man came to the door of the captain's office. He was well dressed in shirt, trousers, and polished boots. He removed his hat. "You wanted to see me, Captain?" he asked.

"Yes, Tate. Come in."

Tate moved into the room and stood waiting. He watched the captain closely.

"I've heard that you know the forest and bayous around New Orleans very well," the captain said. "Is that so?" Kassor had first told Rawls of Tate. The man was a free black and a smuggler. He moved freely about the city and the countryside. He had bragged to Kassor that he had lovers among the slave women of every plantation within twenty miles of New Orleans. Tate had been the source of the information that Dauphin had money in his safe for purchase of horses for a company of cavalry. One of Dauphin's female house slaves had told him.

"I know the country good as any man, captain."

"As good as a Chickasaw?"

"The only Chickasaw I know about is old Panther. He sells honey and furs in the town. Is that who you are talking about?"

"That's the one."

"Old Panther is one damn fine man in the woods. I've run into him now and again. He sleeps with a black woman."

"Could you find where he lives?" the captain asked.

"In two or three days, I think I could. He leaves town going to the northeast. What do you want him for?"

"He killed two of my Marines. Now I'm going to hang him."

"I heard of the shooting. I didn't know it was old Panther who did it. What caused the fight?"

"He had one of our horses and refused to give it up. I want that Indian. I'll pay you twenty-five dollars in gold to help a squad of my Marines catch him."

Tate rotated his hat in his hands. He controlled his expression, giving no sign of his pleasure at the chance to test himself against the Chickasaw. "That Indian is old, but he'll be tough to take. The men you send with me must be ones that know the woods."

"We have plenty of that kind."

"I think some of them won't be coming back."

"That can't be helped. The Indian must be caught and executed for what he did."

"You sent for me, Captain?" Corporal Cooper asked from the open door.

"Yes, Corporal. This is Tate. He will guide you in your search for the Indian. Choose five men who are good woodsmen. Be prepared to leave just at daylight tomorrow morning. You listen to Tate's advice in the woods."

"I'll pick good men, sir."

"Bring the Indian back alive, if you can. But dead, if it comes to that."

"I understand, sir." The corporal spoke to Tate. "I'll meet you out in front of the Cabildo at first light."

"I'll be there," Tate replied.

"That'll be all, corporal," the captain said.

The corporal saluted and left. Tate turned and slowly started to follow.

"Just a minute, Tate," Rawls said.

The black man turned back to the Marine. "Yes, captain?"

"You have a friend at the Dauphin plantation, isn't that so?"

"A good friend, a woman friend," Tate replied.

"Stay at the Dauphin place tonight. Find out what you can about Susan Dauphin, what she might be planning."

"I'll do that, captain. Could I have half my pay now to buy my woman a present? She always takes better care of me when I show up with something pretty for her."

The captain took a gold coin from a pocket. "Here is ten dollars. I want to know about the Dauphin woman, and I want the Indian you call Panther caught without fail."

"I'll do my best to find him. That's all I can promise."

"You lead my Marines to him. They'll do the rest."

Maybe they will, Tate thought as he left the captain's office. He recalled his encounters with the Chickasaw in the forest, and the other meetings with him when he was selling honey on the streets of the city. The Indian with a rifle in the forest was a much different man then the one with his honey bucket in the city. The task of tracking him down would not be an easy one. The woman would be his weakness, as it was with nearly all men. Tate would find the woman. Then the Indian would come to Tate.

## Chapter Twenty-Three

Luke halted the team of horses and wagon at the entrance of the alley that led to the rear of the Sisters of Charity Hospital. He climbed down, tied the left hand horse to the fence encircling a backyard, and slipped quietly forward. The Union military might have stationed sentries to patrol the hospital, and he did not want to blunder into them.

The alley lay blanketed with darkness and he could barely make out the houses. Light showed in a window of the building on his right, but the night absorbed it within a few feet. A dog sniffed at him through a picket fence. It growled once and then became silent and watched him pass.

Luke slowed, creeping the last half hundred steps to the small park behind the hospital. He stopped at the first big tree and pressed tightly to it, blending into the trunk. His sight ranged through the trees and shrubs and along the paved walkway where the sisters sometimes strolled. The park was deserted.

He continued on to the building that contained the stables. Cupping a lighted match in his hand to hide the flame, he checked the horses in the stalls. Susan's mare was in one of the cubicles.

He returned to the wagon and brought it forward. He parked it at the end of the stables.

Luke crossed the park and entered the rear entrance of the hospital. The vestibule and stairway were lighted by a lamp bracketed to the wall. As he mounted the stairs to the second floor, footsteps sounded coming down. A Sister of Charity came into sight.

Luke removed his hat. "Sister, where might I find Miss Susan Dauphin?"

The Sister gave Luke a quizzical look. "Miss Dauphin is in the soldiers' ward."

"Are there still Confederate soldiers there?"

"A few who are too badly injured to be taken to the Union prisoner of war camp. Most of the wounded are now Union soldiers." The questioning expression was still on her face.

"Thank you," Luke said, and went on up the stairs before the sister could say anything more.

Luke halted just inside the door of the ward. The long room was lighted with several lamps. Every bed held a wounded man. Some of the men lay quietly. Others were talking with the occupants of neighboring beds.

Susan was sitting near the bed of a young man with a heavily bandaged shoulder. As she talked with him, she was sewing with needle and thread on a red uniform, apparently mending it. She raised her face from her work at something the man said, and replied to him.

She caught sight of Luke by the door. She started to smile, then caught herself. She promptly laid down the garment in her hands and came up the ward aisle.

When she was very close, she spoke. "You should not be here for you might be recognized." She took him by the arm and drew him into the hallway.

Luke saw she was truly worried about him, and it showed in the tiny crows' feet at the corners of her eyes. "Only the captain and the colonel know me by sight. I'll leave in a minute. I've some news for you."

"What have you found out? Something about the death of my father?"

"I have found two of his murderers, a Marine lieutenant and a sergeant."

Susan leaned tensely toward Luke. "What's their names? Where can they be found?"

"Lieutenant Springer and Sergeant Luttrell. But you don't need to hunt for them. They're dead."

"You killed them?"

"I killed one, and Bouchard killed one. Less than an hour ago."

"You said they were two of the murderers. Who else do you think is responsible?"

"I'm now certain Captain Rawls is the leader of the raiders. He sent Springer and Luttrel with some other men to rob the house while he took the horses from your captain Thacker."

"Then Rawls must not escape punishment."

"He won't. So that you will know all that happened, I should tell you that Springer and Luttrell were with two other men when we found him. Their names were Sam Kassor and Hammlin Fouveaux. They're also dead."

"Why did you kill them?"

"I didn't. Bouchard did. They killed his placee. He took his revenge on them."

"The innocent often get hurt," Susan said, remembering the Marine she had killed in front of the Cabildo.

"The two Marines and Kassor must have recently robbed somebody, for they had a wagon full of silver and gold objects and valuable china. I have the wagon parked out by the stables. I thought you would be the best person to return the stolen things to their rightful owners."

"I'll be off duty in a half hour. I'll take care of that. There are men who will help me," Susan's gaze became tender, and roamed in a slow, lingering glance over Luke's face.

"Have you thought over my request to help me rob the Yankees?"

"Forget about fighting the Yankees. They are professional soldiers, an army of them. I want you to come to New Mexico with me and live in peace at my ranch until the war is over."

"I can't leave New Orleans as long as the enemy controls it," Susan said. Would Luke have asked her to come with him if he knew she had murdered a man today? She thought he would not. "I ask you again, please stay and help me."

"No. I'm sorry, but I can't do that."

Luke watched Susan back away a step. She became totally withdrawn from him, as if his reply had been expected and now she did not care.

"I'm also sorry that is your answer," Susan said. "Good-bye, Luke."

"Good-bye, Susan."

Susan turned away and reentered the ward. She again took up her needle and thread and the Marine tunic. A sob, quickly stifled, came to her as she glanced over the beds and to the empty doorway.

"Bad news?" asked the Marine lying on the cot near Susan.

"Good and bad," she said.

The Marine continued to talk, but Susan did not hear him. She was deeply saddened that Luke would not aid her. She knew a woman could not hold men such as Fletcher and Johnson together in a common cause for long. Luke, a tough and fearless man with experience in the Mexican War, would have been a natural leader.

"There's Captain Rawls," the Marine near her said.

The name cut through Susan's thoughts. She looked up quickly. The captain had entered and was staring directly at Susan.

After a moment of watching Susan, the captain started down the aisle of the ward, speaking pleasantly to each wounded Marine and sailor and shaking his hand. Some of the less seriously injured men climbed out of bed and saluted the captain as he drew near. He returned their salutes. Smiling, he told them to lie back down and rest.

Rawls reached Susan. He halted and stared down at her. "What are you doing here?"

"There are men here who need help," Susan said. She pointed to the far end of the ward. "Those four beds hold Confederate soldiers. But I help all the wounded."

"She's really nice to us, Captain," the Marine near Susan said. "She's even cleaned our uniforms, and now is sewing up the holes."

"I see," Rawls said.

His malevolent eyes probed Susan. Her nerves were on edge with the knowledge of what she planned to do. Could the captain read her thoughts?

"I see," Rawls repeated, but he did not understand what he saw.

He continued on down the ward. At the end he hesitated, evaluating the Confederate soldiers on their beds. He pivoted around, walked to the ward doorway and left without further notice of Susan.

She let her breath out slowly. How awful to be so near the man who helped kill her father and not be able to strike at him.

"Captain Rawls is a damn fine officer, Miss Susan," the Marine said. "He knows you're only trying to help all of us."

"I'm sure you're correct," Susan said.

"You'll be getting a lot of presents soon from the men here in the hospital."

"Presents?"

"Sure. We'll all soon have money. The paymaster is coming ashore tomorrow morning, and all the Marines and sailors will get paid. Then, when General Butler gets here in a day or two, all the soldiers will get their pay."

"How do you know this?"

"A friend was here to visit me earlier today, and he told me. It'll be good to have some money in my pocket again."

"Yes, I'm sure that would be nice."

*\*\*\**

The horse nickered when it caught Luke's smell. It stomped the ground and nickered again, in a plaintive, coaxing tone.

Luke went through the darkness to the stall that held his horse. He had placed the animal in the livery stable on Royal Street and paid the attendant for several days care. He put out his hand and touched the shadowy form of the horse's head that extended out over the top of the half door. "I'm glad to see you too, old hoss," he said.

The horse nudged him with its head and then reached out to sniff at his face. Luke petted the long, bony head. With luck he would find Rawls tomorrow, and the last battle for him in New Orleans would be fought. He would ride away immediately, glad to be gone from the conquered city. For a short time he had thought Susan might go with him. Her presence would have brightened life at his ranch high in the Sangre de Cristo Mountains. But she was not coming. She was locked in an obsessive drive for vengeance upon the

Union military. Luke doubted that she could ever escape alive from the path she trod. The sorrow of that lay heavily upon him.

Luke found a sack of shelled corn and gave the horse a double handful in its grain box. He left, heading toward Exchange Alley.

The streets held few night walkers. Overhead a white moon rode the high heavens. The hard, cold light cast eerie shadows around the unlit streetlight, the abandoned street vendors' stands, and trash piles.

Nearer the river, there was no trash on the sidewalks, and here and there streetlights had been lit and made dull, yellow pools in the darkness. The Union occupying forces were bringing the city back to life.

Luke kept away from the lights, in the deepest murk. He wanted no trouble from the Marine patrols.

Exchange Alley was reached, and Bouchard's dueling gymnasium located. He opened the door with the key Bouchard had given him and locked it behind him. He struck a match, glanced at the large, high-ceilinged interior with its array of weapons hanging on the walls. Bouchard must have created many tough, skilled fighters here. Luke doused the flame.

His mind's eye held the picture of the wide training hall and the door in the end wall. That would be Bouchard's office. Luke went to the door and stepped inside.

He lit a match. The room contained a desk upon which a lamp sat, two chairs, and a leather-covered couch. There was no window to betray him by showing his light to an enemy. He touched the match to the wick of the lamp.

Feeling his weariness, Luke stripped off his outer clothing and lay down, wrapping himself in the blanket on the couch. Sleep would not come. He thought of Susan, beautiful Susan, so consumed with the need for revenge, the need to rob and punish the Union soldiers occupying New Orleans.

His mind jumped to the Marine captain, Rawls. The man would be hard to catch alone. And should he succeed in doing that, the Marine would not be easy to kill.

Late in the night, rain began to drum on the roof of the training hall. Luke pulled the blanket more tightly around himself and finally went to sleep.

# Chapter Twenty-Four

A quarter hour more of morning dusk and then day-light would arrive, thought Susan. She was removing her clothing in a murk-filled corner of the abandoned foundry on Decatur Street three blocks east of Jackson Square. She shivered at the cold, damp wind that came in through the broken windows from the rainy street and washed over her naked body.

In a far corner of the building, eight men were also undressing. She could glimpse the ghostly movements of the white parts of their bodies. Strangely, they seemed to have no heads, for their faces, browned by the sun, were invisible in the gloom. The forms of the men disappeared as they drew on the red uniforms of Union Marines.

Susan had cleaned and mended the uniforms of the wounded Yankees in the hospital. As each garment was made whole, she had folded it and placed it in the clothes locker in the hallway outside the soldiers' ward. After learning of the paymaster's plan to come ashore, she had carried the uniforms wrapped in a blanket to the hospital stables. The wagon Luke had brought had brought her had been ideal for transporting the stolen garments. She loaded them under the tarpaulin, with the gold and silver things the thieving Yankees had taken from some unfortunate southerner, and drove away. Her mare, tethered to the tailgate, trailed along behind.

She had saved the uniform of a slender private for herself. She pulled the pants and tunic on. Her hair was piled on top of her head and the hat was pulled down to hide it. Lastly she buckled a holstered pistol around her waist. The occupying Marines wore personal handguns, even when off duty. Her weapon and those of the men of her group would not be out of place and thus alert their enemies.

Though falling raindrops still drummed on the roof of the foundry, the rain had slackened somewhat from the heavy downpour during the night. The wetness should reduce the number of people on the streets. She had not decided if that was good or bad.

She rolled her civilian clothing into a tight bundle and carried it across the foundry to her horse. The bundle was lashed behind the saddle.

She looked around at the men. She was beginning to think of them as her band of fighters. Waller still wore his civilian clothing. He had a short spying mission to do before he donned his Yankee uniform. Roy was fumbling at the buttons of his tunic. She went to him and finished closing the front for him. He handed her his pistol and she buckled it around his waist.

"Roy, don't you think you shouldn't . . ." Susan caught herself. "We've been through that, haven't we?"

"Yes," Roy said. Susan and he had argued long and hard about his participation in the coming attack on the Yankees. He was regaining his strength. Still, with only one hand he would be handicapped in controlling his horse and shooting his revolver at the same time. The argument had finally ended with his statement that if she did not go, neither would he. When she had refused that condition he had grinned at her, and that ended further discussion.

He lowered his handless arm gently to his side. The wrist end ached like hell if he happened to bump it against something. However, his strength had mostly returned. He would not be a handicap to his comrades for he would shoot as many of the Goddamned Northern men as anyone did.

Susan moved to her mare and laid her arm over the neck of the faithful beast. Jack had provided a horse for Roy, and the entire band of men had mounts. On horseback, they could travel swiftly and most likely escape the pursuers that would surely chase them. Should one of them be set afoot, that person would have little chance to elude capture.

A grim, waiting silence fell upon the group as the men drew into themselves. Susan felt the same sense of withdrawal, of separateness from all the others. The danger to them was absolute, deadly, and was uppermost in all their thoughts. One mistake, one blow of random chance, of bad luck, could cause all their deaths.

However, the Yankee payroll was worth the risk. Mounts could be purchased for Riley's company of cavalrymen. In addition, hundreds of foot soldiers could be equipped with rifles and bayonets to kill or drive away the Northern men who were invading her land. The South did not have to invade and conquer the North. To win the war, the South had only to not lose. How fitting it would be to use the Yankees' own money to help insure the South did not lose.

Even with the knowledge of what the Yankee money would mean to the forces of the South, Susan shivered with the thought that she might have only a few more minutes of life. She breathed deeply of the damp air. The odors of the foundry filled her nostrils—the smell of iron castings, burnt coke, wet molding sand, of lubricating oils.

Scattered around her were the indistinct outlines of many pieces of wrecked machinery. The owners of the foundry had been very thorough in demolishing everything usable. However, the Union engineers would soon make the machinery run again. The furnace would be red with flame and the giant ladles full of molten iron to cast cannon and rifles and swords for the enemy.

The windows had grown a little brighter. She moved to the door that stood slightly ajar. A gray, rainy twilight lay in the street. A large, brown dog scavenged in a mound of garbage at the corner of the foundry. Neither man nor woman was astir in the rain.

"It's light enough that the Yankees could come ashore," Susan said. "Waller, would you go as we planned and watch the riverfront?"

"All right. I'll come back as soon as I'm sure the payroll is on its way."

"Wait until you know which street they'll use to reach their headquarters at the Cabildo."

"I know what to do," Waller said stiffly.

He shoved the door further open and slid out. He humped his shoulders, as if that would protect him against the rain, and walked toward the Mississippi River.

Fletcher pulled the door back to its original position. He turned to Susan. "Waller don't need to be told every little step of what to do," he said truculently. "And neither do the rest of us."

Susan watched Fletcher in the frail light which was leaking in the cracked door and the broken windows.

She noted the uniform fitted poorly on his stocky body. He had turned up the cuffs of the tunic to get them off his hands. His eyes glared out of his broad face at her. She wanted to say something to lessen his antagonism. But what could it be that would not bring a retort from the man, and one she would have to respond to? She wanted no argument with the man at this late stage of the attack.

"Okay," she said.

Fletcher grunted, and lapsed into silence.

The light within the foundry slowly brightened. The horses moved now and again, and there was the stomp of hoof and the clink of bridle metal.

Under the peak of the roof a pair of pigeons stirred on their nighttime perches. With a flutter of wings, the birds launched themselves into the air and darted out a crack high up in the wall. The men and woman on the ground looked up hastily at the abrupt sound.

Susan leaned against the mare. She slowly petted the muscular neck and withers. Yesterday she and the horse had escaped unhurt from the hail of bullets fired at them. Would they be so fortunate this time?

"Waller is here," Roy said. He shoved the door part way open with his good right hand.

Waller came inside swiftly. He wiped the rain from his face with a bandanna.

"The Yankees have come ashore from the Hartford," Waller said.

"What street are they using to come into town?" Susan asked.

"They're moving up St. Peter Street toward the Cabildo."

"How many guards?" Fletcher asked.

"Six Marines with rifles on foot. And there's a seventh man, a naval officer. He must be the paymaster. He had four big leather pouches that he loaded in a spring wagon. He's driving the wagon."

"Just six guards? Are you sure?" Fletcher said.

"I can count, Fletcher. Jesus, you're as bad as Susan."

"We still outnumber them," Roy said. "We can beat them. We've got good luck."

"I don't like this," Fletcher said. "Something is wrong. There should be more than six men to guard a quarter million dollar payroll."

"They probably think they got everybody in New Orleans scared," O'Doyle said.

"Not likely, not after Susan killed one of them right in front of their headquarters," Fletcher said.

"That was your idea that she do that," Roy said.

"To hell with that now," Fletcher said. "What do you think, Johnson?"

"How in Sam Hill can any of us know whether or not the low number of guards is a trap? And I'm not sure it is a low number. We were hoping there would not be many of them so we could whip them and take the payroll."

Waller called out from behind the horses, where he was speedily changing into his uniform. "Maybe that's all that the Yankees feel is necessary to protect the payroll."

"Let's watch them make their delivery of this payroll and take the next one," Fletcher said. "That way we'll know all about how they do it."

Susan had listened to the men discuss the number of guards. She was not certain whether or not six guards had any special significance beyond their normal task of protecting the Union money. However, she did believe that if the New Orleans men disbanded, she could never again pull them together. On the other hand, success in this first mission would bind them as a group, and they could be willing to attack the enemy again. They must go on.

"There's no turning back now," Susan said to all the men. Her voice was strong, but she felt an ice shaft in her stomach at the imminent danger to all of them. Were they going to their deaths?

Susan continued to speak. "There won't be another payday for the Yankee's men for at least a month, maybe two or three. And their army and navy will not remain here long. They'll move on upriver leaving behind just an occupying force. Therefore, the size of the paydays will be small, and most probably held inside the Cabildo. We must go through with our plan and strike now."

"It's a trap of the Yankees," Fletcher said. "I feel it."

"How would they know what we planned and set a trap for us?"

"I don't know that, only that I'm not going."

Susan stared bleakly at Fletcher. If he left, two or three others might go with him. Maybe all of them, except Roy. The group's strength must remain whole to be strong enough to take the payroll.

"You're not leaving," Susan said, her words sharp as pieces of metal hitting. She put her hand on the butt of her pistol.

"You wouldn't shoot me," Fletcher said belligerently.

"You had me kill a Yankee to prove my braver. I put a cowardly southerner in the same category as a Yankee."

"I think she would shoot you, Fletcher, if you tried to leave," Roy said, seeing Susan drawing in like a spring coiling. "Or you'd have to fight her." He was worried about Susan, about the changes that had occurred in her during the past two days. Her hatred for the Northerners and her readiness for violence had aged her, and faded her beauty. At times, a mask seemed to fall over her features, hiding her true thoughts. He believed some of the men were frightened of her, or what she had done at the Cabildo and what she might do if pressed hard.

Waller walked up dressed in his uniform. "Fletcher, I know you're no coward. You're a damn brave fighter. Trap or no trap, I'm going and I want you beside me. Three of us, four counting Roy, got out of Fort Jackson alive after thousands of shells fell on us. Our luck's good, so come along with me."

Fletcher looked away from Susan. "All right, Waller, we'll go to hell together."

"We must hurry," Susan said. She pulled a map from the saddlebag on the mare. "Come close, all of you, and look at this."

She unfolded the map and turned so that light from the outside shone on it. The men gathered around her.

"Here's where St. Peter reaches the waterfront. Waller says the Yankees are traveling up this direction toward the Cabildo." Susan's finger moved along the street indicated on the map. "We're here and can catch them about here in eight or ten minutes. We'll ride up to them, and on a signal, shoot them to pieces."

Susan heard the hoarse breathing of the men standing around her. She wavered in her determination. Was she doing the correct thing? With an effort and a hidden sob, she steeled herself.

"Waller, you saw four moneybags," Susan said. "After the fight, you grab one. Fletcher and Johnson, you each grab one. I'll take the fourth one. Then we'll do just as we planned. Scatter, each man going in a different direction, and ride like hell.

"Later on, after you're no longer being chased, gather in the thick woods where Dosset's lane intersects the main road. Don't go to his house. He's helped us enough. We'll tend to anybody who is wounded, then leave New Orleans, ride upriver to Vicksburg, and use the money to outfit hundreds of Southern soldiers."

Susan fell silent and looked at each man. Their faces were strained, eyes enlarged, and pupils dilated.

"God! I'm proud of every one of you," Susan said with a sudden rush of emotion. This must be how an officer feels leading his men into battle.

There was a shuffling of feet at Susan's words. Some eyes looked away, but then came quickly back to her.

"Hell, you don't have to say that," Waller said. "We've already agreed to go with you."

"That's right," Roy said.

"I know," Susan said, "but I meant it."

"Let's go do it," Roy said.

"Right." Susan shivered.

She shoved the door open. The day had arrived, but dimly under the clouds. The rain had slackened to a misty drizzle.

She went swiftly to her horse, mounted, and rode out of the foundry. The Marine cap did little to shelter her face, and she closed her eyes to a slit against the falling raindrops.

The street was empty. The dog was gone. She and the group of men would be conspicuous riding in the wetness without rain slickers. That could not be helped, and she would not tell the others of her worry.

"Form up two abreast," Susan called. "Stay in formation."

Waller, in a sergeant's uniform, took position beside Susan. Roy reined his mount to the second rank and in the right hand column. There he could hide his handless left arm most easily from the eyes of the Yankees. Fletcher was on his left. Johnson and O'Doyle were just behind him. The remaining men followed in rank two abreast.

The group reached Toulouse Street. A hackney with its leather curtains lowered crossed in front of them and rolled on to the left. A white man and woman sharing an umbrella hastened away in the same direction. The man glanced nervously over his shoulder at what he believed was a squad of mounted Union Marines.

Susan looked to the side at Waller. He was studying her. She smiled, showing her teeth. Waller was proving to be the strong one of the group of men.

Fletcher saw the interaction between Susan and Waller. You're a cold, heartless bitch, he thought. He did not question her bravery, or her desire to hurt the Yankees, but he was damned leery about her judgment. They should not be here riding to rob the Union payroll in broad daylight. Instead, on a rainy morning like this, they should all be in a warm kitchen eating breakfast and drinking hot coffee.

Wilk Row Street was reached and the horses splashed through a pool of water that had collected at the intersection.

"There they are," Susan said in a tight voice. A short block ahead six Marines and a wagon driven by a naval officer had come into the intersection of Decatur and St. Peter Streets. The Marines were in line three on each side of the wagon. The detachment of Union men crossed Decatur and continued on along St. Peter Street.

"We'll ride on as if we own the city," Susan said.

"There, they've seen us," Fletcher said.

"They don't look worried," Waller said. "Our Yankee uniforms are fooling them into thinking we are some of them."

"We'll turn and ride right up beside them," Susan said. "We're going to succeed in taking their payroll."

Susan and the men veered left onto St. Peter Street, a hundred yards behind the Union detachment. The three story stone Montalba Rowhouses lined the full length of the block on the left. Jackson Square lay on the right. The end of the Cabildo was visible three hundred yards ahead.

The Marine guards marched on. Some of them now and again glanced to the rear. The naval officer was more wary, frequently watching over his shoulder as the horsemen overhauled him. Susan thought he seemed to be measuring the distance that separated his group from hers.

Abruptly the officer wheeled his team of horses and wagon to the side. He halted the vehicle and animals crosswise on the street blocking the way. The brake was yanked on. Shouting a command to the Marines, the officer sprang down on the far side of the wagon.

The Marines immediately darted behind the vehicle and took up positions flanking the officer. They raised their rifles and pointed them over the wagon and back along the street at Susan and her band of men.

## Chapter Twenty-Five

"What were Springer and Luttrel doing at that warehouse, Captain Rawls?" Colonel Trotter asked in a vexed voice. "Why were they killed? And Kassor and Fouveaux?"

"Kassor was a valuable informant. He knew more about what was happening in New Orleans than any other man. My guess is that Springer and Luttrel went to the warehouse to talk with Kassor and Fouveaux. As a shipper and someone well known, Fouveaux could have had important information. All of the men were probably killed by rebels." The colonel must not suspect that Springer and Luttrel were at Fouveaux's for any but the most legitimate reasons.

"I suppose that is the reason," the colonel said. "We know resistance to our occupation of the city is growing. The shooting of the sentry in front of headquarters yesterday is a very good example of that. Any leads on who that fellow was?" the colonel said.

"None. The second sentry, who had been inside the Cabildo for a moment, came out just in time to see the killer riding off. However, his view was from the back.

He says that from what he could see, the man was young. He was riding a brown horse."

"Did the sentry shoot at the man?"

"Yes, but he does not know if he hit him or not. A squad of Marines ran out of Jackson Square and also fired at the man as he rode away. Wounded or not, he escaped."

"That was a damn foolish act but a brave one, to ride up and shoot a sentry at the door of our headquarters. Keep looking for the man. Now, about that Indian who killed two of our men on the Ramparts—when will that search begin?"

"They should be forming up out front right now. With your leave, I'd like to go and talk with them."

"Certainly, captain, see them off. I want that Indian brought in."

"Yes, sir."

The captain saluted and left the office. He walked down the long hallway and past the room where a platoon of Marines was kept on duty to help the roving patrols put down any disturbances that might arise.

Captain Rawls went out from under the arches and into the drizzly wetness on the stone pavement in front of the Cabildo. The night was fading, and he could see along the gloomy avenues and into the trees of Jackson Square lying across the street.

Corporal Cooper and his squad of Marines were assembled nearby. The men looked like deformed hunchbacks with their rain slickers pulled up and over the packs on their backs. The captain heard the growl of their voices complaining about the rain.

"Corporal Cooper, have you seen Tate?" the captain called.

"He just went back there out of the rain," the corporal replied gesturing toward the Cabildo.

"Looking for me, Captain?" the black man said, coming out of the darkness of the passageway behind the stone arches. He wore nothing to protect him from the rain. The rifle he carried was encased in a waterproof sleeve.

"Yes. What did you learn about the Dauphin woman? Did you see her? Tell me what you know."

"I saw her. She came to that small house on the plantation way after dark. I sent my woman friend, one of the Dauphin slaves, over to see what she was doing. She was cleaning and oiling a pistol. She was dressed like a man. Then she went to bed. I paid one of my woman's boys to stay awake and watch. He saw the Dauphin woman wake and leave way before daylight."

"Walking or riding?"

"Riding a dark colored horse."

"Anything else?"

"No, sir."

"All right. Go along, now. It's starting to break day-light, and Corporal Cooper is waiting for you."

"Captain, we're not going to catch that Indian in this rain. Those slickers the men are wearing will make all kinds of noise in the woods. We should wait for sun-light."

"It'll quit raining, and you'd better do your damned-est to catch him. That's the colonel's orders, and mine. Find where he lives with his woman, and wait. He'll eventually come to you."

"I'll do my best to find him, Captain." Tate turned away.

The captain stared after the squad of Marines as they went off along the shadow-filled street. Tate was cor-rect. It was very doubtful they'd catch the Chickasaw in his own forest. However, the woman could be the bait that snared him.

The captain's thoughts switched to the deaths of Springer and Luttrel, and the two men with them. He had examined the bodies and the warehouse. The men had not put up a fight, for their weapons had not been fired. It appeared the four had quite simply been exe-cuted. All their wallets and money belts were missing, and so, too, was the wagon loaded with booty from the raid they had pulled during the day.

Coldiron was still in the city. The captain knew it. He had not really expected the man to leave. In some way, the New Mexico man was responsible for what had happened at the warehouse. But to kill four armed men, tough men such as Springer and Luttrel and the others, without them getting off a shot must mean Coldiron had accomplices. Perhaps he had joined with a group of rebel guerrilla fighters.

Had any of the men talked before he died? Did Coldiron now know that he, Rawls, was the leader of the raiders? The captain glanced left and right along the street. The odds were great that Coldiron would be coming for him now that Luttrel and Kassor were dead. The sooner the better, he thought. It would be best for the man to die, and no longer be trouble waiting to happen.

The Dauphin woman might also have a role in the deaths at the warehouse. Where had she been going, armed and in the darkness? Mounted on a horse, she could travel a long distance in a short period of time. The captain recalled his last view of the woman sitting talking to the wounded Marine and mending a uniform. He could feel the hate in her. So why was she at the hospital helping Union men who had conquered New Orleans?

As the last of the night retreated into the cracks and holes of the earth and the rain slackened to a drizzle, the captain stood watching the streets and pondering his questions.

\*\*\*

Luke crossed the gymnasium and went out into the misty rain falling in Exchange Alley. With the heavy downpour of the night and the water sluggishly draining away, the old buildings of the French Quarter seemed to be standing on flood lots. Smoke from the chimneys, beaten down by the rain, was tumbling down the slanting roofs and filling the street. Slops and piles of garbage added their fermenting odor and ugliness.

Luke walked off, his feet getting wet and his lungs breathing the drifting smoke. A bad beginning for the day.

He turned onto Conti Street. Several townsfolk were moving along on private errands. Above the smell of smoke was the odor of freshly baked bread and sweet rolls. An immense hunger surged through him. Bent upon finding Kassor, he had not eaten since breakfast yesterday.

A sign called his attention to a French bakery close by. Near the entrance of the business, a black woman with a basket balanced on top of her red-turbaned head stood under the overhanging second floor and out of-the drizzle. Luke went past her and entered the bakery. He bought a large sweet roll.

As Luke came back outside, the black woman spoke to him. "Kind gentleman, I have something that will make your food even sweeter." She lowered her basket and removed the lid to show a coffeepot and half a dozen cups inside.

"Fresh, hot coffee," she said. She lifted the pot and one of the cups, and made a motion to pour him one.

As she watched him, her black face held a hopeful expression.

"Yes, I'll have one," Luke said, for the woman and her coffee and cups looked immaculately clean.

He paid the woman and stood beside her under the protective overhang of the building eating his sweet roll and drinking the coffee. More people were appearing on the streets, and vehicles rolled by, all defying the rain. The city is beginning to function again, he thought. The irrepressible need of the people to get on with living was growing, regardless of the presence of the Union conquerors.

Luke handed the empty cup back to the woman. He should also get on with living, forget about what happened here. He had recovered a major part of his money and should go directly to his horse and ride out of New Orleans. But he could not. He was almost as stubborn as

Susan in demanding his full measure of revenge from the man who had robbed him.

\*\*\*

"What are they up to?" Susan cried, reining her mount to a quick halt.

The sudden stop by the naval paymaster and his detachment of Marine guards in the street ahead was totally unexpected. Now the Marines held their rifles ready to fire and stared stonily over the wagon at Susan and her band.

"It's a trap, a goddamned trap," Fletcher cursed. "I warned you."

"Where's the rest of the trap?" Waller said. He whirled to look around. "There it is, sure as hell. Look in the square."

Susan pivoted. A platoon of at least twenty Union Marines had broken from hiding in the shrubbery in Jackson Square and was racing toward them. Captain Rawls, carrying a pistol in one hand and a sword in the other, was leading the platoon.

The captain called out to his men and motioned with his sword. One half of the men swerved off to the left. The remainder charged on, directly at the Southerners.

"They're going to block the street behind us and have us penned in," Waller shouted to Susan. "We've got to break out. And do it now."

"It's too late," Fletcher said.

Susan's mind raced. Fletcher was correct. Rawls had planned his trap well. Already it was drawing tight. The stone walls of the rowhouses hemmed them in on the left. Ahead, the wagon and the paymaster guards blocked the way. The group of men with Rawls were forming a single rank in Jackson Square and kneeling in preparation to fire upon the southerners. Behind her, the Marines were already entering the street.

Rawls's group of Marines fired. Gray plumes of gun smoke blazed from their rifles. A blizzard of bullets hurtled at Susan and her band of men.

Pain jolted Susan as something hard slammed into her head. She swayed in the saddle. She grabbed the horn and held on as pinwheels of exploding stars spun in her head. A great roaring sound filled her ears, as if a hurricane blew around her.

"Hold on." Roy's voice reached through the noise to her. A hand caught her by the shoulder and pulled her upright.

With an effort, Susan held herself in the saddle. One of the Yankee bullets had nearly broken her skull. Her senses revived, the bright stars burning away to ash and the terrific noise swiftly lessening. She looked around.

The fusillade of shots had been deadly. Three horses were down on the ground. Tidwell and Compton lay beside them. The men did not stir. Perkins was climbing up on the horse behind Johnson. Waller, still mounted, was holding his shoulder and grimacing. Blood ran down his arm.

Susan's heart cramped within her bosom. She had brought these young men to this hell of flying bullets. She had threatened Fletcher when he had tried to convince her there was a trap and wanted to abandon the attack. She was responsible for the deaths of Compton and Tidwell. Those men who were still alive must be gotten to safety.

Roy leaned close and spoke. "Susan, the Yankees are reloading. We can't fight them, for there's too many. We must break out now, or we'll never make it. Can you ride?"

She scanned the enemy. The guns were momentarily quiet. Rawls's group of Marines were hurriedly reloading their single shot rifles. The other two groups had not fired because Susan's band was directly between them, and thus their bullets could have flown on to strike the other Marines.

"Ride past the Marines in the square!" Susan cried. "Ride while their rifles are empty. Shoot the hell out of them as we go past." And hope the Yankees are not good marksmen with their pistols.

Susan loosened the reins on the mare and kicked her in the ribs. The horse bolted. Susan screamed at the horse and continued to kick it. The stalwart mare straightened in a flat-out-dead-streaking run.

Susan glanced to the left. Roy, good faithful Roy, rode beside her. From behind came the rumbling sound of the horses of the rest of her band that were still alive.

Susan looked back to the front at the Marines in Jackson Square. Captain Rawls was shouting at his men to hurry and reload their rifles.

As she watched the captain Susan felt the burning, primeval urge to kill him, stronger than ever before. Once she had believed that only men possessed that savage instinct to completely destroy an enemy, yet she now felt the desire to do that in every fiber of her being.

She pulled her pistol. She was probably going to die. That would not be so bad if she could take the captain into the world of the dead with her. She pointed her gun and steadied the sights on him as best she could from her seat on the running mare.

The captain faced away from his squad and toward the approaching riders. He raised his pistol and watched Susan as she rushed ever nearer on her running horse.

He called over his shoulder to the Marines. Several lifted their rifles, now reloaded and ready to fire. The remainder of the men pulled their revolvers.

Susan fired at Rawls, her pistol leaping like a live thing. The bullet missed. She shot again quickly. However, the captain was moving swiftly to the side. Her bullet tore a hole in the air where he had stood a moment before.

Pistols cracked behind her as the band of brave young southerners opened fire. In Jackson Square, two Marines toppled to the ground. She heard Roy yell a high, shrill challenge at their enemies.

The squad of Marines with Rawls and the guards at the wagon returned the fire of the southerners. A thundering volley of exploding rifles and pistols lashed out at the riders.

Captain Rawls swung his pistol to track the slender figure on the running horse leading the pack of rebels. His trap was succeeding better than he had hoped. Now to finish it, destroy these bastards.

Susan saw the captain's gun come into alignment and follow her. She knew with certainty that the man would not miss. She jerked back abruptly on the reins, slowing the mare. The captain's gun fired, and smoke jetted out from the barrel.

The mare jerked as the bullet slammed squarely into its head. The animal shrieked in torment as it fell. Susan kicked free of the stirrups as the horse crashed down.

Susan saw the ground coming up to meet her. She hit with a bone-jarring thump. Breath erupted from her lungs.

Half dazed, she lay sucking at the air. More shots crashed on the battlefield. Men cried out near her.

Susan struggled to a sitting position. Her hat had been lost in the fall, and she swept her hair back from her eyes to see. Two horses were bolting away across the corner of Jackson Square. She recognized the figures of O'Doyle and Waller upon the backs of the racing animals.

A burst of gunshots boomed from the Marines at the wagon. Waller's horse went down as if tripped. The man flew over its head and struck the ground. The horse flipped end over end and fell heavily on its fallen rider.

Bullets hit O'Doyle in the back. He dropped his pistol and his arms flew wide as if he were about to embrace a lover. Then he leaned to the side, and farther still. His legs came loose from their grip on the horse. He rolled from the saddle.

All the guns fell silent and Susan looked away from Waller and O'Doyle. On the ground almost against her, Johnson and Perkins lay still and lifeless. Fletcher was climbing to his feet beside his fallen horse. His gaze swept around. He stepped to Roy and helped him to his feet. Roy held his handless arm against his chest. Both men were unsteady on their feet. Susan could not tell if they were hurt from the fall or had been wounded by the hail of bullets, or both.

Susan's throat was constricted, and she fought back tears as she looked at Roy and Fletcher. Her sorrow was not for herself. She would accept whatever punishment came to her. Her sorrow was for the young men she had led so badly. All but two were now dead. Those two would soon follow. She had been so blinded by hate that she had misjudged her foes.

Captain Rawls and his Marines came running into Susan's view. She heard him shouting. "Take the rebels. I want them for hanging."

Fletcher and Roy drew together and stood shoulder to shoulder. Susan started to rise. She must go and stand with them against the enemy. She almost made it to her feet. Then her legs collapsed under her and she fell.

As if of one mind, Fletcher and Roy cast one quick look at her. Roy's expression was one of concern for her. She expected to see something different in

307

Fletcher—condemnation, and hate for her poor leadership. There was only the light in his eyes of a man who sees death coming.

Two Marines sprang at Roy and knocked him to the ground. Before he could rise they fell upon him, and their fists rose and fell.

He fought back, striking up at them. With the heat of the battle hot in him, he forgot his left hand was missing, and he hit with the stub end of his arm as well as with his good right hand. Blood spurted out as stitches were torn open and partially healed arteries ruptured. Blood fell back on him, turning his face scarlet.

He almost broke free once, but the men pulled him back down and hammered and hammered him with hard fists.

Fletcher did not wait for his attackers. He lunged forward, his broad, muscular body driving hard to meet the Marines. He caught a man in each arm and bore them to the earth. His big hands gouged and mauled his adversaries. Teeth shattered under his knuckles. He exploded an eye, bit an ear off.

Other Marines leapt forward and swung the butts of their rifles, plated with iron, down on Fletcher. The blows thudded upon his ribs. He thrust up a hand to ward off the blows. Three fingers snapped. Fletcher snarled like a berserk beast. The iron butt plates slammed into his head.

Susan could not believe the ferocity of the struggling mass of men tearing and striking each other. She heard the curses and wordless cries of the men locked in mortal combat, and the smack and whack of iron and wood striking flesh and bone. Her body flinched at each blow as if she, too, were being hit.

"Enough, damnit, enough!" Captain Rawls shouted. "I want them alive." He sprang in among his men and threw them back from the limp bodies of the two southerners.

The victors stood breathing hoarsely. They stared at the dead rebels and the unconscious ones. They seemed awed by the killings and the vicious beatings they had rendered.

The captain came and looked down at Susan, who sat propped against the dead mare. He wished she had been killed in the battle. "Well, you rebel bitch, I see you are still alive. Your plan was so easy to figure out that a child could have done it. Now I'll hang you."

He turned away and shouted to his men. "Get our wounded to the surgeon at the hospital. And take the rebels still alive there, too. Better put a tourniquet on that one-handed man before he bleeds to death."

# Chapter Twenty-Six

Luke was running within a second after the gunfire exploded. He raced along the street of the Old French Quarter, splashing through the puddles of water and dodging the pedestrians and vehicles. The shooting was near the Union Headquarters. Susan was at the center of it, he knew it. And he was afraid for her.

The clamor of the exploding musketry ceased as Luke came into sight of the Cabildo. He slowed to a fast walk. Most of the people on the street were hurrying away from the disturbance, while a few were pressed to the walls of the buildings and staring with frightened faces toward Jackson Square. A riderless horse sped past with flapping stirrups and hooves clattering on the pavement.

Luke went on and cautiously peered around the corner. Union Marines, at least a platoon, were congregated a block away on St. Peter Street, opposite Jackson Square. Captain Rawls was talking to a figure in a Marine uniform sitting on the street. Several other bodies in similar uniforms lay motionless on the ground. Had the Marines been attacked by Confederates? If so, where were they?

For a moment, because of the distance and the uniform Susan wore, Luke did not recognize her. Then he noted the familiar shape of her and the long black hair hanging below her shoulders. Instantly he knew she had tried to carry out her plan to rob the Union payroll—a plan that had led to her capture, and the deaths of some if not all of her comrades.

Luke felt some relief at the knowledge that Susan was still alive, but her recklessness had made her Rawls's prisoner and no more dangerous plight could be imagined. The captain would surely see that she died. Luke breathed in and out. It was like a shudder. He had not known until this very moment how much the woman meant to him. He recalled their night of lovemaking. That delightful episode had cut a hard groove in his mind, one that would never be eroded away by the passage of time.

A Marine brought a wagon up to the wounded, and five of them were lifted and placed in the bed. At an order from the captain, Susan shakily climbed to her feet and crawled into the rear of the wagon. The vehicle rattled off with an armed escort.

A squad of Marines formed up and marched away along St. Peter Street toward the Cabildo. One Marine was left behind with the bodies still lying on the street.

He placed his back against one of the big trees in Jackson Square and watched warily.

Luke followed two blocks behind the wagon. Townsfolk were in moderate numbers on the street and he should not be conspicuous by his action. He must know at all times where Susan was being held. Perhaps, just perhaps, the Marines that Rawls would place to guard the prisoners might relax their vigilance enough for Luke to break her free.

***

Panther peered through the low hanging limbs of the tree at the squad of white Marines and Tate. Danger comes cloaked in many forms, he thought. This time it came in the form of a big, black man who knew the forest.

Daylight was less than an hour old. The rain fell steadily down from the dark overcast and upon Panther. The leaves of the giant trees dripped and shivered under the fingers of the slow wind. He wore only a shirt, pants, and shoes. All were totally soaked. His Sharps rifle had not yet been uncased and was snug and dry within its greased rawhide covering.

Tate, like Panther, had no rain gear and appeared oblivious to the rain, while the Marines wore cumbersome slickers. The black man was studying the ground and leading the Marines slowly to the northeast. Panther knew the trail the man followed. Panther had grown careless in recent years and sometimes used the same path from his cabin to the city. Luke and he had ridden horses upon it only yesterday. Tate had discovered the route now, even in the rain. He could see the trampled grass and weeds, and was unraveling the path's twists and bends.

The rain slackened. The wind came more strongly. Panther listened to it snuffling along the ground and in among the trees like some great hunting beast. But that was only wind sound. There was a true beast loose in the forest. The beast of death rode Panther's shoulders like an expectant predator.

He slid the greased sleeve from his rifle and hung it over his shoulder. He lifted the rifle, and the wet wind sighed around him as if expressing sorrow at what he was preparing to do. For a fragment of time he was taken aback at the mournful sound. Then his shoulders moved with an almost imperceptible shrug.

He had no fear the soldiers could ever catch him, but they must be turned back before they found his home and Blackberry Woman. Finding her alone in the forest, they might do awful things to her.

He poked the Sharps out through the leaves. The shot must be made quickly for the drizzle would soon soak into the firing chamber and wet the powder in its linen casing.

Tate rose from the squatting position where he had been closely examining the ground. "I'm bettin' this is old Panther's path home, Corporal Cooper," he said. "You mentioned he had a horse, and there's horse tracks here that can be made out even if they are mostly washed away. And I've seen him leaving town coming in this direction. Lake Borgne is off that way a few miles. His cabin must be between right here where we stand and the lake."

"I think I can make out what you're following," the corporal said. "Let's move faster."

"Best not to hurry. We don't want to lose the trail. And I want to see old Panther before he sees me."

"Yeah. Me, too. I saw what he can do with a rifle."

Panther heard the voices of the men above the sibilant hiss of the raindrops falling down through the leaves of the trees. They might look for him, but they would never see him. Instead the Marines were going to see Tate die. Without their guide, they would blunder about in the woods for a day or two and then turn back to the city.

He pulled the stock of the rifle snugly to his shoulder. The sights became aligned on the broad chest of the black man. All right, beast of death, now I'll feed you, Panther thought. He pressed the trigger.

The loud boom of the rifle jarred the air, and shook the leaves, and a heavy shower of raindrops poured down on Panther.

As if punched by a powerful, invisible fist, Tate fell heavily. His body quivered and thrashed about on the wet mat of leaves covering the ground. Then all motion ceased, and he lay lifeless.

Panther immediately sprang away. The plume of gunpowder smoke would mark his position for the guns of his enemies.

He was a hundred feet away and flowing soundlessly like a phantom through the forest when the rifle shots crashed. He laughed without sound, and ran easterly. A quarter mile later he began to circle left back to the location of his ambush on the Marines. He stopped once. Shielding his rifle from the rain, he reloaded it and put it back into its waterproof sleeve. Then he trotted on.

Gradually he slowed to a walk and stole forward the last short distance with a stealth that would have done the true swamp panther proud.

The forest was quiet except for the falling raindrops as Panther came within view of Tate lying on the ground. The Marines were gone, chasing him, but they would soon return when they could find no sign of him.

He went to Tate and knelt down. The man lay face up, the rain falling upon his charcoal skin. The depression of his eye sockets were little lakes of water, through which his unseeing, black eyes stared up from the bottom.

"I have returned to tell you that I'm sorry I had to shoot you," Panther said to the deaf ears of the man. "We have met other times in the forest, and always went on our separate ways in peace. You are not my foe. The white officers in the city are. I will go and shoot them so that they do not send more men like you to hunt me."

Panther heard the voices of the Marines approaching in the wet woods. He climbed to his feet and faded away among the trunks of the trees. The Marines were no longer of danger to him. With Tate dead, they were now blind.

\*\*\*

The Marine captain came, as Susan knew he would. She heard him talking to the two military guards stationed in the hallway outside the locked door of her imprisoning cell.

She was being held in the Parish Courthouse on the second floor, in a cell that was used to hold prisoners on the day of their trial. The furnishings were a cot with a thin cotton mattress, a single, straight-backed chair, a wash-stand, and a chamber pot. Shadows filled the room, for little daylight found its way through the tiny, iron-barred window.

The courthouse was made of stone and was three stories tall. It contained the parish court, offices of the prosecutor, and the offices of other parish officials. The rear third of the structure contained the parish jail. The Union military was using the jail to hold the Confederate soldiers they had captured.

Susan was standing at the window. The bottom sash had been difficult to force up, but she had finally succeeded in doing so. The bars were rusty, for they were decades old, having been installed during the days of Spanish rule of the land. The damp climate of New Orleans had caused the metal to rust heavily. However, in the center of the bars, beneath the layer of rust, the strong iron still lived. The bars had defied her greatest efforts to pry them apart or to break them loose from their recessed sockets in the stone.

She stared out between the bars and down into the narrow street behind the courthouse. She felt trapped, defeated. Her head ached horribly from her wound, a throbbing demon trying to break out of her skull. Roy, Fletcher, and she had first been taken to Sisters of Charity Hospital. There the chief Union surgeon, who now had taken charge of the hospital, examined the wound on her head and stitched her torn scalp back together. The surgeon had told Captain Rawls that he wanted to keep the three prisoners at the hospital for a day or two for observation. The captain had objected. He told the surgeon there were organized rebels that would come and free Susan and the two male rebels. The prisoners must be taken to a place where they could be securely guarded. She and her two comrades had been brought together to the jailhouse. She had been separated from them and brought to this small cell.

Susan moved away from the window and sat down on the cot. She lowered her head and held it in her hands. There were no rebels organized to come and rescue her, and now the Yankee captain had come to question her. Damn him to hell.

Susan raised her head as the door opened and Captain Rawls and one of the guards came into the room. The guard carried a lantern, its yellow flame casting a pale light on the interior of the space.

"Set the light down there on the floor and leave us," the captain ordered the guard.

The Marine lowered the lantern. He glanced once at Susan, and then went out, closing the door behind him.

The captain seated himself on the chair. The light from the lantern lit only one side of his face, leaving the other in deep shadow. He said nothing, studying Susan.

You are a two-faced man, thought Susan, looking at the captain's half-lighted face. One is very evil, and you keep it hidden from your superiors. But I know what you are.

Abruptly the captain spoke. "Where is the man Coldiron?"

"I don't know anything about Coldiron." Susan's voice came out hoarse. Her throat was dry and scratchy, for she had drunk no water since early morning, but she would ask for nothing from the Yankees - especially from this one, who was responsible for the murder of her father.

"You lie," the captain growled.

"If I'm a liar, why do you waste time asking me questions?"

Susan would say not one word more to the captain. The pain within her skull was enough to test her strength to the limit without having to fend off his questions.

The Union officer's face grew hard, and a merciless glitter came into his eyes.

319

"I know Coldiron slept with you at the cottage. Did you have a good night?"

Susan said nothing.

"There was a rebel soldier there, also. He shot one of my men as he rode away. Isn't that so?"

Susan stared at the captain. She could not help that a tiny smile came to her lips.

The captain rose suddenly from the chair and stepped toward Susan. His hand drew back to strike her.

Susan flinched. Immediately a sharp lance of guilt shot through her at the involuntary reaction to the threat.

The captain grinned wickedly and lowered his hand. "You are a coward," he said. "Your two rebel friends did not show fear when I hit them. The one called Fletcher tried to hit me back. Of course I gave him some hard licks for that."

Susan knew she was no coward. Unused to violence, she had, by reflex, drawn back from a sudden threat. I'll show you who is a coward, she vowed, if I live long enough.

"You led your band of men into my trap," the captain said. "I shot them all to hell. But you actually killed them with your stupid attempt to rob the payroll."

A shudder of torment seized Susan. Rawls spoke the truth. She had indeed already murdered most of her comrades, and the two still alive would soon die. The throbbing in her head soared, roaring to a crescendo of pain. Her skull felt as if ready to explode. Her eyes betrayed her and she saw two captains, two foes doubly menacing.

She tried to look away from Rawls, but her eyeballs were set in axle grease and would not obey her command. The world began to spin, and it canted dangerously on its axis. Something awful was happening to her. Clutching her head, she fell backward on the cot.

The captain looked down at Susan. "You're not going to die before I can put a rope around your rebel neck, are you?" He shoved her in the ribs with his foot. "Try not to."

The captain picked up the lantern and left.

Susan never heard the man's words or the door closing. The dark room was spinning, faster and faster. She held onto her head and moaned in pain, and in sorrow at what she had done. Then all the blackness of all the nights of the world came rushing to crowd into her maimed skull.

***

Panther rested on a log in the edge of the woods and looked toward New Orleans lying beyond the cultivated fields of the white men's farms. The rain had ceased in the early morning, but the wind still talked in the trees. He thought the wind had a message for him, if he could only decipher the language.

He considered returning to Blackberry Woman and telling her what he planned to do, and why. However, he was afraid that with her gentle, logical arguments she might persuade him to remain with her and to abandon the thing he knew must be done. It was better not to run that risk.

He waited, with eyes and ears alert for danger. When the day ended, he would go into the city. Many enemies would die.

\*\*\*

"Damn the Union for invading our city," Sophia Dauphin said with vehemence. "And I almost feel like damning my headstrong niece, too."

"Susan, is that all right," Luke said. He had searched out Sophia Dauphin at her home in the Garden District. The task had not been difficult, for he had remembered Susan saying her aunt lived on Napoleon Avenue. He had introduced himself and told Sophia of Susan's attempt to rob the Union paymaster, and of her capture.

"She's like her father, too brave and always totally committed to whatever she is doing."

Luke nodded. He thought Sophia would have the same characteristics. He would soon know, "Is there anything we can do, Luke?"

"She is being held prisoner somewhere in the Parish Courthouse. It is being used to hold Confederate prisoners of war. She will not be in with the men, but rather off somewhere by herself. If I knew the exact location, there might be a chance to slip into the courthouse and break her free."

"That would be very dangerous. Surely the Yankees will have guards every place surrounding the courthouse."

"Yes, they do, but the most dangerous ones would be those inside."

"You would try to help her escape?"

"Yes."

"Why?" Sophia studied the man's face.

"I once asked her to go to New Mexico with me. However, she turned me down. But I still want to help her. Perhaps as her aunt you might be able to find out where she is being held in the courthouse. Would you go there with some clothing and some food and see if the guards will let you see her?"

"Nothing could stop me."

"Stay away from a Union captain named Rawls. I'm certain he is responsible for your brother's death, and the burning of his home. Colonel Trotter would be more likely to let you see Susan."

"You wait for me here. I'll return as soon as I can."

Sophia went to her pantry and filled a basket with food. She added a bottle of water, a towel, soap, comb, and a dress from her wardrobe. She walked hastily to the front door.

"Luke, help yourself to food, or anything else that is here," she said. "A friend of one Dauphin is a friend of all Dauphins."

"Thank you. I will. Do you want me to harness your horse?"

"No. It's best that you stay out of sight. I can harness it. I've done it hundreds of times."

Sophia left. Luke watched her through the window as she walked swiftly to the stables and shortly drove away in a buggy.

***

"Oh, my God, Susan, what have they done to you?" Sophia cried, staring down at her niece lying on the cot. The young woman's face was ghastly white. A bandage encircled her head.

Sophia whirled upon the guard who had let her into the cell and stood near the doorway. "Why did you hurt her so?" she shouted angrily.

"Ma'am, she was like that when they brought her here," the guard said, taken aback by Sophia's harsh voice.

"Susan, can you hear me?" Sophia said taking her niece by the shoulders and shaking her gently.

"Yes, Aunt Sophia, I hear you," Susan said, opening her eyes. "Stop shaking me, for my head hurts so."

"How bad are you wounded?" Sophia asked. She touched the bandage on Susan's head.

"I'm not sure. The surgeon said I might have a concussion. Help me up."

With her aunt's aid, Susan sat painfully up on the edge of the cot. "How did you find me?" Susan asked.

"A friend of yours saw you taken prisoner and came and told me," Sophia said without elaboration. "I have some food and water for you. Can you eat something?"

"Please give me a drink. I don't want anything to eat."

Sophia took the bottle of water from her basket and helped Susan hold it to drink. She was worried at the obvious weakness of her niece. How bad was the wound?

"I nearly failed to get to see you. Captain Rawls had given orders that you were not to be allowed to have visitors. I had to go to the Union headquarters and talk with Colonel Trotter. He is a gentleman and granted me permission."

"What did he say? What are they going to do with me?"

"He told me you must stand trial, a military trial as a spy and for murder."

"A spy? I'm a resistance fighter and should be treated as a prisoner of war."

"The Union officer said you were a spy. That's why he wouldn't allow me to bring you the dress I had in my basket. You are wearing a Union uniform and not a Confederate one, and must continue to wear it until the trial. You will not be treated as a prisoner of war. You are in a very grave, a very dangerous situation, my dear Susan."

"I know. But I can't think about that now. I must rest." Susan lay down wearily on the cot. "Can you stay with me for a while?"

"The colonel said I could," Sophia said, looking at the guard, who was listening to the conversation.

She turned again to Susan. "But just for a little time. Then I will leave. We must see what we can do for you."

"We?" asked Susan.

"I mean I must see what I can do to help you," Sophia said hastily.

# Chapter Twenty-Seven

"Luke, it is impossible to free Susan," Sophia Dauphin said dejectedly. "It can't be done, not by you, not by a dozen men, even if we had that many to help. It would be suicide to try." She had just returned to her home after her visit with Susan. Her eyes were moist as she fought back tears.

"Tell me what you saw," Luke said.

"She is at the Parish Courthouse with the other Confederate prisoners, as you said. But there are half a hundred Marine guards, some at the entrance, others on patrol around the building, and twenty or so inside."

"Maybe there's still a way to do it. Where is Susan being held?"

"She's confined in a cell near the courtroom where prisoners are brought and held on the day of their trial. She said Roy Penn and a man named Fletcher were also being held, but in the main jail section."

"I know Roy. I'd like to help him. And Fletcher, if he's one of Susan's group. Can you sketch out the passageways of the building, and where Susan is?"

"Yes." Sophia took pen and paper from a desk and seated herself. The pen scratched on the paper for a time as she worked. She finished and pointed at her work. "This is the front entrance. A hallway runs completely through the courthouse, passing under the central dome that reaches all the way to the roof. Susan is being held here on the second floor. A stairway goes up here on the right and all the way to the rear." Sophia made an x and drew a line on the paper. "The guards inside the courthouse, at least the ones I saw, are here on the main floor in the large open space under the dome. You would have to go past them as well as the one stationed at Susan's cell."

"Is the window of Susan's cell barred?"

"Certainly. Heavy bars."

Luke picked up the paper containing the sketch. "I'll go and take a look."

"I want my niece to be free, Luke. But she wouldn't want you to throw your life away in a useless attempt to rescue her."

"She must be gotten away from the Marine captain, or she will surely die," Luke said.

*\*\**

The three Marines leaned against the front wall of the billiard parlor and ogled the comely young woman passing on the sidewalk. "Hey, pretty girl, you got any free love for me?" one of the Marines called.

The woman's chin rose, and with an insulted air she hurried on.

The Marines laughed. They paid no attention to Luke as he went by on the far side of the street.

The day had burned away to gray ash. Black pools of water left by the morning rain lay in the street. Townsfolk were out running errands before the night curfew fell. Most people were on foot. A few hackneys and buggies rattled by on the pavement.

By the time Luke left the Garden District and entered the Old French Quarter, the evening dusk had turned to darkness. With the night, an ill-tempered wind had come alive, gusting under a lowering overcast. Luke thought it would storm. That would increase his odds of success in freeing Susan, and perhaps Roy and Fletcher also.

A lamplighter came into sight ahead, moving along the street and reaching up with his long-handled torch to touch off the streetlights. At the next intersection, a second lamplighter was firing the lights on the avenue leading to the docks. The streets at the courthouse would surely also be illuminated. That would hamper Luke's efforts by exposing him to the vigilant guards.

He veered aside from a direct route to the courthouse. First he would go past the Union Headquarters. Maybe his luck was running and he would encounter Captain Rawls. It would be very satisfying to even his score with the Marine officer tonight.

As Luke drew nearer the waterfront, the number of off duty Marines and sailors roaming the ways increased steadily. They were in good spirits as they sauntered along talking to each other. The numerous saloons were doing a thriving business. The sound of music, mostly of pianos and fiddles, and the rumble of men's voices came from the open doors of the saloon!

Several young whores with heavily rouged faces were plying their trade, moving among the military men and smiling and stopping to talk with them. Luke saw a first class navy petty officer talking with one of the girls. They reached an agreement. She took him by the hand and they went off together.

Roving squads of Marines armed with muskets were on the streets to maintain order. Luke kept as much distance as practicable from them. It was wise to avoid the patrols, for Rawls had most likely given Luke's description to them.

He reached the Old Square. The streets here, especially the two abutting the Montalba Rowhouses, thronged with Union military. A large proportion of the men were officers, marine, navy, and—to Luke's surprise—army. The wrought iron gallerias of the upper two floors of the rowhouses held more officers, mostly army, sitting around small tables and drinking. Several girls had made their way up to the gallerias. They were laughing gaily, and drinking and flirting with the officers.

Luke knew the presence of the army officers meant General Butler had arrived in New Orleans. Now there would be thousands of soldiers instead of a few hundred Marines to control the citizens of the city. Luke turned away from the noisy crowd. It would be extremely dangerous to kill Rawls in the presence of so many military men, even if he could be found. The first priority must be to attempt to help Susan escape her captors.

The throng of celebrating Union military thinned as Luke went eastward past St. Louis Cathedral and the Presbytere, and onward along Dumaine Street. Soon streetlights were present only at the intersections of the street. In the dark sections of the blocks, the yellow rectangles of windows threw a little splash of light out on the brick sidewalk.

The curfew had now fallen and only a few night walkers remained on the street. One of them, a man, was weakly illuminated for a couple of steps by the light from a window before he glided back into the murk. He carried a long, thin object in his hand.

Luke increased his pace as the man came on toward him. He had seen that animal-like, effortless way of walking before. The man was the Chickasaw Indian, Panther.

"What brings you into the city at night?" Luke asked when he had come close enough to be heard.

"And what brings you out in the dark?" Panther replied.

The two men halted and stood silently, wondering how much to tell the other.

Luke looked at the rifle in the Indian's hand and then back up at his face almost obscured by the darkness. "I have a friend in trouble and I thought I would go and help her," he said.

"It is good to help a friend," Panther said. "My action is not so noble. The soldiers came into the forest to hunt me. I killed the guide of those men. Now I have come to bring the battle to those who are my enemies. I want to kill some of their chiefs."

"There are hundreds of Union chiefs. You can't beat them all."

"It's not always necessary to win to have fought the good fight."

"That's true."

"You said you go to help a friend and the friend was a woman. Is she the Dauphin woman?"

"She's the one. Do you know her?"

"I saw her with you at the docks the day you bought my honey. Then I found her sleeping in the forest yesterday. We talked a little. What kind of trouble does she have?"

Luke was surprised to hear of Susan sleeping in the woods, but he did not pursue the subject. "She is a prisoner of the Union soldiers."

"Then she and I have the same enemy. What do you plan to do?"

"She is held at the Parish Courthouse, in a cell in the rear. I want to try and free her."

"That will not be easy. I have seen the jail. It has strong stone walls and iron bars."

"And I've been told it has many guards. Even so, I must try."

"There should be enemy chiefs there. So why don't I go with you? Perhaps I can be of help in freeing the pretty woman."

"It will be very dangerous."

"Yes."

Luke studied Panther's dim form. He wished he could see the Chickasaw's face more clearly. What thoughts ran through his mind?

"All right," Luke said. "Let's go."

They went half a dozen blocks through the night shadows and the wind, and came within sight of the courthouse. The large stone structure occupied most of a city square. Streetlamps burned at each corner. Four guards were posted at the double entry door at the top of a flight of four stone steps. Luke knew there would be other guards at the rear entryway and sentries patrolling the perimeter.

"It will be very difficult to break into the building," Luke said.

"And impossible to get out alive," Panther added. "You may get yourself and the woman killed if you try to take her from the soldiers."

"She will soon be dead for they will execute her for what she has done. But there may be another way to free her."

"How would that be done?"

"Have the Marines write a release for her."

"Do you know one that would do that?"

"Not of his own free will. But I'll coax him a little. His name is Captain Rawls. We may find him at the celebration near the square. The curfew has fallen so we must be careful and not get arrested for being on the streets."

335

With long strides, the men hurried back the way they had come. They halted at the junction of Dumaine Street and Chartres Street. The space around the Montalba Townhouses was still thronged with military men, and the gallerias were even more crowded than before.

"You should wait here," Luke said, looking into the dark mahogany face of the Indian. "You would be easily recognized."

"What of you?"

"Look, there are civilians celebrating right along with the military. The Union sympathizers have made their true colors known now that General Butler's army has arrived. I can go among them with little danger. I'll find Rawls and bring him back. With such a lively party as this, he should be here."

Panther sensed the lack of fear in the white man even though what he planned to do was very hazardous. He was a fine man to follow into war. "I will wait," he said.

Luke walked openly along Chartres Street. Rawls and Trotter would know him for certain. He must spot them before they saw him. Trotter would be avoided.

Rawls would be with the congregation of officers on the gallerias of the town houses, Luke reasoned. At the nearest stairway, he climbed to the first level and moved into the press of officers and civilians. As he passed a table, an army lieutenant rose and threw his arm across Luke's shoulders.

"Here's another one," the lieutenant said in drunken, good spirits.

Luke tensed, ready to strike out. He smelled the whiskey breath of the officer. "Here's another what?" he asked.

"A good Union man. Isn't that so?"

"That's right," Luke said, glancing at the three army officers and a well-dressed civilian sitting at the table. "I fought for two years in the U.S. Army, in forty-six and forty-seven. I'm not about to change my loyalties."

"Good man. There must be hundreds like you in New Orleans."

"More likely thousands. Louisiana had a hard time deciding whether it was a secessionist state or not." Luke evaluated the well-dressed civilian. He appeared to be a businessman, probably hoping for an army contract.

"I've heard that too," the lieutenant said. "What's your business?"

"I raise and sell horses."

"Maybe our cavalry could get some of your horses for mounts."

"They already have two hundred of them." And I never got paid, Luke thought. He stepped away from the lieutenant and the man's arm fell from his shoulders.

"Have a drink with us," the lieutenant said. He spoke to one of the seated officers. "Randolph, pour our new friend a whiskey."

"Right," Randolph said. He poured whiskey into a water glass and handed it to Luke. "The good citizens of New Orleans have been generous to us, and we have more whiskey than we can drink."

"Thanks," Luke said taking the offered glass. He took a pull of the bourbon and cast a look around. Nearly all the men on the galleria were army soldiers. "Where are the Marines? I'm looking for an old friend."

"The sailors and the Marines are mostly ganged up on the balconies of the townhouses across the square," the lieutenant said.

"Well thanks for the whiskey." Luke raised his glass to the men and drank. "Maybe I'll see you again later." He placed the glass on the table.

Luke turned back to the stairway, went down, and walked across the square through the scattering of trees.

The first galleria level was crowded with naval and marine officers, and a few army ones. Tables and chairs had been brought from the living quarters to the outside. Coal oil lamps burned brightly on the tables and illuminated the faces of the men sitting and standing and talking in jovial tones. The blue and the red dress officer's uniforms with the gold bars and stripes added a carnival color to the noisy camaraderie of the men.

Three young women had followed Luke up the stairway. As he hesitated, surveying the occupants of the galleria, the women pushed boldly past him. Immediately they were the focus of many eyes.

Luke examined the faces of the uniformed men within view. They were all unknown to him. He moved forward among the officers and their guests.

The gallerias of the town houses abutted one to another to form a continuous platform that stretched the full length of the block. Short, wrought iron railings separated the galleria of each townhouse from the next. There was a constant stirring and mixing of people along the entire level. Luke heard the lighthearted tone of the people's voices. He understood the reason for the festive mood of the Northern soldiers and sailors, and the citizens whose loyalty lay with the Union. A major city had been conquered without a battle, without the destruction of one home or business.

He reached the galleria of the end townhouse and looked down at the street. A Marine officer was coming from the direction of the waterfront. He walked ramrod straight and with a purposeful stride as if on parade. His head was thrust forward in a pugnacious attitude. It was Rawls.

Luke reached under the flap of his vest and checked the position of the pistol in his belt. Somehow he must take the captain prisoner without creating a ruckus and drawing attention. He started for the nearby stairway, then stopped quickly as a man shouted near him.

"Captain Rawls, wait," a corporal of Marines called down from the galleria. "I must talk with you."

Luke stepped hastily back from the railing as Rawls pivoted to look. He hoped he had not been seen.

The corporal hurried to the stairway and went down. Luke noted the man was unarmed. He must have come directly from the Union Headquarters. Luke followed more slowly, stopping in the shadows on the bottom step.

The corporal spoke as he drew close to the captain. "Captain, Colonel Trotter sent me. He is meeting with General Butler, and wants you to join them."

"Very well, Corporal. Tell me what's happening as we go."

The two men set out, talking together. They left the street and took a shortcut to the headquarters through Jackson Square.

Luke crossed the street and went in under the out-stretched limbs of the trees of the square. The light from the gallerias and the even more distant streetlamps reached but weakly here, and the gloom of night lay dense. He pulled his pistol. His enemy was before him, and isolated from all help except for the corporal.

The distance over the square was short and the border already in sight. Luke broke into a trot and speedily overtook the men.

With his feet falling silently on the grass sod, Luke came within three body lengths of the Marines. Deep in conversation, the two men had not once glanced to the rear.

Luke leapt forward and slashed down with his pistol upon the head of the corporal. At the last second, Luke softened the blow. He did not want to kill the man, merely knock him unconscious and prevent him from helping Rawls in any manner.

The corporal's knees buckled and he fell with a groan. Instantly Luke moved on the captain, swinging his pistol in a sweeping horizontal blow. The iron weapon struck the side of the captain's head with a whack.

The captain staggered, then caught himself, for as quickly as Luke had acted, the captain had dodged aside, avoiding the full force of the blow.

Luke lunged, boring in with his attack as the captain's hand darted for the pistol on his belt. Luke chopped down with the pistol upon the Marine's right shoulder. Nerves were stunned in the man's arm. The pistol fell from his numbed hand to the ground.

"Don't move!" Luke ordered harshly. He pointed his pistol into Rawl's face.

The captain ignored the threatening weapon. He shook his arm and worked his fingers a few times. He looked at Luke. "Coldiron, I knew we would meet again," he said.

"But in different circumstances than you had planned. I hold the gun."

"Fortunes of war. Is the corporal dead?" He looked past Luke.

"I don't think so. His head felt hard."

"You had a reason for not killing me. What is it?"

"You're going to write a release for Susan Dauphin, and for her two friends."

"I'll do nothing to free that rebel bitch."

"Oh, yes, I think you will. Then after that is done, you're going to pay me for my horses. In exchange, I'll give you your life."

The captain laughed. "Just like that? An even trade?"

"Yes, a trade. Otherwise you can be certain I'll kill you."

"That's plain enough. But I have no paper or pen."

"I know a place where we can find some. It's just a short walk," Luke motioned with his free hand in the direction of Exchange Alley. "March." He would take Rawls to Bouchard's gymnasium. Writing material could be found there. And Rawls could be tied up and held until Susan's release was obtained.

"Walk faster," Luke prodded the captain roughly in the back with the barrel of the pistol. "If you try to run, I'll blow your spine to pieces." He slid the pistol into his belt. No one must see him holding the Marine captive.

Luke sensed movement behind him, coming swiftly. He spun to face the assault. The corporal had already launched himself into the air. He slammed into Luke. They crashed downward in a tangle of arms and legs.

The captain whirled around. The corporal and Coldiron were fighting on the ground. The corporal was a big man, on top and pounding Coldiron.

Coldiron struck upward, slugging the corporal twice in the face. The blows were delivered but a short distance, yet they dazed the soldier halting his attack. Coldiron heaved mightily upward and flung the corporal aside.

Luke coiled upward to his knees. He must get to his feet to meet the captain's certain attack.

Before Luke could come fully erect, Rawls jumped in and hammered him with two savage chops to the back of the neck. Luke was driven down to the ground with stars exploding in his brain. He shook his head and started to rise up again.

"Grab him," Rawls shouted to the corporal, who was climbing to his feet.

The two Marines grabbed hold of Luke, one on each arm, and jerked him to his feet.

"Got you, you bastard," Rawls snarled. "Now we'll see who dies."

# Chapter Twenty-Eight

Panther crept along, hugging the walls to keep in the shadows of the buildings fronting the street. He heard the boisterous voices of the victorious, celebrating warriors of the North country coming from ahead. They seemed confident men who had no worry that an attack would be mounted upon them by the citizens of the conquered city.

He stopped in the center of the block where the light was dimmest and some night still existed. He held his rifle pressed tightly to his side to hide it as much as possible from any eyes that might chance upon him. He waited, watching for Coldiron. The man had vanished among the Union soldiers several minutes before. Would he reappear?

The minutes dragged past. More military men and civilians joined the throng of people on the gallerias of the town houses and on the streets below.

Three men came out of the trees of Jackson Square and into Decatur Street. Two of them were Union Marines and they held a man in civilian clothing pinioned between them. Panther recognized Coldiron. The man from New Mexico had been taken prisoner.

One of the Marines called out to three Marines passing on the street. "Come help us take this man to headquarters."

"Yes, sir," one of the men replied.

Panther fingered the medicine bundle hanging around his neck. The action he must take came to him with perfect clarity. All the events of the past few days, and of that time a quarter of a century ago when he had fled from the white soldiers and into the swamps, had led inexorably to this point in time. His destiny was fixed, and he knew it. He must prove himself a true Chickasaw warrior.

He searched back through his memory for the warrior chant. It was buried deeply, and for a moment he could not remember it. Then it came to him in its entirety, every syllable, every inflection. He began to chant in a coarse, guttural voice, flinging it along the street toward the two men holding Coldiron and the three hastening to assist them. Panther sprang out of the shadows and into the light.

The Marines whirled to look at him. They pulled pistols. Panther ceased his chant and began to laugh. With contemptuous laughter you can summon battle when you want, and thus if you are to die, you can die erect on your feet, larger than life, giving your life truth and justification. And perhaps, in a battle bravely fought you can wash away your previous cowardice, even terrible cowardice, that has lain so long and so heavily upon your spirit.

He jerked open his shirt and bared his brown chest to the pistols that had appeared in the hands of the Marines and were now thrust so threateningly out at him.

He cried out at the top of his voice, "Soldiers, stand and fight this Chickasaw. Fight bravely so that he can know with certainty that he is truly a warrior."

He raised the rifle to his shoulder, steadied it, found the sights in the frail light of the streetlamps. He shot the man holding Coldiron's right arm. The man flopped backward as the bullet punched a hole completely through his chest.

Panther dropped the empty rifle to the street and pulled his pistol. He was not as skilled with the short barreled weapon as with the rifle. He must be closer. He sprinted toward the gathering of men.

Panther saw Coldiron hit the man that still held one arm. Immediately, the two were locked together in combat, striking each other with fierce blows of their fists.

The guns of the Marines began to crack. Panther saw the red flashes of burning powder dart out at him, faster than a snake's head. Such a pretty color, one Blackberry Woman would have liked.

He was hit. There was little pain. Mostly he felt the shock of the bullets slamming into his body as he ran into them. The bullets twisted him left, then right, trying to knock him off his feet. He must not fall, not yet.

He was near enough now, just a short range to his foes. He began to shoot, the pistol a deadly, barking animal spitting round lead balls. A Marine fell.

***

Luke heard the crushing sound of the rifle bullet striking into the corporal's flesh. The man was hurled backward and Luke's hand was suddenly loose. He folded the hand into a fist and swung a powerful, round-house blow to Rawls's face.

The captain's grip on Luke's arm was broken, and he fell back two steps. Then he lunged to the attack fists swinging.

Luke's anger was like molten lead in his brain. Nothing would stop him from beating the man to within an inch of death. He knocked Rawls's fists away and drove inside. His knuckles thudded into the Marine's face once, twice, three times. Rawls sagged to his knees. Luke kicked him in the ribs, rolling him on the ground.

Luke pivoted to check Panther. The Indian was firing his pistol and charging straight down the center of the street. One of the Marines was on the ground. The other two were shooting rapidly back at Panther.

Luke pounced on the nearest Marine and pulled him down. The man's pistol exploded into the pavement. The bullet ricocheted away with a shrill whine. Luke pummeled the man beneath him with a flurry of blows. The man went limp.

Luke climbed to his feet as Panther came to a halt a few paces away. Luke stared at the Indian in amazement. How had he escaped being killed, running directly into the fire storm from the Marines' pistols?

A flood of voices from the Montalba Rowhouses broke through Luke's awareness. Then there was the sound of a multitude of men running. At least two hundred military men were on the gallerias of the town houses, and many more at the Cabildo. Most of them would be hurrying to the location of the shooting. Panther and he must escape into the labyrinth of the dark streets of the city.

"Are you hurt? Can you travel?" Luke asked. The Indian looked ill, his face strained.

Panther nodded. "I can travel," But he did not know how far. His muscles were weakening, ready to fail him.

"Follow me," Luke said.

He scooped up a pistol lying on the pavement and darted off. He heard Panther's feet thudding on his right and slightly to the rear.

The way was deserted. Any people that had been out on the street, had become frightened by the gunshots and had fled indoors. That was good, Luke thought. There would be no one to tell the Marines which way Panther and he had run.

Conti Street was reached and Luke guided to the right onto it. The shouts of the Union men faded to a low murmur behind. They would need a few minutes to organize a pursuit.

Panther's footfalls could no longer be heard. Luke slid to a stop and looked to the rear.

Panther stood in the street some one hundred feet behind and facing Luke. His body was etched against the yellow glow of the streetlamp at the corner. He began to tremble as he struggled to hold himself erect. He put out his hand as if seeking support on the air. His legs crumpled and he sank to the pavement.

Luke ran to Panther and knelt beside him. The warrior stared up with pain-filled black eyes.

"I can go no farther for I'm badly wounded," he said. "Go on without me."

"Like hell I will. We go together, or not at all."

Luke grabbed Panther's arm and placed it around his neck, and he hoisted the injured man to his feet. As Panther slumped, Luke quickly stooped and caught him over a shoulder. He straightened and moved off carrying the Indian.

Luke moved fast, breathing hard. Shortly he was beyond the last streetlamp and hastened on through darkness. No one was on the street. Luke turned left into Exchange Alley. It, too, was dark and abandoned.

Balancing Panther on his shoulder, Luke unlocked the door to Bouchard's dueling gymnasium. He struck a match to get his bearing, doused the flame, and crossed the wide interior space to the office. His outstretched hand found the couch, and he placed Panther gently down.

"I'll have a light in a minute," Luke said.

He located the coal oil lamp, lifted the globe and lit the wick.

"Let's see how bad you're hurt," Luke said.

He brought the lamp and set it on the chair by the couch. The unbuttoned shirt was pulled aside.

"Damnation," Luke cursed. "You've been hit three times. Why didn't you tell me?"

A bullet had penetrated the center of the stomach, another the right side of the chest, and the third the upper left arm. Blood ran from all the wounds. It was unbelievable that Panther had run several blocks with such severe injuries.

"I think it is bad," the Chickasaw said matter-of-factly.

"I must get you to a doctor."

"No. Take me to Blackberry Woman."

"All right. But first a doctor."

"No. We must leave the city now."

"You can't travel that far. You'll die."

"I will die anyway. So take me to Blackberry Woman. There are things I must tell her."

"Are you certain?" Luke believed the Indian was correct in that he would die regardless of whether or not he was taken to a doctor. The stomach wound was very bad.

"I am certain."

"My horse is about a half mile from here. I'll fetch it and you can ride."

"Do not get caught because of me."

"I'll be careful. Before I go, I must slow the bleeding."

Luke rolled Panther onto his side. All the bullets had gone completely through. Blood was flowing much more heavily from the jagged holes left by the bullets tearing out of the body.

Luke found two clean cotton shirts hanging with other clothing in a closet. The shirts were ripped into pieces, and pads of cloth folded and bound tightly over the wounds.

"That's the best I can do," Luke said. "I should try to find a doctor to tend you."

"Do as I ask. Take me to Blackberry Woman."

Luke touched the hand of the Chickasaw. "You're one hell of a fighter. You hang on. I'll be back."

Panther watched the white man hasten from the room. *And so are you, my friend. Thank you for giving me a reason to fight.*

He lay quietly, conserving his strength. He knew he was still bleeding, his life ebbing away. That did not bother him much, if he could just see Blackberry Woman once again.

Panther watched the lamp flame flicker and splutter. Somewhere inside the wall of the aged dueling school there was the patter of small feet. Then a mouse began to gnaw, like a tiny saw cutting on a thin board.

The sound suddenly ceased as Panther began his death chant. It was almost a song, sad and lamenting yet holding a hard core of strength that could accept the end of the earthly voyage and the one into the unknown of death.

Panther held his gaze on the flickering lamp flame and chanted on and on.

\*\*\*

The blacksmith shop smelled of charcoal, old ashes, and iron. From the livery next door came the odor of hay and manure.

Luke worked by the light of a lantern turned very low. He had cut the blacksmith's thick leather apron into pieces and was tying them over the hooves of his horse. Finishing the last hoof, he blew out the lantern and opened the outside door.

The street was filled with damp murk. He listened hoping there would be no sound of a Union patrol searching for him. The faint bark of a dog far off reached him. A baby cried in one of the houses to his left. That was all, the city strangely quiet.

The horse was brought outside and the door closed. The animal's hooves made only a muffled thud on the pavement as Luke rode toward Exchange Alley. He stopped and listened every half block. Twice he detoured as men's voices reached him from ahead. In a circuitous route, he arrived at Bouchard's dueling academy.

Luke swung down at the door. He led the horse inside and across the gymnasium, each hoof a hollow drumbeat on the wooden floor. The horse whinnied and tossed its head for it did not like the sound and the feel of the wood beneath it. Luke spoke to the animal and laid his arm over its neck to quiet it. He halted at the entrance to the office.

Panther was watching the door as Luke came into the room. "Are you ready to travel?" Luke asked.

"I'm ready," Panther replied. "We must not waste time."

"All right. Let me lift you up in the saddle."

As Luke took Panther in his arms, he saw the bandages were soaked with blood. There was nothing he could do that would completely stop the bleeding from such large wounds. Luke felt a deep sadness at the certain knowledge the Indian was dying.

Panther must also know he was close to death, Luke thought as he placed him astride the horse. The motion of the horse would speed the flow of blood from his body.

"Should we try to find a doctor?" Luke asked. He had to be sure.

"No," Panther said in a firm voice. "Take me to Blackberry Woman."

"So be it. Can you hold on?"

"Yes."

Luke went across the gymnasium to the drumbeat of
the horse's hooves on the planking and out onto the dark
street.

\*\*\*

They went north through the city, the horse with its
rider slumped forward and the man walking and leading.
The night was still without a trace of wind. Overhead
the stars glittered like ice shards flung across the ebony
sky. They reached the edge of the city without encoun-
tering a living soul, and went on across open fields.

Panther clutched the horn of the saddle with both
hands. He had at first felt confident that he could endure
until Coldiron got him to Blackberry Woman. The pain
of the wounds, though great, he could stand. But his
strength was weakening rapidly as his blood drained
away. He was sliding toward death, and the slide was
growing ever steeper. His end was near.

Panther concentrated all his will on the task of holding himself upon the horse's back. He counted every
step of the animal as it carried him homeward.

The yellow-eyed moon rose above the eastern horizon and began to orb the earth. In the new light, Luke

could make out the forest ahead. He looked at Panther. The man's head was bowed.

"I see the woods," Luke said.

Panther lifted his head weakly. "I see it also. That is good." His head sank again.

They came in under the trees and Luke halted. He generally knew where the cabin sat, but he could wander around all night in the deep forest looking for it. "Which way, Panther?" he asked.

The Chickasaw slowly raised his eyes to look at the stars and the moon. He inclined his head and spoke. "That way."

Luke plunged into the Stygian gloom under the giant trees where the moonlight could not reach. He tried to hold a straight course, but almost immediately he came to a swamp and had to make a quarter mile detour around it. He again took up the course Panther had pointed out.

Brushing aside the hanging strands of Spanish moss that hit his face and feeling for the low limbs of the trees, Luke went on through the gloom of the forest. Now and then there were small openings in the canopy of trees and the moonlight stole down from the heavens and cast a pale, silver glow on the forest floor.

Suddenly the ground vanished beneath his feet, and he stepped into water to his knees. He halted his forward momentum with effort and scrambled backward out of the water. Staring hard, he made out the flat surface of a bayou.

"Panther, help me with the direction again," Luke said.

The Chickasaw did not reply.

"Panther, can you hear me?"

Again there was no response. Luke dropped the reins of the horse and went to the Chickasaw. He heard the raspy labored breathing of the Indian as he touched him on the leg.

"Help me down before I fall," Panther said.

"All right."

Luke took Panther in his arms and laid him on the ground. He felt the sticky wetness of the man's blood on his hands. "Damnation," he cursed. Why wasn't there something he could do for the man?

"I can't find my way in the darkness," Luke said. "But when it is daylight, I'll take you on to your woman." The perfectly flat land and the swamps and bayous had defeated him. In his mountains, he could have used the slope of the land to find his way to any location he desired, regardless of the darkness. He yearned to be gone from this wet delta country and the war between the North and South. It was not his war, yet he was becoming evermore bound up in it. He looked down at the dim form of the Indian. Luke could never desert a friend who had come so bravely to his rescue.

"I will not see the sun again," Panther said.

Luke did not know what to say. He remained squatting beside his comrade. Panther's breathing became more labored and shallow.

Panther said something. The voice was too low for Luke to make out the words.

"What did you say?"

"It is not a good thing to die in the darkness."

"I'll start a fire and we'll have light."

Luke collected a small pile of twigs by feeling around on the ground with his hands, and set them afire with a match. He added larger sticks, and the flames grew shooting sparks straight up into the still air. The night reluctantly retreated back into the trees.

"Is that better?" Luke asked.

"Yes. I want you to take a message to Blackberry Woman."

"I'll surely do that. What is it?"

"Tell her I shall wait for her beyond life where the unknown resides."

"All right." Luke felt his throat tighten. "Anything else?"

"Tell her to bury me in some secret, hidden place in my forest."

"I will help her to do that."

"That would be good, Coldiron." Before Panther had found Blackberry Woman, he had thought that when he died he would simply rot away in some lonely place without a ceremony of any kind. Now he would receive a burial by a loved one and a friend. His death had dignity, and so too would his burial.

Panther shuddered. His eyes opened very wide. He saw the blackness run out of the forest with huge, out-stretched arms. It swept past the fire, and closer still. A great howling came from the center of the blackness, but Panther sprang easily to his feet and leapt away, and then he was on a brightly lit pathway leading toward a rising sun. He had been wrong in telling Coldiron he would not see another sun. This one was the most mag-nificent ever. He ran along the pathway, fleet-footed as when a boy. He laughed, for he had escaped the thing that howled in the center of blackness. He truly would be waiting for Blackberry Woman.

Luke watched the fire burn down to the last tiny live coal. He did not stir to add fuel. Feeling the primal mel-ancholy of death and gloom at his failed attempt to res-cue Susan and Roy, he stared broodingly into the sour darkness.

***

"Are you awake, Fletcher?" Roy said from where he lay on the lower bunk in the jail cell. His arm throbbed and he could not sleep.

"No. Just laying here thinking," Fletcher replied from the upper bunk.

"Don't blame Susan for the fix we're in."

"I don't, not now. At first I did, but I didn't have to go with her. I guess I was bound to end up in prison. I didn't know it would be a Yankee prison."

"Do you think that's what they'll do to us, keep us in prison?"

"They lock up prisoners of war and then turn them loose when the peace comes."

"But we were wearing Union uniforms when we were caught. Will that make any difference?"

Roy waited for a reply. He heard Fletcher take a deep-breath, but no answer came.

"I bet it does, Fletcher," Roy said. "I believe we're in a whole lot of trouble. And Susan, too."

"If we're not prisoners of war, then we're spies. They either shoot or hang spies. Which would you prefer, hanging or being shot?"

"Neither."

"Which one, damnit? Pick one."

Roy had seen men torn apart by exploding cannon balls. But never had he seen a man executed by either hanging or shooting. Some of the older soldiers of his company had talked about it. A dozen riflemen would be chosen. They would stand off at an easy range, and on command simply shoot the condemned. He pictured the bullets tearing through his chest. The pain would be horrible, but only for a fraction of a second. Maybe if several rifle balls hit all at once, the mind could not register pain before death came. His thoughts shifted to a hangman's noose snapping taut around his neck as he fell from a scaffold with a hundred pound sack of sand tied to his feet. He shivered at the two prospects.

"That's two damn poor choices," Roy said. "But I would choose to be shot, and hope like hell every man jack of the firing squad was an expert marksman. Which way would you prefer to die?"

"By hanging."

"Why by hanging?"

"I've heard that when you're hung, you get a hell of a hard on as you die," Fletcher said laughing. "Now that's the way to go. You always want to be prepared when you go into a strange place. You don't know what might be waiting for you."

"Don't joke about something like this," Roy said. "I'd want to be shot rather than hung."

"Yes. It's not a joking matter," Fletcher said solemnly. "If I'm going to be killed, I'd want to be shot, too."

# Chapter Twenty-Nine

"Go right in, Captain Rawls, General Butler and Colonel Trotter are expecting you," the army sergeant said as he opened the door of the office.

The captain acknowledged the sergeant with a nod as he strode past and into the room. General Butler had taken over Colonel Trotter's office at the Cabildo, as the colonel had taken it from Mayor Johnson. The general sat behind the desk. Colonel Trotter had drawn a chair up at the end. The captain saw the colonel's daily logs spread in front of them, and a map of the city.

The captain saluted the two senior officers. "I would have been here sooner, sir, but there was some trouble in the street."

The general shoved the papers aside and rested his hands on the desk. He was a man two inches below average height, with a full brown beard and eyes of matching color.

"Captain, we heard the shooting," the general said. "You look the worse for wear. What happened?"

Rawls glanced down at his uniform. It had been badly soiled during the fight with Coldiron. Though he had not seen his face in a mirror, he knew it must be bruised and swollen. He looked back at the general. "It was an attempt to capture me, sir."

"Obviously it failed," the general said.

"Yes, sir, but three Marines are dead and one hurt."

"What of the attackers? How many were there?"

"Two, sir. Both escaped."

"Two men did that much damage to you?"

Rawls felt his face redden with shame. For two men to kill three Marines and severely beat another was inexcusable. "They attacked from the darkness," he said lamely.

"Why would they want to capture you, Captain?"

"One of them said he wanted me to write a release for the prisoners we caught during the attack on the paymaster."

"Who were the men? Did you know them?"

"No, sir. They were strangers to me." Rawls would not tell the colonel or the general one of the men was Coldiron. He wanted no questions about the man.

"It was concerning those prisoners that we wanted to talk with you," the general said. "It is plain from the attempt on the payroll, and now the attack on you, that there is an organized resistance to our occupation of New Orleans. The prisoners must be punished to teach the citizens a lesson."

"The woman, as well as the two men, should be punished," the captain said.

"Colonel Trotter told me one of the prisoners is a woman."

"Sir, she was the leader, not just one of them," Rawls said.

The general's eyes widened with surprise. "Are you certain of that?"

"Yes, sir, most certainly. I saw her shouting orders to the men just before they charged us trying to break, out of the encirclement we had thrown around them."

"Your report said her name is Susan Dauphin, Colonel. What else is there to know about her?"

"She's the daughter of a prominent family here in New Orleans. Their plantation house was burned. She blames the Union for that. Captain Rawls has investigated the matter, and believes blackguard raiders are guilty of the raid. We know our men had no part in it."

"We will be the scapegoat for all such raids," the general said. "It is to be expected."

"What do you plan to do with the prisoners?" Colonel Trotter asked. General Butler had a reputation as a hard man not known for restraint. The people of New Orleans were in for a difficult time under his rule.

"We will publicly execute them," the general said.

"Sir, Admiral Farragut may not be agreeable to that," the colonel said. "Especially executing the woman."

"Damnit, Colonel, I didn't ask your opinion on this." The general's whiskers bristled as his jaw stiffened. "President Lincoln personally gave me orders to conquer this city and prevent its use by the Confederacy. Farragut captured it before I could arrive with my army, but I'm the person to occupy and hold it. I will do that in the way I think most likely to succeed. I plan to scare the hell out of the population so I can free up as many soldiers as possible to send upriver to help take Vicksburg. Is all that clear?"

"Yes; sir," the colonel said.

"Still, you do bring up an interesting point. We'll not execute them out of hand. A trial will be held to hear what defense the prisoners might have to say for themselves. Colonel, since you are so interested in this case, you shall be one of the officers making up the tribunal. I'll also have two of my senior officers present, and one of the navy captains. I shall preside. What do you think of this way of handling the matter?"

"A hearing before a tribunal is the correct way to proceed," the colonel replied. We still should wait for Admiral Farragut, he thought.

"I'm glad you approve," General Butler said, his tone caustic.

Colonel Trotter held his face expressionless. He was glad this man was not his commanding officer. Admiral Farragut was an entirely different type of person.

"The tribunal shall be convened at eight o'clock to-morrow morning to judge the prisoners. Captain Rawls, I want you there to testify as to what occurred during the raid on the payroll."

"My platoon should also be there, General, for they witnessed what happened."

"Yes. Certainly. All the men who had a role in this must be there. All the facts and evidence must be brought out. Do you have any doubts as to the prisoners' guilt?"

"None, General."

"Good. We'll hang them publicly."

\*\*\*

Susan lay on the cot and stared up into the night that filled the cell thick as soot. The darkness seemed heavy, to have a density forcing her to consciously exert an effort to draw it into her lungs.

She felt on the edge of a great deep. She wanted to cry but dared not, for fear that once she surrendered any degree to her emotions she would completely break down. The worst was yet to come. The Yankees would punish her for what she had done. That punishment would not be so bad if Rawls were not still alive.

As she changed positions on the cot trying to ease the ache in her head, someone began to talk with the guard stationed at the end of the hallway. The conversation ceased, and the door opened with a squeak. Susan lowered her legs gingerly off the cot and went to the bars that held her prisoner.

A man with a lantern swinging by his leg came toward her. The lantern light was directed downward, and she could not make out his features. Then as he came nearer, she recognized Captain Rawls. Her feeling of anger and hate for the man ran through her mind like arctic winter.

The captain held the lantern up to throw light into the cell and upon Susan's face. "I see you're still with us," he said.

Susan gripped the cold, iron bars. When the captain had lifted the lantern to see her, she could also see him. Someone had savagely beaten him. That person must have been Luke Coldiron. What had happened, and why hadn't he killed the captain? Still, the bruises on Rawls made her feel better.

"I'm still here, Susan replied. Then her tone became derisive. "Who put the lumps on your ugly face? Was it Luke Coldiron?"

The captain stepped quickly forward. Susan jerked her hands off the bars and moved back in the cell.

"Coldiron will kill you the next time," she said, finding pleasure in goading the man.

The captain laughed. "You have it backward. The next time I'll kill him. Too bad you won't be around to see it."

"Why won't I?" Susan wanted to know what was going to happen to her, even if it were something very bad.

"Tomorrow you hang," Rawls said in a loud, pleased voice.

Susan fell back a step. Death tomorrow. She had unconsciously expected that she would die. However, the pronouncement shook her to the very core. She would die, and Rawls would live.

The captain lowered the lantern. "Well, I must be going. I just came to give you the good news so you could sleep easily tonight." He turned away.

After a couple of steps, the captain pivoted back toward Susan. "By the way, your two friends Penn and Swift will hang with you." With a chuckle, the captain went down the hallway.

Susan stumbled back to the cot and fell upon it. Roy and Fletcher and she were to hang. The thought drummed in her head. Hang. Hang by the neck until dead. She had brought this fate upon the men and herself. Luke had tried to persuade her to give up on her desire for revenge, but she had not, and now the price of failure would be paid.

"I'm sorry, Roy—I'm sorry, Fletcher!" Susan cried out.

Outside the window of her cell a mockingbird began to whistle snatches of a song it had once heard played. Susan focused on the bird's call, trying to identify the piece of music, and in the effort to banish the captain's face and chase his words from her mind. She thought a time or two that she had identified the music. She was never sure.

The mockingbird fell silent. Susan lay in the darkness with growing pain and dread.

*\*\**

Blackberry Woman jerked awake and sprang from her bed. She was halfway across the room before she caught herself.

Trembling at her sudden awakening, she listened keenly and stared around. The cabin was dark and silent.

The window was a faint square of moonlight. She was alone.

She focused on the last moment of her sleep. A man had called to her—"Blackberry Woman," The voice, full of sorrow and longing, had seemed to come from a very great distance. Strangely, she had not recognized the voice, but only Panther used that name for her.

She walked naked outside into the yard. The ground was cool to her bare feet. The stars overhead were a magnificent canopy of glittering points. Surrounding the cabin clearing on all sides, the forest was a high, dark wall. She moved farther out into the yard. A large bat, hunting in the night, spied her and came to investigate. It made two wild, darting descents past her head and vanished as silently as it had come.

Blackberry Woman concentrated on the blackest section of the forest, the one lying in the direction of New Orleans. Never before had Alice LaVeau, Blackberry Woman, wanted to know anything so much as Panther's exact location at this time. Was he hurt? Surely not dead. However, it was not his habit to be gone two days without telling her his plan.

Panther, where are you? Alice LaVeau held the question in the center of her thoughts and willed herself to sense his presence, opening her mind, reaching out across space, beyond the clearing.

She knew not how she knew, but the nearer woods were barren. There was life, yes, but not human. Her mind expanded further like a thin, sentient wave of her very being pushing out through the forest.

She moved beyond a swamp that she knew, and then a bayou. The further she projected her search, the more laborious it became. She could feel the energy of her body being consumed. Maintaining control of the far-flung field of seeking was precarious, tenuous, like holding smoke in her hand. Panther, where are you?

She wondered how far she was "seeing". At the thought, she lost control of her outward-thrusting ring of probing, and it began to collapse in upon her. She caught the cascading wave, barely, and held it. But only for a second. Then the wave broke free of her mind's hold and fell in upon her, shrinking to nothing.

Alice came to herself standing in the yard in front of the cabin. She was staring at the forest. The trees were visible now, and etched against a sky gray with the coming dawn. Hours had passed while she had searched for Panther.

\*\*\*

Luke came to the edge of the woods near the cabin an hour after the sun had poked its head above the horizon. Panther's body, wrapped in Luke's blanket, was draped over the saddle. The limp form was held there by the hands and feet being tied together under the horse's belly, and the waist secured by a rope to the saddle horn.

Luke moved out into the clearing. Blackberry Woman was standing by the cabin door and watching him as if she had been waiting. He thought her face was without expression until he was closer and saw tears glistening as they coursed down her black cheeks. He halted in front of her.

"Panther is dead," Blackberry Woman said.

"Yes. And I'm very sorry about that."

"I know you are, Mr. Coldiron. I don't blame you for his death." Her shoulders sagged, and she began to shake with great, heart-wrenching sobs.

Luke wanted to comfort the woman, but did not know what to say. He felt the moistness of tears in his own eyes.

After a time, Blackberry Woman quieted her crying. She went to the horse and laid her hand upon Panther's blanketed shoulder. "Who killed him?"

"Union Marines shot him. He was killed helping me to escape from them after they had captured me. He died very bravely."

"That would be very important to Panther, and probably also to you. But not to me. I wanted him to live."

"He told me to give you a message."

"What is it?"

"That he will be waiting on the other side of life for you."

Blackberry Woman straightened her shoulders. "He said that?"

"Yes, ma'am"

"Anything else?"

"That you were to bury him in some secret, hidden place in his forest."

"Yes. His forest," Blackberry Woman looked around at the sunlit woods, contemplating what place would be most pleasing to Panther for his grave.

She pulled her attention back to Luke. She pointed at the tree in the yard. "Look, see the honeyguide. It has been perching on its favorite limb since the daylight first came. It is waiting to lead Panther to a honey tree. Did you know, Mr. Coldiron, that the bird will not guide for me? I've tried to get it to, but it won't. Only for Panther. I think it loved that old Chickasaw. Almost as much as I did."

At Blackberry Woman's gesture toward it, the honeyguide lifted its head and trilled its tuneful, honey hunting call. It turned its head from side to side and, with first one eye and then the other, watched the cabin door for Panther to appear.

"It is good to be loved," Luke said. He thought of Susan. Damn the woman. Why hadn't she agreed to go to New Mexico with him? She would have brightened the days at his ranch so very much. He must not think of what should have been.

"If you will show me where you would like to bury Panther, I'll dig a grave."

Blackberry Woman was staring past Luke at the edge of the woods. In intangible ways she could not describe, she knew they were being watched.

"You must leave at once," Blackberry Woman said. "I'll dig the grave."

"I would like to do this for Panther," Luke said in surprise. "A man's burial is important to his friends."

"It is not that I don't want you to help me, but there are men in the trees just over there," Blackberry Woman nodded her head with a slight motion. "I don't think they are friendly to you."

"I understand," Luke said without looking. He stepped to Panther's body, pulled the ropes loose and lowered the shrouded form to the ground. While still kneeling, he reached inside his shirt and into his money belt. His hand came out with a large wad of bills.

He arose and pressed the money into the woman's hand. "This is only a very small payment for what Panther did for me. I want you to have it."

"Bless you, Mr. Coldiron. You'd better go. The men are coming."

"Hide the money. You don't know what they might do."

"Yes. All right."

Luke glanced across the clearing for the first time. "They are Union Marines," he said, watching the armed men come out of the woods.

"Go, Mr. Coldiron," Blackberry Woman said imperatively.

Luke hesitated. He did not want to leave the woman alone to confront the men.

Blackberry Woman saw Luke's concern for her safety. "I'll be all right. I'm just an old black woman. They won't do anything to me."

"I'm not so sure. I'll act like I'm leaving, but I'll circle back and be there in the edge of the woods where I can watch and see what they do."

He swung astride his horse and walked it past the cabin. One of the Marines shouted. Luke paid him no attention. Once the log cabin sheltered him from the guns of the Marines, he lifted the horse to a run. The forest engulfed him.

\*\*\*

"A white man and a black woman," Corporal Cooper said to his band of Marines as he watched the two people by the cabin. "Looks like he's either leaving, or maybe just got there."

"I wonder what the man has tied to the back of the horse," a second Marine said.

"Let's look the situation over for a minute and then go and see," the corporal said.

He and his men were well hidden in the trees and could not be seen by the people at the cabin. They had just now come upon the clearing. After marking the location of Tate's body so it could be found later, they had continued on. The corporal knew that to return from the search for the Chickasaw before two or three days had elapsed would bring the captain's anger down upon him.

The trail had been lost within an hour after Tate's death. However, the corporal had led on in the same direction and come upon the cabin deep in the forest. There was no sign of the Indian. Still, this might be his home, or the people could tell him where it was.

"The man's unloading the horse," the corporal said. "Let's go and talk with him. Spread out. The Indian might be here and make a break for it."

The corporal moved out of the woods and into the clearing. His men flanked him left and right.

The white man looked in his direction, then climbed onto the horse and reined it away.

"Hold up there," the corporal shouted.

The rider ignored the call and vanished behind the cabin.

"The son of a bitch," the corporal said. But he still had the black woman to question.

Blackberry Woman buttoned the top of her dress and brushed back her mop of hair as the Marines approached. Her face was a rigid mask made of black obsidian. It was soldiers like these who had killed Panther.

"Who was that man that just rode off?" the corporal asked, and he poked a finger in the direction Luke had gone.

"Just some white man," Blackberry Woman replied. "What do you want here?"

"What was his name?"

Blackberry Woman shrugged her shoulders. "What do you want here at my home," she asked again.

"We're looking for a Chickasaw Indian named Panther. Does he live here?"

"He used to. But no more."

"Where does he live now?"

"He doesn't."

"What do you mean?"

"I said he doesn't live here anymore. Can't you hear?"

"Then where?" the Corporal asked, his tone full of aggravation at the woman's unresponsive answers.

Blackberry Woman took a deep breath. "He's dead."

"How do you know that? Where is his body? Tell me straight, woman. We mean you no harm. Answer truthfully and we'll go on our way."

"He is there," Blackberry Woman said, and pointed at the blanket wrapped form on the ground.

Corporal Cooper looked at the object. It could indeed be a body.

"Unwrap that and let us take a look," he ordered the nearest Marine.

Shifting his rifle to one hand, the Marine stooped and flipped back the blanket. The upper half of Panther's body lay exposed. His open eyes stared directly up into the Marine's.

"Goddamn," the Marine exclaimed, straightening hastily and stumbling backward.

The honey guide had perched quietly on the limb of the tree as it watched the humans. Now, at the sight of Panther's dead face, the bird squawked loudly and hurled itself into the air. It swooped down, passing so close over the Indian that its feathers touched the upturned face. It zoomed steeply up, beating the air with its wings and screeching wildly. The bird turned on a wing tip and dove back. Its screech became an angry chatter, almost human in its emotion.

The honeyguide hurtled past the corporal, its wings striking the man's hat. The man ducked.

"What the hell is wrong with the crazy bird?" the corporal cried.

The honeyguide climbed to treetop level, then immediately reversed direction and plunged down at the men standing near Panther. The bird screeched and chattered in a frenzied, jumbled mixture of sound. It leveled off and drove straight for the face of the Marine who had uncovered Panther's body. At the last possible instant to avoid crashing into the man, the bird turned skyward. The Marine almost fell in his hasty effort to get out of the way of the threatening bird.

The honeyguide returned again, like a rocket, its mouth wide and shrieking furiously. It zoomed in, attacking a third man, and only veered away at the last fraction of space between them.

With the men ducking and dodging, the bird continued its assault until it had vented its anger on every one of them.

At last the honeyguide fluttered up into the trees. It settled weakly onto its usual perch. It called out in a series of low, mournful notes.

"I'll shoot that damn thing before it starts that crazy flying again," the corporal said. He raised his rifle to his shoulder.

"No!" Blackberry Woman cried. She jumped toward the Marine to knock the gun aside.

The rifle cracked an instant before her fingers could reach it.

The bullet struck the sleek body of the honeyguide, exploding it in a puff of gray feathers and bleeding flesh. The mutilated body of the bird tumbled end over end as it fell. There was the most fragile thump as the bird struck the ground.

"Go find Panther!" Blackberry Woman cried out to the dead honeyguide. "Guide him safely to the other world!"

# Chapter Thirty

The two Marines, one a sergeant and the other a young private, came to Susan's cell. They were both armed with pistols. The private carried a pail of water. He unlocked the cell door and set the pail inside on the floor.

"General Butler has arrived and wants to hear your case," the sergeant said looking through the bars at Susan. "Wash and straighten yourself."

"So I'll be presentable for my execution?" Susan said.

"I hope you get the firing squad," the sergeant said. "I'd surely volunteer for it. Or I'd be the hangman. One of the men you killed was a friend of mine."

The sergeant motioned at the door. "Lock her up, private."

The private pulled the door closed and turned the key in the lock. Susan thought there was a trace of sympathy for her in his young face. Perhaps executing a woman bothered him.

"You've got a half hour, and then we'll be back for you," the sergeant told Susan in a hard voice.

Susan watched after the two men until the door at the end of the hallway closed. The customary time for the execution of a prisoner was dawn, or so it had been in the books she had read. It was full dawn now. Her hands began to tremble. Death, and the unknown that followed frightened her. There was no way to stop its advance. She pressed the palms of her hands against her thighs to quiet them. Her enemies must not see fear in her as they leveled their rifles, or put a hangman's noose around her neck.

Nor should they see any sign of weakness. She removed the bandage from her head and tossed it aside. The ache from the bullet wound was still there, throbbing inside her skull. However, to someone going to her execution, what was a little pain?

She lifted the pail and poured water into the metal washbasin on the stand. She waited for the water to become still and flat and then looked at her reflection in the mirror-like surface. There were creases at the corners of her eyes that had not been there before. The lips were thinner. She had aged considerably during the past three days. The water mirror shattered as her fingers pierced it.

The water was pleasantly cool as she dipped her hands and brought it up to splash on her face. She washed slowly, savoring these last moments of performing such a familiar, routine task. With the comb her aunt had brought her, she untangled her hair and combed it neatly back from her face and over the raw wound.

Susan examined the ill fitting Yankee Marine uniform that she wore. It was badly wrinkled, and stained with dirt from her fall to the ground when the mare had been killed. A person should be allowed to die in the clothing that showed who and what she was. But that was not to be. She brushed at the dirt with her hands, but had little success in removing it.

She sat down on the edge of the cot. What were poor, crippled Roy and Fletcher doing at this time? Were they, too, preparing themselves for the execution? And were they blaming and cursing her for leading them to their deaths?

The door opened at the end of the hallway, and the sergeant and the private came toward her cell. Their booted feet beat drum-like on the wooden flooring.

\*\*\*

Susan came into the large Parish courtroom ahead of the two Marines. She was surprised to find five Union officers, three army, one naval and one Marine, seated behind a long table just in front of the high judge's bench. They stared at her with faces of stone.

Roy and Fletcher sat at the defendants' table. The pain in Susan's head faded away to nothing as she looked at the faces of her comrades, swollen and scabbed with dried blood. She knew they would have equally severe wounds beneath their clothing and the bandages on Roy's arm and Fletcher's hand.

Four Marines armed with pistols stood just behind Roy and Fletcher. Off to the side of the officers, a corporal sat at a small table by himself. Pen and ink were in front of him. He would be the recorder of her death sentence.

"Take a seat there beside the other two prisoners, Miss Dauphin," the army officer in the center directed.

Susan recognized the officer's rank from the gold braid on his dress uniform. He would be General Butler. She walked to the indicated position and sat down beside Roy. Her two guards stepped back to stand with the four already there.

Her eyes met Roy's. He smiled a thin, wistful smile. Fletcher was looking at her. His eyes told her nothing of what he was thinking. Both men turned away from her and looked at the assembled officers.

General Butler spoke. "This is a military tribunal convened to hear evidence against you three and to render judgment. The proceeding shall be recorded. You are charged with murder. There is a lesser charge of attempted robbery. However, that can await the resolution of the more serious offense."

General Butler focused on Susan. "For the official record, state your name and how you plea to the charges."

"My name is Susan Dauphin and I surrender myself to you as a prisoner of war. I demand to be treated as such. You have no right to try me for either of the acts you listed. They are not crimes in time of war. My comrades will make the same claim, I am sure."

General Butler almost smiled. "Your plea will be noted." He looked at Roy. "Your name and plea."

"Roy Penn. And I make the same claim as Susan."

"So noted."

The general nodded at Fletcher. "And you."

"Fletcher Swift. I also tell you I am a prisoner of war."

The general spoke. "All three of you claim to be prisoners of war. Therefore you must be claiming to be Confederate soldiers. Yet you do not wear Confederate uniforms. In fact you have on the uniforms of Union Marines. Those are the very same uniforms you wore yesterday when you killed three Union Marines while attempting to rob the Union paymaster. Please explain this strange situation to this tribunal. The rules of war are very old and very strict regarding the wearing of a uniform of an enemy, so be very precise in your answer. We shall listen."

Susan knew their defense was puny. Worse than that, it had no chance of success. She and her two comrades were lost. Rawls was correct. Their fate was sealed. This hearing before the tribunal was but a charade, for in the end the verdict would be guilty and they would be executed.

She sprang to her feet and spoke angrily. "You are invaders. You come with your big ships and their murderous cannon and your thousands of men and conquer our city. We did nothing to harm you. We wanted no war, yet you make war upon us. Some of your men raid our plantations and homes for personal wealth. My father was killed by such a band of men, and our house burned. And those men go unpunished. Then, when we strike back and fight in the open, face-to-face, we are charged with murder."

Susan's voice softened. "How incredibly unfair your actions are. We beseech you to take us as prisoners of war, for surely we are as much soldiers as any Confederate or Union man or woman can possibly be."

"Then you do not deny shooting the Marines yesterday during your attack on the paymaster?" the general said.

Susan hesitated at the specific question. If she admitted the act, then she pronounced her own guilt and doom. However, she would be found guilty in any event, for there were at least twenty Marines who had witnessed the battle. They would testify against her.

"I was the leader of the band of Confederates. And I alone shot the three Marines. Roy and Fletcher are innocent of killing the Yankees, or anybody. And further, both of the men are Confederate soldiers who fought at Fort Jackson against Admiral Farragut. They are brave soldiers who should be treated with respect, and as prisoners of war."

Roy uttered a gasp. Susan quickly touched his hand in a gesture telling him to remain silent. She had sacrificed herself to try to save him and Fletcher.

Colonel Trotter felt a thrill at the woman's passionate answer and taking upon herself the full responsibility for the killing of the Union Marines. However, her offer to die to save her comrades would not succeed. Had she been a man and Admiral Farragut sat as senior officer of the tribunal, then the offer would have stood an excellent chance of being accepted. But she was not a man, and General Butler presided here today.

"You have acknowledged your guilt, Miss Dauphin, and that is so noted," the general said. "Now we will hear testimony from witnesses to the event, to determine the innocence or guilt of Penn and Swift."

The general called to the sergeant of the guards. "Call in Captain Rawls. Tell the other men to stand by, for we will need them shortly."

\*\*\*

General Butler said nothing until the prisoners and guards had left the courtroom and the sergeant had closed the door behind them. Then he turned to the officers at the table. "Gentlemen, you have heard the prisoners' pleas and the testimony against them. Now you must decide whether or not the woman and the two men are guilty or innocent of the charge of murder."

"Sir, shouldn't we first discuss the pleas?" Colonel Trotter asked. "Is there any basis for their treatment as prisoners of war?"

The general concentrated on the Marine officer. "Colonel, you know the rule of war that applies when a man, and a woman in this case, are caught carrying out a hostile act while dressed in the uniform of the enemy. In case you have forgotten, it states that person is a spy, and as such is subject to being executed."

"But the rule does not say they must be executed. And further, sir, these are not foreign enemies. They are our own people. Until a year ago they were looked upon as citizens and friends. We should show leniency toward them."

"They have shown nothing but hostility for us. Their bullets kill just as readily as any enemy's. Already the Union has lost tens of thousands of men in battles to put down the rebellion of these Southern states. There is only one question in front of us—are these three people guilty or innocent of the charges brought against them? Colonel, you be the first to state your position on this."

"There is no doubt of their guilt, but I—"

"Thank you, Colonel," General Butler interrupted. He turned to the naval officer. "Captain Francis, your vote?"

"Guilty, sir."

"Colonel Haislip?"

"Guilty, sir."

"Colonel Townsend?"

"Guilty, sir."

"I agree with you gentlemen. The verdict is unanimous."

The general spoke to the recorder. "Did you get the officers' votes?"

"Yes, General."

"We shall have a public hanging of the prisoners," the general said to the officers of the tribunal. "The punishment shall be carried out one hour before dark today. Colonel Haislip, make the preparations for the execution."

"Sir, I don't believe there is enough time to build a proper gallows."

"Probably not," the general said. "However, there is a ready answer. The Hartford has been run in to the docks. Since she is the flagship of the conquering fleet of ships, her deck is a proper place to carry out the executions. We can hang the prisoners from the main yardarm. It's more than strong enough to hold all three. Captain Francis, do you see any problem with this?"

"No, sir. I'll go aboard with Colonel Haislip and direct the crew to assist him in the preparation."

"Thank you, Captain. Colonel Trotter, you know the editors of the city's newspapers. Isn't that so?"

"Yes, sir."

"Please inform them of this tribunal and the verdict rendered on the charges against the three defendants. Ask the editors to immediately put out an extra issue of their papers. I want the citizens of New Orleans to know the penalty for harming a Union military man."

"General, that will give the members of the re-sistance time to organize a demonstration, or even an attempt to rescue the prisoners."

"We will have sufficient force on the waterfront to put down any trouble. In fact, I believe any outbreak that is promptly broken will be beneficial to our future control of the city."

"I will have the editors run special editions," Colonel Trotter said.

"Colonel Haislip, turn out enough troops to smash any trouble that arises."

"Yes, sir."

The general raised his voice and called to the sergeant standing near the door. "Bring in the prisoners."

The sergeant opened the door and motioned to the guards in the hallway. Susan, Roy, and Fletcher were marched into the courtroom and arranged standing at the defendants' table.

"A verdict has been reached on the charges of murder brought against you," the general said.

Susan's breath caught. The general's voice was hard as iron, and she knew the verdict. Roy and Fletcher, standing on her left, stiffened.

"Susan Dauphin, you are found guilty of murdering three Union Marines," the general pronounced. "Roy Penn, you also are found guilty of the same crime.

Fletcher Swift, you also are found guilty of the crime. The sentence of each of you is the same. You are to be hung by the neck until dead. The execution shall be carried out one hour before dark this day."

Susan was suddenly very cold, and her brain felt squeezed, as if her skull were shrinking around it. She put out her hand and caught hold of the table to steady herself. They were all going to die.

"I'm sorry! I'm sorry!" Susan sobbed to her two comrades.

"Please don't cry for me," Roy said, catching Susan by the hand and looking into her anguished face.

"Nor me," Fletcher said in a hoarse voice. "Dying is a one man job. You worry about your death. I'll worry about mine."

"Take the prisoners back to their cells, sergeant," the general ordered.

"Move out," the sergeant directed curtly. He chucked a thumb toward the door.

Fletcher pivoted away from Susan and Roy. His head lifted and he led off. Roy fell in behind.

Susan came last. Her heart cramped, and her mind tried to draw back from the certainty of death. But it could not.

# Chapter Thirty-One

"I'm not going to let them hang me," Roy said. He looked straight ahead and spoke in a voice that only Fletcher could hear. "I'd rather be shot dead trying to escape."

Roy walked close beside Fletcher down the long passageway leading from the courtroom to the jail cells deep in the rear of the courthouse. He could hear the tramp of the four guards following a few paces behind.

"The rope scares me, too," Fletcher said. "But whatever we do has to be done before they lock us up. Do you have a plan?"

"We'll be out of their sight for a couple of seconds just after we turn the corner into the cross passageway. We can whirl and jump them when they come 'round."

"We can't whip four men—even if we both had our two hands."

"I know. We'll break past them and run for the outside door."

"My God, Roy," Fletcher said in a hoarse whisper. "You want us to commit suicide. They'll shoot us all to hell."

"That's the best plan I can think up. Do you have a better one?"

Fletcher was silent for a few steps. "No I don't."

"We're going to die in a few hours anyway. This way, we'll either escape or we'll he shot. There'll be no hangman's noose."

"The guards might miss with their pistols," Fletcher said hopefully.

"Yeah, they might. Are you with me?"

"Hell yes." Fletcher's voice was firm.

"All right then. Hit them hard, knock them out of your way. Don't let them catch hold of you."

"At least I'll have the satisfaction of smashing a couple of them. Maybe I can grab a gun."

"Stop talking," one of the guards called roughly.

Life had never seemed so sweet to Roy now that he had pronounced his own quick and certain death. There was really no chance of escaping. If the guards inside the building did not shoot them, the ones outside would. He breathed deeply, wonderfully alive. He smelled not the stale air of the ancient courthouse, but rather the odor of freshly turned soil, and in his mind saw the dark, rich earth of his father's farm rolling away from the moldboard of the familiar farm plow. Some men cursed the hard labor of holding the plow and guiding it behind a team of horses. Not Roy. Not until late in the season when the soil was hard and smelled only of the dust filling his nose. He was proud of the straightness of the furrows he could plow. When he had a series of exceptionally well-done furrows, he'd call his father to come and see them. Roy immensely enjoyed his father's deep voice as he bragged about the quality of his work. Never again would he hear that loving voice. He blinked away tears.

His thoughts jumped to Susan. She felt responsible for the deaths of the others. And now he and Fletcher would soon be dead. That would be terrible for her.

But only for a few hours. Then the rope would end her suffering. I will miss you, beautiful Susan.

Roy heard Fletcher's breathing as they turned the corner into the side passageway. His friend was as scared as he was. The guards were temporarily out of sight behind. The jail cells were directly ahead. The iron-barred door of the cell from which they had been taken earlier still gaped open.

Roy and Fletcher pivoted to the rear. In two or three heartbeats, the guards would appear. Roy lifted his arms. Oh God, how he wished he still had a left hand to hit with.

The four Marine guards came around the corner. Their eyes flared wide in surprise. They reached swiftly for the pistols on their belts.

Roy and Fletcher sprang at the Marines. Roy drove between the two on his side. He struck each one in the chest with an elbow, hurling them spinning apart. Then he was past them and tearing down the hallway.

His pounding feet echoed from the walls. His arms pumped, the handless one feeling awkward. It no longer hurt.

Where was Fletcher? Had he made it past the guards? Yes, there he was, running a little bit behind.

Thunder filled the passageway as the Marines fired their pistols. Roy tensed, expecting to feel the shock of a bullet striking him.

"Roy, wait!" Fletcher called out with pain-filled urgency.

Roy looked to the side. Fletcher was running unsteadily, and leaning far forward, as if his head and shoulders were somehow being propelled faster than his feet. He held a pistol in his hand. He had wrested the weapon from one of the guards.

Now Roy knew why no bullets had hit him. The guards, seeing Fletcher with a gun, had all fired at him. How bad was he wounded?

"Take it," Fletcher cried desperately, holding out the pistol.

Roy reached out and grabbed the gun. Fletcher smiled at him, sad and yet victorious.

"I'll not hang," he said across the distance that separated them.

Fletcher fell as if tripped, and rolled along the floor.

Die quickly, my friend, Roy thought as he faced to the front. He hurtled on a dozen steps, to slide to a stop slamming into the outside door. He stuck the pistol under his stub of an arm and tripped the heavy door latch.

Hope soared in him. Escape just might be possible. He yanked the door open.

A pistol exploded at his rear. The bullets ripped splinters from the doorjamb and hurled them like a fistful of darts into the side of his face. He felt the sting. It was nothing.

He snatched the pistol from under his arm and bolted out the door.

He halted instantly and stood stock still on the wide stoop of the courthouse. Six Marines were drawn up in the center of the street. Every one of their rifles were pointed at the door. They shifted instantly to center on Roy. The shooting inside had alerted the outside guards of the escape attempt.

"Drop the gun," the corporal of the guards barked.

Roy stared at the open bores of the rifles. I don't want to die, he said to himself. Hadn't he said those same words before when he lay on the deck of the boat that had brought him upriver from Fort Jackson?

How long ago had that been? Only a few days, yet it seemed such a long time in the past. He should not be thinking of those things now. The sound of the guards was close behind him in the hallway. If he hesitated, he would be taken prisoner again.

His heart, lonely and bare, struggled within his chest. Fletcher had been victorious. So, too, could he be, for he could choose to die.

Roy cocked the pistol and swiftly raised it. He pointed it at an older Marine with a hard twist to his face.

"Shoot straight," Roy said looking into the old Marine's face.

Six rifles crashed. Six bullets drove into Roy's chest.

\*\*\*

At the first explosion of pistol fire, Susan leapt from the cot where she sat and hurried to the bars of her cell. The shots had come from the rear area of the courthouse. She feared what they might mean to her comrades.

She heard a single pistol shot, and then a volley of rifle fire from the front of the courthouse. Could Roy and Fletcher have made it to the outside?

She stood waiting, gripping the bars with both hands. What had happened? Why didn't someone come and tell her? Were her friends wounded, or dead? Was it possible they had escaped?

No one came, and Susan finally retreated back to sit on the cot. Damn the Yankees. She had a right to know if something had happened to Roy and Fletcher.

\*\*\*

Walt's eyes were fastened on the coffin that held Annette's body. Flowers were piled in a large mound upon the elaborately decorated coffin. He smelled the pleasant aroma of the blossoms, like breathing Annette's perfume again, for the last time.

The coffin had been removed from the hearse and placed upon a portable platform draped in blue satin. Many mourners—half a hundred quadroon placees, and several mulattos and blacks—had gathered to show their respects for the young woman and to grieve her passing.

Just beyond the assemblage of mourners was the head-high stone burial vault that Walt had ordered to be speedily built in the Negro cemetery. The two black workmen who had constructed the crypt stood silently beside it. They watched Walt.

The burial ceremony for Annette had been completed for some time and the mourners waited for Walt to give the order to place the coffin inside the vault and seal the door. He knew they waited, but he could not bring himself to take the final action that would forever separate him from the lovely young woman. Memories flashed through his mind of Annette's smiling face and wondrous, black eyes. She could kiss him from across the room with those eyes. And promise him delightful moments that would be his in the future. Promises she always fulfilled. He could feel the touch of her silken skin under his fingers. Never once in all the months and years they were together had she been anything but a joy to him. If God had created anything more beautiful and wonderful than Annette, he had kept it for himself.

Someone touched his arm. Walt turned to see it was Annette's mother. Her eyes were full of misery. Her hand closed on his arm.

"It is time to bury our Annette," she said.

"How much better it would be if I lay there instead of her."

"God plays strangely with us humans."

"Cruelly is a better term."

"Perhaps so. Give the workmen their orders."

Walt looked at the two black men near the crypt. He nodded at them. At the signal, the gathering of mourners broke apart and went off toward the cemetery gate. He sensed Annette's mother moving away.

Walt remained behind and watched the workmen lift the casket from the satin-covered platform and carry it into the burial vault. They reappeared and began to seal the door of the vault with mortar and stone. He did not leave until long after the men had completed their job and left.

He walked mechanically along the sidewalk of the street. He felt lost. Never before had he not had a purpose in life, a pleasure to look forward to, a duel, a drink, a game of cards, something. And for the past several years he had always had Annette to go home to. The world was now without zest, dead. Or was it that without Annette he was the same as dead?

"Mister, want to buy a paper?" a small, shabbily dressed street boy said, thrusting a newspaper in front of Walt's face. "Read all about the Yankees shooting two spies, and one to be hung, a woman."

Walt paid the boy, merely to remove him from blocking the sidewalk, and shoved the folded paper under his arm. He continued on.

Blocks later, he halted. Without conscious intention, he had guided his steps to Exchange Alley. The door to his dueling academy was before him. Perhaps he could

find a semblance of peace in the old, familiar surround-
ings. He entered.

In the far corner of the shadow-filled gymnasium, he
found a chair and sat down. He let his mind wander
where it willed. Let time go by, for it had no value. Actually, time was something to hurry for it would be
lonely and full of sadness. Would time eventually join
him with Annette? Should he hurry it? He pulled his pistol from its holster and stared at it.

\*\*\*

Luke had started to insert the key in the door of Bouchard's gymnasium when he realized it was unlocked.
Someone was inside. Was it the duelist, or the Marine
Captain Rawls? He drew his pistol and eased the door
open silently.

Bouchard sat in a far corner of the large room. A
pistol was in his hand. He regarded Luke silently and
without expression.

"All right if I come in?" Luke asked.

"Yes," Bouchard replied. At the sight of Coldiron he
recalled the newsboy's words about the Southern spies,
one a woman. He holstered his pistol and picked the
newspaper up from the floor beside the chair.

"Take a look at this," Walt said extending the paper to Luke as he came nearer.

"What's in it?"

"Maybe something about Susan Dauphin. Maybe nothing. I haven't read it."

Luke opened the newspaper and looked at the front page. He stiffened as his eyes scanned the headline.

"Well, anything of interest to you?" Bouchard said, noting Luke's reaction.

"The Union military plans to hang Susan today," Luke said angrily. "They've killed Roy Penn and a man named Fletcher Swift trying to escape. The paper describes an attack on the Union paymaster that the three are said to have done."

"What time is the hanging?" Walt asked.

"Six o'clock this evening on board the Union ship Hartford. I've got to do something to help her."

"That's not possible. You know there'll be hundreds of Union soldiers surrounding her."

"I've got to go and see."

"I'll go with you."

"I'd rather you didn't. I've cost you too much already. Why risk more by going with me?"

"I have lost my woman. I would like to see you keep yours."

"She's not my woman."

For the first time since Luke had entered the academy, Walt's face showed emotion. It was an expression of disbelief.

*** 

The crowd on the dock broke into a wild roar as Susan was brought out of the ship's cabin and into sight on the deck of the battleship Hartford. They surged forward, as if intent on storming aboard and freeing her. She heard their fierce shouts: "You can't hang her!" "You can't hang a woman!"

The wall of soldiers lining the dock leveled their bayoneted rifles at the throng of civilians. The captain of the guard drew his pistol with his left hand and a sword with his right.

"Stand back or we will fire!" he shouted in a stentorian voice. He lifted his sword above his head in preparation to give the signal to his men to shoot.

The front ranks of the crowd saw the deadly determination in the Union officer and his men. They stopped and held back against those pushing from the rear. The human tide slowed and halted. The volume of the Confederate cries gradually diminished to an angry muttering.

Susan looked away from the crowd and out over the river. She was now dressed in the trousers and shirt she had worn just before changing into the Marine uniform. The garments had been found by the Yankees in the saddlebags of the mare. They had been brought to her at noon, and she had been ordered to exchange them for the uniform. Immediately thereafter, she had been taken from the courthouse and marched to the ship.

No words had been spoken about Roy and Fletcher, but she knew they were dead. All her comrades were now dead, and their deaths had been caused by her desire for revenge. Now she was to die by hanging. These were the final moments of her life.

She was glad the river would be the last scene she would see for she had always loved it. It was sad that only Union ships were on the water. Never again would she see the trading ships flying the flags of a hundred countries, nor the whalers from the faraway seas, nor the river craft.

"Do you need some help to walk?" the army sergeant, who was to be the hangman asked, in a kind voice.

Susan saw the noose dangling from the yardarm of the ship and swinging in a little arc. Beneath it was a small platform with a short rise of four steps leading up to the top.

"I think I can make it," Susan replied.

She was chilled. Her teeth were on the verge of beginning to chatter.

She took a step. Her legs felt leaden, the knees wobbly. The sergeant caught her by the upper arm to steady her.

"Just a short ways to go," the sergeant said. "Have courage."

"I don't need your help," Susan said. She straightened to stand more erect. She hardened the control over her legs. She had taken men's lives. She must not flinch from the taking of hers.

She placed her foot on the first step of the platform. The noose swung to a slow breeze directly before her. She could not take her eyes off it.

She breathed deeply. Her life was to be short. Neither man nor woman was meant to last forever, or even for very long.

She lifted her foot to the second step, the third, the fourth. She stood on the top of the raised platform.

The sergeant pulled her hands behind her back, and bound them tightly together with a rough hemp cord. He reached and brought the noose above her head.

# Chapter Thirty-Two

"It's Susan!" Luke cried out to Bouchard above the angry roar of the crowd that surrounded them. His eyes were fastened on the woman moving slowly across the deck of the Union warship. A big soldier walked beside her. He was holding her by the arm.

"They're actually going to hang her," Walt said. "I didn't believe they would."

"I must do something to help her," Luke said.

Luke, his heart racing, flung a look around. He and Walt had pushed their way forward into the dense press of people on the dock. The growls and curses emanating from a thousand Southern throats was a growing storm. The Union soldiers, nervous and taut, gripped their rifles tightly. One movement to help Susan or a violent action upon the soldiers would precipitate a volley of rifle fire. In the packed crowd, hundreds would die.

Walt looked at Luke's bleak face. He was coiled tight as a spring.

"Don't do anything foolish," Walt warned.

"She must not die." Luke's hand clutched the pistol in the belt under his vest.

Walt clasped Luke by the arm. "It's too late. Much too late. Let's hope she dies quickly."

***

Something is wrong, Admiral Farragut told himself as he stared through the round field of magnification of the telescope. He braced himself more solidly against the bow deck cannon of the gunboat Itasca. More steady now, he trained the telescope on the teeming throng of civilians on the dock near the berthed Hartford. A huge gathering such as that one could only mean trouble. What was happening?

"Give me full speed ahead," the admiral called to Lieutenant Commander Kennor, Captain of the Itasca.

"Aye, sir," the commander said. He nodded at the deck officer, who stood nearby and had heard the admiral's order. "Full speed, lieutenant."

The lieutenant stepped quickly to the signal arm connected by a cable to a duplicate indicator in the engine room below. He rang up full speed. There was an answering jangle as a seaman in the engine room moved his indicator to acknowledge the new speed.

The pistons of the Itasca's steam engine began to pound harder. The deck started to vibrate. The bow wave doubled in height and grew a white cockscomb.

In the evening of the first day after leaving New Orleans, the admiral had found the frigate Colorado anchored just outside the bar at the mouth of the Mississippi River. He had boarded the ship and given his orders to Captain Bailey to return to the East Coast and place his vessel at the disposal of the naval department. That night he remained aboard and slept in the comfort of the larger ship. With morning, he again boarded the Itasca and steamed upriver. He stopped and inspected Fort Jackson and Fort St. Phillip, now manned by Union garrisons left behind by General Butler. The soldiers were speedily repairing the damage done to the forts by the cannonballs of the Union flotilla. In a very few days, the forts and their cannon would once again be fully functioning military installations.

"Take me up to the port side of the Hartford," the admiral told the commander. "Then pull away and anchor in the river close to shore." The admiral would avoid the crowd by boarding his flagship on the side away from the dock.

The Itasca came up fast on the berthed Hartford. The admiral saw the Marines on the dock with their bayoneted rifles lowered threateningly, holding the civilians of the city at bay. Aboard the Hartford, twenty or so seamen and an army sergeant were assembled under the yardarm of the main mast. In the center of the gathering, a lone civilian stood on a raised platform.

The Itasca slowed and made the starboard turn to run up beside the Hartford. The commander brought the gunboat in skillfully, backing her down at the proper time to gently nudge the tall wooden side of the flagship.

Admiral Farragut tossed his small bag of personal items up to the Hartford seaman waiting above with Colonel Trotter. He scrambled up the Jacob's ladder to the main deck.

"Welcome aboard, admiral," Colonel Trotter said, saluting the senior officer.

"What's happening here, colonel?" the admiral demanded to know, staring at the young man on the platform and the hangman's noose the army sergeant was ready to place around his neck.

"A hanging, sir. I stopped it when I saw the Itasca coming. I thought it best that you review the matter."

"You did right, colonel." Then the admiral seemed to be taken aback. "Am I seeing correctly—is that a woman?"

"Yes, sir. It's a woman."

"What's the charge against her?"

"She's a Confederate civilian caught in a Union Marine uniform. She was part of, or maybe even led, an attempt to rob the paymaster when he came ashore to pay the men. Three of our Marines were killed and three wounded during the capture of the Confederates. We killed seven of them. We took three prisoners."

"When did all of this happen?"

"Yesterday morning, early."

"And already there's a hanging?"

"General Butler convened a military tribunal this morning to hear the charge against the three prisoners. They were found guilty. The general sentenced them to be hung. The two male prisoners tried to escape and were killed in the attempt."

"So General Butler has sentenced a woman to be hung. Why on my ship?" The campaign had gone splendidly so far, the forts overrun and New Orleans under Union control. Now Butler, in his usual harsh manner, could be stirring the citizens to fierce resistance or outright revolt.

"The general wanted the execution to be done today so as to quickly put fear in the population. There was no time to build a gallows, so he decided to use the yardarm of the Hartford. Immediately after the verdict of the tribunal, the newspapers ran a special edition telling of the execution. The general approved that, for he wanted the people to see the hanging."

The general has his crowd all right, the admiral thought as he looked down at the multitude of angry faces. But will we have to shoot part of the people to keep control'? "Where is the general?"

"Watching from the top floor of the Cabildo, sir."

The admiral stared over the rooftops at the Cabildo. He could see the row of windows of the upper floor, but not the general or anyone who might be standing there. Maybe it is best that you're not here, thought the Admiral. Your presence could complicate what I must do.

"Who was the chief witness against the prisoners?"

"Captain Rawls was in charge of the capture detail."

"Call him over here."

Colonel Trotter raised his arm and motioned to the captain, who had been closely watching the admiral and Trotter. He came up and saluted.

"Yes, sir, admiral," the captain said.

"Colonel Trotter tells me you're the main witness against the woman. Are there any doubts of her guilt?"

"Absolutely none, sir. I caught her red-handed. She shot one of my men. I saw her do it."

"All right, captain. But hanging her here and now is not the correct way to handle this matter." He again looked at the people on the dock. These were his people for he was a Southerner himself and had a home in Virginia, at Norfolk. He had moved to the northern outskirts of Washington, D.C., Shortly before the war had begun. He had joined the Union cause, for he believed the nation must remain as one. No rebellion could be allowed. To accomplish this, the secessionist states had to be beaten. However, the conquering of the people of the Confederate South must be done with the least possible loss of life. Butler's way was wrong. New Orleans could best be controlled with kind firmness, and not by a rule of savage executions.

"The woman shall not hang," the admiral said firmly.

"But, Admiral, General Butler has already sentenced her," Rawls said. "To reverse the sentence now would weaken General Butler's hand for the future."

"Captain, I'd like to remind you of something. The campaign to capture the Mississippi River has been a naval operation from the beginning. General Butler is subject to my authority. I have not yet turned the city over to him. I say the prisoner shall not hang."

"Yes, sir," the captain said. If only the admiral had been live minutes later, the hanging would now have been finished. Bad luck.

"General Butler will disagree with me on this," the admiral said. He will curse and rage, the admiral thought, and he grinned, showing his teeth. "But I am the flag officer of the West Gulf Blockading Squadron. The prisoner is aboard my ship, and protected by my Marines and sailors."

The admiral's tone become conciliatory. "Captain, you know the prisoner is guilty. I'm not dismissing that fact. I'm saying she shall not hang, at least not now."

"Then what do you propose to do?" Colonel Trotter asked.

"I shall send the prisoner back to Washington and ask that her sentence be reviewed by the Secretary of Navy, Gideon Wells."

The admiral spoke to Captain Rawls. "Go ashore and obtain the clerk's transcript of the tribunal's hearing and promptly return back here. Say nothing to the general, or to any member of his staff." The admiral's eyes locked with the captain's. "I will personally inform the general of my decision. Do you understand my meaning?"

"Yes, sir."

"Good. Then you shall transport the prisoner to Washington."

"Me, sir?" Rawls said in surprise.

"Yes, you."

"Sir, I request someone else take the prisoner east. I wish to remain with the fleet here on the Mississippi."

"You shall go, Captain. Your testimony will be important to the department. However, once you have given your deposition, you are ordered to return to your post here on the first available ship. You should be back with the fleet in a month or so. There'll be plenty of fighting left for you. Now I want no more discussion on this. Carry out your orders."

"Yes, admiral."

"Take the Itasca downriver and catch the Colorado before she sails tomorrow morning. You must hurry. Commander Kennor will have to run the river in the dark, but I believe he has enough knowledge about the current and the sandbars so that he can do it. Also, there will be a moon. I'll have the boat refueled with coal while you are ashore after the transcript. Are there any questions?"

"No, sir." Damn the rebel witch. There was great wealth in the city, even after all the contributions the citizens had made to their rebel cause. She was preventing him from taking his share. Once they were at sea he would allow her the freedom of the ship. The first dark night, she would vanish over the side. Then Rawls would transfer to the first ship the Colorado encountered that was bound for New Orleans. He could be back at his post in far less time than a month.

*** 

Hang me, damn you, hang me quick, Susan pleaded silently. I can't stand any more terror at the thought of the rope strangling me. Her legs were trembling, and she was ready to fall. Her eyes had lost their sharpness, and their range barely encompassed the hangman's noose the sergeant held in his hand.

She looked at the sergeant, wanting to know why he delayed. He was staring past her with a questioning expression. He nodded, as if acknowledging some order she had not heard.

The sergeant released the noose, and it swung away from Susan. "Turn around," he told her. "You are not to hang today."

Susan's mind could not readily accept the meaning of the sergeant's words. Had he said she was not to hang? What had changed? She had been prepared to die. Now the sudden reprieve. The one thought solidified in her mind: she was not to hang. She swayed and started to fall.

"Don't faint," the sergeant said, and he caught her by the shoulders with a firm grip. He held her erect. His voice became gentle and kind. "You've done better than most men I've seen brought up to the rope. Don't spoil it now." He squeezed her shoulder hard to emphasize his words.

Susan was glad for the man's strong hands, for otherwise she would have fallen from the platform. She struggled to pull her scattered strength together.

"You got your legs yet?" the sergeant asked.

Susan lilted her head. Life, warm and joyous, was flowing back into her body. "Yes. I'm all right now."

"Good. I'll untie your hands. You owe Admiral Farragut for your neck. He's a fine officer."

Susan, intoxicated with relief by the halting of her execution, turned to look at the admiral. The sergeant had said the officer was a fine man. How could that be since he was the conqueror of New Orleans? His ships with their cannon bad devastated the forts on the river. One of his cannonballs had taken Roy's hand. Poor dead Roy. And how much responsibility did the admiral have for the death of her father?

The admiral was watching her with a studied set to his gaze. Captain Rawls and a Marine colonel were also staring at her. The captain faced away as Susan's attention settled on him. His hate for her was evident. Couldn't the other officers see it?

Susan's eyes followed the captain as he marched off across the deck and went down the gangway toward the crowd on the dock. You failed to get me hung, you bastard.

"Lock the prisoner up, sergeant," Colonel Trotter said. "Captain Rawls will take responsibility for her when he returns."

Susan's blood froze. She had barely escaped being hung, and now she would soon be in the hands of her worst enemy. She had not evaded death after all. It had been merely delayed a very short time.

\*\*\*

"Thank God the navy officer from the gunboat stopped the execution," Luke said.

"With all the gold braid on his sleeve, I judge he must be Admiral Farragut," Walt replied. "He doesn't want a hanging for fear of a riot."

"I am damn glad he stopped it, for whatever his reason," Luke said. "That man coming down the gangway is Captain Rawls. He surely doesn't seem pleased by the turn of events. Soon as he leaves, let's find out what's going to happen next."

The crush of civilians fell silent as Rawls halted at the bottom of the gangway. His eyes ranged over them with a contemptuous air. "Break them up, scatter them," the captain ordered the lieutenant in charge of the Marines lining the dock. "Tell them there will be no hanging."

"Yes, sir," the lieutenant replied. He raised his voice. "No hanging today, folks. Go on about your business. Move out. Clear the dock."

A loud cheer went up from the men in the front of the crowd who had heard the lieutenant's words. They whirled and called out the welcome news to those behind them. The word swept swiftly through the gathering like a wind. A great shout went up.

Luke and Walt moved off buried among the citizens of the city. After a short way, when Rawls had passed and was walking rapidly toward the Cabildo, they halted and looked back at the Hartford. At a command of the lieutenant, the platoon of Marines assembled at the gangway and began to file aboard the ship.

"I've got to find out what they plan to do with Susan," Luke said.

"Better let me do it," Walt said. "I don't think they'll tell you anything. They might even recognize and arrest you."

Luke looked down at his soiled clothing and dirty boots. He rubbed his bewhiskered face. "All right. You would have a better chance."

"Wait here for me."

# Chapter Thirty-Three

"The Yankee gunboat can't be caught," Chesson, the French Creole, said with conviction. "It has an hour's lead on us, twenty miles or more, and the night is almost here."

"If it was anyone but you piloting the boat, I'd agree," Walt Bouchard said. "You can do it."

"I don't think so. We'd have to run at top speed to even have a chance to overtake it. That would be very dangerous in the dark."

"Except for one important fact. You know the river like no other man. That's why I bought half interest in your boat. We must help Luke free his woman from the Yankees."

Chesson spoke to Luke, standing nearby and listening. "The river twists and turns, and new sandbars appear in every flood. During my thirty-five years on the river, I've run aground many times."

"But never stuck fast for long, and never captured by the revenue cutters," Walt said. "You know the river better than the gunboat captain, and he's going to try and run the river in the dark."

"He's a fool." Chesson swung his gaze to look down the Mississippi already darkening with evening shadow. "With a good moon, I can keep us off the sandbars.

But it would be very bad to be caught by the gunboat. She has ten deck cannons and two pivot guns, one on the stern and one on the bow. She carries a crew of at least thirty seamen aboard, and probably some Marines also. They could easily take our boat, or sink it."

"Are you afraid, Chesson?" Bouchard said.

"I'm afraid of nothing," Chesson snapped back. "I just wouldn't like to lose my boat."

"Our boat," Walt corrected the Creole.

Luke watched the growing tension between the two men. Chesson was a large man with gnarled, root-like hands. His face was long, and masked by a black beard streaked with gray. Luke judged him to be about Walt's age. He was obviously not intimidated by the duelist.

Walt and Luke had arrived only minutes before at Chesson's log home on a large bayou downriver from New Orleans. They stood on a long, covered porch facing the water. Luke felt only gloom at Chesson's words.

They had, following the halting of Susan's execution, retreated back across the quay and taken up a position in a side street from where they could observe the Hartford. Two civilians had been allowed aboard the ship, and could be seen talking to the admiral on the quarter deck. Captain Rawls came down the gangway and went hurriedly off toward the Cabildo.

The civilians had left after a few minutes and come along the quay. Walt had known the men, newspaper reporters, and had stopped them as they passed and questioned them about Susan's fate. They had told of the admiral's plans for the prisoner. She was to be taken by the gunboat Itasca downriver today and put aboard the frigate Colorado before it sailed for the East Coast. Admiral Farragut would request that Gideon Wells, Secretary of the Navy, review the case.

Rawls had returned to the ship. Shortly Susan, escorted by Rawls and four armed Marines, left the Hartford. They went the short distance along the quay to the coal dock where the Itasca was being refueled. The four Marines watched while Rawls and Susan went aboard the gunboat and then returned to the Hartford. The last of the boiler coal was loaded into the hold of the gunboat and her lines were cast off. She immediately pulled away from the dock and steamed downriver.

"I need a fast boat," Luke had said, watching the gunboat speed away. "If I could catch the gunboat in the dark, I might be able to slip aboard and free Susan."

"I'm half owner of a fast boat," Walt had replied. "The other half is owned by the best smuggler in all the bayou country. Do you want to use it?"

"God, yes."

"Then come with me," Walt had said. "The boat is a long walk from here and we must hurry."

Luke heard Walt speak to Chesson. "I want you to go with me and pilot the boat. But since you won't, I'll go without you. I'll pilot it myself."

"You'd take the boat without me?" Chesson said in surprise. "Nobody, not even my son, has ever run her unless I was on board."

"I'm going to use the boat with or without you. So make up your mind what you are going to do." Walt's voice had a sharp edge.

Chesson's shoulders hunched like a wounded owl's. Then abruptly his head lifted, and he spread his big hands. His beard parted in a grin of surrender. "I'll go with you. I don't want you to think me a coward. And I want my boat back whole."

"Spoken like a true smuggler," Walt said.

At Walt's words, Chesson glanced at Luke with a questioning expression.

"I've already told Luke that you're a smuggler—the bravest and most skilled in all Louisiana," Walt said.

"That is true without doubt," Chesson said.

The Creole stepped inside the cabin and almost immediately returned with a rifle in his hands. "I may need this," he said. "Come with me."

He jumped down off the porch and led toward the bayou. A pirogue—a boat cleverly crafted from a single cypress log and some fifteen feet long—was tied to a tree on the bank. Luke and Walt climbed into the pirogue quickly. Chesson freed the pirogue and took the stern seat. He picked up the broad-bladed paddle.

"You are in luck for the boat is ready. My son left some time ago to build up steam for a run we were going to make tonight." He lifted the paddle.

The red sun fell out of the sky as Chesson paddled the pirogue out of the bayou and turned along the shore of the Mississippi. He was pulling swiftly and strongly. The pirogue skimmed over the water.

Luke sat amidships. Walt was in the bow and watching forward for the marker Chesson had described to him. The smuggler, fearing the Union military would come to his home and confiscate his riverboat, had moved it to a safe hiding place in a bayou downriver from his cabin.

"There it is just ahead," Walt said.

"I see it," Chesson said.

He swerved the pirogue left and drove it into low hanging branches appearing to be no different from miles of riverbank where tree limbs drooped to touch the water. Within two lengths of the pirogue the leafy curtain parted, and a narrow, twisting bayou stretched ahead.

Chesson drove the craft on along the channel of water overhung by the leaf-heavy branches of the trees. The bayou was a tunnel swiftly filling with the purplish black shadows of night. Mosquitoes were swarming in a dense, buzzing cloud. They pounced upon the men, their long sharp snouts searching for unprotected arms and faces.

Luke turned his collar up. He struck at the mosquitoes, sending some of the pests skittering. He peered ahead where fireflies were hemming stitches in the growing darkness.

He smelled the smoke of burning coal. The smuggler's boat could not be far away.

A moment later, Luke could make out the form of the boat, black and motionless on the water. He judged her length at thirty-five feet with a single, short smokestack and a low center cabin rising not more than a yard above the deck. She was streamlined with her bow curved proudly up. She was built for speed.

Chesson ceased paddling and let the boat coast on. He whistled through his teeth. An answering whistle sounded. A man with a rifle in his hands came out from behind the superstructure of the boat.

"That's my son, Andre," Chesson said.

"Who is with you, pa?"

"Our friend Bouchard, and Luke Coldiron," Chesson replied, driving the pirogue up to the side of the boat.

"Why are they here?" Andre asked.

"To take the boat downriver. We'll make our run some other time. Is the steam up?"

"Yes." Andre held the pirogue steady as the men climbed onto the deck of the boat.

"Bouchard, tie the pirogue to the stern," Chesson said. "We will need it. Andre, cast off from the bank. We have no time to waste."

Chesson moved to the wheelhouse. He bent and checked the reading on the pressure gauge.

"Ready with your line, Andre?" he asked.

"Yes."

"Bouchard?"

"Ready."

The engine labored awake, the screw cutting the water. The boat crept away from the bank and onward through the darkness lying on the bayou. The low hanging limbs brushed the heads of the men, and the black trunks of the trees walked past on the land. The heavy air became a slow breeze. The mosquitoes thinned, some blown away by the wind.

The darkness thickened and congealed as they slid down the bayou. Luke watched the dim outline of Chesson move the helm to keep the boat off the banks that blended without demarcation into the water. The smuggler seemed to have the eyes of a night-seeing animal.

"Watch out for the branches ahead, for we're going to ram through," Chesson called.

He cut the engine. The boat plowed on, shoving aside the obstructing limbs, and broke out into the broad body of the Mississippi River.

The river's current swiftly overcame the momentum of the vessel and halted it. The men and their craft began to float toward the ocean.

All the men were tense, warily scanning the dark river for the lights or the sound of enemy boats. Upstream the faint glow of light from New Orleans broke the night. Downstream, the deep murk lay dense and unbroken. The only sound was the sullen, liquid voice of the mighty Mississippi hurrying toward the Gulf of Mexico.

"I see nothing," Andre said.

"Neither do I," Chesson said. "Do either one of you two?"

"Nothing," Luke said.

"No," Walt said.

Chesson engaged the engine. The boat came alive with a rumble of pistons and a hiss of steam. It moved off with the current.

Luke moved forward and found a seat on a coil of rope. The father and son knew their jobs. The river was their domain, the boat a familiar machine. Let them alone.

The wind created by the speeding boat grew strong on his face. The buzzing fog of mosquitoes fell away behind. From below came the scrape of a shovel and the rattle of coal as Andre stoked the firebox beneath the boiler.

Luke thought of Susan and the danger that threatened her aboard the gunboat with Captain Rawls. She had brought the trouble down upon herself by taking revenge on the Union military. Had enough blood flowed? Were enough of her comrades dead to cool her hatred? It was hard to blame her for her actions. When younger he, too, had found it easy to hate and to kill. Now he fought only when it was absolutely necessary. And now it was necessary to rescue Susan, even if that meant men would have to die. Surely Rawls must die, for he was a thief and murderer.

Walt came and squatted on the deck beside Luke. "It'll be hours before we catch the gunboat," the duelist said.

"If we do," Luke added.

"Yes, we may not. However if anybody can, Chesson is the man to do it. But he'll have to push the boat to its limit."

Chesson called out from the helm. "Andre, come and take the wheel."

A moment later, Chesson came and found a seat on the deck near Luke and Walt.

"We need the moon to see so we won't run aground," he said and swung his arm to point ahead into the darkness.

"It should be up soon," Walt said.

"How long will it take to overhaul the gunboat?" Luke asked.

"I asked about the speed of the gunboats when they first came to New Orleans. I must know about the boats that might chase me if I'm to remain a free man. I believe my boat is three to four knots faster. If that is actually so, then we'll catch the Union boat in five or six hours. With luck, before it reaches the bar."

"Are you at maximum speed now?" Luke asked.

"Yes. We can run like this for a few miles. There is only one channel, and I know the compass heading. The problem comes farther downriver at the Head Of Passes, where the river divides into three branches. Should we take the wrong one, the Yankee boat will get away from us."

Chesson arose and climbed up on the roof of the cabin. He sat down, crossed his legs, and stared ahead.

The boat raced on, the engine throbbing and the water swishing past her hull. The stars drifted along their ancient sky path to the west. Luke begrudged the passage of every second of time.

"There comes the moon," Andre called out from the helm.

"A beautiful thing," Chesson said. "And very valuable to all smugglers."

Luke watched the silver sphere sail up over the horizon. It fought clear of the trees on the riverbank and bathed the broad current of the Mississippi River in a luminous, ghostly light.

Luke stretched himself on the wooden deck. He lay watching the moon inexorably climb the black sky. Now Chesson could run the boat at the top of its speed until the Union gunboat was found.

"While the situation is good, I'm going to sleep," Walt said to Luke. He was tired. All the preceding night, he had not slept. Annette's mother, her friends, and he had held a quiet wake for the dead girl. The lovely face of Annette came to fill his mind, and the sorrow at the loss of her burned his heart. He had seen death so many times, but never the death of someone as deeply loved. He blinked to hold back tears.

\*\*\*

Luke awoke when the chug of the engine died. He sat up hastily. He had not meant to sleep.

"What's wrong?" he asked in the unexpected darkness.

"We've lost the moon," Chesson answered. "Now I must check our position in the channel."

The smuggler turned in the direction where he thought the left bank of the river lay. "Ho! Ho! Ho!" he shouted loudly in a measured cadence through the megaphone of his hands.

He began to count the seconds. At four, a barely discernible echo, weird and hollow, reached the boat. He turned in the opposite direction and shouted out as he had done before. The echo arrived on the count of five.

"We're almost in the center of the river," Andre said.

"Yes, a good position," Chesson replied. "Go straight ahead at half speed."

Luke felt only gloom as he stared up into the sooty heavens. He had also heard the returning echoes from the riverbank and the trees lining it. They could feel their way along by frequently stopping and calling, but precious time would be lost. He hoped the gunboat had also been forced to slow, even more than they had.

"Chesson, how long has the moon been covered by clouds?" he asked.

"A heavy overcast came in about an hour ago. I think a storm is coming."

"Damnation," Luke cursed. "How far have we come?"

"Sixty miles or so. We should soon be at the Head of Passes. The correct channel must be chosen, and that will be most difficult."

Luke lapsed into silence. He watched the black sky and fretted at the wasted minutes.

"What's that?" Luke said. "Is it getting lighter?"

A crack appeared in the dome of the sky. A shaft of moonlight found the hole and streamed down to touch the river.

"Andre, quick, check your compass heading," Chesson said as he strained to make out the river channel ahead.

"One sixty," Andre said.

"Come to one seventy and give us full speed," Chesson said. "That will be a good heading until we reach the Head of Passes.

"One seventy," said Andre.

"The moon and clouds have favored us at the right time," Walt said to Luke.

"It's about time things went our way," Luke replied. He looked at Bouchard sitting on the deck near him. He felt the strong presence of the duelist. A palpable force seemed to radiate from him. Luke was glad the man was here with him.

Walt sensed Luke's eyes upon him and turned. The dead white light of the moon struck the New Mexican in a strange way, making his face oddly animal-like. His nose appeared elongated, like the beak of a huge predator. We go to battle, you and I, Walt thought. We will kill, and one or both of us may die. I have no concern about dying, for I have no fear of death, nor do I have hope of afterlife. But you my friend, do you fear death? I think not. In that we are very much alike. But enough of such thoughts . . .

The clouds fought with the moon for mastery of the night. The clouds won, and darkness flooded in and again ruled the world.

Chesson drove the boat hard, steering by the compass. Now that the chase was growing hot, he too was caught up in it. His heart beat nicely, as it did when a revenue cutter pursued him during a smuggling run. However, he must be ever vigilant and keep Andre safe.

An only son was more precious than any other thing on the face of the earth.

Lightning flashed, shooting a wandering yellow light across the heavens. For a moment the world was brightly illuminated, and wild, boiling clouds could be seen filling the sky south of the speeding boat. Thunder rumbled threateningly.

"The storm is three miles distant," Chesson said, having counted the seconds between the flash and the thunder. "It will hit us right in the teeth. I think we'll lose this race."

# Chapter Thirty-Four

Susan felt as if she were suffocating as she lay on the single bunk in the dark, stifling cabin of the Itasca. Her clothing was wet with sweat. God, how she wanted a breath of fresh air and a drink of cold water.

Rawls had locked her in the cabin on the main deck of the gunboat the minute they had come on board. The sailors had watched her cross the deck, but no one had spoken to her. At the beginning of the trip downriver she had sometimes heard the voices of the crew on the deck. Now the only sounds were the throb of the steam engine laboring in the bowels of the gunboat and a rush of water past her hull.

Thunder crashed directly overhead. The gunboat shuddered at the tremendous concussive force exploding in the air. Susan sprang from the bunk and stood in the center of the cabin. Thunder roared again.

The Itasca slowed as a giant wind hit it head on. There was the sudden clamor of rain pounding upon the decks and the outside of the bulkhead. Thunder bellowed again, punctuating the drum roll of rain. The sound of the storm grew to a deafening roar.

F. M. Parker

Susan knew it was extremely hazardous to be on the river in such a severe storm. The wind could blow a boat aground, and lightning bolts were drawn to anything on the flat surface of the water.

A sudden thought came to Susan, and she cried out, "God, please strike this boat with your most powerful lightning bolt. Kill us all here and now!" She was to die for killing Yankees. It would be so grand if all her enemies on the boat could die with her.

The door of the cabin flung open. A man stepped inside, followed by a cascade of rain. The flashes of lightning silhouetted him. It was the bastard Marine, Rawls.

The captain watched Susan in the almost constant flare of the lightning. He could see the glitter of her eyes. He felt her hatred. She backed away from him until the bunk stopped her. He enjoyed her show of fear.

"You are a troublesome woman. You could cost me a fortune. But I'm going to change that." He laughed a flat, dead sound, quickly born and as quickly killed— by a roll of thunder.

Susan grew tense as a hummingbird watching a snake. She could make out only part of the man's words above the crash of the storm. However those she did hear and his expression told her he had come to kill her. With the crew driven from the deck, and the racket of the storm engulfing them, he could do the deed with no fear of detection.

"Get out of here!" Susan cried, hoping against hope someone would hear her.

Rawls said something, but the thunder drowned him out.

He spoke again. "Take off your clothes."

"No, damn you." Susan stepped around the end of the bunk and pressed her back to the bulkhead.

"Take off your clothes before I knock the hell out of you," the captain snarled.

Susan screamed at the peak of her voice. The cry was absorbed in the wind and the rain and the thunder.

Rawls jumped forward. His arm snaked out and struck Susan viciously. Her head slammed the bulkhead. She gasped with the pain. Half-unconscious, she started to sag to the deck.

The captain caught her. "Stand up, bitch." He propped her against the bulkhead and held her there, with one hand gripping her throat.

He reached out and ripped the front of her shirt open, the buttons popping. The shirt was roughly stripped off her. The buckle of the belt of her trousers was jerked loose. She was flung down on the bunk, and the trousers pulled off her legs.

The captain yanked Susan to her feet and wrapped his left arm around her naked body. He halted his abrupt movements and his right hand fondled her breast. He was aroused by the storm and the struggle with the woman, the feel of her naked flesh. For a moment, he considered taking her then and there.

The captain removed his hand from Susan's breast. He had no time, but for one thing. To kill her.

He dragged Susan, half unconscious, to the door and cautiously peered out into the rain and wind. The cabin was an outside one near the center of the Itasca. He looked both ways along the narrow walkway that ran between the cabin bulkhead and the safety barrier topped with a steel cable lifeline.

In the incessant flashes of lightning, the rain-swept deck was deserted except for the dripping cannons. The forward lookout would not leave his station, and the helmsman could not. The deck officer would probably have found a place somewhere out of the rain. He bodily lifted Susan, a plaything in his hands, and carried her out through the hatchway.

"Now you're going to drown while trying to escape," the captain said. In the investigation that would be conducted, her clothes would be found, adding evidence to the assumption she had taken them off before trying to swim ashore. He drew back his fist to strike her. She must not be in a condition where she could swim.

Susan snapped to consciousness as the deluge of cold rain fell upon her naked body. Rawls held her, his arms tight as a vise around her chest, and was carrying her toward the edge of the boat. In a flash of lightning, she glimpsed the rushing water of the river below her. She jerked her feet up, thrust them against the lifeline, and kicked violently away from the river.

The captain stumbled backward, then caught himself. He cocked his fist. "I'm going to break your pretty face," he growled.

***

"The storm will soon be on us," Chesson said. "It's just out there."

"I agree with you," Luke said. He braced himself and stared hard past the bow of the racing smuggler's boat and into the darkness. The night was charged with the signs and omens of the oncoming storm.

The boat suddenly pitched as a violent wind boiled up out of the darkness and swept over it.

Luke's nose sniffed the wind and his tongue tasted it, tangy and heavy with salt. The ocean was near. There was little time left to overtake the Union gunboat.

Sheet lightning crackled and a bright flash illuminated the southern horizon. The mile-wide body of the Mississippi River and the distant, tree-lined banks became visible, sharply etched.

In the brief life of the lightning flare, Luke saw the branching of the Mississippi into three broad channels. Each stream was as large as an ordinary river. They had reached the Head of Passes. He had sailed past this remarkable place in 1847, as a U. S. Army soldier outward bound for the attack on Mexico. Then he had come this way again when he had returned in 1848, after the defeat of the Mexicans.

One of the river channels, Pass a Loutre, went off almost due east. Then there were Southwest Pass and South Pass. Chesson guided the boat into South Pass.

Lightning flashed in the sky above the boat, like a small sun exploding. Luke's scalp prickled with electricity, and there was the smell of sulfur on the wind.

"I saw something off there ahead on the water," Luke called out through the wind to Chesson. "Did you see it?"

"I wasn't looking," Chesson said as he fought to hold the bouncing, yawing boat on course.

"I saw it," Walt said.

"There it is again," Luke called out. "One tiny light."

In the darkness that temporarily blanketed the river between lightning flashes, a speck of light glimmered. The light vanished as the men looked at it.

"We've found the gunboat," Chesson said. "They're running with a bow light to see ahead. It's now hidden by the superstructure of the vessel. What do you want to do?"

"Run up closer and let's take a look at her," Luke said. "Then somehow I've got to get aboard."

"I'm going aboard with you," Walt said.

"You've already done more to help me than I've a right to expect."

"I'm going with you."

"All right. We both go."

"The Union sailors may spot us in the lightning," Chesson said.

"We've got to gamble that they're busy watching downriver and won't look back," Luke said. "There's no other choice. We're almost to the bar at the mouth of the river. If we're going to get Susan off, it has to be done before they reach the Union frigate."

"Run us up closer to the gunboat," Walt said.

"All right," Chesson said. "Here we go."

The smuggler sped his boat ahead, bucking the invisible river of wind rushing out from the storm. As they drew nearer the gunboat, the clouds lowered to hang threateningly close overhead. The lightning-battered sky began to spill rain. The light on the gunboat was drowned to a mere point.

"The gunboat has slowed," Chesson called over the noise of the thunderstorm. "They're blinded by the rain, and afraid of running aground." He throttled his engine back to a crawl.

Luke held to the side of the cabin as the wind and waves pounded the boat. He ignored the rain swiftly soaking his clothing and laying its cold fingers upon his body. The storm might prove to be an ally.

"Could the pirogue catch the gunboat?" Luke asked.

Chesson evaluated the gunboat, measuring its speed. "With me paddling, yes it could," he said.

"Will you take Walt and me up close where we can climb aboard her?" Luke asked.

"Sure," Chesson said. "Andre, come and take the wheel."

The young man stepped to the helm. He said something to Luke, but was drowned out by a loud rumble of thunder. The noise ceased and he spoke again. "What is your plan? How do I pick you up after it's all over."

Luke concentrated on how Susan might be rescued, and then how to escape from the Union vessel and return to the smuggler's boat.

"Hold this position on the gunboat and watch for us as best you can. We may be able to run the gunboat ashore, or somehow get back into the pirogue and come to you. Worst possible solution would be for us to jump in the river and swim for it." He hoped they did not have to go into the river, for even with the frequent lightning flashes, the chances were slim of being found in the rain and darkness.

"Chesson, do you have a knife?" Walt asked. "I need a way to kill without noise."

"Yes," Chesson said. He removed his sheathed knife and handed it over.

Walt slipped the blade onto his belt. "I'm ready," he said.

Chesson picked up a length of rope. "Let's get it done," he said. "Both of you sit in the middle of the pirogue to keep the bow light and high. With the large waves we could get swamped."

The three men went to the stern of the boat, pulled the pirogue in close, and clambered down into it. Chesson cast loose and took up the paddle.

The smuggler handled the pirogue expertly, keeping it straight to the wind. Still the craft pitched and plunged as it rode up and over the choppy waves. Each time it fell into a trough, a cold, wet spray of water came flying back to slap at the men.

As the pirogue drove south chasing the gunboat, the wind gained strength and the rain fell harder. Lightning shot from cloud to cloud, and bolts darted down to stab the earth. The thunder roared like a battle of cannons.

Gradually the form of the gunboat became more distinct and solid as the pirogue crept up on it. Both masts, the large deckhouse, and the smokestacks took shape. Then the protruding barrels of the deck cannon became visible.

"I can make out the helmsman just forward of the aft deck cannon," Walt said.

"Take us right up to the gunboat's stern," Luke told Chesson. Once they were in close, the cannon would mostly block them from the view of anyone on the deck. Then, when closer still, the overhanging stern would totally hide them.

The Creole bent powerfully to his task. He brought the pirogue into the wind shadows of the large vessel, and thereafter gained more rapidly on it. The pirogue came in under the stern of the gunboat.

"Wait for us as long as you can," Luke told Chesson.

"I will."

Luke grabbed up the coil of rope and carefully made his way to the bouncing bow of the pirogue. He knelt, braced his knees against the gunwale, and looked up through the pouring rain at the stern of the gunboat.

The deck of the Itasca was some ten feet over his head. Extending above that was a safety barrier, a mesh of woven steel supported by steel posts fastened to the outboard edge of the deck. He shook out a loop of rope long enough to reach up and over one of the posts of the safety barrier.

Luke's right hand swooped out and up in a long, curving motion. The loop of rope sailed up and settled over a post. He pulled it tight.

He hoisted himself up hand over hand, and hung peering through the safety barrier. The heavy rain splashed off the deck and into his face, and the stern cannon blocked his view. He caught hold of the barrier and lifted himself higher and to the side, to escape the splashing water and see around the cannon.

A seaman dressed in wet weather gear was holding the helm. Luke knew there would be a bow lookout, and someplace on the ship, an alert duty deck officer. The deck officer could roam at will, and was the most dangerous. Where was he?

Luke muscled himself up the outside of the barrier. As he was ready to throw a leg over the obstacle and drop onto the deck, he halted quickly, his breath sucking in. The figure of a man stood on the port side of the gunboat, not thirty feet distant. He was holding to one of the stays that helped support the aft mast. The man would be the duty officer. He was looking forward, using the visibility provided by the nearly constant lightning to check the Itasca's position in the river channel.

Luke slid over the safety barrier and flattened himself on the deck. A moment later, Walt's head appeared. Luke pointed out the two seamen on the deck.

Walt nodded his understanding. He came cautiously over the barrier and lay prone beside Luke.

"What next?" Walt whispered, pushing the wet hair out of his eyes.

"The helmsman will see us if we try to go forward. You take care of him. Then steer the boat. I'll make that other fellow tell me where Susan is being held."

"Okay. I'll kill the helmsman and throw him overboard," Walt said. He pulled his knife. "We've got to hit them both at the same time so that if something goes wrong and one shouts out, the other man won't be warned. You kill your fellow when you're done with him."

Luke wiped at the rain streaming down his face. He did not want to kill the seaman, for he still felt a comradeship for the Union military, even after the passage of fourteen years. However, the men of the Union had now become his enemies because they held Susan prisoner. For a moment he was angry with her for putting him in this position.

"All right," Luke said.

Walt gripped his shoulder, and crawled away. Luke watched the duelist, a lithe and sensuous menace slithering over the rain-washed deck. The helmsman had but to turn his head during one of the lightning flashes and he would see Walt. But the man's attention remained fixed toward the bow of the gunboat, and he did not know the deadly danger that was stealing upon him.

Luke rose to a crouched position and went a few steps left to put one of the deck cannons between him and the duty officer. Then he turned and moved swiftly up to the cannon and peered over the barrel. The officer had not stirred.

Luke glanced toward the helmsman. The dark form of Walt was flat on the deck barely two body lengths behind the man. Walt rose to his feet as Luke watched.

Specter-like, he sprang upon the unsuspecting helmsman.

Luke pulled his knife and drew in a rain-filled breath of air. He darted around the cannon and leapt on the duty officer. The haft of the knife crashed down solidly on the man's head.

The officer sagged, stunned by the hard blow. Luke caught him by the face with his left hand, clamping his mouth shut. The man groaned, all the fight knocked out

449

of him. Luke lowered his slack body down onto the deck.

The rain fell on the upturned face of the Union officer. In the glare of light from the sky fireworks, Luke saw the man was a naval lieutenant, thin-faced with no beard. He was very young to be an officer and go to war, yet Luke had been as young when he had sailed off to Mexico.

The lieutenant's body jerked as his consciousness returned. His eyes fluttered open. Luke clamped his mouth shut and put the sharp point of the knife to the tip of his nose.

"Be very quiet. Do you want to die?"

The lieutenant shook his head, but Luke felt the man's muscles harden, tensing. He rapped the lieutenant on the head hard enough to add to the headache he must already have.

"Don't try to be a hero. Just answer my questions. Be quick about it, and I'll let you live. You got that straight,"

The man nodded against Luke's hand.

"Where is the woman prisoner being held? Now I'm going to loosen my grip a little. You just whisper to me."

Luke released his hard grip, but held his hand against the lieutenant's mouth.

"She's there forward on the port side at the third hatchway. She's locked up in that cabin."

Luke studied the lieutenant's face in the flashing lightning. "That's not true. You're lying. I know she's on the starboard side. Tell me which cabin."

The lieutenant shook his head vigorously. "No, I tell you. She's on the port side, third hatchway. I saw her just before dark. Captain Rawls has not moved her. I swear it."

Luke believed the lieutenant. "Can you swim?" he asked.

"Yes."

"Would you rather have your throat cut or try to swim ashore?"

"Swim."

Luke clamped the lieutenant's shoulder firmly. "Get up. Slowly."

The officer rose to his feet. He started to turn to the rear.

Luke grabbed the lieutenant by the seat of the pants. Then, before the man could figure out what he planned to do, he lifted him strongly and hurled him over the safety barrier. He fell, his arms outspread and feet kicking. The splash of the falling body striking the river was unheard in the drum of falling rain and growling thunder.

## Chapter Thirty-Five

Luke, feeling his way through the darkness, moved forward on the port side of the Itasca. For the moment the world was black, the lightning building its charge. He passed two deck cannon and entered the passageway between the mid-deck cabins and the safety barrier.

Sheet lightning set whole patches of sky afire, the brilliant intensity almost blinding. In the glare of light Luke saw a man and woman struggling with each other beside the cabins. The woman, naked and startlingly white as snow, was being held around the chest. Her feet were braced against the top cable of the safety barrier, and every muscle of her body was straining as she fought to keep from being thrown into the river.

Luke leapt forward along the deck of the Itasca toward Susan and Rawls. He had to reach them before she was thrown over the ship's side. He saw the Marine cock his fist to strike her.

Luke was close now, and he reached out for the captain. His fingers closed on the man's fist as it descended. He slowed the fist, but could not entirely stop its fall. The bony knuckles cracked against Susan's head.

Luke stabbed with his knife into the captain's side. Kill the murderous Marine quickly. Make the fight short.

The knife stopped abruptly after penetrating only a short distance. The blade had struck something hard, and had not entered the captain's body. A moneybelt, thought Luke.

The captain dropped Susan, and jumped away with amazing speed, spinning to face Luke. He snatched his pistol from its holster.

Luke's blade had wrenched free of the object that had blocked its entry into the captain's body. He lunged in to stab again.

The captain jerked his pistol up. He pointed it directly at Luke's chest. He pressed the trigger.

Luke knew he was surely going to die. His enemy was but a few feet away, and could not possibly miss.

However, no jet of flame lanced out at Luke, no bullet stabbed into him. The gun had misfired. The powder had become wet from the drenching downpour.

The captain recovered instantly from the failure of his weapon. He slashed down at Luke's hand as it was striking out with the keen-bladed knife.

Luke's hand went numb from the savage blow. The knife went flying along the deck. He launched himself at the captain before the man could draw back his arm and hit again with the pistol.

The two strong bodies thudded together with bone-jarring impact. As the men fell heavily to the deck, Luke grabbed the captain's gun hand. He slammed the hand against an iron post of the safety barrier. The pistol went flying ever the side of the gunboat.

Susan backed away from the struggling men and pressed against the bulkhead of the cabin. Her heart hammered with surprise and exaltation at Luke's unexpected appearance. She watched the men, their bodies brilliantly lighted one moment and almost unseen the next, rolling on the deck and striking each other mercilessly.

Both men surged to their knees, and pounded each other like legless giants, with a flurry of powerful blows. She heard the whack of their hard knuckles hitting bone and muscle. Then as if on command, both jumped to their feet.

They sprang at each other, Luke moving most quickly. Luke struck Rawls in the face. Instantly Rawls hit back. Susan did not understand how the men could withstand the brutal blows with which they mauled each other.

Luke's head rang from the hard blows the captain rained upon him. He tasted the copper and salt of blood in his mouth. But the captain was weakening. His last blows had not landed with the power of the first. Now was the time to finish him. Luke drove in, crashing his fists into the hated face. The captain's front teeth broke. Luke crushed his nose, and jumped away.

The captain charged, his mouth and nose pouring blood. Luke stepped quickly aside, intending to hit the man as he went past. But Luke's feet slipped on the wet deck, and he fell against the safety barrier. He stopped himself from going over the ship's side by grabbing hold of one of the stanchions supporting the upper deck.

The captain hurtled past. To Luke's consternation, the man did not halt and turn back for the attack, but continued swiftly on toward Susan, who stood near the bulkhead of the cabin a half dozen paces distant.

Susan made no effort to elude the captain. She moved out from the bulkhead and halted to stand motionless in the center of the passageway. Her naked body seemed frozen, as rigid as white ice. As the captain sprang across the last short space that separated them, both of Susan's arms lifted to point at him, with the hands locked together.

A bright bolt of lightning lanced down from the dark overcast and struck the tall forward mast of the Itasca. With unbelievable speed it ran along the wooden mast, shattering it to splinters. Its power still unspent and enormous, the bolt bore onward, ripping through the two decks of the gunboat to the very keel.

The blazing lightning strike caught the tableau of Susan standing as if transfixed, pointing both arms at the captain, and the captain in mid-jump descending upon her. Both man and woman were oblivious to the tremendous jolt of thunder that shook the boat like a toy.

Luke saw Susan was gripping something that extended beyond her hands and glinted metallic. She had retrieved his knife and held it thrust out at the captain. Every line of her body showed her determination to stab him.

Rawls saw his danger. He tried to twist away from it. He was too late. As he fell upon Susan, she plunged the blade deeply into his chest.

The entangled bodies of the man and woman fell heavily to the deck. But a moment passed, and the captain rose to his knees astride Susan. His hands came up and felt of the knife protruding from his chest. The fingers closed upon the handle, and he tried to wrench the embedded blade out. For a moment the weapon remained wedged between ribs in his chest, and then it came free. He dropped the knife to the deck and put his hand over the gaping wound. Blood gushed out between his fingers. His countenance contorted with pain and fear.

Susan tried to roll from under the captain. Her movement jerked the man's attention back, and he looked down at her with hate. He rocked backward and came to his feet, pulling Susan up with him. Instantly he wrapped his arms around her and pulled her tightly to him. He lunged sideways toward the barrier of the safety railing—and the river just beyond.

The top steel wire of the barrier caught the captain's and Susan's legs. Their momentum carried them onward, their upper bodies moving beyond the deck. They began to rotate outward and downward. A distant lightning flash illuminated them for a brief moment as they cartwheeled toward the black water.

Luke had been stunned by the quickness with which the captain—whom he believed was mortally wounded—had risen and grabbed Susan. He had leapt and almost reached them when the captain threw himself and Susan over the side of the boat. He saw their bodies, the man fiercely clutching the woman to him, plunge into the swift current of the river. They vanished immediately below the surface.

Luke sprang to the safety barrier and hurled himself into the river. He must free Susan from Rawls's death hold. He sank rapidly down through the cold water. Everywhere was pitch black. His hands swept 'round as far as he could reach. They touched nothing except the water. He fought down through the powerful current that pulled him this way and that way. He spun himself, his hands reaching out, searching, searching, in all directions. He had to find Susan. He drove himself deeper, pulling at the water, his legs scissoring.

His lungs screamed for air. The Mississippi here near its mouth was more than two hundred feet deep. How far down was he? He started to fight his way upward, his hands clawing at the slippery water.

The ascent was unending, his hands seemingly unable to gain any purchase on the yielding water. His waterlogged clothing and boots seemed to weigh tons, and held him down. He almost breathed, in a region where there was no air to breathe. Control yourself, make the surface, then dive again. Stroke, stroke. Kick, kick. Stop the damn current from rolling you. Don't let it cause you to waste time.

Luke's outstretched hands broke the surface. His starved lungs pulled hungrily at the sweet, rain-filled air.

"What in hell!" someone exclaimed above and behind him.

Luke whirled around in the water. Chesson was looking down at him from the pirogue. The gunboat had sailed on while he had been below the surface, and he had surfaced almost under the smuggler and his craft.

"Did you see Susan and Rawls go into the river?" Luke asked as he caught hold of the gunwale of the boat to rest.

"No. I couldn't see anything happening on the deck of the gunboat."

"Watch for them. Rawls grabbed her and jumped overboard. He's dead by now, but maybe Susan got free and swam back to the surface."

As he spoke, Luke knew she had not succeeded in doing that. He remembered the expression on Rawls's face, the resolve to hold Susan forever and take her into death with him.

"Wait for me," Luke said. He took a breath of air and dove again into the black water. The odds that he would find Susan and Rawls in this second attempt were small indeed. They would have sunk deeper and been washed farther downstream. But God help him, he must try.

The seconds passed as Luke propelled himself down through the water. He was totally blind. The only possibility of finding Susan was by touch. And he touched nothing but cold, slippery water. At last, his breath gone, Luke fought back to the surface.

Chesson dipped his paddle and swept the pirogue close to Luke. "Anything?" he asked.

"Not a thing," Luke replied between gasps for air. He hoisted himself up and rolled into the pirogue. "Did you hear or see anything on the surface?"

"No."

"Circle here for a while, and let's look for her," Luke said.

"Do you want to do that, or shouldn't we go and get Bouchard off the gunboat before the Yankees kill him."

Luke looked at the Itasca. A tumult of voices rang out as the crew formed bucket brigades to fight the flames that leapt up from the hole where once there had been a tall mast. The red flare of light from the fire illuminated the river for several yards before the downpour snuffed it out.

"You're right," Luke said with resignation. "Quick, catch up with the gunboat and take Bouchard off. Then we can search for Susan;"

Chesson plunged his paddle into the water and shot the pirogue ahead to overtake the Itasca. As the small craft came in under the stern of the gunboat, Walt stole out from behind the aft deck cannon and hurried to the safety barrier. He stepped over, took hold of the bottom cable, and dropped into the water. Walt surfaced, and Luke helped him to climb quickly into the pirogue.

Chesson whirled his craft upstream and sped away from the Itasca.

"Where's Susan?" Walt asked.

"Rawls took her down there with him," Luke said, and he pointed down at the water. He told Walt what had happened. "We've got to search for her," Luke finished.

"Yes, we'll look for her," Walt said. "We'll use the big boat. With the engine, we can cover much more of the river. But you must know, Luke, that there's little chance we can find her in the dark. Maybe tomorrow, when it's daylight and the rain has quit. That's if she broke loose from the Marine, and could swim well enough to make the bank."

Luke did not reply. He could see in his mind's eye Susan's white body caught in Rawls's arms and sinking down through the black water to the muddy river bottom. He shivered at the thought.

*** 

"Luke, Susan's dead and we'll not find her body," Walt said. "It's time we stopped looking. We should return to New Orleans and get the boat off the river."

Luke turned his haggard face to Walt, and then to Chesson and Andre. He did not trust himself to speak. His heart felt cramped within its cage of ribs.

The rain had ceased in the small hours of the early morning. When daylight arrived, the Union gunboat was gone, and they had begun their search. It was now the middle of the afternoon of the third day.

They had run the smuggler's boat up and down the river close to the banks all during the daylight hours of that first day. For miles they had examined every snag, every piece of floating driftwood, and shouted Susan's name into the woods bordering the river. Then, on the chance that Susan might possibly have reached the shore but was unconscious or injured and too weak to answer, they had gone ashore, Luke on one bank and Walt and Andre on the other. For two days they walked the muddy banks, searching the dense brush and weeds. There had been not one sign of her. She was gone forever from him.

Luke looked northwestward across the watery labyrinth of the great delta of the Mississippi River. A thousand miles distant in the New Mexico Territory the Sangre de Cristo Mountains rose to touch the sky. In a high, peaceful valley of those mountains, his ranch waited for him. He must go there, leave this land where Northern citizens and Southern citizens made war on each other. It would be very lonely there without the lovely Susan.

"You're right," Luke said. "Rawls killed her."

"I'm sorry about your woman," Chesson said. "Will you stay and fight the Yankees,"

"No. I'm going home to the Territory. And the sooner the better."

Walt was silently watching Luke's stricken face. He was the kind of man who would grieve a very long time. As for him, everything about New Orleans constantly reminded him of Annette. He should also leave. Perhaps in a new land such as New Mexico, his memories might not be so black and sad.

"If you would invite me, I would go with you," Walt said to Luke. "At least as far as Santa Fe. I've heard there is much gambling in that town. Perhaps there are some duels to be fought."

"That's a great idea, for you'll like Santa Fe," Luke replied. "I'd be damned glad for you to come with me."

"Good. Chesson, get us up the river to Orleans."

Chesson opened the throttle of his boat.

# Author's Notes

General Benjamin Butler became military ruler of New Orleans on May 1, 1862. He was noted for the harshness of his Orders of Occupation. His "Woman's Order" (No. 28) proclaimed that any woman who might by word or movement show contempt for any Union officer or soldier was to be treated as a whore of the town plying her vocation. Other orders levied special taxes against those who aided the Confederacy, and soldiers could search the houses of citizens for arms. Any slave offering testimony against his master was freed. All persons of eighteen years of age were required to take an oath of allegiance to the Union government or surrender their property and leave the city.

The long practiced custom of white men owning quadroon mistresses, placees, ended with the Civil War. Many of the men were killed on the battlefields. Others were bankrupted by the war and could not afford the luxury of the women. The women, on their part, no longer supported by the men, became nearly destitute. Often they used their cottages, owned by them free and clear, as sources of income and rented out rooms.

Most of the placees refused to marry black men, and lived out the remainder of their lives alone.

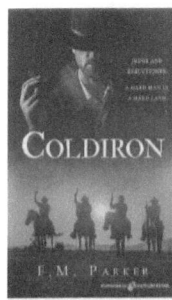